DEATH OF AN OLD LOVE

Juliette slipped an elaborate negligee over her nightgown and went down the stairs. Arthur was in front of the fire, a highball in his hand. He put down the glass and eyed her steadily.

"When I look at you," he said, "it doesn't seem possible that you could wreck a man's life—as you have mine."

She sat down on the arm of a chair and carefully tucked her negligee about her, so that it outlined her body. She was using her sex against him. She had never learned that lost lovers do not return.

"There ought to be a particular hell for your sort of woman," he said slowly. "God knows I loved you, but you took my pride and crushed it. You killed something in me. And now you've fastened onto me like a leech, and by heaven, I can't get rid of you. I'm fed up to the teeth!"

The next morning, Juliette disappeared. A week later, they found her body—with Arthur's hat nearby.

THE WALL

Mary Roberts Rinehart

Kensington Books

http://www.kensingtonbooks.com

KENSINGTON BOOKS are published by

Kensington Publishing Corp.
850 Third Avenue
New York, NY 10022

Second Zebra Paperback printing: June, 1992
First Kensington Paperback printing: July, 1998
10 9 8 7 6 5 4 3

Printed in the United States of America

CHAPTER I

It is odd, how one's ideas can change. A month ago I never wanted to see the island again, or this old house. But it is quiet now. When the sheriff drops in his visits are purely social. He inspects me with a critical eye and scowls.

"Still looking kind of peaked, young woman," he says disapprovingly.

"What would you expect?" I inquire. "If you enjoyed this summer, I certainly did not."

He is likely to grin and, taking out his old pipe, gaze out over the bay.

"Always did say this was the best view anywhere about," he observes, and smokes contentedly.

It was he who finally solved our mystery for us, although toward the end a small army of deputies, detectives, constables and even two New York detectives were working on it.

He worked practically alone, rattling about in his disreputable old car, and once even rather nervously taking to the air.

"Never knew I had a stomach until then," he said.

Then one morning he walked quietly into the District Attorney's office in Clinton. Bullard, the District Attorney, was there, and others, including the New York men.

"Just dropped in," he said quietly, "to say it's all over."

They had thought he was crazy at first. The New York men had smiled, and Bullard was furious. But when he told them the situation changed. All but Bullard crowded around him, applauding him, clapping him on the back. One of the New York detectives even asked him if he didn't want a job with them.

But he only grinned at them.

"Need some brains in this part of the country, too," he said. "Never can tell when these summer folks will break out again."

I was waiting for him in his office when he came back from that conference, and he took off his battered old soft hat, sat down and lit his pipe before he spoke to me at all. Then he said:

"Well, Marcia, I guess we've got to the bottom of it at last."

It had been a long and weary road. He looked tired that day. His eyes were red from lack of sleep. But I can still see him sitting at his desk, in his cluttered office, with Mamie—his stenographer—typing in the next room; and hear him saying:

"Maybe we'd better get at it from the start. It's not a pretty story; but as a matter of human interest and—well, human motives, it's a humdinger."

Which I still consider a pretty good word for it.

So I am still here. The season is over, the summer colony dispersed. Even the bay is empty of pleasure craft. The yachts have gone, the white sloops and schooners, the fast motorboats which always remind me of comets with foamy tails. And the seals have commenced to come back. Only yesterday one lifted his head and looked up at me. Then, as curious as a dog, he came closer to inspect me.

He seemed reassured, for he played about in the water for some time.

It is all familiar and friendly again, this rambling old house, built by my grandfather in the easy money days of the nineties, and called Sunset House, generally corrupted to Sunset. It has been a part of my life, with its garden, its stable now rebuilt into a garage, and with the ravine close by and the pond there, deep at the sea end where long years ago somebody had dammed Stony Creek. My brother Arthur and I had always believed there were fish in the pond, which may have been true, since we certainly never got any out of it.

Even this upper porch where I am sitting with a pencil and pad on my knee is a part of our tradition; for when my father as a young man followed Teddy Roosevelt to Cuba, and was

6

rewarded by a grateful government with one of the worst cases of typhoid on record, he spent his convalescence on it.

According to the story, he would sit there, damning everything from the sea gulls to William McKinley, and Arthur's first lisping words learned at his knee were the secret delight of the servants.

Good heavens, that makes Arthur thirty-nine. It was more than ten years before I came along, and the surprise I caused must have amounted to a profound shock.

But, although the house is friendly, it will never be the same again. I have only to lift my head to see the windows of Juliette's room, now closed and locked, and beyond it the room from which Helen Jordan went out one day, never to come back.

Below me is the rocky beach, uncovered at low water, where the tide once played me so deadly a trick. And each evening, as the fishing boats go out, their decks piled high with nets, I wonder if among them is the one which returned one morning trailing that bit of flotsam which had once been a living creature.

The fisherman landing matter-of-factly at the town dock and calling up:

"Get somebody to call the police station. I've got a body here."

It is hard to think back past all this to the normal life that preceded it. Yet it was normal. Mother had died some years ago, soon after Father, leaving behind her a depressed world she could not understand, a house in New York nobody would buy, this summer place on a New England island, and a modest trust fund; the usual assets of her generation.

"You will always have a home, Marcia," she said, rather pitifully.

"Of course I'll have a home, darling," I told her.

And somehow I had managed. I could not dismiss the servants. Old William had been in the family for forty years, and Lizzie the cook for thirty. Even Maggie, my maid and general factotum, had been originally my nurse, and since both houses were large, I had to have a housemaid as well.

But the money problem was always with both Arthur and

7

me, especially after his divorce and remarriage. It worried me to see his handsome head growing gray at thirty-nine, and the alimony to Juliette every month was often a desperate matter.

It would have helped if we could have united forces in the Park Avenue house. But Mary Lou, his second wife, would not do it. Not that she disliked me; but she is like so many small women, jealous of her big husband and highly possessive. In the end we compromised. She brought Junior to Sunset in the summer, and Arthur joined us when he could.

That was the situation early in June of this year when Mary Lou called me up to say that Junior, their boy, had had the measles, and could I open Sunset earlier than usual.

"He always does so well there," she said, in her slightly querulous voice. "Wouldn't you know this would happen? Measles, of all things."

I observed that measles in a child of four was not unusual, but of course I agreed. The result was that we reached here early in June, the servants by train, and I driving my old but still useful coupé and taking three comfortable days to do it.

All normal. All as it should be. A few seals still about, the island hills beautiful, the village street empty of all but local cars. And to add to my contentment that last morning of the trip, as I crossed the bridge to the island a boy fishing from its rail lifted a hand and yelled.

"Hi ya, kid," he said.

It was extremely comforting, at twenty-nine!

There was always a thrill on getting back to Sunset. Even the servants were excited. And nothing had changed. I remember coming out onto this porch, roofless and open to the sun, with its ancient steamer chairs and the small iron table which holds on occasion my books and cigarettes, and gazing out at the bay below with a sort of thankfulness. For the peace it offered, its quiet and coolness, and the childish memories it evoked.

It was all there. The old stake where Arthur used to tie up a boat and fish for flounders; the broken little pier, relic of more prosperous days, with the float where Arthur—and a pair of water wings—taught me to swim. The shore where we searched for starfish and other loot, to place them in the nursery bathtub and frantically annoy the governess of the moment,

8

the little pools when the tide was out where Arthur made me paper boats and I sailed them. Once I remember we caught an eel, and Father found it in our bathtub. He looked at it and at us with the same extreme distaste.

"You put it there," he said. "Now get it out, and out of the house."

We tried, but it was a desperate business. It ended by the eel slithering slimily down the hardwood stairs, and by Father slipping and following it down, bumping from step to step with an august majesty which sent Arthur and me into hiding in the stables and into nervous jitters for a week.

It was all the same that morning. Even the gulls were there, raucous and shrill at high tide, but at low water settling down to the business of hunting clams. There was only one change, and Maggie commented on it at once.

"I don't like those crows," she said. "They're bad luck, and no mistake."

I saw them then. There were three of them, strutting impudently about among the gulls, and none too welcome, apparently. But I remember that I laughed.

"Why, Maggie!" I said. "At your age!"

"What's my age got to do with it?" she demanded sourly, and retired with dignity into the house.

But I have wondered since. I shall always believe that it was one of them that retrieved the bright gilt initial from Arthur's hat, and hid it where the sheriff found it, above high water mark.

CHAPTER II

That day I went over the house with Mrs. Curtis, the wife of the caretaker. Spring and fall she opens and closes it, but this time she had a report to make.

She stood uneasily in her neat print dress and looked distressed.

"It's about the bells, Miss Lloyd," she said. "Curtis has gone over them, but he can't find anything wrong."

"What do they do? Whistle?" I asked.

She looked almost shocked.

"They ring," she said, in a portentous voice. "They ring when nobody pushes them."

"Probably a crossed wire," I told her. "If they keep on I'll have them looked over."

She let it go at that, although she seemed uneasy. And I may say here and now that the bells still remain a mystery. They rang all summer, in season and out. They cost me a sprained ankle, and they almost drove the household crazy. Then they stopped, as suddenly as they had begun.

Ridiculous? Perhaps. I have a strong conviction that whatever another and better world may be, it is too busy to lift furniture or push bell buttons.

Nevertheless, the fact remains. They rang.

But that day I dismissed them lightly. I went over the house dutifully in Mrs. Curtis's small starchy wake; and since it enters considerably into this narrative perhaps I should describe it here.

As I have already said, it is a big house, sprawled so close to the waterfront that at high tide it seems to be at sea. A long

11

drive from the main road leads in to it, and entering from it to the right are the dining room, pantries, servants' hall and kitchen.

To the left are the family rooms, the library and beyond it overlooking the garden what used to be Mother's morning room, both of them connecting by doors with the long drawing room which overlooks the bay and takes the entire front of that side of the house.

Upstairs are the bedrooms, almost a dozen of them, with bathrooms scattered hither and yon. Both Mother's and Father's rooms are locked off and never used, Mother's room overlooking the garden and Father's next to it. Then comes Junior's nursery and the suite used by Mary Lou and Arthur. My own is in the center, with a sitting room adjoining and this upper porch outside them both.

In other words, with one exception the house and property bear a sort of family resemblance to nine out of ten of the summer estates on the island, built by and for large families, the children eventually marrying or going away and the houses remaining, mute reminders of simpler and livelier days.

That one exception, however, is noteworthy. Mother had always maintained that we children invariably chose the summer holidays to be ill, and after a sequence of chickenpox, measles and whooping cough she fitted up what she called the hospital suite. The one we used was the quarantine room to us always, and the other in those early days was the pesthouse.

"Why the pesthouse?" I asked Arthur.

"Trained nurses are pests, aren't they?" he answered.

Which seemed entirely adequate to me then.

They lay, those rooms, on the third floor of the house, and were accessible only by a steep narrow staircase from the main hallway on the second floor. The day and night nurseries lay beneath them, and how we hated being exiled to them! Mother looking at a thermometer and saying resignedly: "Well, you have some fever. You'd better go upstairs until the doctor comes, just to be safe." And Arthur—or I myself—catching up some books and a nightgown, and then dragging up the steep staircase.

"I tell you I feel all right, mother. What's a fever, anyhow?"

"Go up when you're told. I'll send Fraülein in a minute."

"But listen! I feel fine. I—"

"Arthur!"

There would be a bang of a door above, followed by a sulky silence; and later on Doctor Jamieson would climb the stairs and tell us to put out our tongues.

But—and this, too, is important—we did not always stay there. Arthur was not long in finding a way out. We were convalescing from scarlet fever when he discovered it, lying side by side in the twin beds, with a screen between us at necessary intervals.

He was frightfully bored, and so one night he simply slid down the drain pipe to the drawing room roof, and from there he climbed a trellis to the garden below. He gathered up a starfish or two from the beach, made a triumphant re-entry and put one of the things on me!

I must have yelled, for the nurse came in, and I can still remember Arthur's virtuous face.

"I think she's delirious again," he said, looking concerned. "She thinks she's seeing things."

"What things?" said the nurse suspiciously.

"Oh, fish and that kind of stuff," he said, and crawled into bed, taking his trophies with him.

I had not been there for years when Mrs. Curtis took me up that day. In some ways it had changed. The outer or nurse's room still contained a cot bed, but it had become a depository of everything else, from old window screens to long-forgotten toys, from broken china, chests and trunks to ancient discarded furniture.

Mrs. Curtis eyed it apologetically.

"There's no place else to put the stuff," she said. "I don't know what to do with it."

The other room, the sickroom proper, gave me almost a shock. It was as though no years had passed at all, and I was there once again, an unwilling child being sent to Coventry.

There were the two beds, neatly and freshly made. There was the worn rug, and the bookcase with some of our ancient books in it. Even the small bathroom was ready, with soap and towels. I suppose Mrs. Curtis had kept it like that for years, and I felt

13

distinctly guilty.

But it smelled a little musty, and I went over and opened a window.

"My brother and I used to get out this way," I said. "By the drain pipe."

"It's a wonder you didn't break a leg," said Mrs. Curtis severely.

I went downstairs then, leaving the window open; but some of the gaiety had gone out of the day. It was hard to compare the lighthearted Arthur of his teens with the Arthur of today. I had adored him, but I had seen him go through the hell that only a woman can make of a man's life. And even his freedom had cost him too much. He had been willing to pay any price to be free, however.

"Twelve thousand a year!" I said, when he told me. "But that's ridiculous, Arthur."

"That's Juliette's price, and she sticks to it," he said grimly.

"It isn't as though you'd done anything. After all, you are letting her divorce you, when it ought to be the other way."

"Oh, for God's sake, Marcia!" he groaned. "It doesn't matter where the fault lies. I haven't been perfect, and I'm not hiding behind her skirts. I want to get out of it, and I'll have to pay."

Even at that it had not been easy, for Juliette quite plainly did not want the divorce. Things suited her as they were. She was well if not lavishly supported. Her apartment was large and usually filled with people, and while Arthur worked in his law office and often brought work home at night, her time was pretty much her own. There were stories about her, but I doubt if he ever heard them, and I resolutely shut my ears.

So he bought her off. He did not want to marry again, at that time. He had not even met Mary Lou. But Juliette had made him wretched. He had no real home. She refused to have children, and she was forever and eternally in debt.

Not until she had gone did he discover how much she owed; to dressmakers, to bootleggers—it was still prohibition then— to restaurants and hotels. She even owed at her bridge club. I remember going into the apartment the day she left for Paris and finding Arthur in what had been her boudoir, sitting at her

14

desk with his head in his hands.

He looked up when he saw me.

"See here, Marcia," he said, "what would you pay for my half interest in Sunset?"

I sat down abruptly. The room was still in wild disorder. Juliette had made a clean sweep of her belongings, but she had left behind her a litter of tissue paper, torn-up letters in the fireplace, old evening slippers and half-empty jars and bottles. It had been an attractive room, jade-green curtains and mauve brocaded furniture as a background for her blond prettiness. Always before I had seen it filled with expensive flowers, silver photograph frames with pictures signed to her in terms of endearment, and the thousand and one trinkets with which she always cluttered her life. Now it looked stark and bare.

"I mean it," Arthur repeated. "You like the old place, and it's too far for me to go nowadays."

"You like it too, Arthur."

"I suppose I could still have the quarantine room now and then," he said. "Good Lord, Marcia, how far that seems from all this."

He told me then that Juliette owed the best part of twenty thousand dollars, debts contracted in his name. As a parting gesture she had piled the bills on her desk, and on top of them to hold them in place she had put a grotesque china figure of an urchin with his thumb to his nose. I had never thought of Arthur as a violent man until I saw him pick up that figure and smash it on the hearth.

It seemed to surprise him, for he looked at it and then grinned sheepishly.

"Sorry," he said. "I feel better now. Well, what about Sunset?"

In the end I bought it from him, using more of my depleted capital than I cared to think about, but at least saving his credit and, as it turned out, his happiness. A year later he had married Mary Lou, and the nightmare days were over.

Fortunately I was busy that day, and so I put Juliette resolutely out of my mind. What I wanted was a round of golf;

but what I found waiting for me as I went downstairs was Lizzie, with her mouth set and a long grocery list in her hand.

"I'll trouble you to order some food for the house," she said. "That is, if you want any dinner, miss."

"I do. I want a lot of dinner," I told her.

That pleased her. She even condescended to smile.

"You order it and I'll cook it," she said.

But I did not eat much dinner that night, or indeed for many nights to come.

I got out the car and went to the village in a more cheerful mood. It was pleasant to be back. It was pleasant to meet the tradespeople, most of them old friends. It was pleasant to be clean and cool, and to know that tomorrow I could slip off the old float and swim, even if the water was cold. It was even pleasant to be Marcia Lloyd, aged twenty-nine but perhaps not looking it. I remember taking off my hat and letting the sea breeze blow through my short hair; and that Conrad, the butcher, eying me so to speak between chops, said I looked like a bit of a girl.

"Just for that," I said, "you'll have to give me a slice of bologna sausage. Do you remember? You always did."

He grinned and gave it to me. But he added a bit of advice to it.

"You're kind of alone out there, aren't you?" he said. "No neighbors yet."

"I have the servants."

"They'd be a lot of help! See here, Miss Marcia, things have changed since we've had the bridge, and cars are allowed on the island. Used to be you could go to sleep and leave the front door open if you felt like it. Nowadays—well, I'd lock up the place if I were you. Away off like that by yourself it isn't necessary to take any chances."

I refused to be discouraged, however, and I did the rest of my buying in high spirits. It was just as I left the fish market that the blow fell.

I remember that I was carrying a basket of lobsters fresh and lively from the pots, their claws propped open with bits of stick but their energy in no wise diminished by the seaweed which covered them; and that just as the mainland bus stopped one of

16

them escaped and made for the gutter with incredible speed.

By the time I had retrieved it, my hat on one side of my head and my language totally unbecoming a lady, I heard a cool amused voice at my elbow.

"What would Mother have said!" it observed. "Such language. Don't faint, Marcia. It's me!"

It was Juliette—Mrs. Juliette Ransom as she now called herself—taller and better looking than I had remembered her, but with the old familiar mockery lurking about her mouth. She was extremely well-dressed, and she eyed me curiously.

"How on earth do you keep your figure like that?" she said. "You look about sixteen."

I found my voice then.

"What on earth are you doing here?" I asked.

"I'm visiting you," she said, still in that cool amused voice. "Can you control those lobsters in your car, or do I take a taxi?"

CHAPTER III

I drove her back to Sunset. There was nothing else to do. But I had some satisfaction, after piling her maid and a half dozen suitcases in the rear of the car, in putting the lobsters at her feet. She did not like it, although she still smiled.

"They *smell*," she said. "Do you always have to carry your own food, Marcia?"

"I don't often have to carry passengers."

"No? Then I take it you are alone."

"I am. I've just arrived."

"No Mary Lou? No little Arthur?"

"No."

"Well, thank God for that," she said, and seemed to relax.

"What a train, and what a trip!" she said. "Why in heaven's name bury yourself way up here all summer? Why not Newport? Not that I'm crazy about Newport, but you can at least get away from it."

"Even if I liked Newport I couldn't afford it," I said evenly. "You ought to know that."

I thought she glanced quickly at me. Then she drew a long breath.

"So that's the way it is. I thought it might be."

She said nothing more before we reached the house; I supposed because of the maid behind us. As we turned in at the driveway, however, she leaned forward and looked down at the pond.

"It used to give me the creeps, that place," she said.

I had a chance to look at her then. She was several years older than I was, but she had kept her looks extremely well. As

19

though she had read my mind she turned to me.

"Not so bad, am I? The face isn't yet on the barroom floor, although it's seen a number of barrooms. And so here's the dear old place again! Well, well, who would have thought it!"

I stopped the car at the door, and William's eyes almost popped out of his head when he saw who was with me. Juliette chose to be gracious.

"Well, William," she said. "How are you? And how do you manage never to grow any older?"

He had the grace to color, for it is an open secret that he dyes his hair; that pathetic effort of the old servant to conceal his age. But he was very civil.

"Time passes, Miss Juliette," he said. She had been Miss Juliette while Mother lived, and she was still that to him. "Shall I take out the bags?"

The maid, whose name I learned was Jordan, got out stiffly. She clutched Juliette's jewel case in her hands but made no other effort with the luggage; and I led them both in and up the stairs.

"I'll give you your old rooms," I said. "I suppose you'll want Jordan next to you. She can use the laundry downstairs if you need anything pressed."

Juliette did not answer at once. She had moved to a window and was staring at the bay. The tide was out, and the gulls were busy and noisy on the rocks below.

"Those damned birds," she said at last. "They used to drive me crazy."

I faced her then for the first time. Jordan had disappeared into the next room, and William was lugging her baggage up the stairs.

"See here, Juliette," I said. "You don't like me and you don't like this place. You never have. Why have you come back?"

"Because I have to talk to you," she said. "If you want the truth, I'm in a jam."

Then William came in, and there was no chance for more.

I stood by for a few minutes. Juliette traveled, as she did everything, extravagantly. I recognized the suitcase in which she carried, for any night on any train, her own soft blankets, her own towels, and even a pillow or two. I saw her dressing case, filled with lotions, creams, and all the paraphernalia with which she cared for her smooth skin. I even watched with some irritation while Jordan, taciturn but skillful, whipped my best guest linen from the bed and replaced it with the mono-grammed pale-rose silk sheets which Juliette affected. And I retired when, with her usual complete abuse of all ordinary decency, Juliette began to strip for her bath. Nudity means nothing to me, but long ago her particular form of exhibitionism had palled on me.

It was some time before I could face the servants. I went into my own room and had what amounted to a private fit with the door locked. She had come for something. I knew that. And mixed with this fear was acute resentment. Not only was my peace gone, but Mary Lou's plans would have to be changed.

When at last I went downstairs it was to find Lizzie, lacking a kitchen maid these days, grumpily peeling potatoes. She looked up at me sourly.

"How long's she going to be here?" she said without preamble.

"I haven't an idea, Lizzie. Probably not long, but we'll have to do our best by her."

"I'll feed her all right," said Lizzie, unappeased. "I'll feed that sour-faced woman she's brought with her too, if I have to stuff her meals down her throat. What I want to know is, what's she doing here?"

I never have had any secrets from Lizzie, nor—I suspect— had Mother before me. I put a hand on her militant old shoulder.

"I don't know, Lizzie," I said. "All I know is that she has a reason, and that we'll know it in due time. Perhaps she'll stay only a day or two. She loathes it here."

"Then praise God for that," said Lizzie, and went on paring potatoes.

Nevertheless, and in spite of what was to come, that arrival of Juliette's had its humorous side. One and all, the servants were determined that she should find nothing changed from our more opulent days. Perhaps I had fallen into slack habits. Ordinarily during the season I am not at home much. I am

21

likely to lunch at the club and play bridge, and to dine out on those nights when I am not giving a small dinner myself.

Now the best silver was coming out from the safe in the library, a safe cannily camouflaged by my grandfather by glass doors painted with imitation books which would not have deceived a blind burglar; Mother's old Georgian tea set, the candelabra and even the silver service plates. The pantry was seething with activity, and wide-eyed Ellen was polishing vigorously under William's watchful eyes.

But my hopes that the visit was to be brief were shortlived. Late in the afternoon two large trunks arrived and were carried up to Juliette's room; and suddenly I felt the need of air and action. As a result I took Chu-Chu, my toy Pekingese—so called because of various tracks hither and yon, on carpets and lawns—and went down beside the pond, where Chu-Chu and a red squirrel carried on a sort of daily flirtation, the squirrel plainly refusing to consider Chu-Chu a dog at all. On the way down I turned and looked back at the house, and I was almost certain that I saw a curtain move up in the old hospital room.

I watched for some time but the movement was not repeated, and at last I went on. There was a bench there, out of sight of the house, and I sat down and faced my problem as well as I could.

The pond was very still. At the upper end, where Stony Creek flowed down from the hills to feed it, was shallow; but where I sat near the dam it was deep and dark. What was left of the spring wild flowers formed small patches of color on the banks, and the thin overflow slid over the red stone wall and splashed cheerfully onto the shore below. But the air was cold. I found myself shivering, and so, calling Chu-Chu, who had found an acorn and was pretending to be a squirrel herself, I went back to the house.

Before I dressed for dinner I went up to the hospital suite. Nothing had been disturbed there, but acting on impulse I turned the key in the door at the top of the stairs and took it down with me. I put it in my handkerchief bag in the upper drawer of my bureau, and when Maggie came in to dress me for dinner I showed her where it was. Also I told her what I had seen, and she sniffed audibly.

22

"She's a snooper," she said. "Always was and always will be. But what did she want up there?"

"I'm not certain she *was* there, Maggie."

"Well, she's up to something," she said, slapping the brush down on my cringing scalp as she used to do when I was a child. "What did I tell you about those crows? I'm only thankful your mother didn't live to see this day, miss."

Maggie's conversations with me are rather like those with the Queen of England, when one drops in a "ma'am" now and then, like inserting a comma. Sometimes I am miss to her, sometimes not. Privately and in her loyal old heart I am still little Marcia, making faces when she jerks my hair, and being inspected surreptitiously to see if I have washed my ears. But she was in deadly earnest that day. I knew it when she brought out one of my best dinner dresses and fairly dared me not to wear it.

"Don't let her patronize you," she said, slipping it over my head. "You're better looking than she is any day; and as for that woman she's got with her—"

Here words failed her. She gave me a final jerk and stood back to survey her handiwork.

"Let her beat that!" she said vindictively.

It was half past seven that night before I saw Juliette again. Then she trailed downstairs in a long silver-gray creation with bands of silver fox on the sleeves. It was still broad daylight, and the low sun, streaming in through the big windows in the drawing room, showed her face older and more tired than it had been that morning. There were deep lines around her eyes, and for all her nonchalance she looked worn and harassed. Her earlier cheerfulness, too, was gone. She was irritable and nervy.

"Heavens, what a glare!" she said. "I could do with a cocktail, if you can manage one."

"They are coming."

"Thank God," she said. "In the old days it was sherry. Do you remember? I've never looked at the stuff since."

She relaxed over the cocktails, and she ate a fair dinner, but no sweet.

"I have to watch my figure," she said. "I'm thirty-two, and I

23

can't go on forever being twenty-five. How do you stay so slim?"

She was more than that, I knew; but I let it go.

"I exercise a lot. And I have plenty to do."

It was not a pleasant meal, for all the newly polished silver and Lizzie's efforts. There were long intervals of silence when only William's quiet movements and the lapping of the waves were to be heard. But once she glanced around her and spoke almost violently.

"God, how I hate this place," she said.

There was an obvious answer to that, but I did not make it. As the daylight faded she looked prettier and rather tragic. The candles shone on her fair hair, on her long white hands with their scarlet nails and on her petulant painted mouth.

"I'm sorry, Juliette," I said quietly. "Of course it's home to me."

"It never was home to me," she said, and launched into a barbed attack on all of us; on her home-coming as a bride, and Father at the head of the table, stiff and uncompromising. On the close association between Arthur and me, so that she was often the unwanted third. On the time, a year or so later, when she took sick and Mother sent her to the quarantine room until she had been diagnosed.

"She hated me from the start," she said.

"I don't believe that, Juliette. She was very good to you. Maybe she was a little jealous of you. Arthur was her only son."

"You never liked me yourself."

"You didn't much care, did you? If you had tried—"

"Tried! What was the use? You were too complacent, too rich in those days. And I was nobody. So far as you were concerned I was something he picked up out of the gutter; and you were glad to pay any price to get rid of me at the end."

Enough of that was true to make me acutely uncomfortable. But luckily William reappeared then, and when he brought coffee to the library where a fire was burning, she had made up her mind to be more amiable.

It was there, over a cigarette, that she divulged the reason for her visit.

24

"I want to change the arrangement with Arthur, Marcia," she said.

"Change it? How?" I asked, startled.

"I want a lump sum and call it quits."

I sat quite still. A lump sum, when none of us had any available capital! On the other hand, if it could be managed, an end for all time to the yearly drain on Arthur's resources.

"You said you were in trouble, Juliette. Is it about money? Is that the reason?"

She hesitated.

"I need money, yes. I suppose that's no news to you. But—well, see here, Marcia. I'm young, comparatively; and I'm strong. I'll probably live a long time." She laughed a little. "Look what Arthur will have paid me in the next twenty years. A quarter of a million! That's a lot of money."

"How much do you want?"

"A hundred thousand dollars."

I must have gasped, for she looked at me queerly.

"I have to have it," she said. "He'll be getting off easy at that, Marcia."

I remember the desperation in her voice when she said that, and it made me sorry for her and anxious. The next minute she had lighted another cigarette, and although her hands trembled her voice was steady enough. She knew there had been a depression. She knew our money—Arthur's and mine—was in a trust fund for his children and mine if I ever had any. But there was property, wasn't there? How about selling Sunset? It was supposed to be valuable.

"Sunset belongs to me now," I told her. "I bought Arthur's share. As for selling it, even if I wanted to, I can't. There's no market for big places, Juliette."

She saw that I was speaking the truth, and she looked fairly haunted. She got up suddenly and went to one of the windows, standing there and staring out.

"I loathe night on the water!" she said. "It makes me think of death."

By the time she came back to the fire she was in better control. She even smiled her old mocking smile when I asked her if there was any emergency back of the idea.

25

"You could call it that," she said. "Why shouldn't I want to marry again, and need some capital for the love nest?"

"Is that the real reason?"

She did not reply at once. She sat looking somberly at the fire, and I thought she shivered.

"No," she said finally, and let it go at that.

I felt sorry for her that night. She looked frightened, and I wondered if she was being blackmailed. Before we went upstairs I tried to explain things to her.

"I know Arthur would do it if he could, Juliette," I said. "But you must know how things are. Junior had an appendix operation last spring, and now he has measles. That means nurses and hospital bills. He just manages; no more."

She had no reply to that, and we went up early to bed; Juliette to the long massaging, the creams and astringents which were her evening ritual; and I to write to Arthur.

"I don't know what the trouble is," I wrote, "but there is something. She is worried, Arthur. Do you know what it is? I know the whole thing is impossible, but you will have to tell her yourself."

I left it in the hall with a special-delivery stamp on it and went to bed. But I could not sleep. I was back with the young Arthur who had married her secretly, and then proudly brought her to Sunset. I was only seventeen at the time, but I remembered it well; William and the second man serving—it was lunchtime—and Arthur leading her into the room by the hand. He looked uneasy, but she was calm; calm and smiling.

"This is my wife," he said, looking at Father. "I hope you will all be good to her."

Father got up. He looked stunned. Mother could only gaze at them both, helplessly.

"When did this happen?" said Father.

"Yesterday, sir."

Then Juliette took a hand. She went directly to Mother and, bending over, kissed her on the cheek.

"Try to forgive me," she said. "I love him so terribly."

And mother, who was a gentlewoman first and Father's wife only secondarily, had put an arm around her and held her for a moment.

"Then be kind to him," she said gently. "For I love him too."

Father never fully accepted Juliette. I know that he took a horse out that day and brought it back hours later in a state which set the stableboy to wondering. But the thing was done. We were all helpless.

From the first it was obvious that she was not one of us, if I can say that without being snobbish. She had no family save an aunt, Aunt Delia she called her, somewhere in the Middle West. She had come to New York to study music, and Arthur had met her there. But she was a lovely thing to look at, and if the songs she sang in a sweet husky voice were rather of the music-hall variety, we did our best by her.

She was quick to learn, too; how to dress—her first clothes were pretty terrible, how to ride, even how to talk. And Arthur's pride in her was touching.

"She's beautiful, isn't she, Marcia?"

"Very."

"And you don't mind?"

"Why should I?" I said lightly. "She's yours, and you love her."

But I never really liked or trusted her, and as time went on I found I was not alone. Women did not care for her, but she had a curious effect on men. They clustered about her like flies around honey. It was for men that she sang her throaty little songs, and when the Park Avenue house was too staid for her, it was still men who filled the new apartment. Arthur used to come home and find them there, laughing and drinking.

I lay in my bed that night, remembering all this. But I was seeing her, too, as she had trailed up the stairs ahead of me, her body lithe and effortless as a girl's and her high heels clicking on the hard wood of the steps. At the top she had turned and looked down at me.

"I'm warning you," she said. "I'm staying until something is done, Marcia. It has to be done."

That had been her good night.

CHAPTER IV

Juliette had arrived on Friday, and it was a week before that strange disappearance of hers.

It was a nerve-racking week at that. Juliette herself seemed calm enough, although she reverted more than once to the lump sum idea. Part of the time she spent in bed or in what sounded like long discussions with the Jordan woman; and to add to the general confusion the house bells were actually ringing, as Mrs. Curtis had said. There was a perfect bedlam in the pantry where they registered, so that periods when the servants were rushing over the house to answer them were varied by others when no one answered them at all. As when, after three false alarms one morning a day or two after her arrival, Juliette rang at ten o'clock for her breakfast tray, and was finally discovered in the upper hall in a chiffon nightgown, shouting furiously to an embarrassed William in the hall below.

"What the devil's the matter with you down there?" she called. "I can hear the bell myself."

"Sorry, madam," said William, red to his collar. "We thought it was the ghost again."

Which was against orders, but by that time I suspected my entire household of an attempt to get rid of both Juliette and Jordan. Indeed that day Juliette herself accused us of that very thing. She came out later to where I was sitting on the upper porch, my book in my lap and my eyes on the bay, blue in the morning sunlight. Already the seals had disappeared, and far away a mahogany speedboat was tracing a line of white across the water. I looked up to see her staring down at me.

29

"What's this about a ghost?" she demanded.

"Some superstitious nonsense in the kitchen. The bells have been ringing for some reason or other. I'll have the wiring looked over tomorrow."

She looked amused.

"No idea of scaring me off, of course," she said.

"Certainly not."

She laughed, not pleasantly.

"I'm not easy to scare," she said. "You might tell the kitchen that. And may I have the car? I've ordered a horse. I'm fed up with loafing. No word from Arthur, I suppose?"

"He's barely had time to get my letter."

She was in full riding kit that day, breeches, boots and a well-tailored coat. One of her curious developments had been that she had become a good horsewoman, first here at Sunset when we still kept our own horses, and later after her divorce, when she had cultivated the hunting set of Long Island.

"I suppose Ed Smith still has some horses fit to ride," she said.

"I ride them," I told her coolly. But that seemed to amuse her.

"How hath the mighty fallen!" she said, and laughed.

I had meant to go out myself, but with the car gone I was helpless. Ed Smith's riding academy is on the other side of town, not far from the golf course, and too far to walk in boots. Anyway I didn't want to ride with Juliette. But I was rather resentful when I heard her driving away. I took a swim instead, and although the water was like ice, felt the better for it.

I had just finished dressing afterwards when Arthur called me from New York, and his voice sounded tired and strained.

"Is she there, Marcia?"

"She's out riding."

"What's it all about, anyhow? I can't raise that money. She knows damned well I can't."

"I've told her that, but she's pretty insistent, Arthur. She wants me to sell Sunset."

"I'll see her in hell first."

He was quieter after that. He had no idea what trouble she was in, if any. He would be glad to get the damned alimony out

30

of the way, of course. It was bleeding him white. But the whole proposition was absurd. He couldn't touch the trust fund, and he wouldn't if he could.

"That's for Mary Lou and the boy," he said with finality.

He was furious about her presence at Sunset too. It had spoiled Mary Lou's visit, and Junior's too, and before he rang off he said that they were taking a cottage at Millbank, a small town on the mainland shore about twenty miles from us, and that as soon as Juliette had gone Mary Lou would come to Sunset.

"When is she going?" he asked.

"I haven't any idea. She looks settled for life."

"Well, don't be a fool" were his parting words. "Get her out of there as soon as you can. She's poison."

He hung up, and I was certain that I heard another receiver stealthily replaced somewhere in the house. In the pantry, however, William in his shirt sleeves was reading the newspaper, and Lizzie was working at the range. Maggie and Ellen were in the laundry.

It was then that I remembered Jordan and went upstairs. There was a telephone on my bedside table, but she was not there; and I finally found her in her own room, pressing a dress of Juliette's with what was obviously a cold iron. She gave me a frigid glance.

"Did you want me for something, miss?" she asked, with a mock humility not unlike Juliette's at times.

"I wondered where you were," I said dryly. "And now I think of it, I want to ask you something. Were you by any chance in the hospital suite the day you came?"

"The hospital suite, miss? Where is it?"

"Up the staircase at the end of the hall."

She pursed her lips primly.

"Then I haven't seen it," she said. "I don't go where I don't belong."

I felt beaten. Not only beaten but dismissed. I went to the porch and lay back in my steamer chair, but peace had gone out of the world and even out of the bay. There were other boats there now, a sloop, a yawl with a black hull and spreading sails, a speed boat, a small cabin cruiser. The summer colony was

31

arriving at last, and well I knew how fast the news would spread.

"Juliette at Marcia's? Juliette!"

"So I hear. What do you suppose she's after?"

Knowing Juliette, they would know quite well that she was after something.

It was lunchtime that day when Juliette returned from her ride. I heard the car, followed by her voice in her room and later by the shower in her bathroom. She had never had any sense of time, and I went down nervously to postpone the meal until she appeared. To my surprise, Jordan was already in the kitchen.

"Madam is tired," she was saying. "She will have some tea and toast in her room."

Lizzie turned a red and angry face to her.

"All right," she said. "I heard you. And you can tell madam that this is my afternoon out and she'll get a cold supper. I cook no other meals this day."

But it seemed to me that Jordan looked disturbed, and when later on I met her carrying down Juliette's tray, it was apparently untouched. I thought at the time that the woman had reported Arthur's conversation over the telephone, and that it had upset her; but I know now that something had happened on that ride. Juliette had seen someone, and she was frightened.

I had a number of elderly callers that afternoon. Evidently the news had got about. Old Mrs. Pendexter was the first, her Queen Mary hat higher and more trimmed than ever in deference to the occasion, more than the usual chains around her neck, and her black eyes snapping with curiosity.

"Well, Marcia," she said. "Where's that hussy?"

"Juliette? She's resting. She took a ride this morning."

"What on earth is she doing here?" she demanded. "Has she no decency?"

"Well," I said, smiling as best I could, "you know her. She seems to be settled for a few days anyhow. But she came on business."

"Business! More alimony, I suppose. And that wretched Arthur paying her with blood and sweat. See here, Marcia,

32

you're a lady, whatever that means nowadays. She isn't. She never was, for all her fine feathers. Why don't you kick her out?"

I suppose I was tired and worried. My eyes filled, and she leaned over and patted me on the arm.

"Don't mind me, child," she said. "I'm a bitter old woman. But I've seen you fighting to keep going, with four servants in a house that used to have ten and needs a dozen, and I'm no fool. You're helping Arthur, of course."

She changed the subject then. It looked like a good season. The Burtons were in Europe but had rented their house to a family named Dean; some Lake Forest people, she'd heard. Her own daughter Marjorie was on the way, and the Hutchinsons were due at any time at The Lodge, the next estate to Sunset.

She was followed by others, and sitting where Mother had always sat in the drawing room, pouring China tea and watching William passing English muffins and cake, I was aware of a certain tension.

I finally realized what it was. They were waiting for Juliette. They did not like her. They never had liked her. But she represented a new, defiant, reckless and probably immoral social order about which they were curious. When she did not appear they were disappointed.

"I understood Mrs.—er—Ransom is staying with you."

"Yes. I'm sorry. She's resting just now."

There was a silence. Then someone said that there was a story about a ghost in the house, and I tried to tell them that it was a matter only of crossed wires. But one of the shades, due to some defect in the catch, chose that moment to shoot to the top of the window, and Mrs. Pendexter spilled her tea in her lap!

I was thoroughly shaken and annoyed when they all finally left. Juliette was still shut in her room, and so I had a tray supper in bed that night. And it was that night that I got the first glimpse of the mystery which later on was to puzzle the whole country, and drive me almost to despair. It was a warm evening, and I slipped on a dressing gown and went out onto the porch.

There was a man below, on the beach. He had been looking

up at the house, but when he saw me he pulled his soft hat down over his eyes and moved away.

I was puzzled as well as uneasy, but he did not come back.

The next day was fairly normal. Juliette appeared after breakfast in a sports outfit and topcoat, and asked me if I would walk around the pond with her. Whatever had happened she had got herself in hand, and she had lost much of the mocking contempt of her arrival. When we were out of earshot of the house she asked if I had heard from Arthur.

"I have," I said. "He called up yesterday while you were out. It's just as I told you. He can't manage it, Juliette."

She was silent. We walked down the path, with Chu-Chu ahead of us, and I saw that she was pale under her rouge.

"See here, Juliette," I said, "if you are in trouble, why not tell me about it? We can't help you with money, but after all Arthur is a lawyer. He may be able to do something. Nobody wants you to suffer."

"Why not?" she said. "You both hate me. I suppose there are plenty of reasons, but you do."

"You've cost us a good deal—not only in money. There's no reason for hatred, however. If I can help—"

"Help how?"

I was tired of fencing. I stopped in the path and faced her.

"Stop it," I said. "What *is* the matter, anyhow? Do you want to get married again, and is this money your price? Or are you in a real jam, as you put it?"

"I don't know," she said slowly. "That's the hell of it, Marcia. I don't know."

I remember that she said very little after that. For a time she stood idly throwing pebbles into the pond and watching the circles widen and spread.

"Like life," she said. "A little pebble and look what it starts. The damned things go on and on."

Then she turned abruptly and went back to the house, alone.

I don't know why she stayed on after that. We know now that she had had her warning the day before. Perhaps she had convinced herself that there was nothing in it. Perhaps, too, she still hoped to hear from Arthur or was sure that she could protect herself. Also, there was a certain recklessness in her character. She had weathered too many storms to fear this one.

I think now that she merely conformed to her pattern, and that it was a normal one for her. Probably all of us conformed to a normal pattern, even those of us who were later to be involved. There was no criminal type among us. Desperation and despair in plenty, but with reason behind them; even if that reason was distorted. There was murder, irrational as is all murder, but it resorted to no mysterious poisons or strange weapons; it planted no misleading clues. It arose inevitably, out of an inevitable chain of events.

And so she stayed on, to her death.

Two or three days later Mary Lou and Junior arrived at Millbank, and I drove over to see them.

Mary Lou was unpacking, and she looked hot and resentful.

"Of all things, Marcia!" she said. "To be kept away by that woman! How dare she do such a thing?"

"You don't know her or you would know she dares to do anything she wants to do."

"And you put up with it!"

"What am I to do?" I inquired, taking off my gloves. "This looks comfortable, Mary Lou. You can manage for a week or two. Where's Junior?"

"On the beach with the nurse."

I finally induced her to sit down and take a cigarette, but she was still like an angry child. She is almost my own age, but in many ways she has never grown up.

"I don't trust her, Marcia," she said. "And Arthur is in a terrible state. I hated to leave him. She's always wanted him back," she added inconsequentially.

"Nonsense. He bored her to tears."

"I'm not so sure of that; and I'd like to bet she never bored him."

"Don't tell me you're jealous of her," I said lightly. "Don't join the army, Mary Lou."

"What army?" she asked suspiciously.

"The army of wives who are afraid of her."

She did not smile, however.

"I wish something would happen to her," she said somberly.
"I suppose that's dreadful, but it's true. What good is she to

35

anybody? She's a pure parasite. She takes all she can and gives nothing; and that ridiculous alimony—"

Fortunately the nurse brought Junior then, and we played with a toy cannon until it was time for me to go.

"I've had the measles," he said proudly. "I was all over spots."

I felt better when I left. The cottage was attractive, and Mary Lou had her car to get about in. It was arranged that on Juliette's departure they would come to stay with me, and in the interval Arthur was putting his small sloop into commission and might sail it up later on.

I motored home in a happier mood. The sea was still and blue, and when I crossed the bridge to the island I saw the head of one of my seals, sleek and dog-like. The farmhouses I passed were neat and white, with porch boxes and borders filled with flowers, and the aromatic scent of the pines was familiar and very dear. I took the short cut across through the hills, and looking down saw Loon Lake, small and exquisite in its green setting.

A young man was painting it from beside the road, with the red of the sunset in it, and I stopped the car to look. He was a big young man, in a pair of gray slacks and a sweater, rather shabby. And he gave me a nice smile and asked if I thought he was catching it.

"I like it," I said. "Do you mind if I watch?"

"Not a bit. I was fed up with myself."

How casual it all seems as I write it! Loon Lake below us, the painter working with broad vigorous strokes, his soft hat shading his eyes, and just around the corner sheer tragedy waiting to involve us both.

I sat down on the running board of the car to let the peace of late afternoon relax me. After a time he put down his brush and taking a package of cigarettes from his pocket offered me one and took one himself. Thus seen, he was older than I had thought at first. In his thirties, probably. But he was certainly attractive and undeniably amused.

"One of the summer crowd, I suppose?" he said, idly scrutinizing me. "New York fall and spring and Palm Beach in winter. Is that a good guess?"

I was somewhat annoyed.

36

"Not any more," I said briefly.

"Dear, dear! Don't tell me the depression has hit the island. That's bad for my business, isn't it?"

"How can I tell? What is your business?" I inquired.

He looked extremely hurt.

"Great Scott," he said. "Why do you think I spend hours on that outrageous camp stool, painting rotten water colors? Because I like it?"

"I thought that might be the general idea," I said meekly.

He grinned.

"Sorry. The human animal has to be fed, you know. That's not quite true," he added quickly. "It amuses me, and most people don't know painting when they see it anyhow. I don't myself," he added, in a burst of candor.

He interested me. He was even bigger than I had thought, with broad shoulders and long muscular hands. But looking at him closely I thought he had probably been ill. When he whipped off his hat his forehead was pale, and his clothes hung on him loosely. But he was cheerful, even gay. It turned out that he was stopping at the tourist camp on Pine Hill, not far away, and that he lived, of all unexpected things, in a trailer.

"Ever try one?" he inquired. "Rather fun, when you get used to it; and it has its advantages. No taxes, no permanent domicile, and no neighbors to let their chickens into your garden. Plenty of democracy too, only you probably wouldn't like that. Pretty decent lot, on the whole."

In the end I learned that he had not been well, and that open air had been recommended. He traveled and painted. "Pretty bad pictures, but I don't pretend they're good." And he liked being outdoors. I suspected that he was the usual depression victim, but he was certainly asking for no sympathy.

I summoned enough courage at last to ask if I might buy the Loon Lake picture when it was finished.

"I really like it," I said. "It's not—"

"Not charity," he finished for me, grinning. "Well, I rather hoped you would, as a matter of fact. It's bad, but it's the best I've done yet. I'd like you to have it. If you'll give me your name—"

I did, and I thought he looked at me quickly. But he was quite composed as he wrote it down.

"Let's see," he said. "I think I know your house. Big one on the sea wall, isn't it?"

"That sounds like it."

"And you live there all alone?"

"Usually. I have a guest now."

He shot another glance at me, but he made no comment. Soon after that—and with some reluctance—I went away.

He helped me into the car, and I had an odd idea that there was something he wanted to say. He did not, though, and I left him there, standing bareheaded in the sunlight and looking strangely undecided.

It was some time before I remembered that I did not know his name.

I felt excited as I drove home. Never had the hills looked so green or the farmhouses so white and neat. As a matter of fact I was so abstracted that I drove half a mile past Sunset before I realized it, and had to turn back. I kept on seeing my unknown painter, with his attractive smile, and remembering the idiotic impulse I had had when he took off his hat, of wanting to smooth down his hair where it was ruffled at the back!

I even dreamed of him that night, as I remembered sheepishly in the clear light of the next morning. But in the dream he was not smiling. His face looked strained and hard, and I realized with some perturbation that it probably could look just like that.

One thing that episode did for me. It made Juliette easier to endure that day. For she was not easy to live with by that time. She had been there six days, and the insolent composure of her manner the day she came was entirely gone. She was irritable and worried. I noticed, too, that she avoided the town. When she rode it was into the hills, and her infrequent walks were in the opposite direction, toward the golf club.

"You might as well know that I am staying until something is settled," she said nastily.

"That's up to you," I said. "You are my guest. I can't very well turn you out."

"Always the pattern of all the virtues, including hospitality!" she said, and left me.

CHAPTER V

The days since Juliette's arrival had seen a good many new arrivals. The heat was driving people early to the island, and the estates around us were gradually being opened and occupied. Marjorie Pendexter had arrived, and Howard Brooks, her fiancé, was on the way in his yacht, the *Sea Witch*. The Deans had opened the Burton place. Tony Rutherford had taken his usual rooms at the Broxton House, and little by little the village was beginning to look like a small metropolis.

The last of the seals had gone, the local shipyard was rushing boats into the water, and already one of the sightseeing cruisers was making its tours along the waterfront; and I could hear a blatant voice through its megaphones as I was having tea on the upper porch: "The white house is Sunset, property of Miss Marcia Lloyd of New York. There's Miss Lloyd now on the porch roof, having her supper."

But I found myself rather alone in the excitement. Word that Juliette was with me had evidently been passed around to the newcomers, and either delicacy or prudence kept them away. I did not like it much. Usually Sunset is gay all summer, but now it was as though a plague, in the shape of Juliette, had settled over it.

One day I learned that Bob and Lucy Hutchinson, who had The Lodge, the next property to Sunset, had arrived; and that afternoon Lucy came in to see me. I was upstairs with the electrician, who was going over the bells, and when I went down I found her in the library, restlessly moving about. She gave me only a perfunctory greeting.

"See here, Marcia," she said abruptly. "Is it true that

Juliette is here?"

"For a few days. At least I hope that's all."

"You poor sap," she said venomously. "You know what she is. Once let her get a foothold here and where are you? Where are any of us, for that matter?"

I looked at her. Lucy was the really smart member of the summer colony. The older women watched her clothes and copied them when they could; but what with her slenderness, her bright red hair and the long earrings she affected, the results on some of them were not so good. Only Juliette had ever done it successfully, and there had been one summer when her success had been too obvious. She nearly got Bob Hutchinson himself.

That was in Lucy's mind that day, for she said: "Tell her to keep away from me; that's all."

"I suppose you think I like it!" I retorted.

"Well, get her out of here," she said bluntly. "I mean it, Marcia. By the grace of God I saved Bob, but she cost you Tony Rutherford, and you damn' well know it. If you think that's funny I'm going home."

And go she did, slamming out the front door, meeting Juliette in the driveway and cutting her dead, as I learned afterwards.

I was not too happy when she had gone. Juliette *had* cost me Tony. I suppose that flirtation with her was never serious, and we had still been engaged when she left Arthur; but the hard times hit just then and Tony's firm went under.

"When I'm able to afford a wife I'll come back," he said. "Not before."

Nothing moved him; and of course as time went on the usual thing happened. He drifted off. He did not marry. He found a position and managed to get along. But his letters came less and less often. When they did they were more affectionate than loving, and now and then when he came up from Philadelphia to New York our meetings became a sort of desperate attempt to bridge the gulf opening between us. One day I told him it was all over, whether we knew it or not. He looked surprised rather than hurt.

"As you want it, my dear," he said. "I'll always think you

40

the sweetest girl I've ever known. If things had been different—"

Juliette came down to dinner that night in a vicious temper.

"If Lucy Hutchinson thinks she can cut me," she said, "she'd better think again. I could make a lot of trouble around here if I wanted to."

"You'd better keep your hands off Bob," I warned her. "Lucy is on the warpath."

But she seemed pleased at that, and after dinner, I put on a wrap and went outside. I felt as though five minutes more of her would send me into shrieking hysterics.

It was a beautiful night, and certainly no evening to be alone. I found myself thinking of the painter on the hill, and wondering if I would ever see him again. After all, with a trailer, he might already have moved on. But I dismissed him from my mind. I was no romantic child, at twenty-nine.

On impulse I made a call on the Deans that night, Chu-Chu at my heels. I did not want to go back to Juliette, and across the road and above me I could see the huge mass of the house and that it was fully lighted. Anything was better than another evening with Juliette; I crossed the road, went up the steep driveway and rang the bell.

A footman admitted me, looking surprised, and a butler hovered in the background. I began to feel rather silly, but when I found Mrs. Dean, alone by a fire in the vast formal drawing room, I was glad I had come. She had evidently been lonely, for she was almost enthusiastic in her greeting.

"How nice of you," she said cordially. "Mansfield will be pleased too. You see, we know nobody yet."

"I am your nearest neighbor," I told her. "Marcia Lloyd. And when I saw your lights—"

"Neighbor!" she said. "What a pleasant word that is. It's a long time since I have heard it."

And I wondered, as I have wondered since, if that is not one of the penalties of wealth. There was certainly nothing arrogant about Agnes Dean, however. She picked up Chu-Chu and held her in her lap, a thing the dog detests; and I could see then that she was thin and haggard, and definitely middle-aged, although in the soft light she showed the remnants of great

41

beauty. She was dressed in deep black, and she looked down at it with an apologetic air.

"We lost a daughter a year ago," she said quietly. "That is why we came here. My husband thought I needed to see new people. We have a summer place on Lake Michigan, but it is very quiet."

It was pleasant to sit by the fire and chat about nothing in particular. I did not mention that I had an unwelcome house guest but the Deans had probably heard some of the neighborhood gossip about Juliette.

I gathered that Mrs. Dean was dreading the summer. She had never cared for society and we were credited with being very gay. She had liked her home, and of course when her daughter was living— She broke off, and her chin quivered.

For her sake I was glad when Mr. Dean appeared. I can still see Mansfield Dean as he looked that night, a heavy man with broad shoulders, the beginning of a paunch, and a voice that resounded all over the place. He shouted for a highball, gave his wife an amiable pat that was like a blow, and bellowed that he was delighted to see me.

"I want Agnes to have friends here," he boomed like a church bell. "No use sitting about and fretting." His voice softened. "What's done is done, and people help. I hope they'll come," he added, rather pathetically. "Of course we're new, but there's a lot of room. And later on we can give a dinner or two."

He fascinated me, so sure of himself, of his money and its power; and yet with a certain gentleness about him. He had a pleasant smile, showing big white teeth, and I think he knew that evening that he was a trifle ridiculous and did not mind it. One thing was certain. He dominated his wife, as he probably dominated everyone around him; but he was devoted to her.

"We have had our troubles," he said, "but we have to get along somehow. And we're going to, aren't we, mother?"

His openness disconcerted me. I had a sudden feeling that I did not belong there; as though I was intruding on a tragedy. Agnes Dean sat silent, her eyes fixed on the fire, and after his entrance she said very little. Whatever the tragedy was, it was hers, not his. He could live his man's life, attend to business, play golf, drink his highballs, go to his clubs. But she had no such refuge. She sat there alone with her grief.

That was my introduction to the Deans; but my first impression of Agnes Dean has always remained with me, a small grief-stricken woman in a black dress, with a vast house and the panoply of wealth all about her, and none of it meaning anything to her.

Mr. Dean walked back to Sunset with me when I left. Alone he ceased to boom, and I have wondered since how much of that heartiness of his before his wife was sheer acting.

"I hope you'll come again," he said. "She needs friends. She needs some nice women to talk to. She doesn't talk much any more."

He left me at my gate and for a moment I had a strange feeling that there was a light in the hospital suite. It went out just then, if it had ever been there at all. But, in view of that, it was disconcerting on my return to find William waiting for me with a long face.

"Sorry to tell you, miss. The bells are ringing again."

"Good heavens," I said peevishly, "that man today said the wiring was all right."

"That may be," he said somberly. "Perhaps it has nothing to do with the wiring."

Nevertheless, just to be certain, before I went to bed I went up the stairs to look around. The door was still locked, and soon after I was asleep.

I wakened late the next morning to a bright sun and Maggie with my breakfast tray and an expression which should have soured the cream for my coffee.

"When you're up and dressed," she said, "I'll trouble you to look at something."

"What is it? And where?"

"In the hospital suite," she said, and proceeded methodically to get out my clothing for the day. I looked at her stiff figure with exasperation.

"Why on earth are you so mysterious?" I said peevishly. "What's wrong with the hospital suite?"

"When you're up and dressed I'll show you," she said in a low voice, and lapsed into a dour silence.

43

"Where is Mrs. Ransom? Is she awake?" I inquired finally.

"She's up. She took the car and went to the village for a wave. That Jordan went with her."

"Then why on earth do you have to whisper?"

She made no reply, and as soon as I was dressed I found myself going once more up the steep stairs, I ahead and Maggie following. The outer door was locked as usual, but that was all that was as usual. I opened the door onto chaos. In the anteroom the trunks had been opened and their contents strewn over the floor. Even the mattress on the cot had been taken off, and every box and chest had been searched.

Maggie had followed me in and waited until I caught my breath.

"You were still asleep when Mike wanted one of the screens for a cellar window this morning," she said, "so I got the key and brought him up here. That's what we found. And when I went into the other room, *that* was there."

She led me to the door into the quarantine room proper. At first it looked to me much as I had left it. Then I saw where she was pointing. There was a hatchet lying on one of the beds. It looked quite ordinary as it lay there, but I could not repress a shudder. It was sharp and dangerous.

"Are you certain Mike didn't bring it up?"

"He never put foot in this room."

"Does it belong in the house?"

"No, miss. I've asked downstairs. The old hatchet's in the woodshed, where it belongs."

Save that one of the beds had been slightly moved, the room itself was as I had seen it last. The window was closed, and if anyone had entered by Arthur's old method, via trellis and roof, there was no sign of it.

I saw in Maggie's face a reflection of my own suspicions.

"If you're asking me," she said, "it's that Jordan. She's always snooping around. Only—what did she want, miss?"

I surveyed the two rooms helplessly.

"I haven't any idea, Maggie," I said. "And don't tell the other people in the house. I have trouble enough already."

Everybody was too busy to straighten the place that day, but I did two things before I went downstairs again. I sent Maggie

44

for some nails, and using the blunt edge of the hatchet fastened the window so it could not be opened; and I stood by while William and Mike, the gardener, together put a padlock on the outer door.

I was downstairs in my room hiding the key in my bureau drawer when I remembered that I had left the hatchet where it was, on the bed; although Maggie wanted to go back for it I left it there. It did not seem important at the time.

CHAPTER VI

It was the next day that Juliette disappeared.

I did not like her, but I am glad to feel that at least a part of that last evening of hers was a cheerful one. She had dressed rather elaborately for dinner, and I remembered that she had a number of cocktails before we went in to eat. Apparently the wave had improved her morale, and if she knew anything about the condition of those upper rooms she gave no sign of it.

I, too, was feeling more normal. I had played eighteen holes of golf that afternoon, and I was content to sit still and give her the admiration she always craved.

"That's a lovely dress," I told her. And I can still see her turning around, complacently, in front of the long Chippendale mirror in the drawing room.

"It *is* pretty good," she said. "And I've lost an inch off my waist."

Standing there, tall and slim and smiling, her hair freshly waved, and inspecting herself. Eying her complexion closely in the strong sunset light, and giving a nod of approval. And all the time, as the clock on the mantel ticked on, her span of life growing shorter. The sands in the glass running out.

I am even glad that Lizzie gave her an unusually good dinner that night; and that I said nothing when, later on, she sent Jordan for a long cape with a high fur collar, and stated that she was taking the car.

"I'm fed up with sitting around here alone," she said. "Doesn't anybody ever come in? I thought you were the belle of the place!"

She saw my face and laughed her mocking little laugh.

47

"So I'm the trouble," she said. "Little Marcia's trouble, eh? Well, you know the answer to that."

She went out, and soon after I heard the car. Weeks later we were to wonder about that drive of hers. Where had she gone? Whom had she seen? Had it led to the catastrophe of the next day, and if so, how? But when we did know it was too late to matter.

Tony Rutherford came in just after she had gone.

"Hid in the bushes until she was out of the way," he said, grinning. "Heard she was here. What's the idea, anyhow? And how are you? Bearing up?"

"Pretty well," I told him. "Ring for a drink if you want one, Tony."

He rang and then coming back, eyed me closely.

"Not so good," was his verdict. "Juliette *and* ghosts. Either one would set me running like blazes."

"Not always," I reminded him.

He smiled sheepishly.

"Forget that, won't you? I was an idiot, of course. Maybe I just lost my sense of humor. And she was a lovely thing," he added reminiscently. "God, what a lovely thing she was!"

I was astonished to find how little that meant to me now. There had been a time when, troubled as I was, I would have wanted to put my head on his shoulder and hear him offer his usual comfort.

"Liquor for men and tears for women," he would say. "What would we do without them?"

That night I felt nothing at all. He was as good-looking as ever, as immaculate in his dinner clothes, but I could survey him with complete detachment. He got his highball and settled himself comfortably in a chair by the fire.

"Now tell Papa all about it," he said. "What does she want? Don't tell me she came for love."

"She wants a lump sum instead of alimony," I blurted out. "We can't raise it, of course."

"How much?"

"A hundred thousand."

He whistled. "That's a lot of money. What does she want it for? Want to marry again?"

48

"If she does she's very queer about it. She says she wants to leave America. She seems frightened, Tony."

"It would take a lot to scare her," he observed with a grin. "Better get rid of her, Marcia. She's little poison ivy, my dear. Always has been and always will be."

She came in soon after that. I thought she looked upset, but when she saw Tony she smiled.

"Why, Tony darling!" she said. "After all these years!"

"Only six months, to look at you," he said, grinning. "How do you do it, Juliette?"

She gave him a long look.

"The virtuous life, Tony," she said. "Early to bed and early to rise. You've heard of it, haven't you?"

"Sure," he said. "It gets worms, or something. And who is your particular worm of the moment?"

I listened as long as I could. She got him over onto the davenport beside her, and he looked both gratified and uneasy. But after a while I whistled for Chu-Chu and went out into the grounds. In the servants' hall I could see the household staff still at the table, but it looked like a sober meal, with Jordan at William's right, holding her coffee-cup with her little finger elegantly extended and looking like a skeleton at the feast. Then Chu-Chu, set up a sharp staccato barking, and when I called to her a man stepped out of the shrubbery.

It was Arthur.

There was no moon, and I did not know him until he spoke to me.

"That you, Marcia?"

"Arthur! What on earth—"

"I don't want to be seen," he said. "I flew up this afternoon. Mary Lou thinks I'm out on the sloop. Where can we talk?"

I told him that Tony and Juliette were inside, and suggested the bench down by the pond. When we reached it he lit a cigarette, and I saw how haggard he looked. He had not told Mary Lou he was coming, he said. She hated Juliette, but he had to see her and to see me too.

"I can't carry on, Marcia," he said, "and this last thing has only forced my hand. I'm in debt up to the neck, and with taxes and everything I'm about through."

What he was going to do, he said, was to ask Juliette to take less alimony. If she refused he would go into court and seek relief.

"She'll raise the roof, of course," he said. "But I have to do something. I owe everybody, even the dentist! And what with the office expenses—" His voice trailed off, and I reached over and took his hand.

"I might help again," I said. "I hate to turn off the servants. They've been here so long, and what would they do? But I still have Mother's pearls. We'd better get rid of her if we can. Not only now. For the future. I've stood about all I can. When I think what she's done to us I'm not normal."

He laughed a little, but his voice was hard.

"You're not going to sell Mother's pearls," he said. "I've stripped you of everything else."

At that moment we heard Tony's voice from somewhere above.

"Hey, Marcia," he called. "What are you doing? Hunting pneumonia?"

"I'm coming," I said, and got up.

"It's useless to see her," I told Arthur in a low voice, "but I'll come back for you after Tony's gone."

"Don't let the servants know I'm here."

"No."

I found Tony waiting reproachfully for me at the door.

"I've had an hour's vamping, and liked it," he said, running his arm through mine. "But enough's enough. Come in and save my reputation, won't you?"

I thought there was a change in the tempo of the library when I went back to it. Juliette looked relaxed and comfortable, but Tony was silent, for him. The badinage had gone, and when Juliette asked him to ride with her early the next morning he pleaded a golf engagement and begged off. She raised her eyebrows and gave him an odd look.

"As you like," she said, with a cool little smile.

There was not much more. I remember Tony retailing a bit of local gossip; and also that it had started to rain, and that I hoped Arthur would remember where we kept the key to the garage and go there for shelter. But finally Juliette began to yawn. Tony alone was one thing. Tony with me sitting by was another. She got up at last and Tony took the hint.

"Suffering cats," he said. "It's eleven o'clock. How long are you to be here, Juliette?"

"I'm staying until some business is arranged," she said sweetly. "I can't go until it's finished."

I went with him into the hall, and I thought he wanted to speak to me. But the door into the library was open, and after glancing at it he bade me a perfunctory good-bye and drove off at his usual wild speed. The rain was stopping by that time and a cold fog was coming in, but I did not dare to bring Arthur into the house at once, although the service wing was dark. I would have to wait until Jordan had put Juliette to bed, with all that that implied, from cream on her face to baby pillows and an electric heating pad. Also she had a wretched habit of slipping down to the library at the last minute for a book for Juliette. I knew I would have to wait until they had both settled down for the night.

I left a lamp on and went upstairs, and it was almost an hour before the sounds ceased from the room down the hall. Then I heard a muffled good night from Jordan and the soft closing of her door. It was half past twelve when, having located Arthur and put him to dry by the library fire, I went upstairs again. I thought I heard a bell ringing in the distance, but I had no time to investigate. I opened Juliette's door and went unceremoniously into her room.

She was reading, propped up against her pillows, and with a chin strap around the lower part of her face. She was evidently annoyed, and she looked at me resentfully.

"You might at least knock, Marcia."

"I didn't want to rouse anybody. Arthur's downstairs, Juliette."

"Arthur! What does he want?"

"I suppose he'll tell you himself."

She got out of bed and whipped off the strap, as well as the net pinned to her hair to save the wave. Her face was not pretty at that moment. It was hard and calculating without its makeup, but there was relief and hope in it too. God knows I do not want to be too hard on her. She had wrecked us all, but I

51

know now how uneasy she was. If she had only gone away, disappeared, she could have saved herself. The trouble was that she could not see herself without money, and it seems never to have occurred to her that she could earn it.

I waited as patiently as I could while she made up her face again: powder, rouge and lipstick. While she got out an elaborate negligee, which she slipped on over her nightgown. Then she stepped into a pair of feathered mules, and I can still remember the click they made as we went down the stairs.

Arthur was in front of the fire, and he had found the whisky and mixed himself a highball. He merely looked at her as she came in.

"Well?" she said. "Why all the secrecy?"

He did not answer that.

He put down his glass, still eying her steadily.

"When I look at you," he said, "it doesn't seem possible that you would wreck a man's life—as you have mine."

She made an impatient gesture.

"You seem to have done very well by yourself. Why be dramatic?"

But I think she had still some idea of using her sex against him. She had never learned that lost lovers do not return, and after all he had loved her a long time. She sat on the arm of a chair and carefully tucked her negligee about her, so that it outlined her body; and it must have shocked her when he spoke again.

"There ought to be a particular hell for your sort of woman," he said slowly. "God knows I loved you, but you took my pride and crushed it. You killed something in me. And now you're fastened onto me like a leech, and, by heaven, I can't get rid of you."

She stopped posturing then, and her face hardened.

"Then what are you going to do?"

He told her, brutally but frankly, what he had told me. There would be no lump sum. The depression had ruined us all. He couldn't earn enough to support his family and keep her in luxury at the same time. She could take less money, or he would go to court and apply for relief.

"Luxury!" she said. "On twelve thousand a year?"

She was more reasonable after that, however, although she was both angry and resentful. What she wanted, she said, was to leave America and never come back. She liked Europe, and there was a little place in the south of France that she could buy cheaply. Also she could get a good rate on foreign bonds, and living cost very little. With a lump sum—

"What's the matter with you?" he said roughly. "I know you pretty well, Juliette. You don't want to leave this country. It suits you down to the ground. What have you done that you've got to clean out? For that's it, isn't it?"

She went pale, but her voice was calm enough.

"You would think that," she said. "I haven't done anything. I'm just fed up."

"And what do you think I am?" he retorted. "I'm fed up to the teeth."

It was the impasse again, and at last she gave up. She rose and pulled her dressing gown around her.

"Better think it over," she said. "And I don't mean maybe."

She went out on that, and again I heard the click of her mules as she went up the stairs.

It was the last time I ever saw her.

On account of the servants I put Arthur in the hospital room that night. He had ridden part of the way from the flying field on a truck, he said, and walked the rest; and he meant to leave early the next morning. He was already yawning when I took him up, but he looked around him curiously.

"Queer to be back here, isn't it?" he said. "I feel like a kid again. Remember the time I brought the starfish in, and you yelled your head off? You yelled a lot, Marcia."

"I could do a bit of yelling this minute."

"Why?"

"Having to slip you into your own house and then sneak you out again. How are you going back, Arthur?"

He said he would leave before the servants were up, and thumb a ride back to the mainland. Then he saw the hatchet and picked it up curiously.

"Nice weapon to leave around," he said. "What's it doing here?"

But I did not want to add to his troubles. I made some vague explanation about the window not staying closed very well without a latch, and together we got the nails out again. When at last I said good night he was already preparing for bed. He said he would not undress, but merely sleep for a few hours; and I left him with a distinct feeling that he thought he had faced his own particular dragon and slain it.

CHAPTER VII

It was the next morning that Juliette disappeared.

I was late in getting to sleep and when I wakened and rang for Maggie it was after nine o'clock. Maggie told me that Juliette had already gone in riding clothes, taking the car as usual and leaving me high and dry so far as transportation was concerned; that Mary Lou had called me early, but said not to disturb me; and, characteristically keeping the best news for the last, that Lizzie whose room is at the rear of the house, had seen a man running across the driveway, a bareheaded man with a hatchet in his hand, at three o'clock that morning.

"She says it was a ghost," said Maggie grimly, "but if you'll give me that key I'll see if that hatchet's upstairs where we left it."

I put her off for a minute, but my head was whirling. Nor was I any easier when, an hour or two later, Mike reported at the kitchen door with a hatchet in his hands. Either it was the one from the hospital room or its double, and I could scarcely control my voice.

"Where did you find it?" I asked him.

"Down at the edge of the pond," he said. "At the upper end. It was half in the water."

It was fortunate for me that Ellen went into hysterics just then, and that both Maggie and Lizzie had to look after her. It gave me time to go the third floor and see what had happened. I was shaking with anxiety as I climbed the steep stairs and opened the door. I do not know what I expected, but certainly it was not to find things almost exactly as I had left them.

The bed had been slept on but not in, and beside it was the

book Arthur had carried up, a box of matches and two cigarette stubs on an ash tray. The bathroom was untouched, no towel had been unfolded and the basin was dry—which did not sound like fastidious Arthur. But the hatchet was not in sight, and there was only one incongruous thing in the room, and I stood staring at it with complete bewilderment.

On the bureau where he had left it the night before was Arthur's soft felt hat.

That and the hatchet utterly destroyed any comfortable theory that he had merely left the house early that morning, and that Lizzie had seen him taking a hurried departure against an early dawn. Something had driven Arthur out of the house that early morning. But what? It was absurd to think of the bells, although there was one in the hospital suite which was connected with Mother's closed room.

I was completely confused. William, diplomatically approached, had found all lower doors closed and locked. As a result I had to believe that for some unknown reason Arthur had left the house by his old method, leaving his hat and taking the hatchet with him! It was preposterous, and yet I knew somehow that it was true.

Then where was he? What had happened to him?

I was nearly frantic with anxiety. I remember that I smoothed the bed as well as I could and hid the hat under the mattress, but it was pure automatism. I was just in time at that, for Jordan appeared in the doorway at that minute. She had a wretched habit of wearing rubber-heeled shoes, and of appearing like a jack-in-the-box when she was not expected.

"I was to say, miss," she said stiffly, "that Doctor Jamieson is here to see Ellen, and would you go down?"

She was not looking at me, however. She was staring past me into the room, with a sort of avid interest.

"Lizzie says she saw a man running around the place last night, miss. She saw him under that light on the driveway, and he had a hatchet in his hand."

"I wish Lizzie would keep her mouth shut," I said viciously.

But I saw that she was uneasy. She looked pale, and for some reason I felt sorry for her. Sorry for the slave Juliette had made of her, sorry for the vicarious life she led. I patted her on the arm, and I have been glad since that I did.

"There's nothing to worry about," I told her. "Probably Lizzie had a nightmare."

"I suppose I'm used to the city, miss," she said, and shivered.

Ellen was quieter when, having locked the rooms again, I went downstairs. Juliette was still out, and I had left Jordan on the second floor. It was only later, in the library, that the doctor asked any questions.

"What's all this nonsense about bells, Marcia?" he inquired. "And what about this man with a hatchet?"

"I suppose Lizzie is getting old," I said evasively. "As to the rest, you know how it is. An old house—"

"Maggie says you left this hatchet in the quarantine room."

"I thought so. I may be mistaken. Or it may not be the same one."

Then he made my blood run cold, for he said: "Somebody up to Arthur's old tricks with the trellis and the drain pipe, eh? I suppose Arthur himself wasn't around?"

"With a hatchet?" I said. "And with Juliette in the house?"

"Well," he said, and grinned. "If I were Arthur the conjunction wouldn't be entirely surprising!"

I should have told him then and there. He had looked after me all my life, in the summer, and he had often said that in case he ever became delirious he was to be shut in a sealed room. He knew too much about us all. Arthur's insistence on secrecy, however, was still in my mind. I merely smiled, and soon after that he loaded his bag and folded himself—he was a tall thin man—into his always muddy car and drove away.

It was after he had gone that I made a round of the grounds. But I found nothing. Mike showed me where the hatchet had been found, its head in the mud of the pond, but there were no footprints except his own.

"Looked as though it had been thrown there," he said. "Anybody standing in the drive near the gates could do it."

The excitement in the house was dying down. Ellen was sleeping under a hypnotic, the key to the hospital rooms was again in the drawer, and except that Lizzie was positive that the man with the hatchet had been chasing somebody or some-

57

thing, I had learned nothing whatever. But the bells chose that morning to ring again. They rang from all the rooms, indiscriminately, and I sent again for the electrician.

"Take out all the wires if you have to," I told him, "or the servants will desert in a body."

"There's nothing wrong with the wiring, Miss Lloyd," he told me. "Looks like somebody's playing a joke on you. They don't ring by themselves. That's sure."

It was at noon that the riding academy called up.

"I just wondered, Miss Lloyd," said Ed Smith, "if Mrs. Ransom has come back?"

"Not yet, Ed. Why?"

"Well, I suppose it's all right," he said doubtfully. "But she's about two hours over her time, and I like to keep an eye on my customers."

"I wouldn't worry, Ed. She knows how to ride."

"She does that all right," he agreed. "Good seat and good hands. Has a quiet mare too. Sorry to have bothered you. She'll be coming in any minute probably."

The car was still at the academy, so I was virtually marooned. I went upstairs and telephoned for the house supplies, meanwhile trying to put Arthur out of my mind. But I could think of nothing else. Something had roused him, he had picked up the hatchet and got out the window. Then what?

Even by plane, if he had kept the one that brought him, it was too soon for him to have reached New York. Nevertheless, I called his office, to be told that he was out on his sloop and had given no time for his return. It was only then that I remembered Mary Lou at Millbank, and at one o'clock I telephoned her there.

"How are you?" I said, as naturally as possible. "And how is Junior?"

"All right," she replied. "What are the prospects, Marcia? How soon is she going? I detest this place."

"I can't tell yet. Pretty soon, I think. Any word from Arthur?"

"He's left town to see about the boat. I suppose he's got it out somewhere," she said vaguely. "He called me the day

58

before yesterday and told me. I do hope it doesn't blow up a gale."

I had entirely forgotten Juliette by that time; and it was something after one o'clock, when William was announcing lunch, that Ed Smith called again.

"I think I'd better tell you and get it over," he said. "The mare's just come back. She must have got away from Mrs. Ransom. She didn't bolt. She's as cool as when she went out." And when I said nothing, he added: "I wouldn't worry, Miss Lloyd. Mrs. Ransom probably just got off for something and the horse started home. I've sent a couple of boys up with an extra for her. She generally takes the same trail, over above Loon Lake."

"Did she jump that mare?" I said sharply.

"I guess maybe she did, but those jumps are safe."

Well up in our hills is a small cleared space with two or three low jumps built, and the trail Juliette usually took led to it. But, as Ed said, they were safe enough. I took them myself, had taken them ever since I was a child, and I had never heard of an accident.

"I'm going up myself," he added. "What I want to know, will I sent your car to you? It's here and you may need it."

I asked him to do so, and got my hat and a light coat. Then I saw William in the doorway, and told him.

"Miss Juliette's horse has come back without her," I said. "She is probably all right, but I'll get the doctor and drive to the foot of the trail anyhow. I wouldn't tell Jordan. Time enough when we know what's happened."

I must have been pale, for he made me drink a cup of coffee before I left. Then the car came in, and still dazed I was on my way to the doctor's. Only one thought was in my mind. Had she or had she not told Arthur that she was riding that morning? I could not remember. All I could remember was his desperate face. "Now you're fastened onto me like a leech, and, by heaven, I can't get rid of you."

I found Doctor Jamieson at his lunch, but he came with me at once. He put a bag into the car and, folding his long legs into the space beside me, gave me a whimsical smile.

59

"Don't look like that, girl," he said. "All I've got is a few bandages and some iodine. Probably neither of them needed at that. Most people fall off a horse sooner or later."

His matter-of-factness was good for me. Then, too, once out of the house I felt less morbid. The weather had cleared and the air was bracing, almost exhilarating. The golf links showed a brilliant green on the fairways, and Bob Hutchinson was driving a row of balls from the ninth tee, with Fred Martin, the professional, standing by. Tony was just coming in with Howard Brooks, both looking warm and cheerful. They waved, but I drove on past and into the dirt road which led to the bridle path. At the foot of the trail I stopped the car, and the doctor gave me a cigarette and took one himself.

"Pretty spot," he said. "Relax and look at it, girl. You're tightened up like a drum."

"I'm frightened, doctor."

He turned and looked at me.

"See here," he said, "let's look at this thing. At the least let's say she merely lost her horse. That's possible. Then let's say she's had a fall and is used up a bit—well, that's easily fixed. You're not so fond of her as all that, Marcia. What are you scared about?"

"Suppose she's dead?" I said with stiff lips.

"Why suppose anything of the sort? But just to be practical, she hasn't meant so much to you and Arthur that you couldn't outlive even that. How is Arthur, anyhow?"

"Fine, so far as I know."

My voice may have been constrained, for he glanced at me. "Haven't seen him lately, then?"

Once again I should have told him, of course; told him the whole story. As I write this I find my hand shaking. What if I had told him? Could any lives have been saved? Perhaps not. Almost certainly not. The motives were too deeply buried. Yet I would like to feel that I had trusted him.

But Arthur's story to Mary Lou and his insistence on secrecy were uppermost in my mind.

"Not for some time," I said, and then I heard a horse coming down the trail. It was one of Ed's boys, and he stopped beside the car.

60

"Haven't found her yet," he said, touching his cap. "Mr. Smith and Joe's gone on a ways. One thing, she didn't do any jumping. Doesn't look like it, anyhow."

Over an hour passed before Ed Smith and Joe came back. Their animals were sweating, and had evidently traveled far and fast. Ed took off his hat and wiped his face.

"Only thing I can think of," he said, "she started to walk home and tried a short cut. Maybe she's lost. Maybe she fell and hurt herself. There's a lot of steep places, and she was in boots. If she slipped—"

It was past two o'clock by that time, and the doctor had to go back. I turned the car in the narrow road by which Ed stood.

"What I was thinking," he said, "was to get some of those CCC fellows and let them look around. If she's hurt herself we ought to get her, and even if she's lost it's cold at night. Those boys know the country. They've been cutting trail all spring."

But I was convinced by that time that Juliette was not lost.

It is strange to remember that the picture of Loon Lake was delivered late that afternoon. William received it and carried the small canvas gingerly up to my room.

"There's a person downstairs," he said stiffly, "who says you ordered it. The price is fifteen dollars if you like it and nothing if you don't."

I did like it, and I thought it had been carefully worked over since I saw it. Worried as I was I hastily powdered and went downstairs, to find the painter in the hall, still in his sweater and old slacks.

"Well," he said cheerfully, "how about it? I've made you a sort of double-or-quits proposition. It's worth about seven-fifty, I've asked fifteen; but you don't have to take it at all." Then he looked at me closely. "See here," he said, "you're not sick, are you? You don't look right to me."

"We've had a little trouble. At least I'm afraid so. I—"

I must have looked faint, for he put an arm around me and caught me.

"None of that," he said. "Come into this room, whatever it is, and sit down. And if we can find that high and mighty butler of yours a little brandy wouldn't hurt you. Or me," he added, with a smile.

He put me into a chair and stood over me until the brandy came and I drank it. Only then did he relax and sit down.

"Do you want to talk about it? Or don't you?" he said soberly. "Sometimes it helps."

I felt better by that time. I told him about Juliette, and he listened attentively. When I came to the end, however, he surprised me.

"Did you really care a lot about her?" he said abruptly.

"No. That's partly why I feel the way I do."

"Now listen, my child," he said. "The world's full of people grieving for somebody they cared about. It's sheer sentimentality to worry about the ones we don't. If anything's happened to her, be sorry but for God's sake don't feel guilty."

He went soon after; abruptly, as if he had said more than he should. But I felt comforted, in a way, and almost calm. I stood at a window and saw him going up the driveway, his head up and his big shoulders square and self-reliant. But some of the vigor seemed to have gone out of him. He walked like a tired man.

I watched him until he was out of sight. Not until he had gone did I remember that I had not paid him, or even asked him his name. I found that later, however. It was in the corner of the picture, and it was Pell: Allen Pell.

At nine o'clock that night we still had no news. Jordan was shut fast in her room, and the one glimpse I had of her showed me a stony face and swollen reddened eyes. I sent her a tray at dinnertime but she refused it. But I myself could not eat. Arthur had not reached either his office or his hotel, and there seemed to be nobody at the yacht club.

Then at nine o'clock Tony Rutherford came in, looking grave.

"Sit down, Marcia," he said. "How long have you been walking that floor? You look all in."

He waited until I had settled myself. Then very deliberately he lit a cigarette.

"They haven't found her," he said. "But there are one or two things— See here, did she have any enemies around here that you know of?"

"I suppose plenty of people didn't like her."

"Still," he persisted, "she hasn't been here for six or seven years, has she? That cuts out the new people. Look here, Marcia. Did she wreck any lives around here?" He smiled, but I saw that he was deadly serious. "You know what I mean."

"Only Arthur's and mine. And Mother's last days on earth."

He explained then. They had not found her, but beside the trail and not far from the jumps they had found her riding hat and gloves beside a log, where she must have sat down to rest. And there was a cigarette smeared with lipstick, as though she had been smoking. Apparently the mare had stood there for some time. Unfortunately Ed Smith and his men had mussed up the trail itself.

They had sent for some bloodhounds on the mainland, he said, and the sheriff, Russell Shand, was bringing them over.

"Have you notified Arthur?" Tony asked.

"I've tried to. Mary Lou says he's been out with the sloop, and I can't raise the yacht club."

"He may be back. Suppose I try again?"

He did, and this time he got the night watchman. Arthur, he said, had been there a day or two ago and had taken the boat out for a trial run. At least it had been anchored in the bay, and he had missed it when he came on duty. But he had an idea that it was back now. He could go and see. When he came back he said it was there. He could see its riding lights.

"I wish you'd row out and see if Mr. Lloyd is aboard," Tony said. "If he is, get him to call up his sister. Tell him it's important."

I drew my first breath of the day then. My color must have come back, for Tony gave me a reassuring pat.

"Feeling better, aren't you?" he said. "Whatever's happened, Arthur's out of it. Own up, Marcia. You've been scared, haven't you?"

But I thought Tony himself seemed relieved.

"Arthur is no killer," I said shortly.

"We don't know that she has been killed, do we?"

Less than half an hour later the telephone rang again, and Tony answered it. It was Arthur!

Evidently he was still half asleep, for Tony accused him of it. He was wide awake enough, however, when he was told what

63

had happened, and agreed to take the first train up. If he hurried he could make the midnight and be there by morning; and would I have a car meet him. Also would we break the news to Mary Lou before she saw it in the local papers.

It was all like Arthur, decisive and responsible, and my sense of relief grew. I saw Tony out and, going back to the servants' hall, told William to meet Arthur in the morning. They were all there, nervous and silent, but Jordan was not with them. I went upstairs and knocked at her door, but she would not unlock it.

"I'm sorry, Jordan," I said. "They haven't found her yet. But they will very soon. They have sent for some bloodhounds."

"Thank you, miss."

I waited, but that seemed to be all, so I went away. In my own room I undressed and, putting on a bathrobe, went out onto the upper porch and stared at the bay. By one of our quick turns of weather the air was warm that night, and the tide was lapping in with small advancing waves. The pilings of the old pier showed a faint luminescence at the water line, and for all my anxiety I felt a vague sort of happiness; something I had not known since Tony and I had parted. When I went in I remember standing for some time, looking at the picture of Loon Lake.

CHAPTER VIII

I did not sleep that night. I had called Mary Lou, and the result had worried me.

"Do you think she is dead?" she had asked, and there was a sort of suppressed hope in her voice.

But who was I to blame her? I was sorry for Juliette, if anything had happened to her. She loved to live, had wanted to live. Nevertheless, I faced the situation as honestly as I could. If she was gone for good it meant release for all of us; an escape from the prison of the last few years. She had not left me much, either of faith or of hope, but what was left would be safe.

Perhaps Allen Pell was right. I would be sorry, but I could not grieve.

It was well after midnight when I thought I heard Jordan stirring and got up. Her room was quiet, however, and I did not disturb her. But while I was still up and about I had a shock. I happened to glance out a rear window, and saw someone with a flashlight down near the pond. It would show for a moment as if to direct its holder along the path, and then be snapped off. And it was gradually borne in on me that whoever carried it was moving stealthily toward the garden outside the morning room.

Not until it was close did I raise a window and call out.

"What is it?" I called. "What do you want?"

There was instant silence, and the light clicked off. Whoever held it was in the shadow of the trees, and I could see nothing.

"Whoever you are," I said, thoroughly aroused by that time, "you are trespassing, and I shall call the police."

There was still no answer, but there was a cautious movement below, and by the sounds I knew that the invader was retreating.

I wakened William and we made a careful search; but there was no one around.

I was wide awake the remainder of the night. The tide was full at three in the morning, and I lay in bed listening to it as it eased softly over the rocks below. Shortly afterwards I heard Jordan open her door and come out into the hall, and I got up and spoke to her.

"Won't you let me give you a bromide?" I asked. "You need some rest."

"No thank you, miss," she said tonelessly. "I thought I'd go downstairs and make myself a cup of tea."

She went on down, with that peculiar catlike tread of hers which was almost noiseless, and I went back to bed. But the sight of her had reminded me of something. Had she seen that wretched hat of Arthur's while I was in the hospital room? She might have been there for some time. In that case—

I went to the head of the back stairs. She was still in the kitchen, moving about. I could hear her running water for the kettle and building up the fire in the stove. It would be half an hour or more before she came back, and as quickly as I could I got the key and, passing her open door, went up the staircase in the wing.

I was nervous, but with the lights on the rooms seemed as usual, and I retrieved the hat from under the mattress on the bed and took a quick survey of the place. The bed would have to be remade eventually. It showed signs of having been used. But with Ellen's careful counting of the weekly sheets it would be difficult to account for the extra ones. I got the hat, none the better for its flattening, turned the pillow to its fresh side, and went downstairs again.

But I knew that somehow I had to dispose of the hat. It would be impossible to conceal it from Maggie, and I dared not throw it away as it was. In the end I got a pair of scissors, and I was on the upper porch, cutting it into bits and dropping them into the water below, when Jordan's voice behind me almost sent me over the railing.

"I've brought you some tea and toast, miss," she said.

66

I simply let go of the scissors and what remained of the hat, and they fell into the water. When I turned she was just behind me, holding a tray.

"Thanks," I said. "You startled me. Will you put it in my room?"

I watched her putting it down, and her face was set and hard. She went out again without speaking, but I knew then that she was a potential enemy, and a suspicious one.

The county sheriff, Russell Shand, came to see me early the next morning. He looked tired but indomitable as usual, and I was sitting up in bed when he came in, my tray beside me and my arms and neck bare. He was not abashed. He pulled a chair beside the bed and eyed the coffee pot.

"Got a toothmug or something around that I could use?" he inquired. "I could do with a bit of coffee."

He got up and brought a glass from my bathroom, and not until he had filled it did he give me any news.

"Well," he said, "I suppose you want to know. We haven't found her, but if that mare could talk I guess she'd tell us a story. The dogs flivvered out on us; ran in circles and then sat down. But we trailed the horse from where we found her things down to Loon Lake, and I'm afraid that's where she is."

I must have looked shocked, for he added quickly:

"Maybe not. I'm only saying it looks that way. Either that or she fixed it to look so."

"Fixed it?"

"She might have had some reason for disappearing. It's been done before; and from what I gather she had her own ways of doing things."

"She had no money with her. And where could she go? All she had was her alimony, and we—Arthur—paid that monthly by check. I imagine she is in debt. She always has been. But she'd never run away because of that."

He gave me a shrewd look.

"Well, it looks as though one idea's ruled out," he observed, and went on to elaborate what Tony had already told me.

"No real evidence of any struggle," he said. "Ground was soft enough; but it's pretty thick with leaves and pine needles."

However that might be, that smeared cigarette looked as though she had stopped there for some time, and there was nothing to show how she had left, or been taken away. It was his idea that whoever had attacked her, if that had happened, had put her across the pommel of the saddle and ridden straight down to the lake. There was no trail and the trip itself must have been a desperate one, in full daylight with the possibility of hikers around, and with the slope itself steep and dangerous. Here and there the mare had slipped, and that was how they had followed her. "No horse on earth would take that trip by itself," he said.

"Of course that's the way it looks now," he went on, putting down the glass. "May be some other explanation. But there are some scratches on Eagle Rock, at the edge of the lake, and if I was betting on it I'd say she went in there, or near there."

The searchers had found no footprints along the bank anywhere, and they were preparing to drag the lake.

"They're still looking," he said, "but I figured they could do as well without me. Was she wearing any jewelry when she left?"

"I suppose not, with riding clothes."

He was thoughtful for a minute, tugging at his lower lip.

"If it wasn't robbery, then by the great horn spoon, what was it? Of course she's an attractive woman, or was; but I don't remember a sex crime on this island, and I've been here forty years. Arthur come yet?"

"No. He ought to be here soon."

He picked up his hat from the floor and got up. "The women downstairs say she brought a maid with her. I'd better talk to her."

My heart sank, but there was nothing to do. I told him Jordan was probably in her room, and listened while he rapped and was admitted. Then the car drove in, and I heard Arthur coming up the stairs.

He looked quite normal, grave and weary but otherwise himself. Indeed I had the feeling that once over the initial shock he had already realized that a new and happier life might be opening for him.

"Have they found her?" he asked.

68

"Not yet, but they think—"

I told him what the sheriff had said and he listened carefully. Then he put the question that was in both our minds.

"Does anyone know I was here?"

"No. At least—Arthur, why on earth did you go without your hat?"

"Because I didn't mean to go at all. Not then, anyhow."

The sheriff was still with Jordan, and so he told me the story, talking in a low voice. He had dropped asleep that night in the hospital room, and was wakened by a sound outside the open window. It sounded as though someone was on the drawing room roof below. He got off the bed and listened, and at last he looked out. There was a light fog, but he could see a figure beneath him. It had climbed the trellis from the garden and was working its way over the edge of the roof.

The idea of someone breaking into the house had infuriated him. He had remembered the hatchet, and as cautiously as he could he located it and stuck it in his belt. By the time he got to the window again the man was standing below, apparently examining the drain pipe.

"What I meant to do," he said, "was to slide down and grab him. But he was too quick for me. He jumped into the garden and ran for it. I jumped too, but he had a start. I lost him finally."

"Lizzie saw you, Arthur. She didn't recognize you, but she says you had the hatchet in your hand."

He looked sheepish.

"I did, at that. I had to take it out of my belt, because the darned thing nearly pulled my trousers off."

The rest of his story was equally direct. He had looked at his watch and seen it was only three o'clock, but to get back meant either rousing the house or climbing the pipe again, and he wasn't sure of the last. He weighed a lot more than he had in the old days.

"I was going to leave before daylight anyhow," he said, "and as I had my cap in my pocket I just went on."

It was as simple as that! He always used a cap on the sloop, of course, and he had slipped off from the sloop for that secret visit to Juliette.

He had slogged along for a mile or so, he said. At the end of that time he got a lift from a car, driver unknown, as far as the county seat, and later in the morning he took a train to where he had left the sloop the night before, in a sheltered cove he knew about. He had just got back when I telephoned the yacht club.

"Then it was you who threw the hatchet into the pond?"

"I threw it away. I don't know where it landed."

"This man on the roof? Did you recognize him, Arthur? Have you any idea who it was?"

"Somebody trying to break in. That was enough for me."

"You can't describe him?"

"No. Except that he can run like blazes."

"When did you catch a train?"

"Not until ten-thirty. Why?"

"Arthur," I said desperately. "Juliette left here before eight, and she was due back at the riding academy at ten o'clock. Whatever happened to her, it happened between eight-thirty and ten o'clock. Where were you then?"

He stared at me.

"Waiting for a train. You know how few there are."

"Where were you? Did anybody see you? Can you prove it?"

"I don't know anybody in Clinton. I sat on a bench along the waterfront and slept. I was tired."

"This man who drove you? Have you his name, or the license number of his car?"

"No. He'd spent the night in a tourist camp and was on his way west. He had some coffee in a thermos bottle, and he gave me some. See here, Marcia, *you* don't think I had a hand in this—whatever happened?"

"What does it matter what I think?" I said bitterly. "It's what Russell Shand thinks that matters, if he ever learns that you were here."

We heard the sheriff coming back along the hall and I composed myself as well as I could. He was carrying Juliette's jewel case, a tan leather box with velvet cushions, and after shaking hands with Arthur he put it on the bed in front of me.

"That woman in there says they're all here. Maybe you'd

70

better look, Marcia."

I went over it carefully, but Arthur kept his eyes averted as I drew out its contents. Many of the pieces I recognized; the pearls he had sold some bonds to buy after their marriage, the large square-cut diamond engagement ring, the star sapphire Mother had given her one Christmas as a peace offering, and a familiar brooch or two. But there were some things I had never seen: three bracelets, one of rubies, one of sapphires and one of emeralds, a small jewel-studded watch and a pair of diamond earrings, elaborate and obviously valuable. Even then, though I was sick with anxiety, I resented those jewels, bought as only Arthur and I knew at what cost.

"I didn't know she had all this," I said. "I suppose her insurance people would know if there was anything else."

"The Jordan woman says all she wore was a plain wrist watch on a leather strap."

He left the case with me and he and Arthur went out. Soon after that I heard his car drive away, and learned that Arthur had gone with him. At lunchtime Arthur came back alone, looking white and sick. He ate no lunch, but had a highball or two and smoked incessantly.

"I don't get it, Marcia," he said. "Who would want to do away with her?"

"I imagine the popular idea would be that you and I had at least a certain amount of reason," I said.

He had been up at Loon Lake, it developed. They were still dragging it, with a dozen boats out; and it seemed certain now that she was there. A Boy Scout had turned up her wrist watch on the steep side of the hill where the mare had gone down. It may have caught on a branch and been torn off, for the strap was broken.

There was only one bit of comfort in the whole situation. So far nobody suspected that Arthur had been on the island, and I began to hope that even Jordan was not suspicious. True, he had taken a train from Clinton, but as we seldom used the station there I had some hope that he had escaped recognition.

Naturally both the village and the summer colony were ringing with the news. I was deluged with cards and flowers. Mansfield Dean left a bottle of old port and a note saying that

71

he was there to be used, in case I needed him. Tony was off with the searchers so I saw nothing of him, but Mrs. Pendexter sent some flowers from her garden, and wrote on the card in her crabbed old hand: "Don't worry too much. Plenty of people wanted her out of the way. But it's a little early to hope!" Which was precisely like her, although it seemed callous at the time.

I spent the afternoon on the upper porch. It was a brilliant day. Far out two sailing yachts were moving briskly along, and the *Sea Witch* was moored in the harbor, not far from shore. Around me went on the usual life of the house. I heard the garbage wagon rumble in, stop and go out again, the postman's car and his double whistle, the distant sound of Lizzie— hatchet or no hatchet!—beating eggs in the kitchen for a cake. But I was rather surprised to see Jordan, her black dress blowing around, on the beach, walking aimlessly about. I called down and asked her if she had eaten any lunch, and she said she had. Then she turned and disappeared, walking toward the pond.

On an impulse I got up and went into Juliette's room. It was neater than I had ever seen it, for she had a capacity for disorder. But if I had hoped for anything there to explain what had happened I did not find it. The bed was turned down, showing its silk sheets carefully pressed; the baby pillows of pale blue and rose were piled at the head, her gold toilet set and gold-topped bottles were in order on her dressing table, and the desk by a window was in order. With an ear open for Jordan I glanced over the letters there. They had been brought on from New York, and were mostly unpaid bills. Indeed there was only one letter and that without an envelope. On the surface it seemed of no importance. It was signed Jennifer, and it was largely gossip. It had, however, a rather cryptic postscript:

"Have just heard about L——. Do please be careful, Julie. You know what I mean."

It did not seem important then, in view of Juliette's life as she had lived it. It sounded like a warning against recklessness of some sort, but nothing more. There certainly was nothing to show that it was to loom large in all our lives before it was explained. I merely put it back where I had found it.

At six o'clock Arthur came back. He looked exhausted, but he called Mary Lou at once. Whatever he was feeling he was tender and cheerful over the wire.

"No news," he said. "You're not to worry, darling. Better get the doctor to give you something so you can sleep."

But he was not cheerful with me. All that day his own situation had been increasingly clear to him. He had a motive for wanting Juliette out of the way, and he had no real alibi for the hour of her disappearance. I think it was then that he began to hope that her body would not be found.

"We still don't know that anything has happened to her," he said. "And if it has—"

"I'm afraid it has, Arthur."

He nodded.

"It may," he said. "But it would be damned hard to prove, unless they find her."

I asked him then if he knew any friend of Juliette's called Jennifer, but he did not. He didn't know any of her crowd, and he didn't want to. He paced the floor for a minute or two.

"See here, Marcia," he said. "What brought her here anyhow? She could have put that fool proposition of hers to me in New York. But she didn't. She came here. I don't understand it."

"She may have thought I would be easier than you."

He shook his head.

"I've been wondering," he said, "if she was hiding from something. Or somebody. And that idea of leaving the country! It sounded phony at the time, but maybe there was something in it. After all, that fellow on the roof— Did she seem frightened?"

I thought that over.

"She said she was in some sort of trouble. I thought it was money. But she may have been afraid of somebody. I thought she looked uneasy. She came in from a ride one day and went to bed. She may have seen someone then."

"You don't know who it might have been?"

"I haven't an idea."

He went upstairs after that. I had given him Father's old room, next to Mother's at the end of the hall; a big room, with

73

an enormous walnut bed which had been exiled from the city house, and the sagging easy chair where Father used to doze with an unread book on his lap, after his long rides and a heavy lunch. Juliette and Jordan had the rooms he and Mary Lou had always used.

I waited until I heard him turn on the shower and knew he was all right. Then, starting upstairs to dress for dinner, I was surprised to find Lucy Hutchinson in the lower hall. She was in evening dress, but she looked strained and unlike herself.

"I saw Arthur coming in," she said. "I suppose there's no news?"

"Nothing yet."

She seemed scarcely to have heard me. She said she was going to a cocktail party and on to a dinner later, and just wanted to know if I had heard anything. Then, in the act of leaving, she asked suddenly if she could talk to me privately.

"Bob's up at the lake," she said. "All the men are, apparently. Goodness knows who will turn up for the party. I'll keep you only a minute, Marcia."

She was looking very smart, as usual. She wore a white dress with a short train, jade earrings and jade-green slippers. Also she carried a long jade cigarette holder, and the loose cape she wore was lined with the same color. She had the gift of clothes. But as I took her into the morning room and she went to a window and stood looking out, I could have sworn that she was shaking, and her rouge stood out in purplish patches on her cheeks.

"I think I'd better tell you," she said at last. "I know that Arthur was here the other night."

I stared at her back. I literally could not speak.

"Of course I'm not telling it," she went on. "But if they put me on the stand—what will I do, Marcia? I'm fond of him. There was a time when he could have had me if he'd wanted me, but he didn't. I—well, there it is."

"How do you know he was here?"

"I saw him."

She had seen him. She was driving her car home from somewhere or other, and she and Bob had been quarreling. Fussing, she called it. As a result she had passed the entrance to their place, and so she headed into our driveway in order to back and turn. Arthur was just ahead, in the full glare of the headlights, and he had looked back. She had known him at once.

"Did Bob see him?" I asked, still shaken.

"I think not. He was too busy giving me the devil!"

There was nothing to do but to tell her, and I did so; that Arthur had talked to Juliette the night before, had spent the night here, but had left long before daylight. She was visibly relieved, and as her color came back her make-up was less obvious.

"I'm glad I told you. It's been plain hell," she said, and drew her cape around her. "You know you can count on me, Marcia."

She went soon after, and I saw her out, to the landaulet which she used for parties, and waited until the chauffeur had tucked her in under a rug and slammed the door. But it seemed rather dreadful, as I watched her go, to think that Arthur's safety might lie in her well-cared-for hands.

It was that evening that I found what turned out to be a clue. It looked small and unimportant then, but I have wondered since how much death and downright agony of soul could have been prevented had we known its secret at the time. It sounds absurd, I know, to say that a brown coat button could have solved our crimes, or prevented two of them. Yet in a way it is true. Had we known who lost it, and why—

I had gone out after dinner, a dinner which neither of us had really eaten. The garden has always spelled peace to me, with its fountain splashing down into a little pool with its lotus and water lilies, and with the small goggle-eyed fish which remind me of Chu-Chu. In the center was the green circle of hard-rolled lawn where we serve tea on warm days, with a brilliant umbrella over the table and chairs around it; and against the wall was the rose trellis, now covered with opening buds, but still an adequate ladder in case of necessity.

It showed some damage. Here and there branches were broken, and the peonies at the base were badly crushed. It was there that I found the button. It lay half embedded in the earth, and except that it was brown and that Arthur had worn a gray

75

suit when he followed the unknown intruder, it told exactly nothing.

Nevertheless, I kept it. It might belong to Mike, although he works in overalls. On the other hand, it might explain the man with the flashlight. If he had missed it he might have come back to search for it. I carried it into the library and put in an envelope in my desk, where long weeks later Russell Shand was to refer to it.

"I'm not much up on murder," he said, "and here we had not only no motive, so far as I could see. We didn't even have a clue. Now you take that button you found in the garden. What did it tell us? Only that somebody had tried to get into the house, and we had Arthur's story about that anyhow." And he added:

"Take it from me, Marcia, there's one kind of murder that all the crime laboratories in the world don't help with. That's when the killer just up and kills. No premeditation, no alibi, no nothing. He or she just sees the chance and takes it; and what are you going to do about it?"

CHAPTER IX

It was more than a week before they found Juliette's body.

More than a week of reporters, photographers and long lines of cars containing the merely curious. In the end the sheriff closed the gates and placed a deputy there; but this merely drove the newspapermen to the water. They hired boats, took pictures when any of us appeared, and generally placed us in a state of siege.

The real center of interest, however, was Loon Lake and the surrounding country. For days the search went on there, only to be abandoned when darkness fell. But they did not find her.

One afternoon I went downstairs at teatime to find Mrs. Pendexter settled in the drawing room. She did not so much as greet me.

"I've sent for Juliette's maid, Marcia," she said. "If you want to know anything about a woman, get her personal maid. I've had mine for forty years, and when I want to know my bank balance I just ask her. Has Russell Shand talked to her?"

"Only about Juliette's jewelery, I think."

"Like a man," she sniffed. "What does he know about Juliette's past the last six or seven years? What money did she have? How much did she spend? Who were her lovers, if any? What letters did she get and what were in them? Who hated her? Who was afraid of her? Good gracious, Marcia, I never know I need a liver pill until my Celeste suggests it!"

But it was not easy to get Jordan out of that fastness of hers where she remained locked away; and when she came she proved more than a match for the old lady staring at her through her lorgnette.

"So you're the maid," said Mrs. Pendexter. "How long have you been with Mrs. Ransom?"

"Three years, madam."

"That's long enough to have learned plenty. Who did this? You ought to know."

Jordan merely spread her hands.

"Answer me when I speak to you."

"I have no idea, madam. If anything has happened to her I would say—"

"Say what?"

"One would not have to go far to find people who didn't like her."

"Didn't like her!" echoed the old lady. "Someone kills her and throws her into a lake because he or she doesn't like her! Talk sense, girl. Who hated her enough to do away with her?"

"She was very popular, madam. Wherever we went she was popular. She had only friends."

"Nonsense and rubbish. Get along with you," said Mrs. Pendexter, and put away her lorgnette with dignity.

I was almost entirely shut away. I had not seen Allen Pell again, and I gathered that he was among the searchers. But the season had commenced in earnest. Day after day trucks laden with trunks rumbled along the highway, station wagons passed loaded with servants, and there was the usual procession of cars with liveried chauffeurs.

In town the shop windows showed fresh merchandise, the traffic lights were turned on, a policeman directed the traffic at the intersection of our two business streets; and the local police station was the center of a new and unwonted activity.

Arthur was out all day and every day, coming home late, dirty and exhausted. To add to the general discomfort the town had had several heavy rains and the search had had to be temporarily abandoned. Then one day he told me that he had sent to New Bedford for a diver. "No good dragging any more," he said. "The lake's full of sunken logs and rocks."

That was on the Monday following Juliette's disappearance, and by Wednesday evening the diver, named Oleson, had covered practically the entire bottom of the lake without result. He worked from a flatboat with two assistants, coming

78

up now and then for rest and to get warm, for Loon Lake is icy cold. Owing to the rains it was deeper than usual, and there was more current than under ordinary conditions. Toward the end of the day he concentrated on the outlet into Stony Creek, and there at last he found something.

It was the small leather case Juliette had carried in her riding coat pocket, with her initials in gold on the corner. It was still filled with cigarettes, and case and contents were sodden, as though they had been in the water for a long time.

I identified it that night at the sheriff's office, taking Jordan with me. She eyed it stonily, but a minute later she swayed and we only caught her in time to lay her flat on the floor. I was feeling sick myself. When she came to she tried to sit up, and I had to hold her down.

"Lie back," I said. "You'll be all right soon. Let the blood get into your head."

She stared up at me as if she did not see me. "Dead!" she said thickly. "He got her after all, the dirty murdering devil!"

"Who got her?"

She would not say anything more. The sheriff had gone for water, and when he came back she had her eyes closed and was obstinately mute. Nor did I press her until we were in the car on the way home. Then I asked her, but she merely looked at me in apparent surprise.

"I don't remember saying anything, miss," she replied listlessly.

One thing was certain. The finding of the cigarette case had put new energy into the search. Here was proof that Juliette had faked no crime, staged no disappearance. Obviously its discovery was pure accident and luck. As a result the work went on all night and into the next morning, with practically every able-bodied man on the island joining in it. But now the search had left the lake and with flares and lights of all kinds followed Stony Creek down to our pond. Normally the creek is shallow, but here and there are deep pools, and these they investigated carefully, the theory being that the flood waters after the rain might have carried her for a considerable distance.

They were still searching at dawn. Arthur was with them, as

were also most of the men of the village and of the summer colony, including Tony, Mansfield Dean and Bob Hutchinson. I had not gone to bed at all, and at daylight some twenty of them came into the house and I gave them sandwiches and coffee. They were a tired and dirty lot, crowding into the dining room around Mother's old carved table, and Arthur brought in whisky while I cut bread and ham.

It was when I brought in the sandwiches that I saw Allen Pell. Like the others he was muddy and weary. Arthur had poured him a drink, and he held it in his hand. When I found him he was off by himself, looking at his little painting of Loon Lake, and he made a gesture toward it.

"I'd better change that for something else," he said. "You won't want it now."

I gathered that he had been with the searchers during the entire search so far; but he was with them, not of them. Even that morning he seemed rather detached. I found him later out on the porch, apparently watching the sunrise and eating a sandwich at the same time.

He greeted me with a grin.

"People are queer, aren't they?" he said, apropos of nothing. "After all, why fear death? It's a pleasant road that leads somewhere or other. I've forgotten the rest. Anyhow, the idea is that either we sleep or we wake up to something that must be pretty interesting."

"We don't know which. And she wanted to live."

He was silent for a minute or two. Then he said:

"There are worse things than death. I can think of a number of them."

His tone was so bitter that I stared at him; but Howard Brooks came out just then. And Arthur was asking for more sandwiches. I did not see him again alone that morning.

It was a sombre sort of gathering that early morning. None of the men had much to say, and they all looked weary and dispirited. I gathered that they had found no further clue of any sort; and that they thought it unlikely that the body could have been swept through the culvert under the road and into the pond. Nevertheless, Oleson went down there later that day. This time he wore only a diving helmet and a bathing suit, but it was a strange thing to see him there on the bank among the late irises and peonies, a grotesque figure with an enormous swollen head.

He found nothing at all. Our driveway was still shut off, but the servants from the various houses near by had gathered in small whispering groups, and when he came up for the last time empty-handed there was an almost audible sigh of relief mixed with disappointment. I was at the window, and I saw the sheriff take his hat off and mop his head, although the day was cool. Then as though unable to believe that this was all, that this was the end, he cast an eye along the beach below the dam.

Immediately after that he did a curious thing.

He climbed down the rocks a foot or two, and picking up some small object, examined it carefully. He put it into his wallet, and then proceeded to examine the rocks, both above high-water mark and below. The tide was out, and with his head down he walked along the stony beach until he was out of sight from where I stood.

It was almost an hour later when he rang the doorbell and asked for me.

Arthur had taken Oleson to the train and was motoring on to Millbank, so I was alone. And the sheriff was very grave when I found him in the library.

"I've played fair with you, Marcia," he said. "Now I want you to play fair with me. Do you know anything about this?"

He pulled a dark-brown bundle from his pocket, and I felt my heart stop. It was the remains of Arthur's hat.

He took one look at me and went on: "I'm laying out all the cards. I've got the initial 'A' from a man's hatband in my pocket, and part of this hat has been cut off. I found one piece, and I'll likely find others. I may find the other initials too. Now, how about it?"

"How about what?" I remember saying. "A hat? Anybody can throw a hat away."

"Not anybody cuts it up first. Somebody who finds a hat and wants to get rid of it—that's the person to look for, isn't it?"

"It's preposterous. Who would do such a thing?"

He eyed me.

"What about that bareheaded man running around with a

hatchet?" He inquired. "Maybe old Lizzie had a nightmare, and again maybe she hadn't. Those lights on the driveway are pretty strong."

So he knew that too. I was nervous and confused.

"It may have been washing about for a month," I said, with dry lips. "Maybe a year."

He shook his head, and prodded the felt.

"I'd say it's been in the water off and on for a week," he said. "The tide's like the Lord, Marcia. It giveth and it taketh away. That stuff's been in and out offshore right here for the past several days."

I said nothing. He went on:

"Life's a funny thing," he said. "If somebody had just thrown that hat away I wouldn't have looked at it. Anybody's likely to lose one in the bay. But it's been cut to pieces. Then again, that initial was above high-water mark. That's queer too. Maybe it fell somewhere and a bird picked it up. One of those crows out there; he'd see it in a minute. Or maybe it never went into the water at all. Say it was dropped out of one of your windows, or from that upstairs porch of yours. You might think that over."

I had always liked Russell Shand, with his clear blue eyes and his stocky muscular body. He had the reputation of being beyond political bribery, and of sticking to a case until he solved it. But that day I hated him.

"Where is Arthur?" he inquired.

"He has gone to see his wife. And if you think he killed Juliette you're a lunatic," I said angrily.

He remained calm, however.

He asked to see Jordan, and there was a long interval before I heard him coming back.

"Well, Marcia," he said heavily. "I guess I was right. That maid of Juliette's saw you cutting up the hat, and she says you dropped the scissors. She found them on the beach, and she's got them in her room."

He waited for a while, but there was nothing I could say. All my defenses had crumbled. When he left soon afterwards I went upstairs and took two bromides before I crawled into bed, and I did not get up the rest of the day. I lay there, too tired and too weak to move; as though the very foundation of my life had been taken from under me and a gesture would have meant collapse. But once I got up, and I saw a detective on the beach below the house, carefully searching it.

Arthur came back from Millbank that afternoon to get some fresh linen. Before he left to go back to Mary Lou, he told me about that journey of his to see Juliette. He had tried to keep the visit secret; but it had been Mary Lou he was worried about, not the police.

"She hated her," he said, as if Juliette was already in the past tense. "I couldn't tell her I was coming here to see Juliette."

What he had done had seemed simple enough at the time. He still had the old sloop, weather-beaten but serviceable, and it had already been put in commission, so on Wednesday he had merely stuck a cap in his pocket and gone out to the yacht club. The boat was anchored well out from the shore, and after he and the man from the shipyard had gone over it he bought some provisions in the town and went aboard again. He left word at the club that he might be away for a couple of nights, and as these solitary trips of his were nothing unusual it excited no comment.

He ran under sail for an hour or so, and then started the engine. He did not go up the Sound, however. He turned toward a bay near one of the Long Island flying fields. He was trailing a dinghy, and after he had anchored he rowed himself ashore.

There he chartered a plane, and at dusk it had set him down neatly on the island emergency field. He had got a lift part of the way. The rest of the way he had come on foot.

"It was the hell of a walk," was his comment.

He swore that he had not seen Juliette after that scene in the library.

"Not after she went up the stairs," he said. "I didn't want to see her. All I wanted was to forget her. I've built my life. Why should I let her destroy it?"

I was exhausted when he left me. What with excitement and loss of sleep I must have dozed off just after Maggie had put me to bed. But like most people under strain I slept deeply for an hour or two and then wakened. Chu-Chu was snoring loudly, but outside of that the house was silent. I lay there, wide awake in the darkness. The tide was making small regular sounds, a bit of splash, silence, then splash again. It was some time before I realized that it was not the tide at all.

Someone was rowing a boat just off the shore.

I sat up in bed and listened. The night was very still, and there was no mistaking the faint thud when the boat struck the float, or the muffled sound of someone landing and tying it up. I slid out of bed in my nightgown and went out onto the upper veranda; and it was not difficult to make out the dark outline of the boat, nor—as my eyes grew accustomed to the starlight— the figure of a man moving along on the dock below me.

He saw me too, for he stopped suddenly and looked up. But his next action was certainly unusual. He did not go back. Instead he stood still, turned on a flashlight and, leaning on the rail of the dock, seemed to be writing something. After that he went down on the shore, and a few minutes later I heard a sharp ping as something dropped beside me.

Chu-Chu was still sleeping as I went inside and turned on the light. What I held was a note wrapped around a bit of shell from the beach. "Please come down, I must talk to you."

The signature was merely Pell.

It never occurred to me not to go. I remember how excited I was as I threw on some clothes, including a tennis dress and sneakers. That confidence of mine seems strange now, for I knew nothing whatever about him. For all I knew he might have been the man Arthur had followed. He might have been the man with the flashlight. But I never hesitated.

When, somewhat breathless, I finally crept down the stairs and out onto the front porch, I found him waiting there, where I had last seen him at daylight that morning. He was not much more than a shadow, but his first words were reassuring.

"Are you sure you're warm enough?" he asked.

"Plenty."

"Then where can we talk? Not in the house. This is a private call!"

I thought he was smiling.

"There's a bench down by the pond. But what is it, Mr. Pell? What's it all about?"

84

"What do you think it's about?" he said, his voice altering. "Come along. Where is this bench?"

I led him down to it, and once there he lit a cigarette and gave me one. But those preliminaries over, it was some little time before he spoke again. Then:

"What do you actually know about Juliette Ransom?" he asked at last. "Why did she come back here? There must have been a reason. Did she tell you? She used to be pretty secretive; but after all—"

"You knew her?" I said, astonished.

"I knew her. Yes." He turned and faced me. "Now listen, Miss Lloyd," he said. "I've got some things I want to know, and I can't keep you out here too long. In the first place, did she show any interest in the people here? Ask any questions, or see anybody? You know what I mean."

I was too surprised to grasp all this at first. He had known Juliette! I had seen him twice since her disappearance, and not until now had he admitted it.

"Did you know her well?" I asked, in a thin voice.

"Well enough," he said, almost roughly.

I was thinking fast.

"She knew a lot of the people here," I told him finally. "I don't think she saw them. They—well, they avoided her. But there may have been somebody. She came home one day looking frightened, I thought. At least she went to bed and stayed there. But she kept on with her riding. If she had been really afraid—"

"No," he said slowly. "She wouldn't be afraid. She wasn't really afraid of man or devil. She wasn't that kind. But what brought her back here? To this house?"

"She wanted money," I said. "She wanted to live in Europe."

"In Europe? Did she say why?"

"No. Except that it would be cheaper, and she liked it."

"That's all she said?"

"That's all."

I thought he seemed relieved. He leaned back against the bench and relaxed somewhat. I could see him faintly, and it is odd, everything considered, how completely at ease with him

85

I felt.

"I see," he said. "It didn't matter that you were having a hard time getting along. That wouldn't occur to her. Sometimes I think—"

He did not finish that. He threw away his cigarette and got up. But I sat still, looking at him.

"I suppose you don't care to tell me how you knew her?" I asked.

He stood quite still.

"No," he said. "That's over, thank God. Let's forget it. And forget I've been here tonight. Will you?"

But I could not let him go like that. It was not only that I liked him. It was all too mysterious. He himself was mysterious, clad as he was in an old sweat shirt and trousers, and with that queer background of tourist camp and trailer behind him.

"If you know anything I think you should tell it, Mr. Pell," I said. "After all, if she is dead—"

"If she is dead, I didn't kill her," he replied grimly. "And the angels who keep the book ought to give me a good mark for that."

Whatever that meant, he did not explain it.

He thanked me then rather formally for seeing him, hoped I had not taken cold, and explained that he had stolen the rowboat, as our gate was guarded, and would have to return it. But before he left he did a surprising thing, and did it almost automatically.

He took out his handkerchief and carefully wiped the top rail of the bench.

Back in bed again the entire episode had a quality of unreality. I listened to the sound of his oars die away, and tried to recall all that he had said. Only one thing stood out clearly. He had not killed her, and he thought he deserved credit for it!

He had known her, and known her well. Perhaps he had been in love with her. I thought probably he had. There had been some quarrel, or—after her fashion—she had thrown him over; and he was still bitter. She might be dead. It was almost certain that she was dead. Yet he was still bitter. I tried hard to reconcile the pleasant, rather humorous young man, painting his little picture of Loon Lake by the road, with my visitor that night; but it was difficult. The youth and humor had both gone. He had seemed older, older and very tired.

There was a second incident that night, and I record it for what it was worth. A storm was brewing, and I could not remember whether I had closed the window in the hospital room or not. Wide awake as I was by that time, the thing bothered me, and at last I got up and went to investigate.

I had unlocked the door at the top of the stairs and was about to turn on the light when the bell rang, close beside me. It was the bell from Mother's room, and I stood there, paralyzed with terror.

Then I turned to escape and I fell on the stairs and twisted my ankle. I was in a dead faint when Maggie, aroused by the noise, discovered me.

CHAPTER X

I was still in bed, with my foot bandaged, when they found Juliette's body the next day. It was in a shallow grave some fifty feet back from Stony Creek, and a half mile or so below Loon Lake. She had been struck twice on the head with a heavy weapon of some sort, and she had been dead before she was thrown into the water.

For it was evident that she had been in the water for some time. Her boots were still soggy when she was found, her riding clothes saturated. Yet she had been buried. More than that, she had been buried with some care. Her hands were folded over her breast, and there was a covering of leaves over her face.

Whoever killed her, then, had suspected what had happened; had followed the creek, discovered her and hidden her in that wild spot, almost a mile above the road.

I had my first news of the discovery from Mike, who reported an ambulance on the main road at the foot of the path. He stood in the door of my room and reported in detail.

"I guess it's her all right, miss," he said. "Them police photographers have gone up the trail, and about three carloads of reporters. I expect they'll be taking her to Jim Blake's. Skull's bashed in, they say."

I found myself shivering violently. Jim Blake was the local undertaker, and his name brought with it the sheer horror of what had happened. Up to that time I had not fully accepted Juliette's death. There was always the chance that she had only disappeared. Now she was dead, and was being taken to Jim Blake's. She had loved to live. Now she was dead.

"I thought you'd better know," said Mike. "I'm sorry I

broke it to you like that. But what with her being buried and the lock of the toolshed being broken, seemed like I'd better tell you."

"The toolshed!" I said. "What about it?"

"Somebody's been in it," he replied phlegmatically. "Smashed the lock. Two or three days ago, that was."

"Is anything gone?" I asked, suddenly uneasy.

"I don't miss anything as yet. Things is moved about some, but that's all. Still and all, miss, it's queer to break in and take nothing; and with the shed where it is—"

"Where it is?" I repeated, puzzled. "It's where it always has been, isn't it?"

"It's up against the Hutchinson place. And if I was asked who hated Mrs. Ransom around here, I'd say—"

But this vision of Lucy killing Juliette and then finding and burying her body was too much for me. I burst into hysterical laughter, and it took Maggie and a bottle of aromatic ammonia to bring me around again.

In the end it was from Doctor Jamieson—come belatedly to examine my ankle and pronounce it not important—that I learned all I did learn that morning. For the authorities had not been able to get in touch with Arthur. Apparently he had taken Mary Lou and Junior for a drive, and was still out.

The doctor gave me the story in detail.

It appeared that the sheriff, having finished with the creek and the pond, had by no means finished with the murder.

"What I gather," he said, "is that Shand came back to the office yesterday and held a conference. He said they'd lost a week or more on the lake and the creek, and while in his opinion she'd been in the lake, she wasn't there now. Then where was she? What if whoever killed her had located the body later? He wouldn't want her found at all. There's no murder without a body. But she was a goodsized woman, and this time probably he didn't have a horse. So what would he be likely to do?"

The upshot, according to the doctor, had been that shortly after daylight the sheriff had collected a dozen men, deputies, detectives, and so on, and they had commenced at the lake and worked down, searching the banks of Stony Creek and into the

90

underbrush on both sides. Even then they might not have found her, but one of the detectives had stepped on a soft piece of ground and removed the leaves and pine needles which covered it. What he saw then was the outline of a grave.

They uncovered the body carefully, and the doctor had already examined it. It was in fair condition. There was no question of its identity. And the word got out quickly. They had had to station guards about before the examination was over; they were still there, until a thorough search of the vicinity could be made.

I felt rather sick, but I asked him to break the news to Jordan before he left. He did so, and he came back looking uncomfortable.

"She must have been fond of Juliette," he said. "She's taking the news pretty hard."

"I thought she would. I'm sorry for her, doctor. But she has acted so queerly—"

He looked at me shrewdly.

"You don't think she knows more than she cares to tell?"

"If she does she is keeping it to herself."

"Well, what's she afraid of, Marcia? She looks like a scared woman to me. Why should she keep her door locked, for one thing?"

"I wish I knew," I said, and sighed.

But it was then, and to the doctor, that I told the story about the hospital suite. Not all of it, of course. Nothing about the bell ringing there. That was absurd and not pertinent. Nothing about Arthur's night there. But about the state it was in, and the general mystery. He seemed rather amused at first, for he knew the place well. But before he left he went up there, and he came down looking bewildered.

"It's amazing," he said. "When did it happen?"

"I think it was the day before Juliette disappeared."

"You think she did it?"

"I think she and Jordan did it. But why? What were they looking for, doctor? Juliette hadn't been here for years, and there's nothing of hers there."

"You're certain of that?"

"What could it be? And why should it be important now?

91

Besides, I have been all over the place. There's nothing."

He was thoughtful, however.

"I don't think you ought to keep it to yourself, Marcia. It's queer, any way you look at it."

"I've had enough of Russell Shand and his outfit," I said, and closed my eyes.

He wrote out a prescription for me and left soon after. But the repercussion was not far off. Late that afternoon Maggie roused me to say that the sheriff was downstairs again, and that I was not to get up. He would see me where I was.

The bromides had quieted me, but I was still not too sure of my legs. And it was with Russell Shand standing over me as I lay in bed that he said:

"So you've been holding out on me again!"

"I thought there was such a thing as professional confidence," I said resentfully.

"Don't blame the doctor. He thinks you need protection. If what he says is true—"

"You can go and look," I said, feeling helpless and annoyed. "Maybe it will make sense to you. It doesn't to me."

He was gone for some time. When he came down he stopped at Jordan's door and, after some rather forcible urging, was admitted. His face was flushed when he came in to me a half hour later.

"There's a lot to be said for the third degree," he said, angrily. "If I had my way with that woman— See here, Marcia, tell me about all this. And why in God's name didn't you tell me before?"

"I've had other things to think about."

"There was no other reason?"

I saw that it was no good. He drew a chair by the bed and looked at me thoughtfully.

"I suppose it was in order when you came?"

"Of course. Mrs. Curtis always cleans it."

"Clean sheets on the bed and all that?"

Too late I remembered. I must have looked fairly desperate, for he reached over and patted my hand.

"Why not come clean, Marcia?" he said. "It pays in the end. Somebody has slept in that bed, or on it. I'm making a guess

92

that it was Arthur. I'm guessing too that he left in a hurry, without his hat. And it isn't far from that to Lizzie's bareheaded man with a hatchet. That's right, isn't it?"

I could not answer. Suddenly I found myself crying as though my heart would break. He handed me a large bandanna handkerchief, but I could not stop and at last I felt him give me a sort of apologetic touch on the shoulder and go creaking out of the room.

The day was endless. Endless and terrifying. For I did not fool myself. There was a murder now, with a body, and at any minute the police might appear with a warrant. I knew that if the truth ever came out Arthur was the logical suspect. And there was that wretched story of Mike's. I had no hope that he would keep it to himself. Probably all the servants knew it already.

I lay there in bed, thinking it over. I thought of Mary Lou, and Junior. I thought of Mother and Father, and the old days in the house before Juliette came and peace departed. I remembered Arthur and myself as children, gathering clams and starfish and other queer jetsam of the sea, and the eel that had slithered down the stairs. But most of all I was thinking of Juliette, and Juliette's death.

I lit a cigarette and tried to recall the events of the last few days. It seemed an eternity since she had stepped blithely out of the bus and had said: "Don't faint, Marcia. It's me!" An eternity too since she had thrown those pebbles into the pond, and watched the widening circles, "Like life," she had said.

Now she was gone. What had happened to her? What had occurred, between her arrival and her disappearance, to set such a stage for her? Whom had she seen? Had she been followed to the island and murdered, or was someone on the island guilty?

She had received no mail, and so far as I knew had sent none. Yet she had had friends, such as they were. I had never seen her New York apartment, but I had heard enough to know what it was like, either filled with people or empty while she and her crowd danced the night away, moving on and on.

"Why go home? The night's still young."

And Juliette going on, the center of the exotic gaiety, to

come home at dawn and sleep the day through. Extravagant riotous living it had been, on Arthur's money and mine, but I did not grudge it to her now. Yet that day for the first time I wondered if somewhere in it was not the answer to her death. She had been in a jam, to use her own words. She had even wanted to get out of the country. Not only that. She could have left no forwarding address for her mail when she left New York. Certainly that in itself was unusual.

In other words, had she been looking for some sort of sanctuary when she came to Sunset? It might be. Probably the last place she would be expected to go was where she had come.

I was still there, still thinking—and wondering—when Arthur arrived. He had had the news, but he had not yet gone to the village; and he looked completely devasted.

"I suppose you've heard," he said. "They've found her."

"Yes, Mike told me. And the doctor."

He looked down at me quickly.

"Mike?" he said. "What does he know about it?"

"Only what everybody does, I suppose," I said wearily.

He sat down on the porch rail then and lit a cigarette, but I saw that his hands were shaking.

"I don't need to tell you what this means, Marcia," he said. "They have a murder now and a body. They'll have to pin it on somebody, and I'm the somebody. Why not? I had the motive, and it won't take them long to learn that I was here the night before, or to break down that alibi of mine. They can trace the sloop, and what about the plane? I didn't give the pilot my right name, but I don't suppose he's a fool."

"But plenty of people come here by plane, Arthur."

He looked at me and I think for the first time he realized what I had been through. Anyhow he leaned over and patted me—on my bad ankle, as it happened.

"Poor little sister," he said. "I'm sorry, my dear. Sorry as hell. But it's bound to come out sooner or later. Haven't you seen the papers lately?"

"I didn't want to see them," I quavered.

He drew a long breath.

"Well, your picture has been in them, and mine. And I might as well tell you: a car turned into the driveway the night

94

I came to see Juliette. The lights were right on me. If whoever was in that car saw me and knew me, I'm through."

"I know about that, Arthur. It was Lucy Hutchinson."

He stared at me. "Lucy Hutchinson," he said. "Good God! Lucy!"

"She won't talk. She told me so."

"Listen, Marcia," he said gravely. "There's a woman in this somewhere. Maybe not Lucy, but a woman. Shand got a lipstick of Juliette's from Jordan, and he says the smear on that cigarette they found was not the same."

"You don't think it was Lucy's!"

"I don't know. She walks up in the hills, you know. If she had a golf club with her—"

I found myself gazing at him with a sort of terror.

"Arthur!" I said. "How do you know she was killed that way?"

He looked startled.

"I don't know," he said, avoiding my eyes. "I haven't seen the—seen the body yet. But I gather she was struck with something. Good Lord, Marcia, don't look at me like that. I didn't kill her, and I'm damned sure Lucy didn't. I'm about off my head with worry, that's all."

I relaxed again, and neither of us spoke for some time. I dare say we were both looking back, gathering up our defenses. When Arthur did speak it was to ask about the hat he had left in the hospital suite.

"I'd better get it," he said. "I'll dispose of it somehow. No use making things worse than they are."

He had actually got up to do it before I could stop him.

"You needn't go, Arthur," I said, unhappily. "It's not there. It's gone."

He stared at me.

"Gone? Gone where?"

"I cut it up and threw it into the bay. But I'm afraid—"

I did not have time to finish, for William came to the door just then to say that there was someone on the telephone for Arthur, and soon after that I heard him driving away in the car.

I know only by hearsay of the events of the rest of that day. The message had been from Doctor Jamieson, who was also the

95

local coroner, asking Arthur to make formal identification of the body; and this I gather, white-faced and shaken, he did. Then the sheriff took him to that shallow grave up the creek, now carefully roped off from the sightseers who had already gathered. But I do know that at some time in the interval I saw a detective talking to Mike in the garden, and Mike led him toward the toolshed.

I remember this now, as I say. For a long time it was erased from my memory as though it had never been. Events moved too thick and too fast. There was, for one thing, the arrival of Mary Lou in her car late in the afternoon, a Mary Lou with a sober face, an overnight bag, and the drawing of what purported to be a cat as a gift from Junior.

"I've just heard," she said. "I do think Arthur could have called up and told me. Where is he?"

"Somewhere in the village," I said evasively. "Arthur has Father's room. Send your bag there, and tell William to put your car away."

I was still on the porch when she came back. Death was death to Mary Lou, and although she had taken off her hat, she still wore a black dress. Also, being Mary Lou, she was filled with remorse. It took several cups of tea to restore her to normal.

"When I think of the perfectly poisonous things I've said, Marcia!" she observed solemnly. "Whatever she was she didn't deserve this."

"Someone must have thought she did," I said.

But I realized that she was nervous. She talked too much and too fast. She asked a flood of questions, and I was relieved when at last she went downstairs, to receive the innumerable callers who came, their faces grave—as was proper in a house of death—but their eyes wide with curiosity.

It was a trying time. I went back to bed and lay there, alternately staring at the Currier and Ives prints on the wall and out through the door at the bay, where those wretched gulls sometimes mewed like cats, and again wailed like babies. Offshore at intervals a belated mother seal was teaching its baby to swim. The baby loathed and feared the water, and would turn around and make desperately for the rocks again. I felt rather like the baby, only I had no rock to turn to.

How far we had traveled from the old days, long before Juliette, when Arthur raced up and down the stairs, while I followed him like a small satellite; and Father and Mother pursued their peaceful summer routine. Father always left a victoria and a trap in the stable, and in the summer the horses were sent up in advance. There were no cars allowed on the island, and the days were a quiet ritual of morning calls, afternoon naps, a drive later on, and then dinner, at home or elsewhere.

There was no ostentation; but plenty of dignified living. It may have been dull, but at least it was safe. The morning calls were formal ones, with cards left and sometimes a glass of sherry and a biscuit, and often when there were callers there would be a visit to the garden. How well I could remember them.

"I do want you to see my delphiniums. They are very good this year."

Mother in the garden by the sundial in the long sweeping dress of the prewar days, and later, with a broad hat to preserve her lovely skin. Talk of roses and columbines and pansies, instead of taxes and politics; and then at last William at the door, an open carriage and a pair of handsome horses driving away, and everything still again.

At noon Father would come in in riding clothes, having left his horse at the stables, and Arthur and I, washed and brushed, would go down to lunch. It was my dinner and I was always ravenous, but I preferred the nursery supper upstairs. There was always a frightful decorum about the lunch table. But after lunch I was free to ramble, and I did; along the waterfront or in the mountains, where once Arthur climbed onto a ledge and had to be rescued with ropes.

All normal. All quiet. In the evenings Father and Mother usually dined out. Mother would come into my room in her silks or brocades—quite as though it had been the city—with her handsome earrings and her pearls, and with her hair built high on her head, as she wore it to the end of her life. She would turn around so I could see her, and then stoop to kiss me good night.

"Be a good little girl, Marcia, and go to sleep."

She would trail out then, leaving behind her a sense of loss and a faint scent of the violet perfume which she continued to use long after the new ones had come into fashion.

But Father seldom came in. He was of sterner stuff. Looking back now I think we never really knew him.

I was still back in the old days when I heard Arthur's voice downstairs, and I knew then that I had never expected him to come back.

CHAPTER XI

That was the last peaceful time I was to know for weeks. Arthur was home again, grave but relieved. The authorities had not held him. They seemed to know nothing of his visit to the island. Shand had been decent to him; more than decent. The autopsy had been held that day, and the inquest would take place on the following Tuesday, at the schoolhouse. Apparently the police had asked for more time.

Arthur kissed me when he came in, but his real attention was for Mary Lou. I remember that he held her as though he was afraid to let her go; as if in a shaken world it was good to have her there, loving and believing in him. I did not always like her, but that day I forgave her everything, even her jealousy of me, for what she gave him.

But things were happening that day of which we had no knowledge. There was a conference at the police station late that afternoon. Bullard, the District Attorney, had come over from Clinton, the county seat, and the sheriff was there, as well as the local police chief, the head of the state police, and several detectives. The men from the press associations and reporters from the various newspapers were kept in an outer room. It was a private conference, with Bullard wanting to hold Arthur pending further investigation and Russell Shand opposing him.

"Where's your case?" said Shand. "You think you've got one, but wait until half a dozen New York big shots come up here and throw it away. Maybe he didn't like her. Maybe he was sick and tired of paying her that money. Maybe he was here on the island that night. I think he was, at that. Maybe he ran around bareheaded at three o'clock in the morning with a hatchet. He won't admit it, but say he was for the sake of argument. That hatchet was found before she was killed, and according to Doctor Jamieson the weapon wasn't a hatchet anyhow, not sharp enough."

"Hell bent on clearing him, aren't you?" said Bullard sourly.

"I'll want to be sure he hasn't got an alibi before we hold him. That's all. I'm not willing to be made a fool of, if you are. I admit that sloop story looks queer, but both you and I have done the same thing, Bullard. Why shouldn't a man go sailing if he's got a mind to?"

Months later the sheriff told me that story. They had cleared a table, and on it lay the various articles so far collected: my scissors, the broken lock from our toolshed, what was left of Arthur's hat, and the initial "A," now glued to a card, Juliette's sodden cigarette case, the wrist watch with its broken strap, and an envelope containing the butt of a cigarette stained with lipstick. There were photographs too, of the scratches on Eagle Rock and of the grave itself, uncovered but with the body still in it, one with the leaves over the face and one without. And something else, which none of us suspected at the time. Somewhere near that log on the hill they had found the print of a woman's heel, and the plaster cast of it was before them.

The sheriff eyed it, and then pulled a photograph out of his pocket.

"For that matter," he said, "you've got about as good a case against Mrs. Lloyd as you have against the husband. Better, maybe. We don't know he was here. We know she was."

"What the devil do you mean?" Bullard snapped.

"Looks like she was parked beside the road near the bridle path the morning the Ransom woman disappeared," Shand drawled. "We checked up on all cars and roads right off, and if those aren't her tire marks I'll eat them. She hasn't an alibi worth a cent, at that. I called the garage at Millbank and it seems she got the car about eight-thirty or so the morning of the murder. She called the Lloyd house before that. Sallie Anderson, over at Millbank, remembers the call."

There was a long silence, according to his account.

"That's ridiculous," said Bullard finally. "She's a nice woman. I've met her. I've a sister at Millbank."

"That's the trouble with it," said the sheriff. "All these people are nice people. Marcia Lloyd is a damn' fine girl. I've known her since she was a baby. And Arthur Lloyd's no killer." He leaned over and picked up the lock. "All along," he said, "you fellows have been leaving out the two things that bother me most. First, who got into that top floor at the Lloyd house and tore it to pieces? What were they after? And second, what brought the Ransom woman here? Money? She could have seen Arthur Lloyd in New York. Looks as though she was scared when she came; and she wasn't scared of the Lloyds, or she wouldn't have come here."

Bullard stirred irritably.

"You've got to take the general picture, Shand," he said. "If we can break down his alibi we've got him. He had a motive. Who else had? His wife? Maybe you can see her burying that body, but I can't. And whoever killed her buried her. Knew where to look for her and buried her. Don't forget that."

"Maybe. Maybe not," said the sheriff, and the meeting broke up.

They went across the street to a restaurant for dinner. Bullard was hungry and ate enormously; but the sheriff only ate a sandwich and drank a glass of milk.

"Too much on my mind," Shand told me later. "Seemed like my stomach had sort of shut up."

But Bullard had it all settled by that time. He wasn't worrying.

Even that meal, however, was not to be entirely peaceful. They were still at the table when Fred Martin came in, looking for them, and Fred had a story to tell.

On the morning of the murder he had seen a woman cut across the corner of the course. She was too far away to recognize, but she had carried a walking stick of some kind. She had not gone directly toward the bridle path, but had disappeared into the woods in that direction.

"I didn't think anything of it at the time," he said, "although it was pretty early. About eight-thirty. But I hear the doc says Mrs. Ransom was struck with a heavy weapon, and if what she was carrying was a golf club— Well, I thought I'd tell you anyway."

"No woman did this job," said Bullard, wiping his mouth with his napkin.

The sheriff was interested. Fred was definitely of the opinion that it was a member of the summer colony. The native women were not given to early walks in the hills.

"Kinda queer at that, Fred," he said. "Nobody's come forward and said she was there. The villagers don't use that path. They've got other things to do. And we've more or less checked up on the summer folks. Not all of them here yet, and only one or two regular walkers among them. Seems to me if she knew nothing she'd come out and say so. Who'd be likely to take a walk like that?"

Fred looked uncomfortable.

"Well," he said, "there's Miss Lloyd. She gets about quite a lot. And Mrs. Hutchinson. I suppose we can leave out the older women. They don't walk."

Bullard roused at that.

"Miss Lloyd?" he said. "That's the sister, isn't it? I'd like to see her, Shand. Maybe she's got a motive too. I'd like to bet she hated the Ransom woman like poison."

The result was a visit from them both that night. I had managed to get down to dinner, and we were all in the library, Arthur pacing the floor, Mary Lou knitting, and I absently playing solitaire, when they were announced.

Bullard took the lead, and lost no time in doing it. He started with me.

"I understand you did not leave the house at all the morning Mrs. Ransom left for that ride," he said, his eyes like small bright black buttons.

I was surprised.

"Why, no," I said. "She had taken the car. I couldn't."

"You didn't happen to take a walk?"

"A walk? No."

"I suppose you can prove that?"

"You can ask the servants."

I was puzzled rather than resentful, but I saw Arthur make an impatient gesture.

"Why question my sister?" he demanded. "What has she got to do with it?"

Bullard merely smiled, not too pleasantly.

"Let me do this my own way, Mr. Lloyd," he said. "I imagine we all want the facts. There is a path leading up into the hills from the golf course, isn't there?"

"Yes."

"You didn't take that path that morning? The morning of the murder?"

"I've already said I did not."

"Yet Fred Martin, your golf professional, says you did just that."

I could only stare at him. The sheriff looked irritated; Bullard kept his bland smile, although he shifted his tactics.

"You didn't like Mrs. Ransom very much, did you?" he inquired, almost gently.

"I did not. But if all this means that you think I killed her—" I began angrily.

He held up a plump white hand.

"I haven't said anything of the sort, Miss Lloyd," he said, looking almost shocked. "I am only here, as the prosecuting attorney of this county, to ask some questions."

"As for instance?" said Arthur, scowling over his pipe.

He turned his attention to Arthur.

"Well, what brought Mrs. Ransom here in the first place? Was there any particular reason why she came back just now? I understand—"

He paused, and Arthur flushed. I saw that he was trying to control himself.

"I suppose you've got to do this," he said, "but it's damned unpleasant. Yes, there was a reason. It was money."

"Money?"

"That's what I said. I've been paying her alimony. A lot of it. She took it into her head that she wanted a lump sum instead. That's all there is to it."

"I see," said Bullard, looking smug. "Alimony, eh? And a lot of it. Rather a—" He checked himself. "And so, instead of going to you, she came to your sister? Isn't that unusual?"

"How do I know what's usual in such circumstances?" said

103

Arthur furiously. "All I know is that she damned well didn't get it."

"You refused?"

It was a trap, and Arthur almost fell into it. He caught himself in time, however.

"I called my sister over the long-distance telephone and said it was impossible. You can check the call if you want to."

They left soon after that. Arthur was in a white rage, and Mary Lou was blazingly indignant.

"Well, of all things," she said, as the door closed behind them. "You'd think they actually suspected you, Arthur, or Marcia."

"Perhaps they do, my dear," said Arthur patiently. "Perhaps they do."

I passed a rotten night. It had rained that evening, and the overflow from the pond roared like a small Niagra. Also my ankle was bothering me again. But what kept me awake was a question from the sheriff, after Bullard had gone out to the car.

"Tell me something, Marcia," he said. "Does Mrs. Hutchinson use a pretty heavy lipstick?"

"Yes, what about it?"

He did not answer me. He patted my back and went away. But there was a reason behind that question; and I lay awake and worried over it.

It was still worrying me the next morning. Lucy, who might at a distance, although taller, be mistaken for me. Lucy, who often walked in the hills, and sometimes, after a game of golf, carried a club with her instead of a stick. Lucy, with her mouth heavily made up, so that she stained every cigarette she smoked. And Lucy, who hated Juliette.

I could still see her the evening she came in, in her white dress and jade earrings. She had been terrified that day, trembling.

"It's been plain hell," she had said. But after all it had been a long time since she had been in love with Arthur. I thought now that her fright had been for herself, not for him.

What was I to do? If I told the sheriff about it she could counter with her story about Arthur, and seeing him on the drive.

In the end I took it to Arthur himself. Mary Lou was still asleep, and he was shaving in the bathroom. I sat on the edge of the bathtub and told him, and at first he pooh-poohed the idea.

"Lucy!" he said. "You're losing your mind, Marcia."

He blew out one cheek to run the razor over it, and I wanted to shout.

"That's too easy, Arthur. She's strong as a horse. She often walks in the hills. And she was jealous of Juliette. Bob liked her a lot, at one time."

He merely rinsed his razor and leaning over patted me condescendingly.

"Do all women hate all other women?" he inquired, and grinned at me in much his old fashion. "Keep out of this, my girl. We don't hide behind the Lucy's of this world, do we?"

"But if she did it?"

"Don't be a little fool. No woman did this, Marcia. Look at the facts. She was not only killed. Somebody mounted that mare and, carrying her, rode down to the lake. That took strength. I couldn't have done it myself, and I'm not feeble."

That was on Sunday, and I went to early service that morning. I could not face a churchful of well-dressed and curious people at eleven o'clock. But as I came out I saw the sheriff and two deputies pass in a car, and realized that the law knew no Sabbath.

I did not go directly home. Instead, I drove out to Fred Martin's cottage, a small one on the golf club grounds, and found him washing the breakfast dishes. Dorothy, his young wife, was still in bed. She was soon to have a child, and Fred adored her. He made a sign to me when he saw me, and closed the door before he took off his apron and joined me on the porch.

"Just letting the wife rest," he said. "Ground's too soft for golf today anyhow, after the rain. Well, what can I do for you?"

"I want to ask you something, Fred. Did you tell the District Attorney you saw me cutting across the course the morning Mrs. Ransom was killed?"

He almost leaped out of his skin.

"Godamighty, no!" he said. "I told them I saw a woman

105

there. Then they wanted to know who walked up that way now and then, and I told them. That's all there was to it."

I believed him. There was something sturdy and honest about him. And he was well liked. He had been at the club for five or six years, and many of the members he knew in Palm Beach in the winter as well. Each summer I took a few driving lessons from him, and nothing was more familiar than his muscular figure, in old trousers and a sweater.

"See what you did that time?" he would say. "Tried to kill the ball, that's all. What's wrong? Don't you like it?"

But that morning he was not quite himself. I thought he had lost some of his old directness.

"If you know anything you ought to tell it. We're dealing with a murder, Fred," I said.

"I realize that, all right. But I didn't really see this woman. She was a long ways off. I think she wore a yellow sweater, but that's all I know."

"A yellow sweater!" I said. "I've got one myself!"

"I know that too," he said, and lapsed into silence.

There was nothing to be gained by staying, and so I left, with Fred putting me into the car and standing by until I had gone. But I was not very happy as I drove home. Yellow was a popular color this year, and I knew that Lucy also had a yellow sweater.

Lizzie had the usual country Sunday dinner that day, chicken and ice cream; but I could not eat, nor did Arthur. In the afternoon I drove up into the hills. The weather was beautiful, and I saw Marjorie Pendexter and Howard Brooks, evidently bound on a climbing expedition, and waved at them. But I had been out for two hours before I found Allen Pell.

He was striding along the road, bareheaded, with his hands in his trousers pockets and his head bent; and I thought he looked startled when I stopped the car beside him. He smiled, however, when he saw me. I noticed that even his forehead was now deeply tanned.

"I've been looking for you for hours," I told him.

"You haven't a thing on me. I've been thinking of you for days," he said. "What do I do now? Get into the car, or will you get out?"

"I'll get out," I said, and proceeded to do so. "I want to talk

106

and I can't do it when I'm driving."

"It would be a good thing if more young women knew that," he said lightly.

But he was definitely uneasy. When we found a rock and sat down on it, he seemed rather at a loss.

"Look here," he said. "I'm more sorry than I can say about what's happened. But I can't tell you anything about it."

"You knew her. That's something."

He did not say anything for a brief time. Then he turned and faced me.

"Yes, I knew her," he said. "I was crazy about her, if you want the truth. But that was a long time ago. Don't hold it against me now."

"It doesn't really concern me, does it?"

"Doesn't it? Well, I suppose that was too much to hope. What did you want to ask me?"

For just a minute I had been absurdly happy, but his question brought me back with a jerk.

"You knew her crowd. Whom she played around with, who liked her and who didn't. Are any of them here, on the island?"

"My dear girl, I haven't seen that crowd of hers for more than two years. I wanted to forget the whole damned lot, if you want the truth. And her too. And don't take what I said too seriously. I lost my head for a while. That's all. I got over it in a hurry."

"I hadn't the slightest idea of taking it seriously," I told him. But he laughed and picking up my hand, kissed the palm of it lightly.

"Let's forget her," he said. "We can't help her, and here's a day of days, and you are here. That's enough for me."

It was late when I got home. Mary Lou was pouring tea in the library, and Arthur looked more relaxed than he had been for days. But when I went up to take off my hat I saw William outside Jordan's door with a small tray, and heard her ask who it was.

"The cook's sent up some tea for you," said William stiffly.

"Then put it on the floor. I'll get it."

I was in the hall at the time, and if there was any humor in the situation it was in William's face as he passed me.

107

"She's gone off her head, miss," he said. "If she thinks I want to get inside that room—"

I was puzzled myself, but I did not think the woman was crazy. I waited until, having heard William's steps recede, she unlocked and opened her door. She inspected the hall carefully in both directions before she picked up her tray; and I knew then that she was not sulking, or even necessarily grieving. She was in a state of acute terror.

CHAPTER XII

The next day the case developed, and in amazing fashion. The first surprise came in the morning, and concerned Helen Jordan again. After breakfast she called a village taxicab, and went out in it. She returned for lunch, but late in the afternoon she appeared in my doorway, with her suitcase in her hand.

"I'm leaving, Miss Lloyd," she said, in her flat voice. "I want to thank you for letting me stay. You've been very good to me."

"Leaving, Jordan? There's no train at this time of day."

"No, miss," she said. "I'm not leaving town. I've taken a room in the town.

She gave no explanation, and I did not like to ask for one. But before she left I asked her if she had sufficient money, and she thanked me and said rather obscurely that that was being taken care of. Then she went stiffly down the stairs, and I felt a sense of relief, as though something unfriendly and even sinister had gone out of the house.

Our real surprise, however, came shortly before noon that day.

The season was well under way by that time; the streets of the village crowded with cars, the shops busy, and the Shore Club opened, with its gay parasols over tables on the terrace, and the braver spirits among us already bathing in the pool. But the tourist camp on Pine Hill was filling up also, and on that Monday morning a woman from it drove in to Conrad's for meat.

I was not there, but I now know the story. Dorothy Martin was there at the time, and she and Conrad were talking about the case.

"So Fred saw this woman," said Conrad, scrupulously weighing the order.

"He saw somebody," said Dorothy. "He didn't recognize her. She was too far away. But he thinks she wore a yellow sweater and carried something. A stick of some sort."

"Funny she hasn't spoken up, whoever she is," said Mr. Conrad, eying the scales. "Everybody knows they're looking for her. Not that I think she did it," he added. "It looks like a man-size job to me. But she might have seen something."

It was then that the woman from the tourist camp spoke up.

"If it's a woman in a yellow sweater you're talking about, I saw her myself," she said. "Close by, too. I was out gathering wood that day when she went past. She didn't see me."

As a result of which five minutes later Conrad had shed his apron, put on his hat, and was leading her to the police station, where the sheriff had set up a temporary office. He was there, smoking his pipe and studying a contour map of the island, when Conrad led the woman in and explained.

"You saw her?" he said. "Would you know her again?"

"I certainly would. She was walking fast and carrying a golf club. She was smoking a cigarette too. I don't hold with women smoking," she added virtuously.

Shand looked grave, but nothing shook her testimony. She hadn't been forty feet away. Kind of tall and good-looking; thirty maybe, maybe more. Had red hair and her mouth painted, she said. She had a woman's memory for her clothing too. She wore the sweater, a soft hat and a dark plaid skirt.

It took both Conrad and the sheriff about one minute to identify Lucy Hutchinson, and I believe they went into a panic at first.

They put the woman from the tourist camp in another room, over her protest. Then the sheriff called in the village police chief and a deputy or two, and including Conrad they went into a huddle.

"No proof she did it," said Shand. "But if she was up there that morning she's got a right to tell about it, summer folks or no summer folks." Meaning that as the main business of the island was the people who spent the hot weather there, as a rule

110

they could do no wrong.

"You'll have to be careful, Shand," said Mr. Conrad, mopping his face. "They're good people and good customers. Not only to me. All over town."

"I'll be careful, all right."

The sheriff outlined his plan of campaign then. The police station is on the main street of the village, and any day from ten to eleven one may see most of the women of the summer colony there doing their buying. For that tradition survives among us. Other resorts may telephone for their supplies; most of us go and get them. Tradition dies hard in us. As our forebears did, so do we, although I loathe it. I can still remember my mother, with a groom in livery behind her carrying a huge basket on his arm, testing the tenderness and youth of chickens by lifting a wing to see if the skin broke.

They put the woman—her name was Cutten, I remember— into a window overlooking the street, and the sheriff gave her his instructions. It was eleven o'clock by that time, and still early.

"Just tell me if you see her, Mrs. Cutten," he said. "That's all. And sit back a little. No need for any excitement."

Less than an hour later Lucy, having parked her car, came along the street on her way to the lending library. She did not wear the yellow sweater, and she had an entirely peaceable book or two under her arm. But Mrs. Cutten knew her at once.

"There she is," she said. "I'd know her anywhere."

She was rather surprised when the sheriff made no move. "Sure of it?"

"Absolutely."

"All right," he said. "Go on back to the camp and the family. And don't talk, Mrs. Cutten. You'll have plenty of chance later."

He put in, I believe, an hour or two of good hard thinking after she had gone. Then he got up and smashed his hat down on his head.

"I may have to fight Wall Street, the government and a few foreign nations before I'm through with this," he said to a deputy standing by, "but I'm on my way."

He had no illusions about what it meant as he started out.

111

Both Lucy's family and the Hutchinsons had owned estates on the island for years. They paid high taxes, and were in the forefront of all the village movements. Bob himself had built a new wing for the local hospital. To find then that Lucy had been near by when Juliette disappeared and had concealed the fact was more than a shock. It struck deep into the very roots of the town's life. Nevertheless, he did it, walking in on Lucy when she returned for lunch at one o'clock.

He said later that he did not need to ask a question after he saw her. She looked at him and turned white, though she managed to smile.

"Is the law after me, Mr. Shand?" she said.

"I wouldn't say that, Mrs. Hutchinson."

"Then what would you say?"

She sat down but he still stood, looking down at her.

"I'd say that if people didn't get scared and hide things, life would be a lot easier."

"I suppose that means I'm hiding something?"

"I know damn' well you are."

She still tried to evade it.

"What am I hiding?" she inquired. "I suppose I killed Juliette Ransom and then lifted her on a horse and put her in the lake. What an athlete you must think I am."

But he was not having any persiflage. He took the cigarette from her hand and looked at it.

"Why didn't you tell me you went up into the hills that morning?" he said gravely. "You've been identified by a woman who saw you close by. It was your cigarette we found by that log, and your heel that made the print we've got. Let's not argue about it. That's only losing time."

"You're guessing," she told him, and got up abruptly. At first he thought she was about to walk out on him, but she merely closed the door and came back. "You're guessing, and I'll fight you from here to the Supreme Court, Russell Shand, before I'll let you get away with it."

"All right," he said, picking up his hat. "I thought maybe you and I could have it out all nice and quiet; but if you take this attitude I'll have to go further."

Long weeks later when he told me of that conversation I was to be grateful to her for that day, and for what she did not tell.

112

She must have been tempted. All she had to say was that Arthur had been on the island the night of the murder, and he would have walked over to us and confronted us. She did not say it. She sat there, cornered and desperate, and finally looked up at him.

"You win," she said, quietly. "Where do we go from here? To the jail?"

"Not necessarily, unless— You didn't kill her, did you?"

"No."

"Well, let's change the question. Did you see her that morning?"

She hesitated, and her silence was his answer.

"You saw her. Did you talk to her?"

"That's what I went for. But I give you my word of honor that when I left she was still there, safe and sound."

On one thing she was firm. She would not tell why she had met Juliette that morning. It was a private matter between them and did not involve anyone else. She had wanted to talk to her, and when that morning she saw her starting off in riding clothes, she had got out her coupé and followed her.

"I left the car near the club, and cut across the course," she said. "I knew I could head her off by a short cut. As a matter of fact, I was well ahead of her. I had time to smoke a cigarette before she came. But I'm no fool," she added. "Do you suppose I'd have left the stub there if I had meant to kill her?"

She did say one thing, though. When she started back Juliette was still off her horse and making no move to go.

I knew nothing of this until Tony Rutherford wandered in that afternoon, for a highball and a talk. Now that he felt safe with me he frequently did that! But that day he was being tactful. He approached the matter by indirection, giving me first the small gossip of the colony. Bob Hutchinson had had too much to drink the night before and had quarreled with Howard Brooks. Mrs. Dean was not well and Doctor Jamieson was attending her, the assemblymen were talking about lowering taxes on house property, which did not mean anything, and did I want an Airedale pup.

All lighthearted enough. I listened absently, my mind elsewhere, until he said the thing that made me sit up in my chair.

113

"What do you think of Lucy being our latest suspect?"

"Lucy? Lucy Hutchinson?"

He nodded, grinning.

"Apparently she was the lady in the yellow sweater after all. Been identified! Here! Hold on there! What's the matter?"

I pulled myself together.

"It's absurd, that's all."

"Why absurd? Why shouldn't Lucy take a morning tramp in the hills? She often does it."

He went on. The story was that the sheriff had not only got her identified. He had gone to see her. "But she's still free, white and thirty-one," he said. "You needn't look like that, my dear. Trust little Lucy to take care of herself."

He did not stay long. I dare say I was not an absorbing companion, for I knew well enough that, whether she had already told about Arthur or not, if driven to a corner she would have to tell. I was relieved when Tony finally got up to go.

"Don't take it too hard, old girl," he said. "Better Lucy than Arthur any day, isn't it?"

With which dubious comfort he went away.

But that identification of Lucy was to have an unexpected result the same night.

That evening after dinner Arthur took one of his aimless drives while Mary Lou and I played Russian bank. I had won two dollars from her before she yawned and went up to bed, and when Arthur came back—somewhere around ten o'clock —I was about to call it a day myself.

There was a change in Arthur that night. He looked like a man who had come to a decision; and I found that he had. He ordered a drink and with it in his hand stood in front of the fire, staring at it thoughtfully.

"I'm not going to let Lucy be dragged into this thing, Marcia," he said.

I put down the cards and looked at him.

"What does that mean?"

"I'm going to tell the truth at the inquest tomorrow. I'm sick of dodging it."

"You can't," I said wretchedly. "Nobody will believe it."

"I can't help that. I didn't kill her, and that's what matters."

114

"You can't prove it."

"They can't prove I did. That's something," he said dryly, and finished his drink.

He seemed relieved at his decision. He enlarged on what he meant to do. It was only a matter of time until his alibi would be broken, but it was possible the car could be found, the one which took him off the island hours before Juliette's death. He would have to depend on that or something like it. He was more like himself than he had been for days, but I sat stunned and helpless. I had seen Arthur in one of his stubborn moods before, and there was nothing to do.

In the silence that followed we heard a car outside. It was the sheriff, and his stocky figure was stiff and erect as he came into the room.

He looked at me.

"Better go back to bed, Marcia," he said. "Your brother and I have some things to discuss."

But Arthur interfered.

"Let her stay, Shand," he said. "I suppose it's that alibi of mine. Well, she knows it all. She's tried to protect me, but I've just told her it's no use. I'm telling it all tomorrow. It's a long story. You'd better sit down."

Arthur himself did not sit down. He did not even look at Mary Lou when, having heard the sheriff's car, she slipped into the room. He stood erect on the hearth and quietly and clearly stated his case: the sloop and the alibi, for his wife's sake; his own desperate situation, the talk with Juliette and what he had said to her, and his hasty departure in the middle of the night.

"But that's all," he finished. "I never saw her again. And I never killed her."

Mary Lou was very white. He looked at her then for the first time, but she said nothing. She did not even look at him. To my surprise she got up, and with her dressing gown drawn around her—she had only her nightgown underneath—went out and up the stairs. Arthur followed her with his eyes, but she did not look back.

I hated her that night, that she could still be jealous of a dead woman. And for something more. Toward the end of Arthur's story I had seen suspicion in her face, and he must have seen it too. I know that he sat down as though the courage had left

115

him, and I saw much the same look in his face as had been there the day I found him alone in Juliette's apartment, with those bills and the mocking figure on them.

I do not remember much that followed. The sheriff asked him some questions. Had he seen the man on the roof clearly? What had he—Arthur—done with the hatchet? Where had the car from the camp picked him up, and when? Had anyone seen him as he dozed on the waterfront while waiting for his train? And, rather ominously, had he sent any clothing to the cleaner's in New York since that night?

Arthur answered them all frankly. He had not seen the man on the roof, but thought he was fairly young, from the way he ran. As to the clothing, no, he had sent nothing. They could have his keys if they wanted to look over anything.

I could add little or nothing. I told the story of the hat, and Jordan's discovery of my attempt to destroy it. The sheriff asked me about the night before Juliette's death, when she took the car out before Tony came. But he asked me something else.

"What about this maid of hers, Marcia?" he inquired. "Why did she want to leave this house?"

"I haven't any idea."

"She's afraid of something," he said. "I'd give a good bit to know who or what it is."

I had fully expected Arthur to be arrested that evening. I am sure he did also, for he looked surprised when the sheriff got up and picked up his hat.

"Well, I'd better get some sleep," he said. "My brain feels like mush, and we've got the inquest tomorrow. I'm glad you came clean," he added to Arthur. "I might as well tell you that the pilot who brought you up has made a statement to the New York police. He saw your picture in a newspaper, and identified it."

I went up to bed soon after he left, and out of sheer emotional exhaustion, I slept that night. Sometime after two o'clock I heard a motorboat not far away start up, choke, and after a time start again. It wakened me; but I dozed off immediately afterwards, and not for days did I realize the significance of what I had heard, or that we had had another murder that night.

116

CHAPTER XIII

The inquest was held the next day. They had cleared a room in the schoolhouse for it, and Doctor Jamieson sat behind the desk, looking like a plump and bespectacled teacher, with Bullard and the sheriff close at hand. The six men who constituted the jury were all tradesmen in the town, responsible and somewhat self-conscious. They had already seen the body, I gathered, for one or two of them looked rather shaken.

They sat on the platform in their Sunday best, while photographers' bulbs flashed at them and at all of us as we arrived. Ever since I have wondered at the incredible cruelty of such spectacles. Mary Lou, I know, was white with indignation, and Arthur rigid. But near by in Jim Blake's undertaking rooms Juliette lay dead, and somebody had killed her.

The jury sworn in, Doctor Jamieson made a brief speech.

"As this is the first inquiry of the sort here in many years," he said, "I would like to explain the procedure to the jury. This inquest is an inquiry, a preliminary inquiry under oath. The witnesses are bound to tell the truth or be guilty of perjury. We are to take testimony relating to a grave crime, and that testimony, duly weighed, will lead to your verdict, whatever that may be."

He then instructed them as to the types of verdict they might render and, proof of identification having been given, the first witness was called.

This was, I think, the medical examiner from Clinton who had conducted the autopsy. Condensed, his statement was a follows: The deceased, as he called her, had been dead before

117

she was thrown into the lake. There was no water in the lungs. Her death had been caused by two wounds in the back of the head, both inflicted by a blunt instrument. By that he meant one without a sharp cutting edge. When found, these wounds had been filled with sand and other detritus from the lake or creek, but there was a considerable fracture of the skull. He described the size and nature of the injuries; and he put the time of death, which must have been practically instantaneous, at approximately two or two and a half hours after she had last eaten.

Interrogated, he did not believe that a fall could have caused the injuries. Asked as to the iron shoe on a horse's foot, he was dubious.

"It is possible," he said. "But taking the other circumstances into account I consider it unlikely."

As I have no record of the proceedings, I may be wrong in the order of the witnesses, but I believe that the next one was the detective who had found the body. The grave, he said, was shallow: two feet deep or so. He described his discovery, and the position of the body, adding that the face had been protected by leaves. Also he explained that leaves and needles had been placed over the grave itself to conceal it. It lay about fifty feet from the creek bank, and a mile or so above the main road. He believed the body had been dragged there from the creek, as he had been following a trail of broken branches when he found it. Here Doctor Jamieson stopped the proceedings and drew the attention of the jury to a map on the wall behind him. He got up and pointed out a red line on it.

"In order to assist the jury," he said, "I have had this map prepared. To save time I will say that this cross indicates the log by the trail where the deceased was last seen alive. The location of the grave is shown by this arrow. Testimony as to other marks on the map will be given in due time."

It was given. Witnesses came and went: the Boy Scout who had found the watch, the police photographer with his pictures of Juliette's hat and gloves near the log, of the slides made by the mare on the steep hillside, of the scratches on Eagle Rock, and last of all, of that ghastly grave and Juliette in it, her hands quietly crossed on her breast.

118

The jury passed them from hand to hand, solemnly and not too happily.

They were all there. Oleson the diver, Ed Smith, even William, to testify when she had left the house.

But the spectators were growing impatient. Nobody had yet been thrown to the lions, and the room was hot. Once the proceedings had to be stopped to open the windows. They were growing restless when at last Lucy Hutchinson was called.

She was prepared. She got up, gave a half-contemptuous glance around the room, and going forward was duly sworn. As if in defiance she had worn the yellow sweater, and the room fairly gasped.

But she emerged with a measure of dignity, although with considerable suspicion.

She admitted at once that she had met Juliette that morning on the trail. She had been smoking a cigarette when Juliette rode up and dismounted. They had not seen each other for some time, and they had talked.

"Will you tell us about that conversation?"

"Purely personal matters. We had differed about something, but there was no quarrel."

"Do you care to elaborate that?"

"No. It had nothing to do with her death."

"How long did you talk?"

"Five minutes. Maybe ten."

"Did she indicate any fear? I mean by that, was she at all nervous?"

"Not at all. Very calm."

"Had you carried something with you on that walk, Mrs. Hutchinson?"

"I had carried a golf club."

There was a stir, and Doctor Jamieson rapped for order. Lucy smiled coolly.

"Do you usually do that?" he asked.

"Now and then. I meant to practice later. I've been off on my long shots lately."

"Will you tell us where that club is now?"

"I haven't an idea."

"Will you explain what you mean by that?"

119

"I went off and left it," she said. "Forgot it. That's all."

"It has not been returned to you?"

"No."

"When you left the deceased what was she doing?"

"She was standing beside her horse."

"You did not see her mount it?"

"No."

"Is that the last you saw of her?"

"Not exactly. I looked back at the turn of the path, and she was still there. I thought she might be waiting for someone."

"Why was that?"

"Well, her hat and gloves were still on the ground. And she seemed to be listening. That is, she was looking about as though she heard something."

It was straightforward enough, but it was easy to sense the emotions of a crowd. Lucy had been liked in the village, and at the opening of the inquest sentiment had been in her favor. But it was evident that there had been more to that meeting than she had told. Why refuse to tell what they had talked about? Why go away and forget the club? The thrifty New England soul rejected the idea, especially since she had, as she said, intended to use it later.

I noticed one of the village women draw away as Lucy returned to her seat, as though she did not want to be touched by her.

They forgot her, however, the moment Arthur took the stand. All his long summers there, his personal popularity and the directness of his testimony did not help him. Here at last was the story, and sensational enough to satisfy everybody.

I watched him as he testified, his handsome head well up, his voice calm, his manner straightforward. Mary Lou was holding onto my hand, and I was sorry for her.

I heard her gasp beside me, but Arthur held nothing back; Juliette's suggestion of a cash payment instead of further alimony, his decision to see her, his arrival by plane, and his refusal to agree to her demands because of inability to raise so large a sum.

They were stunned. His presence on the island that night was a real shock, and although he made a good witness, the remainder of his story sounded unreal, even to me: the man on

120

the roof, his attempt to capture him, and his own departure in an unknown car, still undiscovered and unidentified. Nor did Arthur's statement, that he had spent the crucial hours from daylight until his train left, asleep on the waterfront at Clinton, help him any.

Even Doctor Jamieson looked unhappy.

"I have one or two questions to ask you, Mr. Lloyd," he said. "One is this: did you quarrel with the deceased on meeting her, after your arrival?"

"There was no quarrel. I told her that what she wanted was impossible. That was all."

"Did you see her after that?"

"No. I left after a few hours' rest."

"Did you communicate with her in any way?"

"I did not."

"Were you, at any time during that visit, in the vicinity of Loon Lake or the trail above?" he asked.

"Never."

But it was evident that the spectators did not believe him. They stirred in their seats, whispered together. How simple it was after all! Lucy had left the golf club there, and Arthur had found it and murdered Juliette. Even now I find myself shaken with resentment as I write this.

The room was still buzzing when he was excused. He came back to his seat beside Mary Lou, but Mary Lou did not look at him. I could have killed her for that, that day.

I know now that the sheriff had not wanted the inquest to go to these lengths. It had been his idea to make it a brief formality. But Bullard had been insistent, and Arthur determined. It was out of Shand's hands now, and running away with him.

It was probably at his instigation that I was called. I corroborated Arthur's story so far as I knew it. But I saw the sheriff speak to Doctor Jamieson, and the next questions were about Juliette herself.

"Did the deceased appear perfectly normal while she was with you?"

"She said she was in trouble. She wanted to leave the country."

"She did not explain that?"

"No."

"Miss Lloyd, it may or may not be pertinent to this inquiry, but it has been suggested that I ask this question. Have you had any trouble in your house lately?"

"One of the rooms—what we call the hospital suite—was entered and searched."

"When did that take place?"

"On the day before Mrs. Ransom disappeared."

"Was there anything of value in those rooms?"

"Nothing whatever, so far as I know."

"You have no explanation, then, of why this was done?"

"None whatever."

"Do you think this had any reference to the deceased's presence in the house?"

"I think she did it herself," I said bluntly.

I was excused rather hastily after that, and Helen Jordan was called.

But Helen Jordan was not present, nor did a messenger sent hurriedly to Eliza Edwards's, where she had taken a room, find her there. Instead Mrs. Edwards herself arrived, to state breathlessly that her boarder's clothing and suitcase were still there, but that her bed had not been slept in.

Helen Jordan had disappeared.

CHAPTER XIV

The inquest was adjourned following that discovery. I had a fleeting glimpse of old Mrs. Pendexter, her black eyes snapping with interest; of Fred Martin and Dorothy; of Mansfield Dean alone; and, as we went out, of Allen Pell alone and lighting a cigarette, but watching the crowd sharply. Then we were back at the house, Mary Lou to go to bed taking a bottle of aromatic ammonia with her and Arthur to pace the library floor downstairs and drink one Scotch and soda after another without perceptible effect.

"Now where are we?" he demanded. "That woman's gone. She knew something, so she's gone. Cleared out."

"Without her suitcase?"

He stopped and stared at me.

"What do you mean?" he said. "You don't think—"

"I'm not thinking, Arthur. She may be all right. On the other hand, we might as well face it. She may have been murdered."

"Murdered?" he said thickly. "Who on earth would want to murder her?"

"It would be extremely interesting to know," I retorted, and went out to see if Mary Lou's tray was ready.

Lunch—such lunch as we could eat—was over when I heard a car drive up. It was the sheriff, and I found him in the hall, with the door open and the engine outside still going. I did not like the expression on his face.

"Which of your maids here would know what clothes the Jordan woman had?" he asked abruptly. "I want to find what's missing."

"She's still gone, then?"

"She's still gone," he said laconically.

I thought Ellen might know, although Jordan had been rather secretive. I called Ellen, and the sheriff told her to get her hat and coat. She looked terrified and glanced at me.

"It's all right, Ellen," I told her. "You're not under arrest. Do what you're told."

He brought her back in an hour or so. She had not, I gathered, been very useful. All of Jordan's clothes that she remembered were there, except what she had worn when she left us; but she might have had others. However, there was her suitcase and her unused bed, and Russell Shand was in a bad temper and did not care who knew it. He went upstairs and examined her room, and then called for the key to Juliette's room. When I found him there he was staring with some contempt at the rose silk sheets on the bed, and he held such mail as she had brought with her in his hand.

"See here, Marcia," he said. "Do you know any friend of Mrs. Ransom's named Jennifer?"

"No. I don't know any of her friends."

"Then I wish I knew why the Jordan woman thought a letter with that signature was worth taking away with her."

"She took the letter?" I said incredulously.

"She did. We found it in her suitcase."

"I have read it. There was nothing in it of any importance."

"Maybe not. Damned if I know." He took out his notebook and glanced at a notation he had made in it. "'Have just heard about L——,'" he read aloud. "'Do please be careful, Julie. You know what I mean.' Now what does that refer to?"

I had no idea, and said so. He stood looking thoughtfully at the book in his hand.

"Well, by the great horn spoon, you can bet that Helen Jordan thought it meant something," he said. "Why was Mrs. Ransom to be careful about this L——? Was L—— dangerous? It sounds like it." He put away the notebook. "The devil of it is," he added, "that there's a fair chance we'll never know why she took it with her. Something's happened to her, Marcia. You'd better realize that."

"You think she has been murdered?" I said weakly.

124

"Well, look at the facts. She got to the Edwards house all right. She went up to her room, put the suitcase in a closet, took her pocketbook and went downstairs to her supper. After supper she locked her door and went out, maybe eight o'clock. She gave Eliza Edwards the key and said she would be back in an hour or so. But she didn't come back. She hasn't been seen since. Nobody knew her in town, so we can't trace which direction she took; but she left this letter, her bankbook, and a hundred dollars in cash in that suitcase. That doesn't look like running away, does it? Yet from the minute she stepped off the porch of the Edwards house last night she hasn't been seen."

He ran his hand over his bristling hair.

"Now and then," he said, "I read these magazines that deal with crime. Real crime. Well, where do they start off? They've got something. They get a microscope and put a hair under it; or they take the dust out of somebody's pockets and find where he's been and what he's been doing. But in one of these cases we've got a body and no clues; and, by the great horn spoon, in the other we haven't even got a body!"

Some time during the interview I gave him the button I had found in the garden at the foot of the trellis. He stood turning it over in his hand, and his face relaxed into a grin.

"Now if I was a real policeman," he said, "I suppose I'd start with this and go places. But hell, it's just a button to me!"

We buried Juliette from the old ivy-covered Episcopal church the next day. None of her friends appeared, from New York or elsewhere, and Tony hastily recruited a group of men to act as pallbearers, and was himself one of them. Neither Lucy nor Mary Lou appeared, but Arthur and I went together. It was Arthur who had ordered the pall of small green orchids which covered the casket, and except for my own cross of lilies there were no other flowers.

The church was crowded and I myself felt sad and remorseful. Whatever Juliette's faults she had not deserved this, I thought; to lie there shut away forever from the life she had loved, never again to put on her pretty clothes or to lie between her soft silk sheets. Frivolous and selfish she had been, but what could she have done to earn her death?

"For I am a stranger with thee, and a sojourner . . . O spare me a little, that I may recover my strength: before I go hence, and be no more seen."

The words echoed and re-echoed in my mind as the service went on. I wondered if Arthur heard them and was remembering that time when he had brought her to us, and stood uneasy but stubborn before Father's hardening face, and Mother's helpless one.

"This is my wife," he had said. "I hope you will all be good to her."

How pretty she had been that day, and how alluring. Going to Mother and kissing her, and reaching her heart by what she said.

"Try to forgive me," she pleaded. "I love him so terribly."

Acting? Perhaps; but perhaps not. Maybe we had changed her, showed her a side of life she had never known, expensive and expansive living. But Mother had tried hard to make friends with her. When Father wanted to trace her people through a detective agency she vetoed it at once.

"Why?" she said. "It is her future that matters, not her past. Anyhow, that seems respectable enough, and she is Arthur's wife. Don't forget that. She is Arthur's wife."

But she never became one of us, in the family sense of the word. Mother furnished a suite for them both in the Park Avenue house, but it bored her. And I was too young to be a companion to her. In the end she simply moved Arthur away, and when I finally made my debut she was tight at my coming-out ball.

I could still remember the shock that was; Father standing stiff before William, and telling him to get that girl out of the house.

"And never let her come back," he added.

She came back, of course. Even Father had to permit that. But gradually she had drifted away, to take exquisite care of her body, to learn to dress, to gather around her the floaters who drift about New York, and eventually to ruin Arthur, financially and otherwise.

I had tried to be friendly, but she had never liked me.

"If you want your precious brother back, why don't you take him?" she asked me once.

And so I had let her go. I was young and active. I had my own crowd, my own amusements. Now and then, riding in the park, I saw her on a livery hack; and once she cut me dead. I remember going home and crying it out on Maggie's shoulder.

"Now, now, my lamb, don't you worry. She's just common. She always has been common."

But I had never hated her. She had been lovely to look at, gay and reckless. And now there she was, lying in state in the church under her pall of small green orchids. All over. Everything over. And the service going on.

"O most merciful Father, who has been pleased to take unto thyself the soul of this thy servant—"

What was Arthur thinking, there beside me in his morning coat and striped trousers, wearing the black tie which Mary Lou had so bitterly resented that morning? For almost six years Juliette had been his wife, and for at least two of them he had been passionately in love with her. Now she was dead, and there were many who believed that he had killed her.

We stood by in the cemetery until the service was over and they began to lower the casket into the grave. Then Arthur turned away abruptly and I followed him. The crowd opened to let us through; but from somewhere on the outskirts there was a sharp hiss. He appeared not to hear it.

There was a shock waiting for us on our return. Mary Lou had moved into Mother's room and was shut away there! I remember my indignation when I heard it, and Arthur's face. I still resent that childishness of hers; but I know now that it was largely terror. Little by little her small familiar world was slipping away from her, and she could not hold it. Arthur, on the witness stand, telling of deceiving her to meet Juliette. Arthur suspected of killing Juliette. And now Arthur going to her funeral; sitting in the church for everyone to see, standing by while the casket was lowered. It was as though the years with her had been wiped away, and Juliette had been still his wife.

I went up at once, to find her on the small balcony outside Mother's room, with its flower boxes around the railing. She had a sodden handkerchief in her hand, and her eyes were red and swollen.

"What is all this nonsense?" I said sharply. "Can't you forget yourself and think of Arthur? He needs you, and you act like a child!"

"He doesn't need me," she said. "I'm going back to Millbank."

I felt old enough to be her mother just then. What I wanted was to give her a good shaking. But she was pitiful too, and I rang the bell and ordered some tea for her. When I came back she was wiping her eyes.

"Now listen to me," I said, more gently. "You can't escape life by running away from it. I could damn' well do some running myself, if it comes to that. But Arthur needs you. He's built the only life he has around you. If you desert him, what are other people going to do?"

And then she took my breath away.

"I'm sorry," she said. "I suppose I'm scared, Marcia. You see, I was there myself that morning."

"There? What on earth do you mean?" I was shocked because it was not until much later that the sheriff told me all about it.

"I wanted to talk to her," she said hysterically. "We couldn't go on as we were. I thought if I told her how things were she might do something. She'd ruined us. She'd ruined you. Why shouldn't I see her?"

I reached out and caught her by the shoulder.

"Did you see her?" I demanded. "Is that what's wrong with you? Did you find Lucy's golf club and then quarrel with her? Did you—"

"You're crazy," she gasped. "I never killed her. I didn't even see her."

"And you suspect Arthur!" I said. "Arthur, who wasn't even near her. What if I tell that to the police?"

She was shaken, but her story was clear enough. She had telephoned to Sunset early that morning and learned that

Juliette was going to ride. The temptation had been too much for her. She had taken her car and driven over, and at a spot where the road is not far from the bridle path she had stopped it. But she never left it, she said.

"I couldn't," she said. "There was a man on the hillside, and he was getting ready to paint something. I didn't want to be seen, so I just sat still for a while, and then went back home."

"I think you're entirely unbalanced," I told her, and went down to explain to Arthur. On the whole, dangerous as it might be, that statement of hers relieved the tension between them.

"You're an idiot," he told her. "It was a fool thing to do. Now give me a kiss and go and fix your face. It needs it!"

But to me privately he showed some apprehension.

"Sooner or later they'll learn about that," he said, "and they'll suspect her of driving over to pick me up that morning. If they do there'll be hell to pay. What got into her anyhow?"

The next few days were quiet. Mary Lou was herself again, repentant and loving. I worried over the bills as usual. Why is there no sympathy for the people with houses and servants who can't get rid of either of them? And meals in the servants' dining room resolved themselves into small courts of inquiry, with no regrets for the missing Jordan.

For Jordan was still missing. The search followed the general lines of the previous one, but with less excitement. Perhaps we were getting used to murder and sudden death. But no clues had been found, and no body. Bloodhounds, given one of her gloves, made nothing of it in the village. Taken on a route encircling the settlement they followed the bay path for a mile or so without enthusiasm, and then gave it up.

The adjourned inquest was postponed once more. I tried to pick up my life as best I could, played some golf and some bridge, even went to a small dinner or two. Eventually Mary Lou went back to Millbank and Junior, leaving Arthur with me. And the excitement was dying away. It was as though, with Juliette dead and buried, everybody wanted to forget her. As for Jordan, I think only the police and ourselves believed that anything had happened to her. Nobody knew her. She might have had her own reasons for taking a stealthy departure, but the colony was not particularly interested.

Mrs. Pendexter chose that time for one of her huge parties,

and on her insistence I went. With Tony, as a matter of fact, and wearing a new white chiffon dress and Tony's orchids.

"Of course you're coming," she said to me over the telephone. "What was Juliette to you but a nuisance? Don't tell me you're hypocrite enough to go into mourning for her."

"I was thinking of Arthur."

"Stuff and nonsense," she retorted. "Nobody thinks he did it, or would blame him if he did. As to that Jordan woman, I knew when I saw her that she would come to some bad end."

The party was for Marjorie and Howard Brooks, and as Howard had brought up his yacht, it was moored to the Pendexter dock and brilliantly lighted. Part of the time we danced there, on the deck, and Howard showed me over the boat. It was a beautiful thing, and he said he was planning to go on to Newfoundland in it, taking Marjorie and a party.

"She'd like it if you could come," he said. "It wouldn't hurt you to get away, either." He smiled. "Juliette alive was a strong man's burden, but Juliette murdered is a lot worse. Better think about it."

"I didn't know you knew her," I said.

"Not well. I saw her now and then. I have a place on Long Island, you know, and I'd see her about. Not my sort, of course."

He let it go at that, and I could not pursue the subject. We went over the yacht, its bedrooms, each with a bath, its imposing quarters for the owner, the bar, the living rooms. But I was wondering. Just how well had he known Juliette? Just how long had he been on the island when she disappeared? A day or two, at the most. And he was not the type that would kill, I thought. He was too self-controlled. He was strong enough, broad-shouldered and muscular. On the other hand, he had a sort of shy modesty that made the whole idea seem idiotic.

"Silly thing to have a yacht this size," he said. "But Marjorie likes it. I hope you'll come along."

"I may be able to, if Arthur gets out of this mess," I told him.

"Of course he'll get out of it," he said heartily.

But I never made that cruise; and the time was to come when, needing Marjorie badly, I was to look out over the bay and see that the *Sea Witch* had gone, taking her with it.

CHAPTER XV

The investigation was still going on. One day I saw Arthur with Russell Shand in the grounds, examining the door of the toolshed and then apparently retracing his direction the night he had climbed out of the hospital room after the unknown intruder. So far as I could see the man, whoever he was, had first made for the Hutchinsons' grounds. Once there, he had apparently doubled on his tracks, for Arthur and the sheriff reappeared beyond the garage and followed the driveway toward the gate.

It looked as though the sheriff was coming to the conclusion that there was something in Arthur's story, and I felt happier than I had for a long time. It was also hopeful that a group of fingerprint men and photographers came over from the county seat that afternoon and went up to the hospital rooms. They were there for a long time, but a careful search revealed nothing of interest or value, and I could see that the sheriff was puzzled.

"What," he said, "would Juliette Ransom have been looking for in that attic of yours?"

"I haven't any idea."

"Well, she was there," he said. "Her prints are all over the place. They match up with the ones in that bedroom of hers. If we knew what she was after we'd know a lot. How long since she's been here? To live, I mean."

"More than six years. Seven, I think."

"Queer," he said thoughtfully. "If I hadn't been over those rooms with a fine-tooth comb, I'd say one of two things. Either she came back to hide something there, and that's unlikely. Or she came to get something, and somebody got her first. At least that's what it looks like, or why did she stay on, when she knew she couldn't get that money from Arthur?"

The idea that there was something hidden in the room interested him, and later that day he took a detective up again. They sounded the walls in both rooms and even lifted a loose floor board or two, but they found nothing.

Before he left that afternoon he told me something that only added to my bewilderment. He said that Jordan had visited him at the police station the day of her disappearance. She had driven up in a taxi and, sitting across the desk from him, had said she wanted to leave Sunset.

"I'm afraid," she said. "I guess I know too much. So I thought—"

"Afraid of what?"

"Of being killed."

"Who would want to kill you?" he asked.

She had shut her mouth firmly.

"I'm not accusing anybody. I just want to be safe, and I'm not safe in that house."

That is all she would say. She not only wanted to leave the house. She wanted to leave the island. But she was needed for the inquest, and he could not let her go. Further than that she would not explain. He had done everything but threaten her with arrest, but she remained stubbornly mysterious.

"I'm not talking," she said. "Not yet anyhow."

That was all he got out of her. He had given in at last and got the room for her at Eliza Edwards's, and she went there that same afternoon. Where she went from there he did not know, except that it was probably to her death.

As I have said, I made an attempt at normal living during that interval. The Shore Club had opened the first of July, and now and then I stopped there on my way home. One day I saw Mansfield Dean there, an enormous figure in a pair of bathing trunks and nothing else. He was entirely unself-conscious, and he walked across the lawn and asked me if I would go to see his wife again.

"She's been sick," he said, "and she liked you. I know you have plenty on your hands, but she's pretty lonely. She's used

132

to having young people about."

He looked pathetic, I thought. Evidently he was worried about her; and so I went that same afternoon. I found Mrs. Dean on the terrace, and I was shocked at the change in her. Thin before, she was emaciated now. She gave me a friendly smile, but her hand was bloodless and cold. She did not directly mention our trouble, nor did I; but once I turned from the panorama of bay and sea before us to find her eyes fixed on me with a curious intensity.

She colored above her pearls and looked away quickly.

People had been very kind, she said. Quite a number had called, but of course she had not been able to see them. Later on she would get about more.

"It would please Mansfield," she said. "He is gregarious. He likes people. And of course, for the last year or so—"

She was silent for a moment.

"I think my life ended then," she said, and closed her eyes.

I felt awkward and constrained. There was nothing to say, although I tried. She did not really hear me; she seemed far away in some distant tragic past; and I left her like that, polite but detached.

Those days before Jordan's body was found were the longest I have ever lived through. Arthur, asked to remain within call, spent much of his time at Millbank. He looked older and very tired. I saw little of Tony Rutherford after the Pendexter dance, and Allen Pell had apparently left the hills and was painting from a small boat. Once I saw him tied to a channel marker a hundred yards from the house, and he waved to me, but did not come in. But most of the time he spent on one or another of the islands. I saw him there several times through the field glasses, clad in old white duck trousers, and once he was moving along a beach. He was walking with his head down, as though he was looking for something, and I wondered what that something was.

Then one day the first clue to Jordan's fate was discovered.

The butler to one of the families along the bay path, a man named Sutton, had been taking a swim and landed to rest, on the rocks at Long Point. The path there was some twenty feet above him, and he climbed to it and sat down.

133

He had been there five minutes or so before he saw something. Below him, and above high-water mark, was a woman's bag, firmly wedged between the rocks.

He was interested but not suspicious. He opened it, sitting down comfortably to do it. Inside was the usual lipstick, a few dollars in money, a key or two, a fresh handkerchief and a partly used package of cheap cigarettes. But there was a slip of paper also, and Sutton opened and read it. It began without salutation:

> I would like to have a talk with you, but not here. The quietest place would be the path along the sea wall after dinner tonight about nine o'clock. Let me know if you care to do this, and if you need funds. A.C.L.

Sutton was no fool. He recognized the initials, and as soon as he was dressed he went to the police station. The sheriff happened to be there. He took the bag and read the note, and later on he had Sutton show him where the bag was found. When he sent for Arthur late that afternoon he was sitting behind the shabby desk, with the bag in front of him.

"Did you ever see that pocketbook, Arthur?" he asked.

Arthur stared at it.

"I don't think so."

"Well, I have," said Russell Shand. "The last time I saw it a woman was sitting where you are now, holding it. And she said: 'I am afraid. I guess I know too much. I want to get out of that house.'"

Arthur was pale but composed.

He admitted the note immediately, but said that it had been written a day or two before Jordan disappeared. He had gone to the sea wall, but she had not come. As for the reason for the note, he had felt all along that she held the key to the mystery of Juliette's death; but it was difficult to talk to her at the house. That key, he was certain, lay in the past few years after Juliette had left him. He absolutely denied any knowledge of Jordan's disappearance; or of her death, if she was dead.

"Why should I kill her?" he demanded. "If she knew anything incriminating about me she had had plenty of time to

134

tell it."

"Had she made any demand on you for money?"

"Blackmail, I suppose you mean. No."

The sheriff was hard and truculent that day. Until then he had believed Arthur innocent, but now he was not so sure.

"You say you were out for a drive the night the Jordan woman disappeared. Where did you go?"

"Back into the hills. I had no objective."

"Did you get out of your car at any time?"

"No."

"Were you near the bay path at any time?"

"Absolutely not."

"How well did you know this woman, Arthur? The Jordan woman."

"I had never seen her until I came here, after my—after Juliette had disappeared. I never exchanged a word with her."

"But you admit that you wrote this note."

"I did. I have explained that."

The sheriff blew up then.

"You've got to get a better story than that," he said. "By the great horn spoon, Arthur, I've stuck by you as long as I can. But you're coming clean now. Why didn't she meet you? Did she ever explain that? And why write to her at all! Couldn't you have talked to her? Not deaf and dumb, was she?"

"I don't know why she didn't meet me," said Arthur unhappily. "She stayed in her room, with the door locked. As for the note—" he colored—"I slipped it under her door. Good God, sheriff, I had to see her somehow. She knew who killed Juliette. I'm certain of it."

But there was no murder still, at least not officially, and he came home to dinner, to say nothing about the bag, to refuse food, and to prowl around the house until late that night. Once I remember he came to my room, where I had in despair gone to bed, and asked what had happened to the house bells. They were ringing in the pantry from empty rooms.

"Why don't you have them looked after?" he demanded irritably.

"I have," I told him.

"Well, it's a damned nuisance," he said, and went off again.

135

It was the next morning that Jordan's murder became an established fact. She had been missing for two weeks by that time, and it was a fisherman, out all night with his nets, who found her on his way home at daybreak.

He was a practical man, not unused to the tragedies of the sea. He saw the body floating, face down, and with a gaff he managed to hold it until he could get a rope around it. Then, still practical, he merely towed it to the town dock and called up to a man fishing there.

"Get somebody to telephone the police station," he said. "I've got a body here."

He was smoking his pipe quietly when the chief of police arrived. A crowd had formed on the dock overhead, the intent silent crowd of such occasions. The chief drove them back, and in due time the body was taken out of the water and to the mortuary. There was no question of identification. The underclothing was marked with indelible ink and she still wore the suit she had worn in the sheriff's office.

It took no lengthy examination to discover the hole in the back of her skull, or that there was a piece of rope around her neck.

CHAPTER XVI

It was evident that she had been murdered. Doctor Jamieson, straightening from the preliminary examination, merely shrugged his shoulders.

"Back of the head bashed in," he said. "Then towed out to sea."

He believed she had been dead before she was put into the water. The rope around the neck was too loose for strangulation. As for the rope itself, it looked like part of a boat's painter. It had been cut with a sharp knife, and the knot was an ordinary double one. But the weapon had not been the one which had killed Juliette. This wound looked as though it had been made with a rock.

I was fairly dazed by the situation. Arthur had been sent for at once, and came home looking sick.

"I'm in for it now," he said. "I wish you'd go over to Mary Lou. Tell her about Jordan, but let the rest wait. I'd better not leave the island."

He told me as much as he knew, and that he was to be interrogated that night. Bullard was away for the day, and wouldn't be back until late.

I went to Millbank, and to my surprise Mary Lou took the news better than I had expected.

"Jordan!" she said. "Why, he didn't know her. It's all ridiculous." And she added, with that occasional shrewdness of hers, "I suppose they have to have a scapegoat, and Arthur happens to be it. But it may help him, Marcia. He couldn't have killed them both."

I spent the day there, and felt the better for it, building sand

137

castles for Junior on the beach, and later talking idly with Mary Lou as she knitted on the veranda of the cottage. But it seemed strange, as I drove myself home that night, to think that life was going on much as usual. There was a dance at the Shore Club that night, and from the house I could see the colored lights around the pool, and even imagine I heard the band.

People dancing, or gathering in the bar, the women dressed in bright clothes, the men in conventional black and white.

"Hear they found that woman's body."

"Yes. Queer story, isn't it?"

Life going on, and Arthur in that shabby office at the police station, sitting in a hard chair and confronting Bullard, like a red-faced bulldog, across the desk. The sheriff was there, and the local police chief, as well as two or three detectives. But it was Bullard who did the talking; looking pompous and grim. It went on, I learned later, for hours, as if they meant to wear him down, or to trap him.

"You say you never saw her that night. What explanation did she give for not keeping the appointment?"

"None. I didn't see her. She stayed in her room. I began to wonder if she had found the note."

"How did you give it to her?"

"I've already explained that. I couldn't get near her, so I slipped it under her door."

Coloring unhappily, but keeping his head up. "I was convinced that she knew something. My first wife—Mrs. Ransom—often talked to her maid, whoever it might be. As a matter of fact"—he hesitated—"I was aware that during our life together she frequently received mail addressed to her personal maid."

"Letters from men?"

"Some of them. I found one or two she had overlooked after she left me."

"Then, if I get your meaning, you thought that this woman, Helen Jordan, might know of some man who had reason for making an attack on Mrs. Ransom?"

"That was my idea. I wasn't sure, of course."

"That night you waited on the bay path and she did not come—did you see anybody, Mr. Lloyd?"

138

"No, I believe it was bank night at the movies."

"How long did you wait?"

"From eight to almost ten."

"And she did not come?"

"No."

Bullard with the note in his hand, glaring across the desk; and Arthur still quiet, still composed.

"What did you mean by what you say here? About her possible need of money?"

"I should think that explains itself. She was no longer employed, and she had been sick. After all, Mrs. Ransom had brought her to my sister's house. I felt I ought at least to see that she got back to New York, and be looked after until she got another position."

"Very kind of you," said Bullard. "It's unfortunate she didn't see things that way. She told the sheriff once that she wasn't safe in your house. What did that mean?"

"I have no idea," he told them. "Unless she referred to one or possibly more attempts to break into the place. I didn't think she knew about them. She may have, of course. Or," he added, "she may have heard from the servants that the house is queer." He smiled faintly. "Something went wrong with the bells some time ago, and they claim it is haunted."

But he had no alibi whatever for the night of her disappearance. He said he had driven aimlessly about through the hills, and so far as he knew had not been seen. He had not stopped for gasoline. He had not stopped anywhere.

They were not inhumane. At some time during the evening someone sent across the street for some coffee, and he drank it. But as time went on even the sheriff looked grave. Somebody asked him if he carried a pocketknife, and he produced it. It was sharp, and one of the detectives tried it on the rope; that rope which had been around Jordan's neck. Arthur watched, pale with fatigue, and Bullard's eyes full of hard suspicion.

"It does it, eh?"

"Does it, all right."

But they did not arrest him that night. They knew as well as he did the weakness of the case against him. He could run a motorboat, of course. They had seen him doing it for years. But he knew the sea, and so did they.

"Why should I have killed her?" he demanded. "If she had had any knowledge dangerous to me, is it reasonable to think that I would have given her all that time to disclose it? As it stands, I never spoke to her. I didn't even know her name until my sister told me." And he added: "Suppose I had killed her and wanted to dispose of the body. Would anybody but a lunatic—somebody who didn't know the currents here—have put that body into the water without a weight tied to it?"

"There might have been a weight, at that," said Bullard.

But Arthur looked at the rope and smiled.

"There's no knot in it," he said.

They could understand that sort of talk, the local men at least. More or less they all knew the sea and its way in such matters. And there was Arthur, straight and handsome, facing them with a half-smile and clear direct eyes.

"Whoever towed that body out and cut it loose didn't know much about the tides around here," he said, and sat quiet.

Strange, all of it, it must have been: the shabby room filled with drama, the reporters on the street smoking and grumbling, that body forever still in the mortuary, and at the club people dancing or sitting out under the stars.

"Hear they found that woman's body."

"Yes. Queer story, isn't it?"

Except for what Arthur had told me, I knew nothing of all this that night. I did know that with the discovery of the body we would be deluged again with reporters, and so I had the gates closed and locked after Arthur left and put Mike on guard there, with orders to keep everybody out.

Arthur had left at six o'clock, and I had hoped that he would get back for dinner. But he did not come, so I ate alone, with a depressed William moving in and out of the shadows.

"The soufflé is spoiled, miss. Lizzie says she can send in some fruit."

"I'm not hungry, William. Have you heard anything?"

"Nothing, miss. Not since this morning."

It was still faintly twilight when I finished, and calling Chu-Chu went out into the garden. The sun had set in a blaze of rose and green, the tide was low and the gulls were feeding

140

clamorously. The usual starfish and sea urchins littered the beach, and among them stalked those wretched crows. I was eying them with resentment when to my surprise a dark head lifted itself from the water, some distance out from the shore.

It was late for seals. I watched it curiously, and when it rose again nearer the land I saw that it was not a seal. It was a man; and a man who was fully at home in the water. Most of the time he swam under the surface, with hardly a ripple on top; but now and then he rose for air and looked toward me. When he came closer I saw that it was Allen Pell!

He was like an answer to prayer that night. I had missed him more than I cared to acknowledge, and I found my heart beating fast when I recognized him. I was even trembling when I made my way along the dock to the float, to find him still in the water, but smiling up at me.

"Sorry to be so informal," he said. "D'you mind standing as if you were merely looking at the landscape? I've gone to the hell of a lot of trouble to pretend I'm an amphibian."

He pulled himself up onto the float, and I saw that he wore only a pair of bathing trunks. But for all his smile, he was shivering and his lips were blue.

"Not up to my usual form, I'm afraid," he said apologetically. "Listen, I've got to talk to you, and I can't keep my teeth still. How about some brandy and a blanket? I'll hang around here until you get them. I tried the drive," he added, "but the gates were closed, and a gentleman with a shotgun seemed suspicious. So I went back to a boat I've hired and—"

"Good heavens! Has Mike got a shotgun?"

"It looked like one to me, lovely lady; and I've seen a lot of them in my time."

I ran back to the house then, with Chu-Chu thinking it a game and yapping at my heels. Nevertheless I was gone longer than I had meant to be. I found Arthur's flask, mercifully full, and a towel and a warm dressing gown; but with them under a blanket over my arm I met Maggie in the upper hall, and she stared at me.

"And where," she said, "are you taking that, miss?"

"I'm going to sit outside, Maggie. It's a lovely night."

"Then I am going with you," she said firmly. "You don't go

141

out of this house alone at night. Not with murder all around."

It took both time and effort to get away from her, and I was fairly desperate when she followed me down the stairs and even out into the garden. The air was chilly, however, and at last she went grumbling back into the house. I was, I think, just in time. Allen Pell was having a fairly substantial chill when I reached him.

He shook like a man with ague for some time, and I was beginning to be frightened when at last the brandy and the warm dressing gown and blanket began to have their effect.

"Sorry," he said. "Devil of a way to visit a lady, isn't it?" And he added: "You're a pretty fine girl, Marcia Lloyd. Blood tells, doesn't it? I'd like to have known your mother."

That upset me. I had a quick memory of the old peaceful days, with Arthur and myself on that very beach, and Mother in her garden in her wide sun hat, showing her delphiniums. Suddenly I felt that I was going to cry.

"Don't," I said, "or I'll howl like a wolf."

He reached over and put a cold hand on mine.

"Sorry again," he said. "You've been pretty heroic so far. It won't hurt you to cry. But for God's sake don't howl. I don't want to be found here."

When I was calmer he told me how and why he had come. He had been in the water for an hour, swimming far out to escape observation, and most of the way it had been against the tide.

"But I'm here," he said, "and that was the general idea. Now, what about your brother? They can't tie *this* on him, can they?"

"They're trying to. He's there now. At the police station."

I told him how things stood. Indeed I told him all I knew, and he was very attentive. He sat with his arms hugging his knees, gazing out over the water and listening.

"Will they arrest him?" I asked. "Do you think they have a case?"

"God knows," he said roughly. "There is this in his favor. They'll hold off if they can. The sheriff's a decent chap, and you've got to remember that the summer people can do no wrong. But I gather that this Bullard is a swine." He stirred and faced me. "See here," he said. "Look back a little, will you?

142

Was Mrs. Ransom here any time since her divorce? Or—I'll change that—any time in the last three years?"

"No. I saw her now and then, but only in town."

There was a longish silence.

"These rooms of yours, what you call the hospital suite. You think she was looking for something there?"

"Somebody was, apparently."

"Maybe you've got it wrong. Maybe she was hiding something."

"I don't know what it could have been. I've searched the place. So have the police."

"Any loose floor boards? That hatchet looks like something of the sort, if she put it there."

"The police have been over it. They've even lifted some of the floor. There was nothing."

He made a gesture.

"Then that's that," he said, and lapsed into silence again.

It was no time for romance that night, with Arthur in trouble as he was. But it was a comfort to have him there, close at hand; even if he did look slightly absurd, rolled in blankets and clutching the flask.

"I wish you would tell me something," I said. "How did you know Juliette? She doesn't seem the sort of woman you would know, somehow."

"Meaning the trailer?"

"Good heavens, what sort of snob do you think I am?" I asked indignantly. "Meaning you, yourself."

He did not answer that. He drew a long breath.

"How does any fool of a man know any woman like that?" he said. "I met her and fell for her. That's all. Too much," he added bitterly.

But I persisted.

"Where was that? In New York?"

"Does it matter?"

"Of course it matters. Everything matters, just now. Do you have to be so mysterious? It's rather silly, isn't it?"

He looked at me soberly.

"No, my dear," he said, "it is not silly. It's just damned necessary. Someday I'll tell you why, but not now. And if you are wondering why I'm interested, I'll say this. Arthur Lloyd and I are brothers under the skin. He was lucky, though. He only married her."

He did not elaborate on that. He got up and threw off the blanket.

"I'll make it back all right," he said, eying the beach. "The tide's ready to slack." But he did not go at once. "I forgot to tell you," he said. "I'm working on that alibi of his at Clinton. Living the way I do, I get in touch with all sorts of people. They won't talk to the police, but they'll talk among themselves. I have a line on a man who is supposed to have said he saw him that morning, asleep on the bench. If I can locate him, it will help."

He stood looking down at me for a minute, as if uncertain about something. Then he slid noiselessly into the water and remained there for a moment, holding to the edge of the float.

"Good night, Marcia Lloyd," he said. "We'll fight it out on this line if it takes all summer! Just remember that."

I stood there awhile after he had gone. Then I gathered up the blanket, robe, and the flask. I felt lonely and depressed, as though something strong and vital had gone with him, as though I could not face the empty house again. When I turned back it was to see, far away along the curve of the bay the lights of the Shore Club, and it was strange to think that people were gathered there, dancing, moving about, talking.

"Hear they found that woman's body."

"Yes. Queer story, isn't it?"

To my great relief, Arthur came back, after midnight. He looked exhausted, and I saw at once that he did not want to talk.

"I'll tell you tomorrow," he said. "Just now I'm all in. Go to bed like a good girl, and stop worrying."

I did so. I did not expect to sleep, but eventually I did. And it was that night that Maggie chose, for the first time in years, to walk in her sleep.

The weather had changed. There was a threat of storm in the air, and so I closed the doors onto the upper porch before I went to bed. It was a shock, therefore, to be aroused by cold air roaring over me, and to my horror to see a white-clad figure on

144

the porch itself.

I could scarcely move, but at last I raised myself on my elbow, and at that the figure turned and came inside, closing the door carefully. Not until the dim hall light fell on her face did I see that it was Maggie.

I sat up and watched her, and she did a curious thing. After the sheriff's last visit to the hospital suite I had placed the key in the bureau drawer, where I had always kept it. Now she opened the drawer and took it out.

I could see her plainly. The room was quiet, except for the wind outside and the small friendly thud of Chu-Chu's tail on the floor. She stood still for a moment, with the key in her hand. Then she moved slowly into the hall. Following her to the door I saw her go to the foot of the stairs to the hospital rooms and stand there, looking up.

Perhaps I roused her. Perhaps she wakened herself. In any event the next moment she started back, and without seeing me went quickly to her own room and closed the door.

I found the key on the floor of the hall the next morning, and I have wondered since. Suppose she had gone on up that night and I had followed her? Would we have solved our mystery then? Would that buried memory of Maggie's have helped us? I do not know, but weeks later I was to see the rusty old cage where Arthur once had kept his white mice, and to remember what Maggie had forgotten.

CHAPTER XVII

The discovery of Jordan's body had started a sort of reign of terror on the island. The story of an unknown killer spread everywhere, and women refused to leave their houses at night unaccompanied, or to allow children on the streets after dark. Nor was it only the townspeople who were affected. Most of the summer places at once employed guards, and one reporter, trying to climb over our gates, narrowly escaped a load of buckshot from Mike.

For once more reporters were pouring into the town. We were a major sensation now, with all that that implies. There was nothing we could do about it.

Arthur told me his story the morning after that long interrogation; told it briefly and clearly. It had not been too bad, he said. At least they had used no third-degree methods on him. When he wanted water he got it. There was no blazing light in his eyes. He could smoke, and did. But he was not too optimistic.

"Bullard's determined to get me," he said. "Unless they get somebody else first. Better carry on as usual," he added. "The more normal we are the better. There may be some bad days ahead."

I had a visit from Mrs. Pendexter that day. Acting on Arthur's suggestion, I had played eighteen holes of golf with Lucy, and we had resolutely said nothing about the situation. When I came back, anxious for a bath and change, I found Mrs. Pendexter's old Rolls in the driveway, and she herself in the drawing room, having tea and in deep conversation with William.

"Smart man, William," she observed after he had taken an uncomfortable departure. "Wouldn't put it past him to have done away with the Jordan woman himself. Hated her like poison, of course." She looked at me with her sharp old eyes. "Police pinning that on Arthur too, I suppose?"

"I don't see why they should," I said defensively.

She chuckled.

"Why not?" she demanded. "She knew a lot. She knew all that Juliette knew; you can bet your bottom dollar on that. Why she came, what she was afraid of, what she was looking for up in those rooms, everything."

She moved, and all her chains and bangles clinked.

"Birds of a feather," she said. "I told you you were a fool, Marcia, to let them stay here. Whoever did away with one did away with the other, and I'm not sure my own Marjorie doesn't know something about it."

"Marjorie! You can't mean that, Mrs. Pendexter."

"Oh, I don't think she's done any killing," she said cheerfully. "But she knew Juliette. So did Howard Brooks. And for an engaged pair they've acted mighty queer the last week or two. Maybe that girl of mine will talk to you. I can't get a word out of her."

She went away soon after that, leaving me in a state bordering on stupefaction. But I dismissed it from my mind. The whole island was rife with suspicion by that time, for every attractive man about had at one time or another been attentive to Juliette, and as the days went on old jealousies were renewed, old fears.

Nor did the inquest help the situation when it took place. It left us precisely where we had been before.

There was no difficulty about identifying the body. Swollen and hideous as it was, Jordan's large teeth, her hair and a ring she wore were undeniable. Also both Ellen and I were able to recognize her clothing, Ellen of course in a state of semihysteria. After that the fisherman, a laconic individual who might have been describing the hooking of a halibut, told about finding her.

"I saw something bobbing about," he said, "and ran over to see what it was. It was her, all right."

The injury was described, a jagged fracture at the back of the skull; the rope which had been cut from the neck was produced, and some time during the proceedings the butler, Sutton, told about finding the bag on the rocks.

"I opened it," he stated, "and that letter was inside. I read it and—"

But it was evidently no part of the police program to introduce Arthur's note, and he was sharply shut off. One thing came out in his testimony, however. The place where the bag was found was where the bloodhounds had lost the scent.

Later on that location, presumably now the scene of the murder, was carefully described. Nothing else had been discovered there, however, either on the path or on the rocks below.

So far all was well, or as well as it could be. It was after Sutton had been excused that I had what amounted to a shock.

Allen Pell was called!

He came forward, tall and sober, and as he faced about I thought he glanced at me. That was only momentary. He did not look in my direction again for some time. It was evident that he had been interrogated before and that he expected to be called; for he had abandoned his usual slacks for a dark suit which made him look strange to me.

"Mr. Pell, you are an artist, I believe?"

"I paint pictures. There is a difference."

"Where do you live?"

"I have a trailer at the camp on Pine Hill."

"Any permanent home?"

"None at present."

"Now, Mr. Pell, I believe you have rented a small motorboat here. When did you do that?"

"Three weeks ago."

"Will you tell us the purpose of that boat?"

"I have used it to go along the shore or among the islands, and to paint what I see. Sometimes for fishing too."

"Can you tell us where that boat was on the night of the fifth of July?"

"So far as I know, it was anchored off the small dock at the foot of Cooper Lane."

149

"When did you take it out after that?"

"A few days. I don't remember exactly."

"Did you notice any change in it?"

"The rope was gone. That is, it had been cut off. There was an end of it still fastened to the boat."

"When did you make that discovery?"

"I had gone out to one of the islands. When I tried to tie up the boat the rope was too short."

"Did you later on buy another rope?"

"I did."

"Have you any explanation as to what happened to the original one?"

I thought he hesitated.

"I could guess," he said finally. "That looks like it on the table."

"Did the boat show anything else? I mean, had it been used since you last took it out?"

"I'm not certain. It had less gas than I expected. I may be wrong about that."

"There was nothing else disturbed? No blood? No signs of a struggle?"

"None whatever."

There was a pause. Doctor Jamieson glanced over some notes on his desk.

"Now, Mr. Pell, think carefully over this. Did you see the deceased at any time during her stay here?"

"No. So far as I know I never saw her."

"Have you ever known her?"

"No. Never."

I had been frightened by these last questions, and I thought his eyes rested on me reassuringly. It developed, however, that he had a complete alibi for the night of Jordan's disappearance. From eight to eleven o'clock he had sat on the step of his trailer and talked politics with one of the men at the camp. Nevertheless, although it was a cool day, I saw him wiping his hands on his handkerchief when he left the stand, and I suspected that he had not told all he knew.

Little more was developed after that. Jordan had eaten her evening meal at Eliza Edwards's, had gone upstairs and locked

150

her room, giving the key to Eliza when she left the house.

At the corner drugstore she had been seen going into a telephone booth. There had been a number of calls from the booth that night and this call could not be traced. After that she had not been seen again. How and when she reached the bay path and whom she met there remained a part of the mystery.

Some rumor of that letter of Arthur's had gone about, and certainly the crowd was disappointed when it was not introduced. I gathered that the police had their own reasons for suppressing it. Nor was Arthur called. Except for that interrogation of Allen Pell, the inquest limited itself to the identification of the body, a description of the injury, and an attempt to trace Jordan's movements after she left the Edwards house.

The homicide man from Clinton was present, with the usual photographs, and the jury eyed these macabre exhibits as they were handed to them, taking them gingerly. Then they went out, into what was the office of the school, and brought in their verdict soon after.

Helen Jordan had been murdered by some person or persons unknown.

I was slightly dazed as I stepped out of the schoolhouse into the summer sunshine again. Allen Pell was not in sight, but the sheriff was waiting for me on the pavement.

"Well, that's that," he said, looking not unpleased. "Busy, Marcia? If not, how about taking a little drive with me? Send Arthur home. He looks as though he needed it. And I'd like a quiet place to talk. That office I've borrowed is as private as a canary's cage."

He turned his old car back into the hills, and he was rather taciturn as we climbed. When we reached the top of Pine Hill he stopped the car, and looked down to where Loon Lake, long and quiet and blue, lay beneath us.

"What I'm wondering," he said somberly, "is whether we're through or not."

"Through?"

"That's what I said. Two women are dead. Maybe one deserved it. That's not for us to say. The other one died because she knew something. How many people do you think may know what she knew?"

It was a sickening idea, and he made a slight movement, as though putting it out of his mind.

"All right," he said. "Now let's get down to business. Who gets Mrs. Ransom's estate, if any? What about her family?"

"I don't know," I said vaguely. "She came from somewhere in the Middle West."

"That all you know?"

"Yes."

"Queer," he said. "Doesn't Arthur know? He married her."

"She said she had no people."

"She had to have a couple of parents. That is, it's usual."

"She never mentioned them, except to say that they were both dead. She was raised by an aunt. I don't remember her last name. She called her Aunt Delia, when she spoke of her at all—which wasn't often."

He turned that over in his mind for some little time. Then:

"What about her apartment in New York? Ever been there?"

"No."

"I suppose her furniture goes to somebody? And that jewelry of hers."

"I imagine her creditors will claim it," I said. "I suppose she owed everybody. She always did."

He was silent again, staring down at Loon Lake. He took out his pipe, filled and lit it before he spoke again.

"Here's the way it is," he said. "Bullard's hell-bent on getting Arthur. Me, I'm not so sure. Seven years is a long time to hate any woman. I'm inclined to believe that it's too long. And I'd like to see that apartment of hers. Unofficially. Just slip in and look around. We got the New York fellows to take a look-see after she disappeared, but they didn't find anything."

"I have her keys," I said doubtfully. "I could send her trunks down and be on hand to receive them. I've thought of doing that. The superintendent of the building would probably let me in. I shall have to send them somewhere anyhow. If you went with me—"

"Fine," he said, and gave me a vigorous pat on the knee.

152

"Get off as soon as you can, and I'll follow you. No need to go together. This darned place would think we had eloped!"

Which, considering his age and his matronly wife—not to mention half a dozen children—seemed to strike him as highly humorous, for he chuckled at intervals all the way back to the house.

I told Arthur the sheriff's plan that same day, and he seemed dubious.

"Not that I want the stuff," he said, "or you either. You'll probably find that her creditors own it anyhow. They'll have had an administrator appointed to take it over probably. But I don't like you mixed up in this."

He agreed finally, and Maggie and I spent the afternoon in packing. It was rather a nuisance that Mary Lou chose that particular time to come over, although I knew she hated Millbank and was lonely there.

She watched us jealously as we packed those fineries she herself could not afford, and which Juliette would never use again: the evening dresses, the expensive sports clothes, the vast array of spike-heeled shoes and slippers, the pillows and elaborate sheets, the blanket covers edged with heavy lace, and the diaphanous underwear with which she had more or less covered her body. She had an elaborate gold-fitted dressing case, and another with straps to hold her endless bottles and cosmetic jars. It seemed to me impossible to have achieved all this on what was a substantial but not princely sum, and as I packed in the heat of that July day I found myself wondering where it had all come from.

Mary Lou was in no doubt, however.

"She dressed like a kept woman," she said. "Who do you suppose bought them for her?"

"I suppose a good many of them are not paid for," I told her.

But Mary Lou remained grim.

"I notice I have to pay *my* bills," she said.

I was sorry for her. She had been protected all her life, and now she was facing ugly reality.

Jordan was buried the next morning from Jim Blake's undertaking parlors. Arthur did not go, nor Mary Lou. But Eliza Edwards attended, wearing a heavy black crepe veil, and a few of the townspeople were also there. Eliza and I sat together, and she took occasion to whisper to me.

"Somebody ought to represent her folks, if she has any," she said. "I thought I might as well."

As we were going out I thought I saw Allen Pell; but he had disappeared when I reached the street.

I had ordered Jordan's grave next to Juliette's, and so we left them there together, mistress and maid. All the small important things behind them now, packed in the trunks at Sunset, or to be forgotten in the mists of time. The glamour gone, and only two graves, with my flowers on one and on the other—

I looked again. There were flowers on Juliette's grave also. They were fresh, and they looked expensive. They puzzled me, and I stopped in at the local florist's that morning and asked about them. He knew as little as I did.

"It was a telegraph order from New York," he said. "It's to go on every week until discontinued. No name given."

It was mysterious. Or was it? I stood in the shop, with its roses and carnations behind glass doors and its garden flowers and potted plants about me, and considered that. Someone out of Juliette's immediate past had loved her, or grieved for her. Did that mean anything? It did not sound like that crowd of hers, hard and unsentimental and interested only in living, not in dying.

Someone who had loved her? But did women like Juliette inspire love? I thought not. They inspired passion, wild reckless infatuation; but the spiritual overtones would be lacking. As for lasting sentiment—

I got the name of the New York florist, not without difficulty, and that night when I took the train for New York it was in my bag.

The train rattled on. Somewhere was the baggage car, with those trunks and bags of Juliette's; and somewhere, probably in a day coach—he was thrifty New England always—was Russell Shand. He had decided to go with me after all. But lying in my compartment I could not sleep.

I had met Tony Rutherford on the village street that day, and there was a brown button missing from his knitted golf

154

coat. When I pointed it out he smiled.

"I need a wife, Marcia," he said. "The darned thing's been gone for weeks."

"Bring it up and I'll sew it on," I told him. "I think I found it, in the garden."

It was a moment before that registered. He looked suddenly acutely uncomfortable.

"Thanks," he said. "I'll hold you to that." Then he was off.

I lay in my compartment on that rattling train and wondered. Tony in the garden. Tony climbing the trellis, and Arthur above him at the window. It was fantastic; and yet everything about our murders had been fantastic.

CHAPTER XVIII

It was not easy to enter Juliette's apartment the next day. Probably we made a queer combination, the sheriff looking as though he had slept in his clothes, as he doubtless had, and I myself certainly tired and not too tidy. Around us, in that impressive lobby, were Juliette's bags, and her trunks were on the way by truck.

The superintendent eyed us with suspicion.

"But I'm her sister-in-law," I protested.

"So *you* say."

"But I am," I said crossly. "How on earth could I have all this stuff otherwise?"

"Listen," he said. "I'm not saying you are, and I'm not saying you're not. But I've had a dozen cousins of hers here already, and about as many brothers. Reporters," he added, seeing that I looked bewildered. "Sob sisters. From the press."

The sheriff was enjoying himself hugely, but I was furious.

"What about these bags of hers? They have to go somewhere."

This left the man unmoved.

"She's got a storeroom in the basement. Or had," he added. "They can go there."

But the truth finally came out. Arthur had been right. After her death Juliette's effects were in the hands of her creditors, and her apartment was closed and locked. It was only when the sheriff took a hand that the man weakened.

"There's some pretty valuable stuff in these bags, and more coming," he said. "I don't suppose these creditors will object to that, will they? And you can come along if you like. Then

157

you'll see we don't aim to take anything."

That was the way we finally got into the apartment, with a scowling superintendent watching our every move. The rooms were hot and musty, and while he was raising a window the sheriff had a chance to speak to me.

"Take your time," he said. "He's just showing how important he is. He'll get over it."

But with the shades raised and the window opened the superintendent promptly forgot us, and I did not blame him. The place was in terrific disorder. Russell Shand gave one look at the desk drawers open and papers strewn over the floor, and into the bedroom beyond, where the mattress from the bed lay on the floor.

"Looks as though you're a little late in being careful," he said. "Or did these creditors of hers do this?"

The superintendent looked stunned.

"It's those reporters," he said at last. "I'll swear I locked the place up and kept it locked. What's more I gave orders—"

He gulped and looked appealingly at the sheriff, but that gentleman was unmoved.

"Well, a five-dollar bill will go a long ways these days," he said, "unless you want to buy a meal with it. Looks like somebody in the building sold you out."

I glanced at him, but he was imperturbable. I knew then that he was less astonished than I was, and when the superintendent had fussily departed to find the guilty individual, he admitted it.

"It's like this," he said. "All along I've thought she had something somebody wanted, and wanted bad. Either she took it with her or she left it here. That is, unless she had a box at some bank. We'll have to find that out."

I shall never forget the next few hours. The apartment was typically Juliette. A large living room was done in modern fashion, with much chromium and glass. A small room adjacent, and evidently meant to be a library, contained no books whatever. Instead, there was a built-in bar at one end, fully stocked and complete even to a brass rail. Her bedroom was different. It was typically feminine, having a canopied bed, the head and foot covered with quilted satin, and an enormous toilet table which was really a shelf of glass with the entire wall behind it a huge mirror bordered with lights. There was a rose-colored chaise longue, piled high with pillows, and the tub and other fittings of the bathroom were of the same color.

Over the tub was another mirror, painted with birds around the borders, and the sheriff eyed it with disapproval.

"Looks as though she kind of liked herself," he said, and turned away.

He wandered about for some time before he let me put the place to rights.

"Now if I was one of these smart New York dicks," he said, "I'd have the fingerprint outfit here in no time, and I'd end up just about where I began. Outside of that— Well, I'd say somebody whose prints aren't recorded anywhere has been here, because he didn't wear gloves; that he had plenty of time, that if there was anything here he wanted he got it, that he didn't wear gloves because he had to wash his hands before he left, and that they were plenty dirty at that. And I don't think he was any reporter. Too thorough for that. But that's as far as I go."

He brought a cake of soap from the bathroom washstand and took it to a window.

"Not so long since he was here, either," he went on. "I'm no soap expert, but—"

He took an enormous penknife from his pocket and dug into the cake.

"If I was guessing, and I am guessing, I'd say under a week," he commented. "Dry outside, but pretty soft just under the surface. Now if the storybooks are true we'll find part of a railroad ticket somewhere about, and know that somebody came here from the island within the last few days. Only things don't work out like that. Not for me anyhow."

He moved rapidly about the place, with the light tread of so many heavy men. The superintendent had not come back, and at last he turned to me and grinned.

"All right," he said. "You aren't your mother's daughter for nothing, so if you want to straighten up I'll put that mattress back on the bed."

I did the best I could, which wasn't much, and some time

later I found him at the desk in the living room. He had picked up the letters and papers from the floor and was carefully going over them.

"Funny thing," he said. "You get a pretty good idea of any human creature from his desk, or hers. Far as I can see, it didn't worry her a mite that she owed bills everywhere. She just went on, and she seems to have moved pretty fast at that. One day out of this calendar of hers would put me in bed for a week."

I saw then that he had what I called the Jennifer letter in his hand, and that he was carefully comparing its large square writing with various letters which lay before them.

"Can't seem to get it out of my head," he observed, mopping a red and dirty face. "Why did the Jordan woman leave everything else of Juliette's when she went to Eliza Edwards's, and then take this? What's important about the darned thing? Unless it's the postscript. And who the hell is Jennifer? That's a name for you! Jennifer!"

"We might find it. She may have a private telephone directory somewhere."

"What's that?"

"A book or something, where she kept the numbers she used most."

There was one, and that as it happened was the first real lead we got, although it led us to a dead end. The name was scrawled in, merely "Jen" and a Regent number; but an operator said that the telephone was temporarily disconnected, and with a shrug of his broad shoulders the sheriff hung up the receiver.

"Getting nowhere pretty fast," he said resignedly. "Look here, we'd better eat. I think better on a full stomach."

The heat was terrific when we went out onto the street. I called a taxicab and directed it to a hotel. Russell Shand, who at home drives like something fired out of a gun, swore all the way and braced himself for catastrophe. Over the meal he relaxed, although the grand manner of the head-waiter rather daunted him.

"Looked as though he didn't think much of me," he chuckled as he sat down. "Maybe I'm spoiled. What would he do if I flashed a badge on him?"

"He'd be more impressed if it was a dollar bill."

The menu bothered him, and I finally did the ordering. It was while we waited for the food that he drew out of a pocket a brief newspaper clipping and, putting on his spectacles, read it out loud:

"'The marriage of Miss Emily Forrester to Mr. Langdon Page has been indefinitely postponed.' Ever hear of either of them?"

"Never."

He examined it carefully, rear and front.

"Found it in the Jordan woman's room," he said. "Under the bed. May mean something, may not. No date, no place. Probably New York, but maybe not. Still, it's likely to be a big city somewhere. If Nellie Morgan was writing that up home she'd say: 'The *Star* is sorry, but it looks as though Lang Page and Emily Forrester are not getting married this year. Bad luck, folks.'"

Which, while partially true, is a libel on as neat a small-town newspaper as I have ever seen.

He turned it over, with a twinkle in his eye.

"Now if I was a real detective," he said, "I'd learn a lot about it from the fact that a woman on the other side of it is advertising Pekingese pups for sale, with only a post-office box number. But being what I am—"

We went back to the apartment after lunch. Juliette's trunks had arrived, and in view of the claim against them, I left them as they were. The sheriff, though, was painstakingly going through the address books and calling numbers. With the exception of a florist and her liquor dealer, it was soon apparent that Juliette's familiars did not spend the summer months in New York; and before three o'clock the sheriff went to her bank, to return rather chagrined.

"Funny thing," he said. "At home I could walk into the bank and Ed Howe would tell me anything he knew on a case like this. Those fellows downtown acted as if I was out to rob the place. Maybe I could have got it from the police at Centre Street, but we've pulled a pretty fast one today. And anyhow"—he grinned—"I'm just a hick country sheriff to them, mussing up two good murders, and I'd as soon not let

161

them know I'm in town."

One piece of information he had received. Juliette did not have a box at that particular bank. Nor, he imagined, a balance.

The clipping continued to interest him. He took it out again and examined it.

"Maybe it's a clue, maybe it isn't," he said. "One thing's sure. Either Juliette or Jordan thought enough of it to cut it out and keep it. And there's this to say for it. The Page fellow's first name begins with an 'L,' and I've got that Jennifer letter on my mind. Looks like they were society people, too. Who else bothers about putting that formal sort of notice into a newspaper when there's a fuss and a wedding is called off?"

There was a copy of the Social Register about, and I got it. He was surprised and interested when I showed it to him, but no Emily Forrester or Langdon Page was listed.

The sheriff took it and glanced through it.

"Don't it beat the devil?" he inquired. "Here we are in America, where everybody's supposed to be free and equal. But a handful of people get into a book like that, and all at once they're different!"

He made a final round of the apartment before we left. Aside from two servants' rooms, the dining room, library and living room, there were three or four guest rooms, and the whole layout seemed to puzzle him.

"How did she do it?" he inquired. "Even if she didn't pay her bills, she had to pay some of them. And this apartment cost her six thousand a year. I got that from the elevator man, for fifty cents! Now, with no reflection on her, was she doing that alone or was someone helping her?"

"You mean, was someone keeping her? I wouldn't know that, naturally."

He looked uncomfortable. He still has an idea that I know nothing of the facts of life.

"Well, something of the sort," he said. "My own guess would be no. Women of her sort usually want marriage, with plenty of money. They play around, but the real idea is safety, with some man legally providing for them. I've been seeing a lot of them in the summer for forty years, and that's the way it looks to me."

162

"What you mean is that, if she was spending more than she had, where did it come from," I said.

He ran his hand over his head in what was becoming a familiar gesture to me.

"Well, that's what I'm asking myself," he said slowly. "Maybe she had something on somebody, if you know what I mean."

"It sounds like blackmail."

"With a woman like Juliette Ransom you can't leave that out, Marcia."

He was silent for a time. He lit his pipe and moved about the room.

"There's something else too," he said. "Where did she come from, Marcia? Who were her people? You don't know, and as far as this place is concerned she might have come out of an egg."

I was dirty and tired before we finished that day. I managed to get in a shampoo and manicure; and with the brutal frankness of all beauty parlors, André came in and suggested that I needed a facial.

"You 'aven't been sick?" he inquired. "Sickness, it is bad for the face."

But I told him I would leave my face as twenty-nine years had made it, and he left me, looking disgruntled.

One thing more I did that day. I saw the florist who had received the weekly order for flowers for Juliette's grave. After I had explained he went back and examined his books, only to return with a blank look on his face.

"I'm sorry," he said. "The order is confidential."

I didn't tell the sheriff about my visit to the florist. Its implications were too frightening.

I slept badly on the train that night. Except for the discovery that someone had been there ahead of us, the trip seemed to me to have been entirely futile. As a result I found myself bitterly and resentfully going back over the past six years, years of struggle for Arthur and deprivation of a sort for me, while Juliette had lived her extravagant carefree days.

For it had been a struggle. Poverty is a relative matter. We were not poor, in the ordinary sense of the word. I had been able to keep the servants, and save them from going on relief. So far I had kept up my taxes and retained my property. But the demands on both Arthur and me were heavy, and lying in my hot berth that night I wondered.

Had Arthur known and resented that riotous life of hers, lived largely at his expense? He must have. The people she played with were constantly in the newspapers. They staged the first treasure hunt in Manhattan. They took prizes, sometimes largely unclothed, at some of the less reputable costume balls. During prohibition days they patronized the best speakeasies. During the Harlem vogue they were there. They preferred Miami to Palm Beach, but were photographed in scanty bathing clothes anywhere from Nassau to Bermuda. During the racing season they went to the tracks. During the hunting season some of them followed hounds, usually on horses belonging to other people. They went to bed at dawn and rose at noon, they kept going on a diet largely of cocktails, highballs and champagne, and they succeeded pretty successfully in copying a half-world which probably never existed outside fiction and the movies.

I faced the problem squarely that night. Either Arthur had known all this, and in desperation ended it; or it was in that pleasure-seeking life of Juliette's that the key lay to her death. I did not think that it lay on the island. The life there was too quiet for her particular crowd, and I remembered something she had said to Arthur when she was preparing to leave. "Well, thank God I'll never have to go to Sunset again."

But she had been killed on the island. Then why, and by whom?

I dozed off while puzzling over this, and wakened to dress and to find William, white of face and shaken, waiting on the platform when the train pulled in the next morning.

"I'm sorry to have bad news, miss," he said. "There's been a little trouble at the house."

"What sort of trouble?" I asked apprehensively.

"It's Maggie," he said. "Either she fell down the stairs from the hospital rooms or somebody hit her on the head."

CHAPTER XIX

It was almost twenty-four hours before Maggie was fully conscious. Even then she had no explanation. I thought she had probably been walking in her sleep again, for the door to the hospital suite had been found open and the key still in it. However she got there, she remembered nothing, except that when she wakened she was in her bed, with an icecap on her head, a trained nurse in the room, and Doctor Jamieson sitting beside her.

That was not until the next day. Arthur, uneasy and alarmed, had sent Mary Lou back to Millbank, and had spent much of the time since either with Maggie—he had always been devoted to her—or with one of the county detectives in examining the scene of the attack.

When she was able to talk he was there, holding her hand and looking more weary and desperate than ever.

"Try to remember, Maggie. What took you up there, in the middle of the night?"

"I don't know," she said dully. "I must have been dreaming." Which is her own euphemism for her occasional sleepwalking.

"You didn't see anybody?"

"I didn't even know I was there."

That was all we could get out of her, but it was evident that she had been there. Not only was the key in the door. Beside a bed in the far room they had found one of the long hairpins she used, and it had a bit of blood on it. Not only that. The window over the drain pipe had been opened with a jimmy, or some such tool.

But the whole affair was puzzling. Maggie had been struck down in that room; but when Ellen found her early the next morning, still unconscious, she had been rather neatly laid out on the hall floor at the foot of the stairs. And there was a pillow from Jordan's room under her head!

That day Arthur urged me to leave the island and go back to the New York house.

"I want you out of this devilish business," he said. "I've got enough to do to worry about myself. If this keeps on—" He smiled faintly. "If Bullard could do it, he would pin this last thing on me too. Maggie knows too much, so I try to get rid of her by banging her on the head."

I refused to go; but I told him then about that trip to the city, and of the condition of Juliette's apartment. He dismissed it with a shrug.

"Probably reporters," he said. "They get in everywhere. Like termites!"

As for the rest, he had never heard of Langdon Page or of Emily Forrester. He knew no one, on the island or off, who had been an intimate part of Juliette's life after their separation; he vaguely remembered a Jennifer, called "Jen," but had forgotten her last name.

Maggie's trouble, however, had shaken him. For the first time since Juliette's death we went back that day to our old friendly intimacy. He knew nothing of Juliette's death. "There must have been a lot of people who wanted her out of the way." But why kill the Jordan woman? She had seemed inoffensive enough, what little he had seen of her.

"But why write that note?" I said. "Why on earth not have seen her here?"

"I had a fat chance, didn't I?" he said dryly. "I tried to once, and she slammed the door on me."

But he had felt responsible for her, and also, he said, she had worried him.

"The way she acted wasn't normal," he said. "She was afraid, and I knew darned well it wasn't of me."

"Are you sure of that, Arthur?"

"Good God, yes," he said impatiently. "Are you beginning to wonder, like the rest of them?"

Nevertheless, it was good to be together again, in our old frank companionship. We were on the upper porch at the time, smoking, with Arthur as usual on the rail, and the gulls circling about noisily over the water. But there was one question I had to ask him, and I did it then.

"Arthur, could it have been Tony Rutherford you saw on the roof that night, and followed?"

He stared at me in amazement.

"Tony? Great Scott, no! What on earth would he be doing there?"

"I don't know," I said. "But I think I found a button from his golf coat below the trellis, in the garden."

He laughed at that. I had caught the detective fever, he said. Somebody always left a cuff link or a button about for the police to find. And if I knew what was good for me I'd take a nap and leave the matter to the authorities.

Nevertheless, his face, when he left and went into the house, was thoughtful.

I did not take a nap. I swam off the float that afternoon, and afterwards sat in the sun and thought of Allen Pell. It was hard to fit him into that life of Juliette's as her apartment had revealed it. Yet he must have been a part of it, have stood at that bar of hers—or behind it—mixing drinks, laughing, talking. There must have been other times, too, when the crowd had gone and only the two of them had been there together. But I did not want to think of them. I went up to the house and dressed for dinner, feeling considerably depressed.

It was that night that I began to wonder if Arthur had a part in the mystery after all.

I had been in and out of Maggie's room all day, and at midnight I relieved the nurse so she could go down to her supper. Lizzie had left a thermos of coffee and a tray for her in the dining room, and I told her not to hurry.

"Please don't leave her, Miss Lloyd," the nurse said as she went out. "She seems to be asleep, but now and then she tries to get out of bed."

She went on down, and I sat beside Maggie's bed for some time. It was strange to see her there, asleep, her work-roughened hands still, her hair in two long braids on the pillow.

167

I had forgotten that she had such pretty hair. It was a long time since the days when, waking in the morning, I had watched her hurriedly combing it.

"Now just be patient, Marcia. I've got to get some clothes on, haven't I?"

"Well, you don't have to comb your hair forever."

She was sleeping quietly now, and I was in the bathroom, putting fresh ice in the icecap when I glanced out and saw someone with a flashlight near the shrubbery. As I watched, the light moved toward the toolshed, and focused on the lock there.

I was frightened. I remember standing still, staring out, and in the silence I could hear the nurse clattering china and silver below. Then I dropped the icecap and ran to Arthur's room.

He was not there. He had not even gone to bed. I stood in the doorway, gazing in. There was his book. On the table was a still smoking cigarette. But he was gone.

When I went back to the head of the stairs he was coming in by the front door. The hall was dark, but I could see the vague outline of his body, and hear him quietly closing the door. I slipped away then, but standing in the door of Maggie's room I heard him come stealthily up the stairs, and shortly after his door closed.

When I went back to Maggie I found that she had one foot out of the bed, and was trying to get up. I put her down again, and when the nurse came up I left them. But as I got into bed that night I knew that, for all his frankness that day, Arthur had still not told me all he knew.

I slept soundly that night. I suppose the mind reaches a point where sleep is pure escape. When I wakened the sun was shining into my room, and Arthur's shower was running. There was a comforting odor of coffee and bacon from below, a fisherman's boat was on its way in, loaded with cod, and the most impudent of the crows was on my table outside, busily throwing away one cigarette after another.

It was all normal, even to the huge red jellyfish drifting about. But when I went out to drive away the crow I saw that there was something else there, only partially submerged and drifting in with each wave, to recede before the next one. It looked like a man's handkerchief, rather gaudy in color, and I had a sickening feeling that I knew it.

One thing was certain. I had to get it. Looking back, I am not sure why I felt that this was necessary. I did, however, and after dressing hastily I went downstairs. The old fishing tackle was still in a hall closet, its lines moldering, its hooks rusty. The rods, though, were in good condition, and I took one and went out onto the veranda. It was not so easy as I had thought. The thing slipped away, came back, and was lost again; and William's face was a study when he finally found me there, still making frantic jabs for it. He was imperturbable when at last, somewhat flushed, I brought it in.

"I saw it floating," I said unnecessarily. "I think it belongs to Mr. Arthur."

"Yes, miss," he said. "Your tray has gone up, miss."

He knew it was not Arthur's. It was not only gaudy in color. It was smeared with paint, and I was certain I had seen it before. I dried it and hid it, but it was to worry me for some time to come.

I remember the rest of the day chiefly for certain things which seemed comparatively unimportant at the moment. One was the sheriff, calling up from the county seat.

"Here's something to chew over, Marcia," he said. "About that New York business. Pretty nearly every man on the island's gone back by train at one time or another; but in the last week or so not so many. Fred Martin from the golf club, to see a sick mother. I've talked to Dorothy, and the mother's a fact. Mr. Dean, probably to pick up another million or so. And young Rutherford and Bob Hutchinson together for one day, to order some cups for the golf tournament. That's about the list from your neighborhood."

"It's an impossible list," I said uncomfortably.

"Well, it is and it isn't. At least two of them knew her."

That was all he had to say, except that the Page-Forrester matter was still on his mind.

"You might ask if anybody knows those names," he said. "People have a way of knowing other folks in the same walk of life. You know what I mean. They meet here and there. Anyhow it won't hurt."

It seemed a thin thread to me, but as Russell Shand said later, by that time—so far as our crimes were concerned—he

169

had sunk for the third time and a straw looked as big as a log to him.

But that day should have been marked in red ink on my calendar, for it was then that Mrs. Curtis told me something which neither she nor I recognized as having any bearing on the case; but which was to loom large before we reached the end.

She had been repairing some curtains, and after she had been paid she did not go. She stood, looking at me uncertainly.

"I don't suppose it means anything, Miss Marcia," she said, pulling nervously at her cotton gloves. "But I told Mr. Curtis at the time, and he says now I'd better tell you. It was three years ago last spring, when I came to open the house. Maybe you remember. There was a bill for glass in a cellar window."

"I don't remember, but that's not important."

"Well, the first thing I always do is light the furnace. The house is damp, and it takes a good while to dry out. So I went down into the cellar, and that window was broken. The boards had been taken off and put back again, loose; and there was glass on the cellar floor."

"You mean somebody had broken into the house?"

"That's what it looked like. I told Mr. Curtis that night, and the next day he came up and went all over the place. There was nothing wrong that we could find. Nothing missing either. There had been a leak in the roof over those hospital rooms, but that was all we found—except that Mr. Curtis thought a car had been driven in not long before. Of course, that's not unusual. People drive in sometimes to see the bay. The view's good from here."

Weeks afterwards I was to remember that conversation; to see Mrs. Curtis standing uneasily by the door, and to know that she had told me something that day which was vitally important. But it was too late then. The thing was done.

I was showing her out when the postman whistled, and I promptly forgot her. Not entirely. I told Russell Shand about it when I next saw him. But the fact that someone had sought shelter in the house more than three years ago did not seem important to him either.

CHAPTER XX

The day seemed interminable. But Maggie had improved greatly. She even remembered something of what had happened.

"I guess I was walking in my sleep," she said sheepishly. "Anyhow, when I woke up I was in the dark corner of a room somewhere. On my knees too, as if I was looking for something. I was pretty scared, it being dark and everything. I know I got up, and— Well, that's all I do know."

"You don't remember hearing anything? Any sound? Anybody moving?"

She merely shook her head and then clutched at it.

"It still hurts," she said. "No, miss. That's all."

Outside of Maggie's statement, that day was remarkable for only one thing.

I had a visit from Marjorie Pendexter. She came shortly after lunch. A tall girl, taller than I, I remember her sprawled in a chair, with the drink she had asked for at her elbow, and looking at me with eyes that were haunted.

"I've got to talk to someone or go crazy, Marcia," she said feverishly. "It's about Howard. He knew Juliette, and— Well, at one time he liked her. You know what I mean. He'd met her about, at house parties, and so on, and you know how men fell for her."

I stared at her incredulously. She was wearing her engagement ring, a square-cut diamond, and she kept twisting it about her finger.

"Well, really, Marjorie!" I said. "If you're going to worry about all the men who liked her you'll have to worry about half the males on this island."

She did not smile. She lit a cigarette, inhaled and exhaled deeply before she spoke again.

"I suppose it does sound idiotic," she said. "But he's not like himself, Marcia. He's worried about something, and he keeps putting off a cruise we were going to take. He meant to take the *Sea Witch* to Newfoundland, but now I don't know when we're going. Marcia, do you think she was blackmailing him? Juliette, I mean. You knew her better than I did."

"I wouldn't know a thing like that," I said. "He has a lot of money. It's possible. But I don't think he killed her, and you don't think so either."

"No," she admitted. "But you know what she did to men. There was one poor devil—" She let that go. "He has a frightful temper, Marcia. It's over in a minute, but it's there. If he met her that morning on the path—"

"Well, the probability is that he wasn't within miles of her," I said briskly. "What about this poor devil you mentioned?"

"Went crazy about her," she said. "Took to drinking and killed some people wtih his car." She got up. "She deserved what she got," she said viciously. "I'm not sorry for her. But somebody's going to the chair for doing his good deed for the day, that morning up on Pine Hill; and I'm plain scared."

She swore me to secrecy before she left, and when she got into her roadster I thought she looked better, as though talking it out had done her good. But as I watched her go I realized what a change had come over all of us.

It was not only the police and the reporters, both still overrunning the island. It was suspicion and fear. People eyed each other with an unspoken question in their eyes. Bob and Lucy Hutchinson next door were reported as being at daggers' points, and it had even interfered with the usual informal summer distractions, bathing parties on remote beaches, picnics and the long hikes which were always a part of the life.

In a way, the island at that time was divided into three schools of thought, as old Mrs. Pendexter put it: those who believed Arthur guilty of the murders, those who suspected Lucy, and those who never had an idea in their heads anyhow.

Unfortunately for the Arthur group Lucy's golf club was

172

found about that time, and quite a number shifted. It was found half buried on a hillside, and the excitement began all over again. It had no fingerprints on it, but there was certain grisly evidence that it had been the weapon in at least one of our deaths.

Fortunately the bells were quiet during that brief interval. That fact at least prevented the servants from leaving in a body. I had my hands full, what with Arthur sitting for hours gazing at nothing, and Mary Lou in and out of the house. She would not bring Junior to Sunset, especially after Maggie was hurt, but she drove back and forth. Alternately gentle and loving to Arthur, and again retiring into a remoteness that made me want to slap her.

One day she said:

"I'm standing by, Marcia. Whether he did these things or not. You know that."

"You can't possibly still believe—"

"Oh yes, I can," she said, with an unnatural composure. "You haven't known how things have been with us. I hated Juliette myself. I wanted her dead. If I had seen her that morning and there had been a golf club lying by I don't know what I would have done. Maybe he felt that way too."

"He detested her, Mary Lou. I heard him talking to her here. He said: 'You're fastened on me like a leech, and, by heaven, I can't get rid of you.' If that's love—"

She had turned rather white, but she was still calm.

"It's not very far from love to hate," she said in a flat voice. "And somebody got rid of her. Remember that."

I had no reply to that. I was seeing Arthur at the tool-shed, and his stealthy re-entrance into the house.

It seems extraordinary now that life went on more or less as usual during that brief interval of what I call peace, for lack of a better word: I played tennis at the club, lunched out, dined out, and generally tried to be normal in a strange new world. Maggie was up and about. Morning after morning Lizzie demanded the day's menus, and I had to face the thought of food. But Arthur himself was eating little or nothing, although for a time the police were letting him alone.

One day, needing exercise, I climbed the path beside Stony

Creek. There was no sign of that shallow grave where Juliette had been buried, but at one place the ground was trampled, and there were broken branches all about. I shuddered as I passed it.

It was on the way down that I heard heavy footsteps on the path, and saw Mansfield Dean coming up. He had not seen me. He was striding along with his head bent, like a man lost in deep and not too pleasant thought. So far lost that when he finally saw me he looked almost shocked.

He recovered in a moment, however, and was his own hearty self again.

"Well!" he said. "Is this your walk too? I thought it was mine!"

"It used to be," I told him.

He nodded understandingly.

"Of course. Not so pleasant now. Still—" He drew a long breath. "That's all over now. We can't bring them back, and maybe sometimes we wouldn't want to."

He took out his handkerchief and wiped his face.

"Too much good food and drink in this place," he observed, more cheerfully. "No place for a man who has to watch his blood pressure." Then, as though I might take that amiss: "Fine people, though. They've been splendid to Agnes. Everybody's called. I tell her she'll have to keep books on her visits."

I thought he looked tired, as though his wife's condition had worried him. Perhaps, as Mrs. Pendexter said, he was a self-made man and proud of the job; but he was a simple and natural person. Kindly too. He started to move on, then hesitated.

"I understand those fools of policemen have shown some sense at last," he said, with some embarrassment. "It's a pity your brother has been bothered. I'm sorry."

"They have to do their duty, I suppose."

Long weeks later I was to remember how he looked that day, his big muscular legs bulging in their golf stockings, his coat over his arm, and his eyes filled with a sort of shy friendliness. I watched him as he went on up the path, his head again bent, and I felt he had already forgotten me.

I sat on a rock beside the path, and looked down to where, far below, I could see the roof of Sunset among the trees. It had been a happy house for many years, until Juliette came into it. Now she was dead, and for days she had lain in that shallow grave somewhere above me on the hill. Why? What had actually happened, that day when Lucy Hutchinson had talked to her, and looking back at a turn of the path had seen her still there, as though she was waiting for somebody.

Had she been followed to the island and killed? And was Jordan's death merely secondary to that first crime? Certainly the arrival of the two women had set loose a number of forces, still mysterious and certainly deadly.

It was late in July now, but it seemed a long time since the day I had first come to Sunset, and looking out from the porch had had my first view of the bay; the gulls soaring to drop and break their clams on the rocks below; and Maggie gazing down at the three crows, and saying that they meant bad luck. A long time since the postman's double whistle had meant the small excitement of the day, and a boy on a bicycle with a telegram, a large one. A long time and another life since Arthur had combed the pool at low tide, and I had followed him like a small and reverential satellite.

It was late when I got home. The local caterer's wagon was driving into the Hutchinson place loaded with the gilt chairs which with us mean a party. It was probably Lucy's method of holding her chin up, but I resented it that day; and when I found Mary Lou on the veranda and mentioned it, she was fiercely indignant.

"It's outrageous," she said. "After all, Bob was crazy about Juliette. Everybody knows it."

"That was years ago. I don't suppose he has seen her since."

"He saw her six months ago."

I could only stare at her. There were times when she seemed incredible to me. All the problems, the careful balancing of this against that, motivations, human relationships, and she had not thought that fact worth the mentioning.

"You saw them? Together?"

"Certainly they were together. They were lunching at that French place on Sixty-third Street."

I could have shaken her, but Mary Lou was Mary Lou, and

Arthur loved her.

"Why haven't you said so before?"

"I'm no scandalmonger," she said virtuously. "I certainly don't go about telling tales on Arthur's first wife. Besides," she added more humanly, "I like Lucy. I like Bob too, for that matter, if he is a fool about women."

Queer, that mixture of childishness and astuteness which was—and is—Mary Lou. I had never thought that Bob Hutchinson was a fool about women. He was big, active and not too intelligent. For all their bickering he had always seemed to be in love with Lucy. Yet as time went on we were to learn that Mary Lou, who knew him hardly at all, knew instinctively what we had never guessed.

"Did they see you?" I asked.

"No. They left soon after I went in."

"Did they seem friendly?"

She thought for a moment.

"He looked pretty serious. She was smiling. She was wearing a lot of orchids. Why, Marcia? Surely you don't think Bob did that awful thing?"

"I think he is as likely a suspect as your own husband," I retorted indignantly, and left her.

But I thought that over after I had gone up to dress for dinner. Juliette seldom left things as she found them. She could go into any peaceful community and set it by the ears. She was not deliberately malicious. She never gossiped, for the reason, I dare say, that the affairs of other people were of no importance to her. But two days anywhere, and the men were gathered around her, while the women formed a sort of tacit mutual defense society against her, somewhere else.

Now, though dead, she was still leaving discord and suspicion behind her.

But Bob Hutchinson! It seemed incredible. He had a quick temper. I had seen him break a golf club and throw it away, in a fit of anger. He had certainly been infatuated with Juliette at one time. But he had seen her recently. He had even taken her to lunch.

Bob was still in my mind when we went in to dinner that night, and unfortunately I tried to speak of him to Arthur.

176

"That man you chased from the roof that night, Arthur," I said. "You must have some idea what he was like. At least you could tell whether he was large or small, couldn't you?"

He put down his fork and spoon and shoved his chair back.

"I wish to God," he said violently, "that I could eat one meal in peace. No, I haven't any idea what he looked like. I've said that before. I've said it over and over. If I knew who it was I'd go out and get him. I suppose that hasn't occurred to anybody!"

He slammed out of the room. Mary Lou, who had stayed to dinner, looked frightened, and William disappeared abruptly into the pantry.

"I told you," said Mary Lou. "He's not like himself at all. It scares me, Marcia."

Small as this is, I have related it here not only because it shows our general nervous condition. It show what Russell Shand was later to state in other words, that we were dealing with people rather than clues; with people and their interrelations, their reactions and their emotions. Indeed up to that time we had virtually no clues, or none that seemed to mean anything. I had found a button in the garden, Jordan for some reason or other had carried away the Jennifer letter but left all the rest of Juliette's mail, Mary Lou's car had left tire marks on the shoulder of the road, Lucy Hutchinson had dropped a rouge-tipped cigarette and left the print of a heel on the hill, somebody unknown had buried her golf club, and somebody equally unknown had broken the lock of our toolshed.

But also somebody, still unidentified, had killed two women and had tried to dispose of their bodies. And what about Maggie, and the attack on her?

The one new element, as I saw it that night, was Bob Hutchinson's possible recent relationship with Juliette.

Mary Lou went upstairs directly after dinner. She went slowly, as though hoping that Arthur would call her back. He did not. He sat in the library with his untouched coffee beside him, and when I found him there later he was looking at the framed photographs of his wife and Junior on the table.

"At least," he said harshly, "with that dammed alimony out

177

of the way, they'll have enough to live on."

I shivered.

"I wish you wouldn't say such things, Arthur."

"Why not? This thing's closing in on me. Even Shand knows it. They'll arrest me sooner or later. If they don't, the newspapers will try the case and force them to. Either way I'm through."

I felt entirely desperate that night. By ten o'clock Mary Lou had not come downstairs again, and Arthur was simply holding a book, not reading it. I threw on a coat and went outside for some air, and it was then that I decided to see Bob Hutchinson and talk to him; that night if I could.

But the party was still going on, and so I walked up and down the driveway until it was over. It was a dark night and cool, and I had reached the gates again when I was suddenly aware of a man close at hand. He was hardly more than a shadow, standing beside a tree and looking toward our lighted windows. I must have startled him, for he hesitated a second and then plunged headlong down the bank toward the pond.

Had we not had so many reporters I might have been alarmed. As it was I was merely astonished. I stood still and listened as he reached the pond, circled it and climbed the bank on the other side. The sounds were distinct, and it was a long time—weeks, in fact—before I realized that only someone familiar with the place could have made that escape in the dark.

It was not quite eleven o'clock when the cars began to leave the Hutchinson driveway, by which I gathered that it had been a dinner for the older group, without bridge. This was borne out when I saw Mrs. Pendexter's old Rolls emerge, followed by the Deans' vast limousine, and the coupé from the rectory.

There were other cars too. Evidently Lucy, under a cloud of sorts since the inquest, had been solidifying her position. There must have been most of the older substantial members of the summer colony there that night. In a way it was a triumph for her. They had come, rallying around her, her mother's daughter and Bob's wife, and therefore one of them.

But I felt bitter as I saw them go. They had not rallied about Arthur. They had never entirely forgiven him for marrying Juliette. Now, if they secretly applauded him for getting rid of her, by divorce and perhaps by something much worse, they were openly resentful of the scandal. The tradition of their privacy still obtained.

"Give you a list for my dinner?" they said to the press. "Certainly not. How do you know I am giving a dinner?"

And I was Arthur's sister. I realized that with Juliette's murder something of the taboo had been extended even to me. We had both broken the law and made the front page of the newspapers.

As a result I was in a fighting mood as the last car turned into the road. I had no plan, unless it was to confront both Bob and Lucy, complacent after their party, and ask them some questions. Why had Bob met Juliette in New York? What actually happened at that spot near the jumps where Lucy sat and waited, smoking her cigarette and with her golf club beside her? And was it Bob who had tried to get into the hospital rooms the night Arthur saw somebody there? Bob, who knew that route by trellis and drain pipe as well as I did.

The light under the porte-cochere blinked out as I approached the house; but the lower floor was still brilliant, and I stopped outside one of the drawing room windows and looked in.

It was a large room. Now it was like a stage setting with two characters behind the footlights. Bob and Lucy were both here, Lucy in black with scarlet slippers and a scarlet belt; smoking a cigarette by the fireplace; Bob in tails standing by a table. The French door was open and I was about to go in when I was stopped by Bob himself.

He had picked up a highball glass, and holding it, stared over it at Lucy.

"Well, thank God that farce is over," he said.

Lucy stiffened.

"So what?" she said coldly.

"You've proved your innocence up to the hilt, haven't you? Poor Lucy, such a rotten position to be in. But carrying on. That was the idea, wasn't it? Always carrying on."

She threw away her cigarette.

"I think you've had too much to drink," she said bluntly.

He surveyed her, from head to toe.

179

"The brave girl!" he said. "We must go to her dinner. After all, we knew her people. We must rally round the flag. So they rallied, and to hell with them!"

He put down his glass suddenly and flung out onto the terrace. It was so unexpected that he almost touched me. But he did not see me. He went down to the edge of the beach and dropped onto a bench there. I followed him, and when he saw me he looked startled and uneasy.

"Oh, it's you, Marcia. Pity you didn't come three minutes sooner. You'd have heard a little exchange of pleasantries," he said.

"I heard it, I didn't know what it meant."

"It sounded fairly obvious, didn't it? She thinks I killed Juliette Ransom, and I'm not so damned sure she didn't. There you are. And if you think," he added savagely, "that we are the only people who feel that way, I'm here to tell you that every woman on the island whose husband ever said a decent word to Juliette is wondering the same thing."

"But perhaps with less reason, Bob," I said.

He glanced at me and then looked away. Inside the house the butler and second man were putting out the lights. There was no sign of Lucy, and he drew a long breath. He got out his cigarette case, offered me one and took one himself before he spoke again.

"All right," he said. "Let's have this out. What are you talking about, Marcia? You've got something on your mind."

I told him, rather cautiously at first. He had been seen with Juliette, lunching with her, six months before. That didn't amount to much. Anyone could do that. But he had been crazy about her years ago, and I had a right to know if he had been seeing her in the interval. We knew nothing about her life, or her friends. If he was one of them—

"See here," he said roughly. "Cut out the preliminaries. Do *you* think I killed her?"

"I haven't the slightest idea," I said honestly. "I only know Arthur didn't."

He laughed shortly.

"Get this," he said. "I know Arthur's in a jam and I'm damned sorry. But until that day six months ago I hadn't seen

180

Juliette Ransom since her divorce. That's hard to prove, but it's a fact."

"You saw her then, anyhow."

"I did. I met her on the street and asked her to lunch. Why not? Knowing Lucy, I didn't tell her about it. That's all there is to it."

And that was literally all there was to it, apparently. He knew none of Juliette's friends, he had never seen Helen Jordan, and—I was to believe it or not—he had never been in Juliette's apartment.

When at last he got up he flung his cigarette away savagely.

"I wish to God I'd never laid eyes on her," he said.

He took me back to the house, leading the way through the short cut in the hedge. He was silent and not too friendly, but once at the door he spoke again.

"Are you going to tell Lucy?"

"Not unless I have to, Bob."

"Things are going pretty haywire with us just now. No need of making them worse. How about the police?"

"I haven't decided yet. If what you say is true—"

"Listen," he said gravely. "I didn't kill her. I don't know who did. That's the truth. You'll have to believe me."

Then he was gone, and I was in the house again, with only a night light burning in the lower hall, and Arthur sound asleep in his chair.

CHAPTER XXI

I went downstairs the next morning to find the sheriff on the front veranda, looking out over the bay. He smiled when he saw me.

"Always did say this was the best view anywhere around, Marcia," he said. "I came out here so I could smoke my pipe." His eyes twinkled. "Never forget the time the silver was stolen here—that's why the safe was put in—and I lit it in the library. Your mother just about took my head off."

He became serious after that. He didn't like the way things looked. Of course he was only a country law enforcement officer, and he supposed a man with real brains would have had somebody behind the bars before now. Himself, he wasn't so sure. No use hurrying things anyhow.

I listened, rather puzzled.

"Are you trying to say that you think Arthur is innocent?" I asked hopefully.

But he shook his head.

"Don't go too fast," he said. "I'm saying that this thing's a lot deeper than it seems on the surface; that's all. We've got two crimes, both different. One's a crime of passion. Maybe nobody went up that hill to kill Juliette Ransom. Maybe nobody meant to kill her at all. I've been mad enough myself to cut a fellow's throat if I'd had a razor in my hand at the minute. But the Jordan case is different. That looks cold and premeditated. Somebody arranged to meet her and put her out of the way. She knew too much. I'd give a good bit to know what she did know, at that."

After that he seemed to be thinking out loud, rather than

183

talking to me. Granting Arthur hadn't done it, who on the island would have hated Juliette enough to have struck her that murderous blow with the club? A discarded lover? A jealous woman? He glanced at me when he said that.

"I'm not thinking of Arthur's wife," he said dryly. "Not that she couldn't have done it. You take these small home-loving women and they will fight like tigers when they're roused. But she is out of the Jordan business. I've checked that. She was here in the house the night the Jordan woman disappeared. You and she played Russian bank. Remember that?"

I nodded. It was my first realization of the pitiless publicity in which we had become involved. Our every act was known, and even my own servants, faithful for years, had evidently told all they knew.

The sheriff tapped his pipe on the railing and watched the ashes fall into the water.

"Not that I think a woman did it," he went on. "Both look like jobs for a man, and a pretty strong one at that. But about Arthur now—it's six years or more since Juliette Ransom left him. Seems to me that's a long time for anyone to hold a grudge, especially a murderous one."

"Why think it was someone who belongs here? She could have been followed, couldn't she?"

"Maybe, maybe not. Whoever did it knew the island pretty well. That's as far as I go. Knew where Juliette was going to ride, and when. Knew Loon Lake. Knew that toolshed of yours. Knew this house too, if he got in and hurt Maggie. And whoever killed the Jordan woman knew more than that. He knew where to lay his hands on a boat, and how to run it when he got it. What outsider would know all that? No. I come right back to the summer people every time."

It was true, and I knew it. Our colony is like similar ones everywhere. Its members come from as far west as Chicago and St. Louis, and as far south as Baltimore and Washington. It meets and then separates for the rest of the year, unless to meet casually at Palm Beach or the Riviera. But the island is a part of its life. It has a proprietary interest in it, and it knows it as well as the natives.

"Only thing I can think of is to figure who were her friends

184

when she used to come here," he said. "Who liked her, and who didn't. And which of them has been seeing her since. You'd know that, Marcia."

I hesitated.

"I believe she saw Marjorie Pendexter now and then," I said, "and she's met her since. Howard Brooks too. They all hunt, you know."

"Brooks? The fellow with the big yacht?"

"Yes."

"Well, that's something," he said, and got up. It was then that he made an observation which made me vaguely uneasy.

"What about this fellow from the camp on Pine Hill?" he inquired. "Pell's his name. You and he are getting pretty thick, aren't you?"

"I wouldn't call it that. I bought a picture from him."

"Swam over from the foot of Cooper Lane to bring it, did he?"

He was smiling, but his eyes were on me, keen and intent. I could feel the blood in my face.

"I suppose that's meant to be funny," I said. "That night he was out swimming. He stopped here to rest."

"It took him about an hour and a half to rest, down there on the float with you," he said quizzically. "And a cold night too! I just happened to see him. I was looking over the boats along the shore, and there he was."

He became sober after that.

"Better be careful, Marcia," he said. "We don't know anything about this fellow. Pell may be his name, and maybe not. But I don't know any better way to hide out than to take a trailer and keep moving."

It was that day that I told him about Mrs. Curtis and the broken cellar window. He went downstairs before he left and took what he called a look around. But he apparently thought it unimportant, for soon after I heard him driving away.

The rest of the day was quiet. Arthur took Mary Lou home and was to stay a day or two at Millbank; and save that the bells rang once or twice nothing happened. I played a round of golf with Tony; but he did not refer to the button, nor did I. Seeing him there on the course, debonair and cheerful, I could not

185

suspect him of anything, unless perhaps when unobserved of slightly improving the lie of his ball!

On the way back to the club he took my arm, and astounded me by asking if I had entirely ceased to care for him.

"Things are looking better now, Marcia," he said. "And I've never forgotten you. You know that, don't you?"

A few months ago that would have touched me. Now it merely surprised me.

"I don't know anything of the sort, Tony. You have managed extremely well without me, haven't you?"

He looked hurt, and dropped my arm.

"If that's the way you feel about it," he said sulkily, "I suppose it's no use."

"No," I told him. "It's no use. I'm sorry."

The next morning I received a note from Allen Pell. At least I could guess that it was from him. It was unsigned, except for a rough drawing of a man sitting at an easel, with a squirrel on his shoulder and what purported to be a cow chewing at his hat.

The note itself was brief:

"Did you ever take tea in a trailer? If not, it may be an amusing experience. How about this afternoon at five? You need not answer. Just come if you can."

I was excited and happy, I remember, and late afternoon saw me on my way up the path again. I had not gone a half mile, however, when I saw a woman ahead of me. She was sitting on a rock, gazing out over the bay, and when I got closer I saw that it was Agnes Dean.

She smiled when she recognized me, and I noticed that she was thinner and more fragile than ever.

"Isn't this rather steep for you?" I asked.

"I'm not going much farther; but I sleep badly, so I thought maybe a little exercise—"

Her voice trailed off, and I sat down beside her and took off my hat.

"I suppose I'm not used to the quiet," she said. " 'The green stillness of the country or the dark gray town.' It's funny how few people know Longfellow any more, isn't it? Mr. Dean likes the island, but then he goes about more than I do. He likes noise and excitement; I suppose most men do."

Her voice was the voice of a tired woman, and I wondered if Mansfield Dean himself did not tire her. He was cheerful and exuberant, fond of people, fond of living. Then, too, he had loaded her with possessions, and probably they tired her also.

"I wish I could be gayer, for his sake," she added, and sighed.

But she seemed more normal that day than I had ever seen her. She had lost some of her self-consciousness, and after a brief hesitation she said: "I hope you don't mind my speaking of it. I'm terribly sorry about your trouble."

"It's all rather a mess. Of course my brother had nothing to do with it. His own wife! Even if they were divorced, she had been his wife."

She was silent for a minute. I offered her a cigarette, but she refused.

"I ought to go back," she said. "But I have wondered—I hear so much and I know so little, Miss Lloyd. What was she like, this Mrs. Ransom? Or would you rather not speak about her?"

It was my turn to hesitate, but there was something so tragic and yet so simple in her that I could not take offense.

"I suppose she was a mixture of bad and good, like the rest of us," I told her. "She was what she was. Probably it wasn't her fault. She made trouble, lots of it, but usually it was not deliberate; merely selfish. If that's vague—"

She seemed to consider that.

"I've known women like that. Men's women, mostly. I suppose men liked her?"

"Some of them went crazy about her."

For just one wild moment I wondered if Mansfield Dean had ever met Juliette. She seemed to sense it, for I saw her smile faintly.

"I'm afraid we did not move in her particular circle," she said. "It must have been a gay one. And of course we did not live in New York."

She got up and brushed the pine needles from her skirt. Then she looked at me directly.

"I suppose it is sad, but perhaps the world is better without her, Miss Lloyd. Women who are heartless and cruel can wreck many lives."

She left me after that, rather abruptly, as though she had realized that the conversation was unconventional, to say the least.

Poor Agnes Dean! I can see her as she looked that day, her lips blue and her breathing difficult. I watched her down the hill, going back to Mansfield, to her big house, and to her servants. She had said that she had a hairdresser's appointment, and I knew that some time that night she would put on one of her handsome dresses, color her blue lips, and play the game as her husband wanted her to play it.

I went on and up the path, to find Allen Pell waiting for me at the top, as though he had known I would come.

"Whether by car or road, I knew I'd catch you here," he said. "Ever see a tourist camp before?"

"I'm afraid I never have," I admitted.

"Then you've missed a lot of fun. I'm inclined to think you've missed a lot of fun anyhow," he said, looking at me quizzically. "You people do, you know. Why not join the proletariat and see the world?"

"I've never had a chance," I said. "Until now."

That made him laugh. He was glad to see me, I thought. But seen in the strong light he had somehow changed. He seemed to have lost weight, and there were deep lines from his nose to the corners of his mouth which I had not noticed before. But he laughed that off when I spoke of it.

"Me?" he said. "I'm as strong as an ox. Don't waste any pity on me, my dear. At this minute, with you beside me, I could lick a carload of tigers."

The camp looked pleasant when we reached it. But strange too. It was the open road with a vengeance, small tents everywhere, open fires and cars. Here was family life, open and unashamed, with bits of washing hanging out, children playing, men reading newspapers, and women preparing supper.

But I felt a pang when I saw it. It had been a picnic ground in the old days, with a good spring walled in, and I knew it well. Here Arthur and I used to be taken in the surrey to meet other children from similar vehicles, and there in the woods was the

188

long table where we ate our supper, with the benches still on either side of it. I suppose I showed what I felt, for he eyed me.

"Why the sudden melancholy?" he inquired. "Have we profaned some sacred spot?"

"It's nothing. We used to come here on picnics, Arthur and I. That's all. I don't know why I always have to be low in my mind when I see you. I'm not like that, really."

"It's my normal effect on a lot of people," he observed gravely. "If I could tell you of the tears which have been shed on this manly bosom—!"

Which made us both laugh, and certainly relieved the tension.

I was rather surprised when I saw his trailer, set a little apart from the others, at the edge of the camp. It was large and exceedingly comfortable, and the coupé attached to it was a substantial one. Up to that time I suppose I had taken his poverty for granted, and I think he enjoyed my astonishment.

"Not so bad, is it?" he said. "Well, how about coming into the sitting room and having some tea?"

There actually was a sort of sitting room. That is, the front end held two easy chairs and a table, as well as a bookshelf and a radio. He ushered me in with considerable manner.

"Sitting room, bedroom, kitchen and bath," he said. "Cold water all the time, and hot on bath nights. Now sit down in the parlor and I'll fix the tea."

"Hadn't I better do that?" I asked.

"My dear girl," he said. "I am one of the best cooks on the road. You should taste my fried eggs! As for tea, I'll show you in just a second. China or India?"

"China."

"That's fine. That's all I have," he said, and retreated to the stove somewhere at the rear.

It looked very domestic. The only inconsistency was Allen Pell himself, big and rather awkward, fussing over his tea-kettle, and after helplessly trying to cut thin bread and butter, turning it over to me.

"I'll be the hell of a good wife for somebody yet," he said. "But I can't cut bread. Let's see what you can do."

I cut it, and he watched me.

189

"To be honest, just for once," he admitted, "it's the food business that gets me. The rest is all right. No ties, quiet nights and the open road. I wasn't cut out for a cook, and that's a fact."

He was pouring boiling water over the tea, and he grunted when he set down the kettle.

"You seem to think you weren't cut out to be a painter, either," I reminded him.

"A painter? God forbid," he said piously. "Someday, when I know you better, Marcia, I'll tell you about that. And now here's your tea. Lemon or cream?"

Thinking it over later, it was a sort of Mad Hatter's tea party that afternoon. People came and borrowed things from him. He ran out of cigarettes and borrowed some himself. I had to inspect his bed, which was a couch in daytime, and to admire his refrigerator, which he claimed to have cleaned for the purpose. I remember saying that I would like a trailer of my own, and that he smiled at the idea.

"What?" he said. "No butler? No maid to dress you?" But he added more soberly: "Just now you rather like the idea. Sunset among the trees, wood smoke, camp clothes, and no parties. It looks pretty good. But how about rainy days, and cleaning up? You wouldn't like it, and you know it."

By a sort of tacit agreement we had avoided discussing the tragedies. I had been thinking, however. There was something wrong with the picture. He was no painter. He painted, but that was different. He did not need the money. And there were other things. There was that handkerchief of his, spotted with paint, which I had found floating in front of the house. There were a dozen other puzzling incidents. And all at once I stumbled on what seemed the only possible explanation. He was lighting a cigarette at the time, and I summoned all my courage.

"I wish you'd tell me something," I said. "I don't think you are what you pretend to be. If that's true—"

He threw away the match before he spoke.

"None of us are what we pretend to be, are we?"

"That's no answer."

He turned and looked at me.

190

"And what am I, my good woman?" he inquired lightly.

"I think you're a police officer of some sort, in—well, in disguise."

He laughed out loud at that. Then he sobered.

"Listen," he said grimly. "There isn't a policeman in the world I'd lift my hand to help. Let's get that clear. As for the rest— Well, I happen to believe that your brother Arthur is in a hell of a jam, and that he is innocent. In fact, I'm damned sure he's innocent."

I gasped.

"Does that mean that you know who is the murderer?"

He did not reply directly.

"Let's say this. Say I think I know why those women were killed. That's different, isn't it?"

But I had stood all I could.

"It isn't fair," I said hysterically. "It's wrong. What you know, whatever you know, you ought to tell it. Why wreck us? We have never hurt you."

I looked at him. He had a dogged look in his face, but his eyes were full of pity.

"Put it this way, my dear," he said. "If it becomes necessary I'll tell what I know. I promise you that. But get this straight too, Marcia. If you try to force my hand or go to the police with this, I'm through. I'll have to be."

"You are protecting somebody, aren't you?"

"I'm protecting myself," he said quickly.

He shifted to Arthur after that. He thought he had found a man who saw Arthur asleep on the bench that morning of Juliette's death; but he was away. When he came back in a day or two he would be certain.

"That's the first thing to do," he said. "Get your brother's alibi fixed up. He mustn't be indicted. I gather Bullard wants to hold him for the grand jury, and you know what that means."

"I'm afraid I don't."

He sat still, staring out to where the sun was shining low through the trees.

"It's not very pleasant," he said at last. "The prosecuting attorney runs the show, and he runs it the way he wants. His opening address is an indictment in itself. He brings in his own

191

witnesses, and if he wants a true bill he generally gets it. In this case he wants it. Don't forget that."

That upset me. I cried a little, and he waited patiently while I fumbled for a handkerchief.

"I'm a fool," he said. "See here, Marcia—you don't mind my calling you that, do you? And my name is Allen in case you haven't heard!—I'm going to tell you something. Your brother will never go to the chair. I promise you that, on my sacred word of honor."

I left soon after that, more lighthearted than I had been for days. It was six o'clock, and suppertime was approaching at the camp. Open fires and a sheet metal stove or two showed women bending over them, and there was an appetizing odor of food mixed with wood smoke in the air. Allen Pell eyed it with something like affection.

"Nothing wrong with America when you can see this," he said. "Plain people living plain lives, but sound to the core. Maybe you and I have missed something in life, Marcia."

He took me to the top of the path and left me there.

"Not necessary for the local gentry to see us together," he explained, with his attractive smile. "And don't worry too much, my dear. We'll see this through together."

Those were the last words I heard him say for a long and weary time. I left him there on the path, a big figure in slacks and a sweater; and when I looked back at the turn he was still standing there, looking after me.

CHAPTER XXII

This is not a love story. In a way it is the story of a story, hidden from us at the time but underlying everything that happened. Now and then, like one of the seals in the bay, it emerged for a moment; then it sank back again, leaving behind it despair and death. But that evening, as I left Allen Pell on the trail, I felt that I was leaving something of myself behind me. As indeed I was.

It was that night that he disappeared.

I can write that now, here on this upper porch, with the hills turned to a tapestry of red and brown and yellow, and the autumn sun warm on my bare head. But for a long time I could not. I could not even think of it.

It was as though a new life had been opening for me. Then, without warning, it was gone.

I did not know it until the next night, when matters had come to a head between Bullard and the sheriff. Bullard had sent for Russell Shand and stated flatly that he was tired of delay and being ridden by the press; that he intended to take Arthur into a magistrate's court, have him held, and call a special grand jury at once.

"I've let you play around with this case long enough," he said. "Maybe you've forgotten it, but we've had two murders in this county. If you think I'm going to wait until we have another—"

"Who's to be the next?" said the sheriff, with interest. "Unless you're looking for a lunatic. If it's a lunatic it isn't Arthur Lloyd; and if it's Arthur Lloyd, who else would he want to kill? Looks as though he's about cleaned up."

"Don't be a God-damned fool," said Bullard, bristling. "And don't play me for one. I've got a case, and you know it."

"You've got two murders. That doesn't mean you've got the killer."

Arthur was still at Millbank when I received a more or less faithful account of this over the telephone that night. Apparently time was short and if Arthur's alibi was to be established it should be at once. If Allen Pell could help I had to see him that night.

I had sent the servants to the movies in the car, and so I had to go on foot. It had been half past ten o'clock when I got the sheriff's message, and not much later when, armed with a flashlight, I started up the Stony Creek path again. I remember that the lights were all on in the Dean house as I passed it, and knew that there had been a dinner party. I remember, too, again feeling resentful that life should go on as usual, that people gave parties, drank cocktails and champagne, walked or trailed in to elaborate food and service, as though there was no such thing as death by violence, or punishment for the innocent.

It was a horrible trip. I had never taken that path at night, and certainly not in a dinner dress; and as I went on it seemed strange and unfriendly. At one place I lost it entirely, and stepping onto some soft ground realized with a shock of horror that this might be where Juliette's body had been buried. In places, too, the path was steep and in the dim light from my flashlight it became rocky and precarious. As I climbed the noise of the creek sharpened as it fell in small cascades over the ledges.

I still do not know whether I was followed that night or not. I had stopped in the comparative silence beside a pool, and I thought I heard a small sound behind me. I turned, but the path twists at that point and there was no one in sight. Nevertheless, there had been a sound, like a foot against a rock, and I called out sharply.

"Who's there?" I said.

Nobody answered, and at last I went on.

The camp was quiet when I reached it. In one tent there was a light, evidently from a candle, and one trailer showed a lamp

194

and a man reading beside it. Otherwise it had settled down for the night, a series of large lumbering shadows not unlike a herd of elephants in a clearing.

The Pell trailer also was dark. I knocked at the door, and receiving no reply, called as cautiously as I could. Careful as I had tried to be, however, the man who had been reading not far away heard me. He emerged, located me, and came over.

"Looking for Pell?" he said.

"Yes."

"I haven't seen him about today. Kinda queer too. He's usually in and out." He eyed me more closely. "You'll be the young lady who came to see him yesterday. That right?"

"Yes."

"Wait a minute," he said, and went back to his own trailer, where a woman now stood on the step.

"Here's a lady asking for Pell," he said. "Haven't seen him, have you?"

She shook her head.

"Haven't seen him since he started off with that girl yesterday," she said.

"You didn't see him come back?" I asked incredulously.

"I don't know as he did come back," she said. "I didn't see him. But there was somebody there last night. It wasn't Pell. Looked like an older man. Heavy-set fellow. I saw him going in."

Even then I was not apprehensive, although I was uneasy. The visitor, she said, had stayed quite a little time, a half hour or more. It was only his outline she had seen. He had drawn the curtains before he turned on the lights inside. "He acted like he knew the place," she added.

Her own idea at the time had been that it was one of the summer colony, but of course she did not know. Some of them had bought pictures from Mr. Pell, she thought. The one thing she was sure of was that it was not Allen Pell himself.

She seemed to enjoy talking, and perhaps she sensed drama of some sort. They all liked Mr. Pell, she said.

"He was pleasant," she went on. "The children liked him too. He'd draw pictures for them, and he generally had candy for them."

But for all that, he had kept rather to himself. Not like a young man somehow. "He would sit sometimes inside there at night—you could see him—just looking at nothing."

He was not around much in the daytime, she explained. "Out on the hills, mostly." And she added, with a look at her husband: "We had an idea he wasn't too anxious to be seen around here. He used to watch the cars when new folks came. Might have been in some sort of trouble, we thought."

That was a new idea to me, and it made me more uneasy than ever. Nor was it reassuring to find that the door of the trailer was locked. I gathered that he had not been in the habit of locking it.

"The man who was here must have had a key," I said. "Either that or— Perhaps we'd better break a window. He may be inside, sick or—"

I could not go on. I was certain by that time that something had happened to him, and I felt sick and dizzy.

A small interested crowd had already gathered, but my idea met with immediate opposition. Apparently the law of private property was carefully observed. One man, though, who was a locksmith on holiday, offered to try to open the door. This was approved, and with the aid of a flashlight, a file, and innumerable offered keys he finally succeeded.

It was characteristic of the increasing anxiety that when I stepped forward a woman caught me and held my arm.

"Let the men look first," she said. "With all the killing that's been going on, I'd wait if I was you."

I stood while two or three men entered the trailer, and I do not think I breathed until one of them reappeared.

"He's not here," he called. "If the lady would like to come inside—"

I found myself shaking violently. Around me the crowd was quiet, intent. Somebody back in the shadows said perhaps the killer was loose again, and was instantly hushed. But I was able to climb the steps and, once inside, to control myself better.

There was no sign of Allen Pell. On the small table were still the remains of that tea the day before, the small cakes from the village pastry shop, the cut bread, the butter, our cups. And as conclusive evidence that he had not come back, his hat lay

196

where he had left it, on the couch.

I must have swayed, for one of the men caught me.

"Get her out of here," he said. "And don't touch anything. Somebody better call the police." And to me: "Don't worry, lady. He may have fallen and hurt himself."

They got me out somehow, and the night air revived me. The light shone on a circle of friendly faces, grave and concerned. Someone brought a camp stool, and I sat down. Someone else left for the small administration building and a telephone. But there was a delay. Whoever was in charge had gone off for the night, and the place was locked. It was an impasse until a state policeman roared in on a motorcycle and found us there.

"What's the trouble?" he inquired.

"The painter fellow's missing," he was told.

"What do you mean, missing? How long's he been gone?"

"Looks like yesterday evening. This young lady came to see him, but he isn't here."

He saw me then and recognized me. He touched his cap.

"I wouldn't worry too much about him, Miss Lloyd. He knows his way about. He's all over the place."

But he looked at me curiously. It was about midnight by that time, and I must have seemed a queer figure, in a sleeveless dinner dress, clutching my flashlight, surrounded by a constantly increasing group of campers, and seated on a folding camp chair. But the policeman was young and serious.

"Let's get this clear. You came up to see Mr. Pell. When was that?"

"I've been here a half hour. Maybe more."

"Did you have any reason to think anything was wrong? Is that why you came?"

"No, I had to see him about something. It was important. It couldn't wait."

He looked uncomfortable, as though he did not believe me. But he persisted.

"When did you see him last, Miss Lloyd?"

"I had tea with him here yesterday. He walked part of the way home with me. I"—I almost lost control—"I don't think he's been back since. The table is there, just as we left it."

He glanced around at the crowd.

197

"Anybody see him since then?"

Nobody had, and he took off his cap and wiped his forehead, his face sober in the light from the open door.

"I'd better get you back home," he said. "Then I'll report it. Where's your car, Miss Lloyd?"

"I walked up."

"Alone?"

"Yes. My car was out."

There was a little movement among the crowd. Most of them knew the short cut by the creek, but that I should have taken it on foot that night and alone evidently made them suspicious, not so much of my motives as of my character.

"The servants have my car," I said lamely. "Mr. Pell had some information for me, and I had to have it at once. It was about my brother."

That, too, was unfortunate. They knew about Arthur. Some of them had helped in the long search for Juliette's body, and later for Jordan's. If there was any mischief afoot they were ready to associate Arthur with it. Even the state trooper gave me a quick glance.

"We'll have to get you back," he said. "Somebody here drive Miss Lloyd down?"

I may have imagined it, but I thought the crowd hesitated. Then the locksmith volunteered, and the crowd opened silently to let me pass.

What with shock and fear I collapsed that night, and much that I know of the next few days is from the sheriff. The fact remains that for the third time that summer the search started for a missing person. Not that night. The police had contented themselves with locking the trailer again and making a few routine inquiries. But the next morning, with all the now familiar routine of bloodhounds, boys from the CCC camps and amateur searchers of all sorts, it was a ghastly time. But one thing Allen's disappearance did for us. It left me in a state bordering on delirium, but at least it held Bullard's hand.

Arthur had an unimpeachable alibi for the day Pell had vanished. He had spent the entire afternoon and evening at home with Mary Lou. The servants testified to that, even the neighbors. Some of them had been in to tea, two others—old friends—had dined and played bridge.

Not that Bullard was willing to concede anything.

"How do we know this case is connected with the others?" he demanded. "Fellow falls over a cliff, or just goes off about his business. That any reason for letting Lloyd give tea parties and play bridge?"

It was soon apparent, however, that Allen Pell had neither gone voluntarily nor fallen over a cliff. The dogs, following his trail to the path, and some forty feet down, stopped at that point; and it was Russell Shand who first saw the rock there, with blood on it.

He came to break the news to me, sitting beside my bed and trying to treat it with a reasonable amount of hope.

"It's like this, Marcia," he said. "He may be— Well, considering what's been going on, we have to face the fact that somebody may have done away with him. On the other hand, there's a good chance the other way. First place, the blood may not be his at all. Second place, that stone hadn't been lifted. Looks more as though somebody fell on it."

I roused myself.

"Fell on it?" I said. "Knocked him out, you mean? Then what about the man in the trailer that night? Who was it? It wasn't Allen Pell."

He filled and lit his pipe, with that slightly guilty look he always had when he did so in the house. He had it going well before he answered.

"I don't know who he was," he said. "But so far as I can make out he was cleaning up the place."

"*Cleaning* it!"

"Fingerprints. And a damned good job he made of it. Maybe that makes sense to you, but by the great horn spoon, it doesn't to me." He took a turn about the room, puffing like a locomotive. "Here's a man who has lived in a trailer for weeks, perhaps months. Now a trailer's not the size of a barn; even that one of Pell's. And he was a big fellow. Practically every time he moved he had to touch something. Yet that place hasn't a print; not even on the dishes! Only ones we found were around the door where those men unlocked the door for you, and we've traced them."

I listened in silence. I was remembering a night by the pond and Allen Pell wiping the back of the bench before we left. Had he himself come back and, for reasons of his own, gone over that trailer? But what reasons?

The sheriff had more to say. Fred Martin, walking up the path soon after I came down that day, had seen nobody and nothing, but thought he had heard a car starting on the road before he reached it.

"He might have hurt himself, and someone picked him up and took him to be fixed up. Or a car might have hit him. Whoever did it might have carried him off. That's happened before this."

"I thought that stone was forty feet away from the road."

"He might have staggered down the hill before he fell."

But neither of us believed that. I told him why I had gone to the camp that night, and he was properly indignant.

"I wish to God you'd let me handle this case," he said angrily. "What was the idea? Why didn't Pell come forward if he knew anything? What's all the secrecy about? And who is the fellow anyhow? Don't tell me he's a painter! If I was to give a guess he'd know more about a polo pony than a paint palette."

With which alliterative statement he glared at me furiously.

"You people always stand together," he said accusingly. "I know you. I've seen it for forty years. You may differ among yourselves, but you present a united front to the rest of the world. And Pell's one of you, isn't he?"

"I don't know anything about him. I suppose he is what might be called a gentleman."

He looked at me angrily.

"Gentleman!" he said. "You'd think gentlemen were a class apart! We've got more gentlemen working with their hands in this county than in all of New York. All right. Let that go. He knew someone who might have saved Arthur, and he kept it to himself. And unless I miss my guess he knew a lot more. So now we're back where we started. Suppose you tell me what *you* know, before something happens to you."

I felt crushed and guilty. The sheriff looked like a different man. His old easy friendliness was gone, and he was regarding me with hard blue eyes.

"Come on. Out with it."

So I told him. The night by the pond with Allen Pell—except that I left out the part about Juliette—the other night on the float, and that statement of his, made at the camp, that Arthur would never go to the chair.

"So he knew something," he said, more quietly. "Well, I'll tell you this, Marcia. That fellow had something to hide, including himself. If he knew Juliette Ransom he may have killed her. Why not? He was in the hills every day. If Lucy Hutchinson is telling the truth, Juliette looked as though she was waiting for somebody when she left her. Why wasn't that Pell?"

"And I suppose," I said indignantly, "that he went off without a hat, leaving that blood on a stone to throw you off the scent!"

"I've seen queerer things than that," he said, and stamped out and down the stairs, slamming the front door in William's face.

CHAPTER XXIII

I did not see him again for almost a week. The days dragged on. We had a series of storms, and again the creek poured a heavy stream over the dam like a small Niagara. Maggie was up and about, at night tying a string to her big toe and from that to the foot of her bed, to prevent walking in her sleep; and I, too, was convalescing, looking like a ghost when I saw myself in a mirror, but trying to keep my head up and my chin out, whatever good that may do.

Arthur was back and forth. I gathered that this last mystery had cleared matters between Mary Lou and himself, as well as with the police, for he seemed more like himself. But the general situation was nervous to the point of hysteria, and I crept downstairs one night to dinner, to discover that the authorities had put a guard on night duty around the house. His name was Tate, and after that I had coffee and a tray left for him under the porte-cochere before William went to bed.

The excitement of course was for the crime, if it was one; not for Allen Pell himself. The summer colony knew little or nothing of him. But one day, walking out to the gate—I was still rather tottery—I saw Howard Brooks going by in his car. He did not see me, but he was gazing straight ahead with a sort of blank look on his face; like a man whose thoughts were far away and not too pleasant.

The time came, of course, when I had to get about again, to write notes of thanks for the flowers that had come in, to have my hair trimmed and my nails done, to pick up my life as best I could. But the heart had gone out of me, to use a phrase of Maggie's. One day I even got into considerable trouble, owing largely to my state of mind.

Once again we had had the usual influx of reporters, and one followed me into Conrad's one morning, and touched his hat apologetically.

"Sorry to bother you, Miss Lloyd," he said, "but do you connect this Pell story with your—with Mrs. Ransom's death, and the other one?"

"Why should I?"

"You think not, then?"

"I haven't said that. Or anything."

"It was you who found that he was missing, wasn't it?"

Just then I caught Conrad's warning eye, and I said no more. The result in the press was startling, in spite of that. I was quoted at length as having stated that there was a possible connection among our three mysteries. Also as having visited the camp late at night and growing hysterical at the discovery that Allen Pell was not there.

Arthur, coming over the next day, read it grimly and turned an unbrotherly eye on me.

"What's all this trash?" he demanded. "Do you mean to say you went to the camp to see that fellow? At night?"

"I walked up after dinner. The servants had the car."

"What for? This article makes you look like a lovesick schoolgirl. Don't tell me you had been meeting this man! I can't believe it. Who is he? What is he?"

"I don't know whether he is even alive," I said, and choked. "As for why I went there, he was trying to help you."

But Arthur was outraged.

"Who the devil asked for his help?" he almost shouted. "I don't know him. Never heard of him. It wasn't enough that I've been plastered over the front page of every newspaper in the country. Now you've got to do it!"

He was nervous, of course. But then we were all in a state of unstable equilibrium. These are the overtones of crime, I suppose. Any crime. The things that never reach the public. The suspicions and angers, the tight nerves, even of the innocent, the breaks in old friendships, never to be healed, even in family relationships.

For I think Arthur has never forgiven me entirely that

204

publicity, tying us once more with what began increasingly to look like another crime.

The police had not been idle during that interval. The usual alarms had gone out over radio and teletype. A detective had traced the trailer and coupé to where they had been bought, for cash; and there was no doubt that Allen Pell had been the purchaser. The transaction had taken place in Boston, early in June, and the dealer had secured the license plates. Allen had registered at a local hotel of the respectable but not showy type; had registered as from New York, and was clearly remembered. Among other things he had taken the examination required in Massachusetts for a driver's license and passed it. Then one day he had driven the trailer to the hotel, put his bags in it, paid his bill and departed.

He had had no visitors and his bill showed no telephone calls, except one or two local ones, probably to the dealer. There was, however, no Allen Pell in the New York telephone directory.

I did not know this at the time; but the repercussions from that wretched press article were already manifest. It seemed to me that everyone called during the days that followed. Lucy Hutchinson came in one morning, left her umbrella in the hall, damned the weather to William, and came in to where I was trying to read by the fire.

"See here, Marcia," she said. "As one of the suspects, I certainly have a right to know something about this revolting situation."

"I don't know myself, Lucy."

"You look like death, Bob walks the floor at night, Tony looks like a scared rabbit and revokes at bridge, Howard Brooks has called off a party, we've had another crime—which ought to let me out, for I didn't know the man—and you're the one who discovers it. And at midnight, up at that camp! It doesn't make sense."

"It never did make sense," I said wanly. "But there's no mystery in my part of it, Lucy. I had tea with him the day before he disappeared, and he said something that made me wonder."

She raised the two thin lines she called her eyebrows.

205

"Tea?" she said. "In the trailer? That was going some for a Lloyd, wasn't it?"

I must have colored, for she busied herself with a cigarette.

"Sorry," she said. "He may turn up, you know. Where does he come in in all this, Marcia? I don't suppose he killed Juliette. Did he know her?"

I evaded that.

"He had found someone to support Arthur's alibi at Clinton. He didn't tell me who it was. When I learned Bullard wanted to arrest Arthur, I went up to find out."

"Leaving me to hold the bag!" she observed, without resentment. "He was gone then, was he?"

"So far as I can find out he never went back, Lucy. He left me at the top of the path. That's all I know."

"At a guess, somebody didn't want him to tell what he knew," she said shrewdly. "I'm sorry, Marcia, but it doesn't look so good, does it? If he had to be put out of the way."

"No," I said dully.

She did not stay long. This third crime, if it was one, she considered let both Arthur and herself out. She was safe anyhow, she said. She had played bridge the afternoon of Allen Pell's disappearance, and dined out that night. Before she left she gave me a long look.

"Do you happen to know if Pell was one of Juliette's discards?" she asked.

"He knew her. I think it was a good while ago."

But she only whistled softly and went out, and through the window I saw her plodding back through the rain, her feet slapping in galoshes and her umbrella low over her head.

Queer, how life went on much as usual after that. People meeting at the club, at dances, on the street.

"Any news yet about the painter fellow?"

"Haven't heard any."

I had to do something to fill in the time. One morning I took Maggie and a nervous Ellen up to the hospital suite, and we put it in order again. Maggie thought she remembered the corner where she had been when she was attacked, and that she had seemed to be looking for something. We examined it carefully, but there was nothing there. The wall was neatly papered with

206

the nursery design I remembered from my childhood, a sea of blue with ships and whales scattered over it; and the baseboard and floor were solid and intact.

"It seems so silly, Maggie," I said. "What could you have been after? There must have been something in your mind."

"I don't know, miss," she said, looking bewildered. "But I think it had to do with Mr. Arthur."

Allen Pell had been missing for fourteen anxious days by that time. Over at the sheriff's office in the Clinton courthouse all sorts of clues had been coming in, to be run down without result. And, although I did not know it, the sheriff himself was doing a bit of literary composition. I saw it later, and it ran as follows:

Dear Sir or Madam: I am interested in a Pekingese pup for my youngest child. Said dog must be housebroken and of a gentle disposition. Price not too high. Yours very truly, Russell Shand.

The address he gave was his house, not his office; and Mamie, his elderly stenographer, typed quite a number of them.

"County paid the time and I paid the postage," he told me later, when the matter came up. "Cost me about two dollars. Not so many cities that run a real society column."

Arthur had spent most of that interval at Millbank, and it was about that time, too, that I had a call from Mary Lou. Owing to the rain and cold, Junior had been sick and I had not seen her for some days. When she came in I sensed a change in her. She pulled off her driving gloves and answered my questions about the boy absently. She asked for a cup of coffee, and when it came I saw that she could hardly hold the cup.

"I've had plenty of time to think things over," she said. "I know now that Arthur didn't kill Juliette, Marcia. I was a fool ever to think it. But I do believe he knows something."

"What could he know?"

"I think he buried her," she said quietly. "Found her and buried her."

I could not think of anything to say. Once again I saw Arthur at the toolshed with that flashlight in his hand, and his stealthy re-entrance into the house that night.

"Why on earth would he do that?" I asked at last. "Why would he have to break in to get a spade? He could have got the key, easy enough. It hangs in the kitchen entry."

"Not that night," she said, with the same deadly calm. "I stopped just now and asked Mike. He had it in his pocket that night."

"But why, Mary Lou? If he hadn't killed her—"

"Because he still cared for her," she said. "You wouldn't understand, Marcia. You see, he had never forgotten her. He was devoted to me, but she was his first love." She drew a long breath. "She was everything I was not. Reckless and popular and gay. And beautiful, Marcia. Men don't forget beautiful women. Not entirely."

She began to pull on her gloves automatically.

"He never really got free of her," she said. "He never even had a chance to forget her. Every now and then he would see her picture in the newspapers, and each month when he made out her check he had to remember her all over again. So when he found her body—"

She got up, with that new maturity of hers in her face.

"Have the police examined the toolshed?" she asked.

"They've looked it over. Not very carefully. Why?"

"Because he has lost his key ring, Marcia. The gold one I gave him. He doesn't know I know it, but he has. He's worried about it. If they find it, there or near that grave, they'll arrest him. That's all they need."

She had come to ask me to find it, if I could, and that day after she had gone I examined the shed as well as I could; the lawn mowers, the hundred and one things any gardener accumulates. But it was not there. Nevertheless, as I pulled about the crocks and sacks of fertilizer I was remembering several things. Not only Arthur with the flashlight, trying to get into the shed. Long before that, with Juliette in her dressing gown and mules, and Arthur in front of her, white to the lips.

"When I look at you," he had said, "it doesn't seem possible that you would wreck a man's life as you have mine."

What had he meant by that? Was there something more

208

than the mere problem of her support? When he looked at her was he thinking of what life might have been with her had she cared for him? Then later: "God knows I loved you, but you took my pride and crushed it. You killed something in me. And now you're fastened on me like a leech, and, by heaven, I can't get rid of you."

Was Mary Lou right, and had he never been able to get rid of her? Did she haunt his mind? If men leave an indelible mark on the women who have loved them, do women do the same thing to men?

One thing that day or two of activity did for me. They filled in time, let me forget the problem which absorbed all of my days and most of my nights. That afternoon, however, it was to be brought back to me in full force, and of all people by Mrs. Pendexter.

I saw the car stop in the driveway, and a militant old figure alight and address someone inside.

"Are you getting out? Or shall I have to drag you?"

There was a brief pause. Then, slowly and unwillingly, Marjorie followed her, protesting indignantly.

"But I tell you I'm not sure."

"I'm not asking you to be sure. Who is sure about anything?" demanded the old lady dauntlessly, and prodded her into the house.

The argument was still going on when I reached the drawing room.

"Don't be a fool," Mrs. Pendexter was saying. "If you know anything now is the time to say it."

"But I don't, mother. At least I'm not positive."

"All right. Here's Marcia. Tell Marcia what you told me, and don't hold out on it either. She says she knew this Pell person, Marcia."

"Mother!" said Marjorie. "I didn't say anything of the sort. I only saw him once. I said he reminded me of someone. That's all. I don't even remember who it was he looked like."

"Go on," said the old lady inexorably.

"Well, that's all—except that I thought he knew me too. He had been painting, and he pulled down his hat and picked up his stuff. That's really all."

209

"No, it isn't," said Mrs. Pendexter. "Tell her when and where this was."

"It was on Pine Hill, the morning Juliette was—the morning she disappeared. It was close to where it happened, Marcia."

But she had really nothing much to say. She had got out of her car to gather some lupine, and was on her way back. She "hadn't wanted to be mixed up in anything" and so she had said nothing. But she had seen Allen Pell there, and later on she saw Mary Lou sitting in her car some distance away. She had not seen Lucy at all, nor Juliette.

"All that happened must have been after I left," she said. "I took the lupine home and put it in water, and— What good is all this, mother? I couldn't identify the man, and he is missing anyhow."

But I was not so certain, after they had gone. Marjorie was a direct person, with the straightforwardness of all people who like horses and the open air. I felt certain that she was holding something back, and that it was concerned with Allen Pell. She might pretend all she could, but I believed she knew who he was. Knew it well, and for some reason would not tell me.

Just what had she said, that day weeks ago when she came to see me? I spent most of the afternoon trying to remember. Then, after giving it up entirely, it came back to me that night after I had gone to bed. Something about a poor devil who had gone crazy about Juliette and took to drinking, with tragic results.

Could that have been Allen Pell? He had certainly been bitter about her. Arthur had been lucky, he said. He had only married her. And, after stating flatly that he had not killed her, there had been something about deserving a good mark for not having done so; "from the angels who keep the book" he had said.

It was possible. I knew that, lying in my bed in the dark, while Chu-Chu snored on her pillow and a sleepy gull mewed outside. And what was it the sheriff had said? "I don't know anything about this fellow. Pell may be his name, and maybe not. I don't know any better way to hide out than to take a trailer and keep moving."

I shut my eyes. There was the motive, if it ever came out. At

210

least the police might think it adequate. She had driven him to drink, and he had killed some people as a result. Then, too, why was he here, on the island? Was that accident? A coincidence? Had he followed her? Had she seen him, that day she rode into the hills and came home frightened?

I could not stay in bed. I got up and went to the telephone in my sitting room, and there called Marjorie. She was still up, she said, playing bridge; but her voice altered when I asked my question.

"I want you to tell me something," I said. "I promise to keep it to myself. Who was the man who killed those people with his car? I mean, what was his name?"

There was rather a long pause. Then:

"That's all over and done with, Marcia," she said. "Why bring it up? It was two or three years ago."

"Then it certainly won't hurt to tell me," I said urgently.

There was another pause. Then her voice again, flat but decisive.

"I've forgotten it," she said, and hung up the receiver.

When I looked out over the bay the next morning I saw that the *Sea Witch* had gone on its long-deferred cruise to New-foundland.

CHAPTER XXIV

It rained almost steadily for the next few days. Water rolled down the face of the old house like tears, and in the little pools on the upper porch I could see drowned insects floating. The islands in the bay were soft green smudges, as if someone had drawn them with a crayon and then rubbed them. The bay and the sky merged in a mutual gray, so that it was hard to tell where one ended and the other began. The tides swept along, carrying with them the flotsam of the shore, dead trees, boxes and barrels, and all day the bell buoy off Long Point rocked and rang.

The gulls had disappeared to hug a lee shore somewhere. The small pleasure craft had left or swung neglected at their moorings. Even my upper porch was bare of furniture except the swing, which creaked back and forth dismally; and I had a strange feeling of being alone with myself, as though the active world had gone and I was its lone survivor.

One day I put on a raincoat and galoshes, and walked to Eliza Edwards's in the village. It seemed to me that all our mysteries must be connected somehow, and there was a bare chance that the police had overlooked something. Eliza had little or nothing to say, however. It was clear that she resented with all her New England soul the publicity she had had, and the inability to rerent the room Helen Jordan had occupied.

She did not ask me in. We sat on her small vine-covered porch, and she pursed her mouth at my first question.

"I've told all I know. She just came, left her stuff and went out. I never saw her again."

"Surely she said something?"

"She asked where the bathroom was, and she wanted a key to the house. I said I only had one key, and I hadn't seen it for a year. Nobody in this town is a thief," she added virtuously.

"I wish you'd think back," I said urgently. "She didn't say where she was going? She walked in, ate her supper, and walked out again. Is that all?"

"She asked if I had a telephone and said she'd be back in an hour or so."

"I suppose you have no idea whom she wanted to call?"

She had not. Almost every roomer she got asked the same question. Generally she sent them to the corner drugstore. She had no idea whether Jordan had gone there or not. All she knew was that she had eaten a good dinner and never so much as said it was good, and had then gone out. She had worn a hat and carried a handbag, and she had locked her bedroom door before she left. It was evident that Helen Jordan's disappearance and death were a matter of grievance to her.

"Not to mention the police tracking in and out for days," she added somberly. "Wear and tear, I called it; but they just laughed at me. I pay my taxes on the dot, and—"

She went on for some time, but I learned something that day, although it seemed of no importance then. Eliza thought she had seen the woman before.

"She was no beauty," she said. "But I've got it in my mind that I've seen her somewhere. She was so plain that it stuck out, and it's easier to remember an ugly face than the other kind. Not lately. Must be quite a while back."

"Here? In town?"

"Might have been here. Might have been somewhere else. I don't leave the island much."

I thought back. Jordan had hardly left Sunset at all after her arrival. She had gone with Juliette once, to the hairdresser's, but that was about all. Eliza merely sniffed when I mentioned the beauty shop. She had no time for such goings-on, she said contemptuously.

But she had relaxed by that time. She agreed to let me see the room Jordan had occupied for the brief tragic interval before her death; and I added to what she called the wear and tear of her carpets by following her upstairs. The room was small and

214

bare, and a glance told me that there was nothing of any value to be discovered there. A neatly made bed, a pine bureau and chest of drawers, two chairs and a small table, and all spotlessly clean, furnished it. There was no stove or fireplace, and wherever her suitcase had stood, it was now at the police station.

It seemed difficult to believe that a woman, any woman, could slip from life into death and leave so little behind her; a letter—not addressed to her, a handful of possessions in the New York apartment, a suitcase at a police station, and this empty room.

"Was this the way she left it?" I asked.

"All but the suitcase. The police have got that. Somebody's in a good bag, if I do say it," she added darkly.

It seemed clear that Eliza had little faith in the forces of law and order. But that was all that was clear. I tried to think.

"How did she act that night?" I asked. "Did she seem excited? Or worried about anything?"

"She didn't seem the excitable kind. No. She looked kind of determined. I guess she was that sort, though."

I left the house, still puzzled. Jordan had decided that night on some course of action. She had gone to a telephone and then walked along the bay path on Long Point. She had carried the handbag, and left the key to her room with Eliza. And locked in that room had been only one thing of any possible importance; what the sheriff called the Jennifer letter.

Was it important, after all? Had she kept it merely for her own purposes, perhaps in the hope of securing a situation with "Jennifer"? I could not tell, of course. Yet it is curious that on that very morning the Jennifer of the letter was going through a difficult time of her own, in the cabin of an incoming ocean liner.

I knew that Russell Shand had always considered that the letter had some bearing on the case; but I did not know he had enlisted the New York police to help him. They had traced her name through the telephone number in that book of Juliette's, and it must have been a shock to her when two detectives from Centre Street met her ship at Quarantine.

It was a long time before I heard that story, and then it was

215

from Russell Shand himself.

"They didn't think much of me or of that letter either," he said cheerfully. "It stood out all over them; a country sheriff with two murders on his hands and maybe three, and messing them up to beat the band! The lady was Fifth Avenue and Southampton, and that griped them."

Her name, it had turned out, was Dennison, Mrs. Walter Dennison; and she traveled with a maid and a dog. What is more, she had the best suite on the ship. The detectives were uncomfortable when they realized what they were up against.

At first she thought they were ship reporters, and she received them with the proper air of resignation plus straightening her hat in case of photographs. The disillusionment must have been a shock.

"Sorry to bother you, madam. We'd like to ask a question or two."

"For the press?"

They grinned and said no. She stared at them.

"Then who are you?" she demanded.

One of them flashed a badge, and she went pale.

"If you are from the customs—"

"Nothing to do with customs, Mrs. Dennison. Did you know a Mrs. Juliette Ransom?"

Her color came back, but she still looked wary.

"I did. She is dead, isn't she?"

"Yes. You probably know the circumstances. Mrs. Dennison, we have here a copy of a letter which seems to be yours. It was found among Mrs. Ransom's effects. Will you glance over it and identify it?"

She did so, with the two men watching her. When she came to the postscript they thought she stiffened, but she handed it back calmly enough.

"It is mine," she said. "What about it?"

"Do you care to identify the man whose initial you used in that letter?"

"Certainly not. It was a purely personal matter."

"'Have just heard about L——. Do please be careful, Julie. You know what I mean.' That sounds like a warning, Mrs. Dennison. Was this L—— liable to do her bodily harm?"

216

"Of course not. Mrs. Ransom was reckless sometimes. She did a good many foolish things. I was merely telling her to behave herself."

They did not believe her.

"This L—— was a man, wasn't he?"

"Yes. That doesn't mean anything. She knew a lot of men. And now," she added haughtily, "if you'll give me a chance to get ready to leave this ship, I'd appreciate it."

They got nothing more from her as the liner moved up the river to its dock. In fact, she ordered them out of her room. Once landed she left her maid to see her trunks through the customs, and still ignoring them marched to her waiting car and got in. But she did not go to her apartment on Fifth Avenue. Some time during that ride uptown she had her bags transferred to a taxicab and quietly disappeared.

"That's what set me on the trail," said the sheriff, long after. "All along I'd thought that letter was important. Now I knew it."

It was August by that time, and August is the gay time on the island. Usually my calendar then is filled from morning until night, from club pool to lunch, from lunch to golf or a sail on the bay, and after that cocktails here and dinner there. But during the early part of that month I did little or nothing.

When it was clear I sat on this upper porch where I am today, and listlessly watched the activity in the bay. Now and then a speedboat would pass, trailing a surfboard with some youngster erect on it. Yachts came and departed, brilliant with paint, their brasswork gleaming in the sun, and once in a while I saw Lucy Hutchinson, usually the head and front of the August season, sitting lethargically on the bench by the sea wall where Bob and I had talked.

Sometimes she saw me and waved, but mostly she ignored me. She looked thin, I thought, and Bob was said to be drinking heavily.

Then one day a British battleship came in, and Tony Rutherford asked me to go to the club to help make it gay for the officers at tea. He seemed to hold no resentment for what had happened on the golf course.

"It's only tea. Put on your prettiest dress and come along;"

217

he coaxed. "We can't have all dowagers, Marcia. No use letting the English think the average age of America is over fifty. Be good, won't you?"

I went and felt better for it. Death and danger seemed far away. The uniforms were dignified, the men charming; and behind them in the harbor—as a background—was their great gray ship. I did my best, and apparently made a conquest of one of the junior officers, for I could not lose him. But as I was leaving I saw Lucy, and she drew me aside into the cardroom and closed the door.

I was shocked when I saw her, close at hand. Her smartness was gone, her face looked ravaged; and after lighting a cigarette she dropped into a chair and stared out at the crowd on the lawn.

"What do you do," she said finally, "when you think you are losing your mind?"

"You'd have plenty of company just now," I said, feeling suddenly tired and lost.

She glanced at me quickly.

"I'll change that question," she said. "What do you do when you suspect your husband of everything from unfaithfulness to murder? He denies both, of course," she added.

"I don't think he killed Juliette, Lucy," I said. "If that's what you mean."

"Why not?" She shrugged her shoulders. "He used to be in love with her, years ago. He's big enough and strong enough to do anything. And he's not been the same since she was killed. He's been like a crazy man. Of course, if he was still in love with her—"

"You don't believe that, do you? Not seriously."

"I don't know what I believe," she said. "He took her to lunch last winter. That's all he admits, but how do I know it's true?"

"A good many men take women to lunch without killing them later," I said impatiently. "Be yourself, Lucy. What if he did? You lunch with men day after day, don't you? I expect a good many of them make love to you too. It's customary. You'd be disappointed if they didn't. But you are still alive, even if you do look shot to pieces."

218

She did not resent that. She lit another cigarette and fitted it neatly into her holder before she spoke again. Then:

"I'm fond of Bob," she said slowly. "I'm— Well, it's more than that, of course. I'd have fought and killed to hold him, if it would have done any good. And after I thought the affair with her was over we were happier than we had ever been. I thought I'd got him back. He wasn't even drinking. Then it started again, last winter. He came home one night—well, plastered is as good a word as any, isn't it?—and it's been going on ever since." She turned and gave me a direct look. "Just why was Juliette murdered, Marcia? Have you any idea?"

"The general public seems to think that Arthur did it, for obvious reasons," I said bitterly.

"That's nonsense, of course. You must have some theory. Who wanted her out of the way? Was she dangerous to someone? Was she blackmailing anyone?"

"The police have been over her bank account. It's all right. If she was getting money she got it in cash."

"But you think she was spending more than she got from Arthur?"

"She always did that."

She thought that over.

"It's not like the old days," she said. "Credit's not as easy as it used to be. She had to pay some of her bills, and that crowd of hers had no use for people who couldn't spend pretty freely. Sometimes I wonder if she was blackmailing Bob."

She got up. She looked as though she had not slept for a long time; and it was typical of Juliette, I thought, to leave behind her a trail of devastated women: Mary Lou, fighting her own suspicion; Lucy, haggard and uncertain; Marjorie Pendexter, and myself. Even Jordan certainly gone to her death because of some secret knowledge she had possessed of Juliette's affairs.

Lucy was preparing to go, powdering her nose, reddening her lips; but doing it abstractedly. She looked up at me.

"These men!" she said, with a sort of sullen anger. "You love them. You do all you can for them. And then they run out on you, and you find there's another woman. He walked out with her after that time he lunched with her, and bought her a diamond bracelet!"

219

"Juliette! How do you know?"

"I know all right. His secretary paid the bill, and she wrote me the other day, to ask if I didn't want to insure it!"

There was nothing I could say. She stood still, holding her vanity case.

"What about this Allen Pell?" she said. "He's in this too, Marcia. Somewhere. Have the police any idea who the man was who went to that trailer of his just after he disappeared?"

"Nobody knows. They haven't traced him."

She drew a long breath.

"Sometimes I think I *am* going crazy," she said. "Bob was out in the car that evening. I don't even know where he went."

I found my junior officer still on duty when I went out, and I had some difficulty in getting away. Also, as a result of anxiety and the long rainy spell, I went down with a feverish cold the next day. Maggie sent for Doctor Jamieson, and it was Doctor Jamieson who added a new angle to the case of Allen Pell.

He tapped me, announced that I would live, wrote a prescription and then sat back to talk. It seemed that Agnes Dean was down again, and that Mansfield Dean was taking it very hard.

"Funny thing," he said. "These big men who marry fragile women like that and worship them! Of course she has come through a lot. Still, what's the use of nursing old griefs? Dean rates something."

It was not until he got up to go that he mentioned Allen. I remember that he looked tired that day. As I look back over this record I find that at some time or other I have said the same thing about most of us. But he looked worried too, and what he had to say put a new light on the situation.

"There's one thing the police have overlooked," he said. "Here's a strong man and a young man. I've met him now and then along the roads, and liked him. But you can count on this. Whoever hit him that afternoon was somebody he knew and trusted. He didn't expect what he got."

"But no one really knew him, doctor. Not well anyhow."

"Someone knew him too well for his own good," he said dryly, and left me to lie wretchedly in bed, thinking that over.

CHAPTER XXV

As it happened, that night ended the bad weather. When I wakened late the next morning it was to sunshine and the wailing cries of the gulls. My cold was better too, and if there had been any real cheer in the world for me just then I would have felt it over Lizzie's strong clear coffee, her crisp bacon, and a rose fresh from the garden which is Mike's occasional contribution to my breakfast tray.

After I had dressed and been bundled into the sweaters Maggie forced on me I went downstairs and out into the garden. I was still there, dutifully inspecting the Canterbury bells, when the sheriff drove in.

He took one look at my nose and shoved me back into the house.

"Looks as though you needed somebody to look after you," he said, apparently forgetting the terms on which we had last parted. "I can't even go away for a week without something happening to you."

"I didn't know you'd been away."

He tried to appear reproachful, but he only barely missed looking triumphant.

"Sure I have," he said. "Been doing some traveling too. Thought maybe you'd like the law out of your pocket for a while."

"Did you learn anything?" I asked eagerly. "About Allen Pell?"

He shook his head.

"No, but I learned a lot about something else."

He had put me into a chair in the library, and now he sat

down and looked me over.

"It's a funny world, Marcia," he said. "I don't get you people at all. I've got a farm outside Clinton, and when I breed my cattle you can bet I know all about who's who, or what's what." He looked uncomfortable then, as if he had been indelicate. He went on rather hurriedly. "Yet here's your own brother, born and brought up like royalty, and what does he do? He marries a girl he doesn't know a thing about; her folks, if any, or where she came from. All he knows is that she has a pretty face and he wants her."

"And look where it's brought him," I said bitterly.

"Well, look where it's brought her too," he said, not unreasonably. "Anyhow, once it's done it's done. Nobody looks her up. Nobody knows anything about her."

"What was the use?" I asked. "She was Arthur's wife."

"Sure she was. But did any of you know her real name was Julia, and that she'd been married before? No? I told you, I handle my cattle better than that."

I could only stare at him incredulously.

"Married before?" I gasped. "Are you trying to tell me she had a husband when she married Arthur?"

"Not necessarily. He may have died, or she may have divorced him. But let's get back to this. First of all I had to trace her, and that took time."

Nevertheless, he had done it. It still seems incredible to me, but what with the police radio and a good picture of her, added to the nation-wide publicity, he had done it. "Not alone," he said. "I had a lot of help, both in New York and elsewhere. But I've had an idea all along that this trouble didn't begin here. You Lloyds may kill—I've seen a look in *your* face once or twice I didn't like much—but I don't think you kill for money or money reasons. That set me off. Or up, if you like. I went part of the way by plane."

He seemed rather proud of that, although he gave me a detailed description of himself in the air, with a paper bag for certain emergencies and a feeling that he was being pretty much of a damned fool for the risk he was taking. "Never drew a full breath till I was down," he said. But he came back to Juliette after that.

"First thing," he explained, "she came from Kansas, and when she left there her name was not Juliette Ransom. It was Julia Ransom Bates. Her folks were dead and she lived with the old aunt she told you about. That part was true enough. She's dead too, but plenty of people remember both of them. According to them, Juliette was the usual small-town pretty girl. Decent, I guess, but shaking her curls and making eyes at the traveling men in the hotel, and driving the local boys crazy. She wasn't popular with the women, but the men fell for her like ripe apples.

"Anyhow she was eighteen when she lit out one day with a salesman for something or other, one of the hotel crowd, and she married him the next day in Kansas City. I saw the record."

I said nothing. I was seeing her that day when Arthur brought her into this very house, looking young and innocent and appealing.

"Well, that's the story," he went on. "She never came back, the aunt died, and the next line-up we get she's in New York studying music; or pretending to. She's smart and she's good-looking, and Arthur meets her and marries her. Then when she gets her divorce from him, she doesn't go back to Bates as a name. Not stylish enough, most likely. She's not Julia Bates. She's Juliette Ransom, which is the name she used when Arthur married her."

It was amazing, all of it. What a long way she had gone, this Julia Ransom Bates Something-or-other Lloyd; from the main street of a small town, ogled by the boys on the corner and eyed appreciatively by men in hotel windows, to our house on Park Avenue and this one on the island; and later on to that gay and exotic crowd which lived so fast and precariously in the night clubs and bars of wherever it happened to be.

One thing was certain. When Arthur brought her to us as his shy young bride, she had been already an experienced woman. "Try to forgive me," she had said to Mother. "I love him so terribly." She had been no mean actress, Juliette.

But the sheriff was not through. He reached into his pocketbook and drew out a letter.

"There's something else, Marcia," he said. "Helen Jordan came from that town too. If Juliette was the pretty girl of the

223

place, Helen was the ugly duckling. Worked in a grocery store, had no family and no prospects. Then two or three years ago she sold what furniture she had and went east. She wrote one or two letters back to a woman she knew, and I got hold of this one. Maybe it means something, maybe not."

He gave it to me. It was written in a surprisingly good hand, and was undated.

> Dear Mabel: Well here I am, and I don't mind saying it is a new world and no mistake. Day is night and night is day, with my lady sleeping until all hours, and the place looking like hell upset no matter what I do.

There followed a long description of Juliette's apartment, her clothes and so on. But the last two paragraphs seemed pertinent:

> You would hardly know Julia. She's looking prettier than ever, and that's going some! But she has something on her mind. She acts scared, and you know that isn't like her. Some trouble about a man, I suppose. There are plenty of them.
>
> As for me, I am sort of companion and what have you when we're alone, and a maid otherwise, black silk apron and all. But it is easy and I am seeing life as I never knew it was lived. And what a life! So I don't mind. I'll write you more later.

I looked up. It was, I knew, a pretty accurate picture of life as Juliette had lived it, but it told me nothing new except that part about being frightened. Still, two or three years ago was a long time.

"Is that all?" I asked. "Were there any other letters?"

"One or two, but about the same. This woman seems to have been the only friend she left behind. She never mentioned Juliette's being scared again, if she was scared. It looks as though, whatever it had been, it was over."

"It may not have been," I said. "She was nervous when she came here. She said she was in trouble."

He looked doubtful.

"It must have been some trouble," he observed, "to last almost three years."

He went back to Allen Pell then. All search on the island had been abandoned, but he said it was still going on farther afield. Although I knew that that might mean nothing, it gave me at least a margin of hope.

And then, only a few days later, I learned that he was still alive!

Arthur was at Millbank, and I was alone in the house. Also our spell of good weather had broken. Another storm was threatening, and Maggie, who is afraid of lightning, insisted on closing the house early. The result was that the house was stuffy, although it was cool outside, and when the storm finally broke I was in the morning room, with the door open onto the garden trying to read.

Suddenly I heard Tate shout, and the sound of running feet, followed by a shot and excited voices.

"Lemme go. I haven't done anything."

"What did you want in that house?"

"Jeez! Can't a man ask to sleep somewhere out of this rain? Take your hands off me."

I went to the front door, to find Tate marching along the driveway toward it, holding by the arm a disreputable-looking individual, unshaven, drenched with rain and shivering with cold and terror.

"Shooting at me," he said resentfully. "Shooting at me for ringing a doorbell. Who are you anyhow?"

"That's my business," said Tate, and asked me if he might use the telephone. There was one in the hall, and still holding to his prisoner he called the police station. The man stood sullenly beside him, dripping small pools onto the carpet, and I felt sorry for him. But when I asked him if he would like some brandy he shook his head.

"And get put away for being drunk and disorderly!" he said. "No, thanks, miss. This cop's got nothing on me and he knows it."

The servants had been aroused, and were appearing in various states of undress. I managed to get rid of them.

"It's nothing," I said. "Just a man looking for shelter. There's nothing to worry about."

When I came back the tramp was looking at me. He had sharp little eyes, for all his evident fright.

"Any reason why I can't stand by that fire in there?" he asked. "I've just come out of a hospital."

He looked it. He was wasted and pale, and after some argument with Tate he was allowed to warm himself in the library while a car was sent to pick him up. He was still there, resigned but unhappy, when the car arrived.

The incident seemed unfortunate but unimportant, my only feeling being that at least the local jail was dry. As a matter of fact, he was kept overnight and dismissed the next morning, with a stern adjuration to leave the town and the island at once. But this was to prove a mistake, as it turned out. I know now that he had not come to ask for shelter. He had come on a definite errand. But I saw him out with some relief that night, and it was not until the next morning that I understood.

I had not gone to sleep until toward daylight, and the unfortunate result was that I slept late. When Maggie's disapproving face appeared with my breakfast tray I thought the displeasure was for me. It was not. Propped against the coffeepot was a soiled envelope, dry but showing signs of having been wet, and with my name and address, almost obliterated, printed on it with a pencil.

"That tramp must have left it," said Maggie stiffly. "William sent it up, dirt and all. It was behind a cushion on the library couch."

She stood over me, filled with curiosity, and she was indignant when I sent her out before I opened it. Like all personal maids long in one position, she lived a purely vicarious life, which was mine, and normally I had no secrets from her. But I had a strange feeling about that letter, although when she had gone and I opened the envelope I found myself at first unable to grasp what it contained. There was in it a single sheet of note paper, without date or place, and on it merely seven words, also printed in pencil and with a shaky hand. They were: "Your man is Jonas Tripp, of Clinton."

But the signature was unmistakable. It was what looked like

226

a bus, but might have been meant for a trailer.

My first reaction was purely nervous. So great was my relief that I lay back on the pillows and found myself shaking all over. Allen was alive. Whatever happened to him, he was still alive.

It was some time before I remembered the note and looked at it again. What man? The tramp? There were plenty of Tripps around, but I had never heard of a Jonas. "Your man is Jonas Tripp, of Clinton." Then at last I understood. Jonas Tripp was the alibi witness Allen Pell had found, and Arthur was saved. I felt a wave of relief that set me to trembling again.

All this had taken time, and when I rushed to the telephone in my sitting room it was to find that the tramp had already been reprimanded and released. I tried for Russell Shand then, but he was out somewhere; and so I spent most of the morning in my car, desperately trying to find my man on one of the roads leading to the bridge and the mainland. But after the fashion of his kind he was evidently avoiding the main highways. I did not find him, and I have never seen him since.

I shall always remember that day as one of alternate hope and anxiety. I called Arthur at Millbank and gave him the name of Jonas Tripp, but I hadn't the heart to mention the news of Juliette's first marriage. He seemed rather skeptical, but agreed to try to locate him. But my first relief about Allen Pell had been succeeded by fear. He was ill somewhere, or hurt. The tramp said he had just come out of a hospital, and I felt sure that that was where Allen had given him the note. But why not have said so? Why not have told me where he was? Perhaps the messenger was to have given me the details. Still, why the caution of that note, printed and unsigned?

It dawned on me then that, wherever he was, he did not want to be discovered, that he was deliberately in hiding. Why? From whom? The police?

It was a bad time, not improved by a brief call from the sheriff himself late that afternoon. He was in a hurry. He did not come in, and I talked to him in the driveway beside his rattletrap car.

"What about this tramp last night?" he inquired. "Kinda queer some ways, wasn't it?"

227

"I don't know. We have them now and then," I said evasively.

"Light in the back of the house and so on?"

"I suppose so. I think William was still downstairs."

He fiddled with his hat.

"Lights on and servants up," he said. "Yet this fellow comes to the front door. What's more, the island's not too friendly to vagrants and they know it; but he comes right along to this house. Looks as though he might have had a reason, doesn't it?"

I must have looked uncomfortable, for he gave me a hard look.

"I didn't ask his reasons," I said. "He looked cold and he was certainly wet. I suppose he saw the lights of the house from the road."

"He passed a dozen other places before he got to this one."

But he asked no more questions, although he made a few uncomplimentary remarks on our local police for releasing the man before he himself had heard about him. I had an uneasy feeling as he did it that he was studying me, but at last he got back into the car and settled himself.

"Don't be surprised at anything you hear," he said, almost airily. "At least it's made Bullard happy, and that's something."

I did not know what he meant. It did not greatly concern me at the time. I was busy wondering if I had been right in not telling him about that note; and when the news came, at four o'clock the next afternoon, it was simply stupefying.

Fred Martin had been picked up at his house near the golf club and taken to Clinton for interrogation.

CHAPTER XXVI

It seemed incredible. Everybody knew Fred and liked him. Liked Dorothy too. It was almost time for her baby to come, and at least a dozen women I knew were knitting an afghan for it. Not Fred. There must be some mistake. He had been at the club for five years or so, and his sturdy figure and old cap were as familiar to us as the water hazard at the eighth hole, or as the very greens he watched so carefully.

Tony Rutherford brought me the news. He had been at the club when it happened, and he looked more indignant than I had ever seen him.

"It's an outrage," he said. "These county policemen! What do they know? Why on earth pick on Fred? I doubt if he ever saw Juliette, and as for the Jordan woman—"

He merely voiced the resentment of the entire colony. Yet it had its advantages, that arrest of Fred Martin; at least so far as we were concerned. It was obvious that if Fred was guilty Arthur was innocent, and the result was that almost the entire summer colony, by ones and twos, dropped in for tea that afternoon.

That shift in public opinion could have amused me once, but now it did not seem to matter. What started as an informal gathering turned rapidly into an indignation meeting. People continued to come, and I remember that we ran out of cake almost at once, and that William was dodging about frantically, carrying cinnamon toast and anything else Lizzie could fix in a hurry.

It was entirely futile, of course. Nobody knew precisely why Fred had been detained, except that it had to do with our murders. Even that was partly surmise, based on Dorothy's hysterical statement that he had nothing to do with them. Mansfield Dean, driving past Fred's house, had heard someone hysterically crying, and had stopped his car. He found Dorothy alone, face down on her bed, wailing that Fred was innocent, and that the police had come and taken him away while he was eating his lunch.

He told that story himself, standing with a teacup in his hand and looking unhappy at the recollection. Part of it we knew. Fred spent his winters at a Florida club and his summers with us. The club provided a small house, and he earned a fair amount by giving lessons. He was a natural golf player, starting as a caddy years before in some Middle Western state. Then in Florida about two years before he had met Dorothy. She had been a schoolteacher, young and a bit above him in some ways, but devoted to him.

The rest of the story came from Dorothy herself, sobbed out to Mr. Dean as she lay on her bed.

According to her, Fred had been the same as usual that summer. Maybe a little more silent—he was a cheerful man ordinarily—but she had laid that to the trouble on the island. He did not like to leave her alone at night. When he joined the searchers he had made her lock herself in.

But, still according to her, Fred was as bewildered as everybody else at the mystery. She would see him sometimes in the evening, apparently trying to puzzle the thing out. Now and then he spoke of it.

"Do you think he had ever known Mrs. Ransom?" Mansfield Dean had asked her.

She shook her head. No. How could he? She had been gone before he came to the club. Possibly he had seen her in Florida, but what could that mean? She, Juliette, wouldn't know him. She might have met him on the golf course, but she didn't play golf, did she?

It was pitiable, but it answered no questions. True, Fred could easily reach the bridle path from the club. True also, he liked to hike and was often seen on free afternoons up in the hills. But there it ended. It was incredible that he had murdered Juliette and disposed of her body in Loon Lake. It was equally incredible that he had killed Helen Jordan on the bay path, got a boat, tied a rope around her neck and towed her out to sea. Not Fred, giving his patient lessons, standing cheerfully with his hands in his pockets and saying:

"See what you did? Lifted that shoulder again!"

I left them there, and went to the telephone. Dorothy said he had not come back, and I knew she was still crying. I called Mrs. Curtis and asked her to go there and look after things, and when I returned it was to hear our amateur detectives still arguing back and forth, and Mrs. Pendexter's high thin voice.

"I'm no murderer," she said. "Not but what I'd like to be now and then. But whoever disposed of the Jordan woman was a fool."

"Why?"

"That boat had an anchor in it, didn't it? Why didn't he tie it to the body? Even I would know enough to do that, if I'd killed a woman."

"Are you sure you didn't?" somebody asked; and in the laughter that followed the party broke up.

Mansfield Dean was the last to go. He had waited deliberately, and with his car at the door he asked me if I would go up to dinner at the house with him.

"Just as you are," he said. "We're not fashionable, Miss Lloyd. We dine early when we're alone. Agnes is better, and I don't like to think of you here by yourself. After all," he added, "you should celebrate a little. Whatever is behind this Fred Martin affair, it doesn't hurt your brother's case."

I went, waiting only to brush back my hair and wash a bit. After my old car, his big limousine was luxuriously soft, and I leaned back and shut my eyes.

"That's right," he said. "Try to forget it. We won't talk about it tonight."

He lived up to that; a fine man, I thought, Mansfield Dean, with all his money; and a comforting one. Not a very happy one though. When I opened my eyes as we swung into the driveway I saw him as I had seen him the day I met him on the path above his house; with his head bent and his face a mask of sadness.

It altered as soon as I sat up.

231

"Here we are," he said. "A cocktail will make you feel better." He put a large friendly hand over mine. "Remember, no mysteries tonight. Just a little gossip, eh?"

As a result, for three hours or so that night I listened to his big voice booming, ate delicious food at a bright table in a bright room, and tried to forget my troubles.

Agnes Dean was quiet. Now and then her husband tried to draw her into the conversation, but it was as though she had to bring herself back from a far distance. He found occasion to tell me when she left the room after dinner that Doctor Jamieson was seriously worried about her, and I sensed tragedy in his voice.

"I don't think he is very hopeful," he said. "A man builds a life, works and gets somewhere; and then all at once he knows it doesn't matter. There are other things . . ."

His voice trailed off, and the next minute he was bellowing for hot water. "This coffee's like ink." And Agnes Dean was back in the room again.

He walked home with me that night. He was not sorry for himself. I could see that. But he talked about his wife. They had come to the island because of the stimulating air, he said; but her condition was partly mental. She should have been kept in bed, but inactivity depressed her. "I suppose I ought not to be telling you my troubles," he added apologetically. "You have enough of your own."

It was one of our rare warm summer evenings. Usually sunset sees a chill in the air, but that night was lovely. He stopped once, I remember, and looked up at the stars.

"Queer," he said, "but a sky like that always makes me feel that there is a God after all."

I knew what he meant. He was facing the death of his wife, and was trying to comfort himself; an unimaginative man, given to having his own way in life, and now confronting something he could not control.

There was a message from Mrs. Curtis waiting for me when I got back. The police were still holding Fred, a detective had come over with a warrant and searched the house, and Dorothy was sick. Mrs. Curtis had sent for the doctor.

I took the car and went out at once. It did not require much

232

experience to know what was happening, and I sent for a nurse from the hospital immediately. I stayed throughout the night, and just at dawn Dorothy's baby was born, a son.

I remember Dorothy's expression when we told her. It was almost defiant.

"I'm calling him Fred," she said, "after his father."

It was some days before I learned the full details of that arrest. They had taken Fred at noon. Russell Shand and a deputy had gone for him, calling him away from the lunch table.

"We want to ask you a few questions, Fred," the sheriff said. "No use bothering your wife. Better come along quietly."

Fred had not seemed surprised.

"Does this mean that I'm under arrest?" he asked.

"Not unless you won't come otherwise."

He had gone back for his cap, and Dorothy saw him.

"I'll be back in an hour or two, honey," he said.

She protested.

"What is it?" she asked. "You haven't finished your lunch."

He told her he was not hungry, but she followed him to the door. The two men were on the porch, and she saw them. She knew them both, and she faced them gallantly, her distorted body rigid.

"What do you want him for?" she demanded. "He hasn't done anything."

"Nothing to be excited about, Mrs. Martin," said the sheriff gently. "Just want to have a little talk with him."

But she looked at Fred, and was suddenly terrified. He was like a man going to his execution; stiff, and as if he did not really see her, or indeed see anything at all.

"You're arresting him! How dare you? How dare you come to this house and do a thing like that? Everybody knows him. Knows he's incapable of anything wrong."

Fred turned to her then and put his arms around her.

"It's all right, honey," he said huskily. "Don't get excited. Remember the kid."

That was his good-bye to her. He turned around and waved to her from the car. She did not wave back; she stood gazing after him, as though she would never see him again.

233

They took him to Clinton, and to the courthouse there. They were all silent on the way over. Once Fred asked to stop and buy some cigarettes, and the deputy went into the store with him. At the courthouse he was taken to the sheriff's office. Bullard and a couple of detectives were waiting, but so far as I can learn it was Russell Shand who asked that first amazing question.

"Just answer this straight, Fred," he said. "When and where did you marry Julia Bates?"

He must have known all along that it was coming; that long-dead past of his, rising now to confront him. Nevertheless, it was some time before he answered.

"In nineteen-twenty-three," he said thickly. "We ran away."

"How long did you stay together?"

"Less than a year. I was traveling then, selling sporting goods, and playing some golf on the side. I didn't like the way she carried on while I was on the road."

"So you left her?"

"It was about an even split. We were both satisfied."

"Was there a divorce?"

"She wrote me she'd got one. In Reno."

"But that's all. You got no papers?"

"Well, I was on the road a good bit. Things get lost. No. I never got any."

"When and why did you change your name?"

He looked surprised at that.

"I didn't change it. It was Theodore, but everybody called me Fred. I don't know why. Guess my mother started it. She didn't—" he gulped—"she didn't like the other."

Then they pulled their trump card. Bullard did it, leaning forward, his plump face vindictive.

"Isn't it a fact," he said, "that you afterwards learned there had been no divorce? And that you learned it from Mrs. Ransom herself?"

He was silent for a long time. The room was still, except for the ticking of a wall clock. Then he shrugged his shoulders.

"That's right," he said. "I didn't know it until she came here this summer."

"You were married by that time. Your wife was going to have a child. Then Mrs. Ransom saw you, and told you. Your wife was not your wife. Your child would be illegitimate. And so you killed her."

He jumped to his feet.

"It's a lie," he shouted. "I wanted to kill her. God knows she deserved it. I could hardly keep my hands off her. But as God is my witness, I never touched her."

That was Bullard. When the sheriff took up the interrogation he was less brutal.

"Why did she tell you, Fred?" he inquired. "She was sitting pretty, the way I see it. As the divorced wife of Arthur Lloyd she was drawing a fat alimony. If it came out that the marriage to Arthur Lloyd wasn't legal she stood to lose it, didn't she?"

"She knew I wouldn't talk. How could I?"

"That wasn't the question. Why did she tell you?"

"She wanted money," he said sullenly.

"Did she come to the island for that purpose?"

"No. She didn't know I was here. I just happened to meet her. I'd been walking. She was riding, and I nearly dropped dead when I saw her."

Bullard leaned forward again.

"Where was that? That meeting?"

"Up in the hills," said Fred defiantly. "I'd hiked up there, and we met. I think she was scared at first. She looked that way. She didn't have much to say either. Just 'Hello, Fred. What are you doing here?' But she must have thought it over. She called me at the club the next day, and I met her later on. That was when she told me about the divorce."

"And asked for money?"

"She'd talked to somebody. Mr. Rutherford, maybe. He knew I'd saved a bit. I'd asked him what to do with it. I didn't know about her alimony then. I didn't even know she'd married Mr. Lloyd. I didn't know anything about her at all. What I wanted was to keep her quiet, until—"

"And you did keep her quiet," said Bullard roughly.

They went over and over that part of the story. Juliette had not followed him to the island. She hadn't known he was there. The idea of getting money from him must have been a

235

secondary one. After all, the little he had wouldn't amount to much. But he had thought she looked worried. She had said something about getting all she could lay her hands on and then leaving the country. He hadn't paid much attention to that. She had always threatened to go somewhere else when things did not suit her.

It was then that they switched to Helen Jordan.

"Did you know her?"

"No. That is, there was a girl in Julia's town by that name, or something like it. I never knew her."

"Did you know she was here with Mrs. Ransom?"

"No. Not until she disappeared."

"Ever see her?"

"Never."

"But it would be natural, if Mrs. Ransom saw you, that she would mention it to this Jordan woman?"

"How do I know? I tell you I hadn't seen her for years." His voice rose. "She'd changed her name to Juliette Ransom, and that didn't mean a thing to me."

They switched again. Had he a telephone? On the night Helen Jordan disappeared had she called him up? Did he meet her that same night on the bay path? Could he run a motor launch?

He must have grown dizzy with that interrogation, going on as it did for hours. They let him smoke, but he had had no lunch. When they brought in two or three other men and lined him up with them he was unsteady on his feet. And he was apparently utterly bewildered when they brought in a man from the camp on Pine Hill and asked him to look them over.

"Size and build," said the sheriff. "We're not asking for a positive identification."

The man was cautious. He eyed them all, even asked them to turn around. In the end he nodded and was taken out of the room. Not until long after did Fred know that he had selected him as having the general proportions of the mysterious visitor to Allen Pell's trailer, the day he disappeared.

They held him. Even the sheriff knew the motive was there. They put him in a cell that night, and at least they saw that he had a decent meal. But he did not eat it. He sat with his head in his hands, wondering about Dorothy, wondering how to get out of the trouble he was in. It had hit him suddenly, whereas the authorities had had several days to prepare; ever since the sheriff's return, in fact. For in one of Jordan's letters which he had not shown me was the name of Fred Martin.

"Things have certainly changed," Jordan had written, "since the time when she ran away with Fred Martin. You'd think, to see her, that she had never heard of him! Or of Reno."

They had had time to look up the records too; time enough to have the records at Reno checked, and to discover that no such divorce was recorded there; time to check over Fred's activities also. He told them that on the night of Jordan's murder he was at home with Dorothy, and that on the morning Juliette disappeared he gave a golf lesson at nine-thirty.

But it was not far from the club to the bridle path. He would have had time to do what was done, and be back for the lesson. And so far as Allen Pell was concerned, he admitted that he had been in the hills that afternoon.

He maintained, however, that he had not gone near the camp, nor had he even seen the trailer. And as far as going there that night, he denied it absolutely.

"Why would I go there?" he asked. "I'd seen the Pell fellow around, but I'd never talked to him. I didn't even know his name until there was all this fuss about him."

It was some weeks before I saw that record, taken down in shorthand by a clerk from Bullard's office and later transcribed. It seemed rather pitiful to me. Bullard was exultant. After Fred had been taken away he leaned back in his chair and grinned at the sheriff.

"There's the case!" he said. "Sewed up in a bag."

The sheriff lit his pipe before he answered.

"Maybe," he said. "Fellow looks guilty as hell. But it seems to me the bag isn't big enough, Bullard."

"What do you mean by that?"

"Doesn't hold it all. Too many odds and ends left over. What about that letter Helen Jordan carried away and locked up in her suitcase? You can't get an 'L' out of either Theodore or Fred Martin. And what's the idea of wiping the fingerprints off that trailer? Who got away with Pell anyhow? Martin didn't even know him. And to go way back, who tried to get into the Lloyd house, and did get in? Got in more than once, maybe; once to tear up the place, and the second time to throw Marcia Lloyd's maid down the stairs—or whatever happened to her. Who broke into that apartment in New York and went over the Ransom woman's effects?"

That last was a mistake. Bullard laughed.

"I thought you said Fred Martin was in New York that week. Sure he would go there. He'd killed her. He had to be sure there were no other letters out of that past of his, no marriage certificate. He'd done the job. Now he had to mop up after it."

CHAPTER XXVII

All that took place, of course, in Clinton. But I have said that this was a case of human reactions and motivations, rather than of clues; of the effect of crime on a group of normal people, neither better nor worse than their fellows. And the immediate effect of all this on Arthur was shattering.

Save that Fred was under arrest in connection with the murders nothing else was generally known. Sometime that evening the sheriff drove to Millbank and saw Arthur. He stopped his car outside on the road and went up to the cottage; and through the window he saw Junior in his night clothes, hanging onto his father and shouting for him to play, with Mary Lou standing by.

The sheriff is a sentimental man, so he went back to his car again and sat there for a while, smoking his pipe. Then, when the lights went on upstairs he went back to the cottage. Arthur was alone, and he stepped inside and spoke to him.

"Mind if I see you for a minute, Arthur? It's not official."

He smiled, and Arthur grinned back, rather wryly.

"Sit down," he said. "And since it's not official, how about a drink?"

The sheriff shook his head.

"I'd as soon see you outside. I have an idea you won't like what I've got to say."

"I thought it wasn't official."

"Well, it's not, at that. But it's damned unpleasant if it's true."

They went out together; and on the lawn, sitting side by side on a bench, Arthur heard that story. What passed through his

239

mind I do not know. Perhaps he was seeing Juliette, in that festive hat and frock she had worn at their wedding; looking out with bland childlike eyes and solemnly taking him for her husband, when she already had one. Certainly that incredible duplicity of hers was the first thing he mentioned.

"Married!" he said. "To Fred Martin! I can't believe it. I don't believe it."

Then he sensed something further.

"But look here," he said. "You don't mean—" He steadied himself. "She had divorced him, of course."

The sheriff knocked his pipe against the arm of his chair.

"Well, that's it, Lloyd," he said. "We don't know for sure. She wrote to Fred that she'd been to Reno, but there's no record there. And when she saw him here she said there hadn't been any divorce at all."

Arthur sat still, in a stunned silence.

"Good God!" he said. "And I lived with her for years!"

That was his first thought. It was later that he remembered the alimony, the constant nagging worry about money for her, his continuous anxieties, even the deprivations. It must have been a bitter pill to swallow. He had paid her a small fortune, and if the sheriff was right she had not been entitled to it.

I believe he did not go to bed at all that night. Toward morning Mary Lou wakened, and found him in the cottage living room.

"What in the world is the matter?" she asked. "It's four o'clock."

But he could not tell her. Not the truth anyhow.

He reached up and pulled her down on his knee.

"My darling," he said. "I have just learned something that—well, that bothers me."

"What?"

"Apparently Juliette had been married before I met her."

She stared at him.

"So that's the woman you couldn't forget!" she said. "A liar and a cheat! A cheap woman, hiding her past and carrying on with anybody who attracted her! What fools men are!"

She was sorry afterwards. She cried and he tried to comfort

240

her. At last he carried her up to their room and put her into her bed; but when she moved over and made room for him he kissed her and went away again.

Juliette had made a fool and then a tool out of him. But it was not only that. Jonas Tripp was still away, his alibi for the murder still uncorroborated; and sitting alone that night, with Mary Lou and Junior asleep upstairs, he wondered if Juliette had not provided a new and convincing motive for his having killed her.

There was plenty of activity now. One night Tate did not appear, and I gathered that with Fred under lock and key in the jail at Clinton we were supposed to be safe again. Then suddenly there came real news of Allen Pell. On the third day after Fred Martin's arrest a hospital a hundred miles down the coast reported a case which might or might not have been the missing man. At least both the date and the appearance of the man in question coincided. A detective, sent there at once, brought back the details.

It was a curious story. On the night of Allen's disappearance, or rather about two o'clock in the morning, the night porter on duty had heard the bell ringing frantically, and ran to the front door. There was a car in the driveway, and two men were on the steps, one lying still and the other bending over him. The one on the steps was unconscious and bleeding from a wound on the head.

The stooping man did not straighten. He was holding a handkerchief to the wound, and he spoke in a husky voice.

"I struck this fellow with my car," he said. "Better get some help and carry him in."

The porter went to get an orderly, and when the two came back with a stretcher the injured man was alone. Both car and driver had gone.

That was the story, belated as it was. The porter could describe neither the automobile nor the man who had driven it. The incident itself was not unusual. Motorists were not infrequently moved to pity but anxious to escape recognition; and the injury was not a fatal one. Pell—if it was Pell—had had a bad concussion and a deep surface cut at the back of his head.

241

They had put him in a semipublic ward, where he had lain in a stupor for several days. When he came out of it he did not know where he was.

"How did I get here?" he asked the nurse. "What happened to me?"

"A car hit you," she told him.

"And where is this? Where am I?"

He seemed bewildered when she explained, but he asked no more questions. He gave the name of Henry Lewis, and said he had no fixed residence. As to his injury, he said that the last he remembered he had been on a road some miles from a hospital, and that he knew nothing more. The intern who dressed the wound the night he was brought in said, however, that it appeared to be several hours old. The blood was clotted and had changed in color.

He was impatient to get up and leave, but it was two weeks or so before he was up and about. He insisted on going, and as he had still some money in his pocket they let him go.

"Some money?" asked the detective. "How much?"

"He had two hundred dollars when he came in. I thought later maybe the fellow who brought him put it there. Lewis seemed surprised to find it. He had about a hundred left, I think, after he paid his bill. The rate is low here in the wards."

There was apparently no doubt that it had been Allen. He answered the description, even to the slacks and sweater I remembered so well. But there was no further trace of him. Once more radio and teletype sent out their description, without result, of his weight, height, coloring, and even of his clothing. The press played up the story, and he was generally believed to have been the third victim of the unknown killer.

I was entirely certain myself that it had been Allen. It tied up with the tramp, who had been in a hospital himself; but though relieved, I was still anxious. And the story, as the sheriff pointed out, was not consistent.

"Why the Henry Lewis stuff?" he demanded. "If he is straight, why not come back here and tell what happened to him? The papers are full of it. And what about this tale of his, of being on a road some miles from that hospital? How did he get there? His car and trailer are still here."

"He is alive anyhow," I said inadequately.

"Alive where? See here, Marcia," he said. "You were a friend of his—if that's the word, after seeing the way you took his disappearance! Did he ever tell you anything about himself?"

"Nothing—except that he didn't like the police."

He grinned wryly at this.

"May have his reasons for that," he said. "May have had his reasons for the trailer too. It's a pretty anonymous way to live. No permanent location. No neighbors to watch. Just trundling along from place to place. A fellow could hide out that way pretty much as he pleased; especially if he knew somebody was after him." He smiled. "When I take this to Bullard he'll say Fred Martin was after him!"

Fred was not without friends during those days. I was looking after Dorothy. The baby was adorable, but she herself still lay in bed, her face white against the pillows, and the nurse reported that she could not eat. But the golf club had taken up a subscription for Fred's defense, and retained a lawyer for him. His name was Standish, and on learning the Pell story he gave it to the press.

"Nothing," he was quoted as saying, "will be explained until we know why this man Pell was injured and then spirited away. Martin did not know him, and he has a clear alibi for that night. He and his wife were at the late movies, and had ice-cream sodas at the drugstore afterwards. I demand that this man be produced and made to tell his story."

But Standish was a voice crying in the wilderness. Demand or no demand, a special session of the grand jury indicted Fred a few days later.

I know something of what took place there. Little Bullard, pompous and pontifical: "Gentlemen of the grand jury: As prosecutor of this county it becomes my duty to present to you a most unhappy and sensational crime. In this district, known for its freedom from grave derelictions of the law, there took place, on the eleventh day of June, last, the murder of an innocent woman. That this murder was followed by a second

243

one is not within our purview today. We are concerned only with the original crime, the motive for which crime, brutal beyond my imagination to portray, we will endeavor to show you as this session proceeds. On this day the victim, known as Juliette Ransom, went to her death, and we will show you that this death was caused by an injury to the head, inflicted by a heavy weapon.

"For fear she was not dead, however, her body was then placed in Loon Lake, where flood waters carried it later on to where it was recovered, or near by. An attempt had been made to conceal the body in a shallow grave, but this attempt failed."

"Through the efforts of the police certain facts have been discovered which will be presented to you in due time, both by the police and by various witnesses. These facts point to a certain individual as being guilty of this crime, and after hearing the testimony it is your duty to decide whether or not to present a true bill against him."

"Gentlemen of the grand jury, the case is now in your hands."

The twenty-three men sat in their hard chairs and watched him. They knew him. Knew he needed a scapegoat for the case; but knew also that by that time all the country wanted a scapegoat. Known as the Rock Island murders, the crimes had been exploited from coast to coast. Nor, I dare say, were they ignorant of the reporters, gathered outside in the halls and eagerly searching the faces of the witnesses. An indictment was a story, the big story of the summer when the news was short. Wires had been leased, there was a radio sound truck in the street, and photographers crowded the pavement and halls.

I have nothing to say against the grand jury. It had been put on the stage and given its lines. Even its props had been provided: the grisly photographs of Juliette as she lay in her grave, Lucy's golf club, which she had left at the scene of the crime, the wrist watch found on the hillside, that sodden cigarette case rescued from the lake.

There were not many witnesses: the detective who had found the body, the Boy Scout who had located the watch, the two doctors who had conducted the post-mortem; and a few others, including Ed Smith, to say that she had been in good spirits when he put her on her horse that morning of her death. But there was put into the record that damning testimony of her early marriage to Fred Martin, and her statement to him that there had been no divorce.

The verdict was settled then and there, although the session lasted two full days.

I was the one selected to carry the news to Dorothy. She lay in her bed, painfully thin, looking at me with sunken red-rimmed eyes. But she was intelligent. I did not have to tell her.

"They've indicted him, haven't they?" she said. And when my face told her the truth, she still held on to her self-control.

"He didn't do it, of course," she went on drearily. "He might have wanted to. She had played him a dirty trick, the worst anybody could. And what about the baby?" Her voice broke. "That makes it worse for Fred, doesn't it? But he never did it, Miss Lloyd. Never. He was too kind, too gentle. If it wasn't for the baby I wouldn't want to live."

She would carry on, I knew, whatever happened. Her child might not be legitimate, but it was Fred's and hers. I found myself quietly crying as I got into the car that day and drove back to Sunset.

Arthur went back to New York and his neglected law practice that night. I could see that he still seethed with resentment against the trick Juliette had played on him. And although he liked Fred, he thought he was probably guilty.

"I wanted to kill her myself," he said. "If he had more guts than I had—"

It was that same night that the *Sea Witch* came back. I looked out at the harbor to see it at its mooring, and later in the day I had an unexpected visit from Howard Brooks.

He began without preliminary.

"What's all this about Martin?" he asked. "All I get is fury from Mrs. Pendexter and a sort of general hysteria from the rest. Did he do it? Kill Juliette Ransom, I mean?"

"I don't think he did. No."

"Suppose you begin at the start, Marcia," he said. "What have they got on him?"

I told him as best I could. He sat very still, his face expressionless, until I had finished.

245

"Thanks a lot," he said. "That damned wireless of mine broke down the day after we left. I've been pretty much cut off."

Then he went, getting into his car and driving off without further explanation; but I thought he looked strange when he left; uneasy and apprehensive.

CHAPTER XXVIII

Apparently our murders were solved to the public's satisfaction at last. The reporters went away again, and we had almost a feverish round of gaiety, part of it out of sheer relief and part of it because the season was coming to a close. For early September would see the colony largely dissipated, to meet later perhaps in Palm Beach or California or the Riviera, or not to meet at all until next summer.

Except for those two graves in the cemetery, Allen Pell's impounded car and trailer in the local garage, and Fred Martin staring at nothing in that cell of his in the county jail, everything was apparently as it should be. There was no warning of further trouble to come, and indeed my own particular cloud began to lift, leaving me happier than I had been all summer. The first thing to happen was a note from Allen. It had an undecipherable postmark, and the message was brief. Merely, "Don't worry. All my love." The signature was a seal's head, rising above the water; and from that time on I watched the bay carefully.

The other thing was the return of Jonas Tripp. All along I had felt that the sheriff did not consider the case closed. When he telephoned me that Tripp was back I realized that Arthur must have told him about his alibi. I went to Clinton to see the man. I found him in his back yard, peacefully inspecting a row of cabbages; a positive little man with most astonishing tufts of hair emerging, brush fashion, from his ears and nose. But he confirmed Arthur's alibi without reservation.

"Sure I saw him," he said. "He was sound asleep, but I knew him all right. I remember wondering what he was doing there."

247

Tripp had gone to Canada to visit his wife's people, and had not known he was needed until he came back the day before. Then he had seen Bullard, and Bullard had not believed him. He told me that with his bristles quivering with indignation.

"He asked me what I'd been paid to clear Mr. Lloyd," he said. "And I asked him if he was being paid to persecute people. He didn't like that," he added cheerfully.

All in all, except for my poor Dorothy, life began to take on a more normal aspect. The wave of suspicion had passed. Bob and Lucy Hutchinson had patched up their differences, and Lucy looked happier than I had ever seen her. They gave a picnic on one of the remote beaches one day, or what they called a picnic; that is, we ate on the ground, but there were men to serve the cocktails and the food, and as Tony said, the only real difference was in the knees. Marjorie was there, and I thought she avoided me.

She did not look well, and Howard Brooks had not come at all.

I suppose none of us really thought that Fred Martin would be found guilty when he was brought to trial. I did not realize the strength of the case against him. I remember going over my evening clothes with a cheerfulness that seems incredible now; and just before Labor Day I gave a dinner party. Perhaps it was a gesture, like that one of Lucy's weeks before. Perhaps it was out of sheer relief. Anyhow I gave it, with results so startling that I shiver when I think of them.

Yet it began quietly enough. Once more William got out the extra silver, and Mrs. Curtis came in to help. Even Mike was cherishing his late flowers for the house. There was an air of bustle everywhere, of furniture and floor polishing. The days were shorter now. By seven o'clock it was twilight, but long after evening fell I could hear the suppressed activity below stairs.

Lying upstairs I remembered the parties of my childhood: the florist augmenting the garden flowers with his own, the candles and centerpieces on the long table, the gilt chairs with their rose cushions, and the caterer's men in their shirt sleeves, making canapés in the pantry. Mother rustling down the stairs, holding up her train, with her pearls around her

248

neck, her diamond solitaires in her ears, and her hair built high in the braids and curls she wore until after the war.

She would move around, her train over her arm, inspecting everything. Then she would join Father in the drawing room, and I would be sent up to bed; to see from my window the first pair of lights turning in at the drive, and to hear the sound of horses trotting.

"Now, come away from there and get to bed," Maggie would say.

I was thinking of that as I went downstairs the night of the dinner. How far we had gone since those days! Especially Arthur. Arthur and the war. Arthur and Juliette. Arthur and Mary Lou. Arthur and our murders. And now Arthur free at last, busy and working.

I drew a long breath of sheer relief, and after glancing into the dining room, stepped onto the veranda and looked out over the bay, still faintly opalescent after the sunset.

Then suddenly I knew I was not alone. I turned with a jerk, to see a man with his back against the wall of the house in order to escape observation from the windows, and to hear a familiar low laugh.

"Allen!" I said incredulously.

"Be careful, darling," he said. "One shout and I'm out! Are you all right?"

"Yes. But you, Allen. Are you well again?"

"Well enough. Come over here, won't you, where they can't see us. I want to hold you, just for a minute. I'm so frightfully in love with you, Marcia. You know that, don't you?"

I did know it. It seemed to me that I had always known it. And nothing else mattered that night except that he was there, alive and warm and strong. I simply put my head on his shoulder and sniffed.

"You know too much," he said, almost roughly. "Worse than that, you know me. That may be dangerous. I'm earnest. Deadly earnest, my dear."

All sentiment had gone out of his voice. He dropped my hand.

"You're not safe. Nobody's safe," he said somberly.

He would not explain that. He knew about Fred Martin, and

he said flatly that Fred would never go to the chair. Then he glanced out over the water to where a small cruiser was anchored offshore. It showed only its riding lights, and he nodded toward it.

"That's how I came," he said. "I'll have to get away pretty soon. But I hate like hell to leave you here alone. You will go, darling, won't you? Soon?"

"I've got to see Fred Martin through this, Allen. I've promised his wife."

He gave a sort of groan.

"Don't you ever think of yourself?" he said. "Or of me?"

"Always of you," I told him, and for the first time he leaned down and kissed me.

"I'll have to go," he said huskily. "I'll watch you as well as I can. But I'm dodging the police, my darling, and that's not as easy as it sounds."

As it happened that was his good-bye to me, for I heard Mrs. Pendexter's high-pitched voice in the hall, and when I looked back for him he had gone.

I suppose the dinner that night was all right. I never have known. I must had talked. I dare say I smiled. Women are good actresses, all of them. But I sat facing a window, and we had not finished the soup when I saw the lights on the cruiser moving out toward the open sea.

I felt deserted and lonely.

It was after the meal, while the men were having cigars and brandy in the library, and the women coffee and liqueurs in the drawing room, that Marjorie Pendexter called me into a corner and said she wanted to talk to me.

She looked feverish that night. Her face was flushed, her eyes almost glittering. But she was steady enough, as though she had made a decision, and meant to stand by it.

"I'm going to tell you something, Marcia," she said. "Fred Martin never killed Juliette. I know it."

"So does anybody with any sense."

She did not hear me. She was busy with her own unhappy thoughts.

"I think I know who did," she said, and shivered. "But if Fred's innocent—Marcia, this Allen Pell who's been missing; I

250

knew him. So did Howard. Why did you call me up that night? Did you know who he was?"

I put a hand on a chair to steady myself.

"Only that Pell was probably not his name."

She pulled herself together at that. She even lit a cigarette, and inhaled deeply and exhaled before she spoke.

"I imagine you're right," she said. "I think he was Langdon Page, and that he is on parole from the penitentiary."

I must have shown the shock, for she looked at me quickly and asked if I wanted a glass of water. I shook my head.

"From the penitentiary?" I managed to ask. "For what?"

"For manslaughter."

For a minute the room faded away, all the lights, the women's bright dresses, the flowers. I heard Marjorie telling me to sit down, and I did so. But just then the men came trooping in, and she had to leave me. I did not see her again until she and Howard were leaving. Then she said merely that she had had a lovely time, only she had lost fifteen dollars at bridge. She evaded my eyes, and when at last I was alone I did not dare to telephone her. Our night operator has a pretty dull time of it, and I did not want her listening in.

When I did call the next morning I found that she and Howard, with one or two others, had started on a short motor trip to Canada, and I was left with that one word of hers to ring in my ears, day and night. Manslaughter!

Much of the puzzle was clear to me now; the reason why Allen's prints had been erased from the trailer, the absence of identifying marks on the clothing there, even that absurd pretense at painting. Allen Pell was Langdon Page, he had killed some person or persons with his car while he was drunk, and he had been drunk because of Juliette.

There was only one question I could not answer. Had he hated her enough to kill her?

CHAPTER XXIX

Lacking Marjorie, I had to know the story somehow. I could not sit still that day. When I tried to walk my knees shook. When I sat out on the upper porch I found myself searching for the small cruiser I had seen the night before. When my lunch came I drank some coffee and sent the rest away untouched.

It had always been Mother's custom to thank the servants when a dinner had gone well, and I have done it ever since her death. That day, however, I forgot the dinner entirely, and it was only a reproachful William who reminded me, as he took away the tray.

"Were things to your liking last night, miss?" he inquired.

I roused myself.

"I'm sorry, William. I'll see Lizzie later. Yes, it went beautifully. I'm afraid I'm tired today. I forgot to speak about it."

He cheered visibly.

"The lobster was especially fine, I believe, miss."

"It was indeed. Will you tell Lizzie that?"

Having been thus tactfully reminded of my duty, I went the rounds later myself. But early that afternoon I found myself at the public library in town, asking if there were any back files of New York newspapers.

There were none; nor, I was assured, were there any at Clinton. At four o'clock I went back to the house and announced to Maggie that I was going to the Park Avenue house that night for a day or two, and she could come along to make my bed and cook my breakfasts. Perhaps my manner was strange, for she looked at me queerly. She was willing enough, however. Like the others, she looks forward to summers on the island, as an escape from the drab monotony of all service, no matter how loyal. Like the others also, the end of the season finds her fed up with the country, and anxious for the city again: its pace, its noise, its general feeling of active living everywhere.

More than that, she had completely lost confidence in Sunset. It developed as she packed that day that the bells had started ringing during the party, with nobody upstairs at all; and that William, pouring champagne into Mansfield Dean's glass, had heard them and spilled it.

"It didn't hurt the table," she said. "But it upset him. I'll be glad to get away from whatever rings them, miss."

I paid no attention. I went out onto the porch and stood looking down at the beach. Those wretched crows were there again, strutting impudently about.

There was no sleep for me in the train that night, and the city was hot when we got there the next morning. Early as it was when we arrived, small heat waves were rising from the streets, and our taxi driver was in his shirt sleeves. The house looked dirty and dreary, its windows shuttered, the pavement unswept and dusty. It had been wired as usual for the summer, and I had telegraphed ahead to have it opened. We descended from the taxi, however, to find a wretched-looking young man on the doorstep, turning a worried face to me.

"Miss Lloyd, isn't it?"

"Yes," I said. "Is anything the matter?"

He looked even more uncomfortable.

"I'm sorry. It looks as though somebody had been in the house. The service is okay. I've tested it. But I've had a look around, and"—he smiled faintly—"I don't suppose you leave your bureau drawers on the floor!"

Maggie gave him a ferocious look.

"Are you telling me—" she began.

"He is telling *me* something, Maggie," I said, effectually shutting her up. "Do you mean," I inquired incredulously, "that someone has broken into the house?"

"I'm afraid so. Although how they did it—It's not all over

254

the place," he added. "Just some rooms on one of the upper floors."

And that, as it turned out, was the fact. There had been a cursory inspection of the lower floors. Here and there drawers had been opened and not entirely closed. But the real search had been made in the rooms Arthur and Juliette had occupied after their marriage. They consisted of a double bedroom, a large sitting room and a bath, and when Arthur and Juliette took an apartment the rooms had been left as they were.

Juliette had done them over, after her own flamboyant fashion, and that morning they bore a sort of family resemblance to her apartment the day the sheriff and I had seen it. I could only stare around me helplessly, with Maggie muttering and the young man—still nameless—practically wringing his hands.

"I'm sure I don't see how it happened," he said. "The wires are all right, and the basement windows are barred. I've been down there. It's—it's most mysterious."

He was completely unnerved when I finally got rid of him and sent Maggie downstairs to make some coffee and open the windows. But left alone I had no solution of the mystery.

The whole suite was filled with memories for me. Coming home from boarding school to hear Arthur and Juliette quarreling there. Arthur coming back there, after the break, and bringing such few personal possessions as a man salvages under such conditions; a few books, some papers, his pipes, his clothing. Juliette, looking into the place one day for some purpose or other, long after their separation, and laughing unpleasantly.

"There's the old wall safe," she had said. "And I had nothing to put in it!"

It was there now, open but empty.

I examined the rooms as best I could. So far as I could tell, nothing had been taken. The safe—there was one in every bedroom—had been empty for years. A photograph of Juliette still hung on the wall, but Arthur's books were gone long ago. The closets were empty, and the bathroom showed only the extra guest toothbrush in a cellophane holder, although someone had recently washed there. As for the rest, the dust

255

sheets were off the furniture, the carpet had been lifted, the mattresses were off the beds and all the drawers stood open, with some left on the floor.

I did not attempt to straighten the place. I went down to my own room and bathed and dressed again. Maggie had brought up coffee and toast by that time, as well as considerable indignation. But I left her as soon as I had eaten, her head tied up in a duster and her face still flushed with fury.

Looking back, I think I had gone through the previous thirty-six hours in a sort of automatism. Now, however, my head was clear. I was thinking as coldly and clearly as a machine. All emotion seemed to have died in me.

The next few hours I spent at the public library. The building was comparatively cool, but the search was a long and tiring one. I forgot lunch entirely. It seemed to me that for endless hours I had been going through newspaper files, filled with endless tragedies. But by four o'clock that afternoon I knew what I had gone there to learn.

It was all there: the identity of Allen as Langdon Page—his full name was Allen Langdon Page—supported by many pictures, his antecedents, his college, his inherited wealth, and his ultimate catastrophe. But I still knew nothing whatever that would explain the murder of Juliette Ransom, or that of Helen Jordan, her companion and maid.

The story was not an unusual one. I had lived the life of my day and generation, and no part of it was strange to me. But it was both sordid and tragic. Allen had been at a weekend party on Long Island, drinking heavily. On Sunday the party had moved to a country club, and the drinking had gone on. Then, at eight o'clock of a late spring night three years before, he had suddenly left in his car, heading toward New York.

The result was horrifying. He had either gone to sleep at the wheel—he did not remember—or he had suddenly passed out. What was certain was that he had run through a traffic light, killed a woman and her grown daughter, and critically injured her husband. Not only that. He had not stopped his car! Two or three blocks farther along he had turned sharply into a side street, hit a lamppost, and was found unconscious lying on the cement roadway. He claimed to have no recollection of what had happened, in the hospital and later at the trial. But he had put up no defense.

"If I did it I'll take what's coming to me," he had said.

His lawyers had fought for him. He had an excellent record. He was not normally a drinking man. He had inherited his father's business and was a hard worker. They challenged the jury panel until the court's patience ran out and the jurymen already selected were betting quarters on whether or not the next would be chosen. There was a vast array of counsel.

His wealth was against him. The press pictured him as a typical playboy, throwing money right and left, and he never spoke for himself. He sat tight-lipped and silent throughout the trial. There was a photograph of him leaving the courtroom after the verdict. He looked as though all the vitality had been drained out of him. He had faced the camera steadily enough, but he must have felt, at twenty-eight, that life had ended for him.

I had missed it all, had never even heard of it. That spring I had spent in England, and it was probably over when I came back. But it was a good thing that the story did not dawn on me suddenly. Even as I got it, bit by bit, I felt sick and my head throbbed wildly. Nothing that I had known of him suggested the reckless drunken man who had committed that crime, and received an eight-year sentence for manslaughter as a result. Nothing except what I now knew was the prison pallor under his tan, when I first saw him.

Yet, sitting there in the library, with the noise of the streets coming in through the open windows, a number of things fell into line. He had served less than three years of his term. Then he was paroled. He had not seemed to be interested, however. He had stood by while the cameramen photographed him as he left the prison. After that he simply disappeared.

I went back over the story again, but there was no mention of Juliette in it. The woman who had been killed was named Verna Dunne, and her daughter had died an hour or two later. According to the husband's story, they had been on their way home from church on that Sunday night, and they never really saw the car that struck them. They were, I gathered, simple God-fearing people, and they had probably never heard of

Langdon Page.

"I don't know what happened," said the husband from his hospital bed. "We were all together, and Millie had her mother's arm. The lights were with us. Then I heard Verna scream. That's all I remember."

But there were some other facts that set me to wondering. The week-end party had included not only Marjorie Pendexter and Howard Brooks. Mrs. Walter Dennison had been there also. What did that mean? Or did it mean anything? It explained one thing, of course; that was Marjorie's reluctance to identify Allen. She probably thought that he had killed Juliette. After all, when a woman drives a man to drink and then to prison—

I found myself shivering in spite of the heat. After all, why not? He had been on the hill that morning. He knew horses; one of his activities had been polo. He could have ridden down to Eagle Rock, carrying the body. And he had loved her once, and might have buried her.

I thought of that order for flowers at the cemetery, and held my head in my hands. Had he done it, after all? He had denied it; but he had said, too, that no innocent man would suffer for that crime. He might even have killed her and felt justified. Prison did strange things to men. But in my heart I did not believe it. I remembered his strength and gentleness, even his humor, and I did not believe it.

Nevertheless, there would be a strong case against him the moment he was identified and his affair with Juliette known. I knew what the sheriff would say. What in different words he did say later on.

"He was crazy about her, and I've known that kind of crazy love to turn to hate before this, Marcia. Now take Fred Martin. He had a way out. He could buy it. All she wanted from him was money. But this Pell or Page or whoever he is—he hadn't any way out. It was over. Nobody could bring the dead woman back. It's human nature to blame somebody else, when you can't face the thing yourself."

"She'd have seen him somewhere when she was out riding, and she came home scared. She wasn't scared of Fred. She told him what she wanted. But she might have been scared of Pell.

More I think of it, the more I'll bet she was scared of him."

But that bag—as he himself would have said—also left over too many odds and ends. If all this was true, then who had attacked and carried off Allen himself? Left him at a hospital with two hundred dollars in his pocket, and disappeared.

For one wild moment I considered Samuel Dunne, the little plasterer, sitting in court and still bandaged. "I heard Verna scream. That's all I remember." Suppose, hearing that Allen was out on parole, he had followed him to the island, found him talking to Juliette and in his fury killed the wrong person? I dismissed him at once, however. There had been no vengeance in that meek testimony of his; only tragedy and quiet acceptance. Providence had sent him this to bear. It was God's will.

Nevertheless, I determined to see him. I took down his address, returned my papers, took a taxi and went home. It was late by that time, and Maggie, opening the door for me, was shocked at my appearance. Being a Scot, she is dour when things are going well, but the essence of emotional sympathy when there is trouble. So now she gave me one look and hustled me up the stairs.

"You take a bath and get into bed," she said, "and I'll have a tray ready in a jiffy."

She started the bath water and left me. My bed was ready, and I began to undress. Then, what with heat and emotional exhaustion, I suddenly saw the floor rising to meet me and quietly fainted. When I came to I was still there, the bath water was overflowing the tub, and Maggie was in the doorway with the tray.

CHAPTER XXX

I was in bed for two or three days. Our city doctor was away, and Maggie brought in a pleasant young man with a round vacuous face and a pair of intelligent eyes behind horn-rimmed spectacles. He knew about Arthur's trouble, as who did not; and being a wise young man he let me talk.

"Why not discuss it?" he said. "I have an idea that you have been bottled up too long. That's why you blow off the lid."

I did talk. With certain reservations I told him everything, from the morning Doctor Jamieson and I sat waiting at the foot of the bridle path to Fred Martin's arrest. Then rather sheepishly I told him something about the bells. He looked interested but not amused.

"It would be idiotic," he observed, "to think we know all about this universe of ours." And he added as he got up: "I had an old grandmother once. She was as shrewd and keen as they make them; but if I had told her I could turn a dial and hear a man talking in an ordinary voice in Moscow, she would have sent for the preacher to pray over me."

He left me confused, but somewhat reassured.

I improved rapidly. Maggie overfed and coddled me, and in the intervals put the house in some sort of order again. My mental state was better too. I was less emotional. Now that I saw the case in clearer perspective I was confident that Allen was innocent. Why would he kill her? Why, if he had, remain on the island? He could have escaped, but he had evidently not considered it.

Arthur came in to see me at that time. He looked better, although he was still resentful of the trick Juliette had played

261

on him. But the search of his rooms overhead puzzled him.

"What were they after?" he asked. "There was nothing valuable around, was there?"

"Not unless Juliette had put something there," I said. "She could have, you know. She still came in now and then, and she had the run of the house."

"Put what there?"

"Well, papers maybe."

He smiled.

"Still the girl detective!" he said. "What do you mean by papers?"

"Suppose she had divorced Fred, after all? She'd have something to show for it, wouldn't she?"

He looked unhappy, as he always did when he was asked about Juliette. But he did try to think, going painfully back into those almost-forgotten years of his life with her.

"I'm not certain," he said. "I seem to remember something of the sort. A flat tin box with a lock. I saw it only once or twice."

"Did she take it away with her?"

"Probably. She took everything else!"

"Then where is it, Arthur? She didn't have it with her. It wasn't in her apartment here in town; I've been all over it. It certainly isn't here, although someone may have thought so."

"Who would want them?"

"Fred Martin, for one."

"Why would Fred go around hunting for a thing like that? She was dead, Marcia. She wasn't threatening him any more. He was safe, so far as he knew."

But the facts were there. He might smile wryly, as he did, over what he called "the papers" and my attempts at detection. He could not deny that someone unknown to us had been searching frantically for something, at Sunset, in Juliette's apartment, and now at the house.

"If there is anything at all," he conceded, "it must be important. She's gone, but it's still important. I'm damned if I can think what it is."

It was an uneventful few days that I spent in that bare room of mine, with the rug in storage, the curtains down and the breeze, when there was a breeze, coming in hot from the canyons we call our streets. One thing happened, however, although the results were not what I had hoped.

Mary Lou, back to see that Arthur was comfortable, came in and brought some roses; by way, I imagine, of apology for her past suspicions.

"I've been such an idiot, Marcia," she said, looking at me with tragic eyes. "I suppose I care too much. I've always adored him, and when that woman came back—He despised her, Marcia. I know that now."

"I wouldn't say that to the police," I warned her.

But with her usual ability to surprise me she told me before she left that Jennifer Dennison was in town, at a hotel; and after she had gone I called her up. She seemed surprised and not too pleased when I gave her my name.

"I thought that was all over," she said. "Haven't they arrested somebody?"

"Yes. I'm not trying to involve you, Mrs. Dennison. I just want to clear up something, for myself."

"But I really don't know anything," she protested.

Nor did she apparently, when I finally induced her to come. Maggie brought her up to my room, and she walked in, a small blonde woman in her late thirties, looking cool as only blondes can look in the heat.

"I'm sorry you're ill," she said, shaking hands and eyeing me. "Of course I can't think why you want me. But at least, here I am."

She sat down and took out a long holder—all Juliette's woman friends seemed to use them—and carefully inserted a cigarette.

"I suppose it's still about Juliette Ransom?" she inquired.

"It's about Langdon Page, Mrs. Dennison, and the postscript to that letter of yours." She looked uneasy, but she said nothing. "You knew him pretty well, didn't you?"

"How well does anybody know anybody else in this town? I saw him about. One does."

"He was fond of Juliette, wasn't he?"

"You can call it that. It was a crazy sort of infatuation. He wasn't really a drinker, but they had a quarrel, I suppose.

263

Anyhow that night—I suppose you know all about that too."

"I've read the papers. I came back to do that."

"Then you know as much as I do," she said flatly.

"Not entirely," I retorted. "I'm rather interested to know why you warned her against him. You said, you remember, to be careful."

"Did I?"

"You did. And you wouldn't explain that to the police."

"Why should I?" she asked coolly. "I'd been through a lot. I didn't want any more notoriety."

"Even if it sent someone to the chair?"

She looked startled for a moment.

"Don't be theatrical," she said rather sharply. "That's absurd. He might have been resentful. After all, she'd driven him to drink, and not treated him too well at that. But that's all."

I did not believe her. It sounded as though she had rehearsed it. It was too smooth, too specious. As for the rest, she was willing enough to talk. I could not have looked very formidable, lying there in bed, and I had an idea that she was mildly curious, about me and about the house.

It was the usual story of a spring week end in the country; the club a nucleus for the places around, golf or riding in the morning, lunch, and pretty steady drinking the rest of the day. Marjorie and Howard had been there, among a dozen others, in one house party. Langdon Page had not appeared until late on Saturday, having driven out. He had had a good bit to drink already, and he kept it up on Sunday. He was usually cheerful, but as the day wore on he grew silent and sullen. Someone at the club had asked him where Juliette was, and he had said he didn't know and he didn't care.

"We liked him," she said. "He wasn't one of the regular crowd, if you know what I mean, but we'd seen a lot of him through Juliette. I remember Howard Brooks offered to drive him back to town that night. He was in no condition to do it himself. But he refused."

She got up to go, and I thought she was relieved.

"There is just one more question," I asked. "Who is Emily Forrester? Is she one of that crowd? Do you know her?"

264

"Emily Forrester?" she said, and looked at me with real surprise. "I never heard of her. Is she mixed up in this too?"

She left soon after that, putting her holder back in her bag and powdering her nose before my mirror. She is not important in this record. She was, I imagined, not very important anywhere. One of those negligible women who hang to the fringes of this group or that, buying a popularity of sorts; shrewd, a little hard, but incapable of rousing any stronger emotion than tolerance.

I have never seen her since.

But as I lay back on my pillows I wondered about some things she had told me. Howard Brooks was not only a member of the house party. He was a friend of Allen's. It was odd how Howard's name came up, again and again, Marjorie worried and suspicious, that cruise of the *Sea Witch* at a crucial time, and his visit to me. What had he wanted to discover that day? Did he know that Fred was innocent? Looking back, I felt quite certain that he did.

The next day I was up and about. The doctor eyed me with disapproval.

"Still pretty shaky," he said. "Queer thing. If you had to get up and earn your living I'd understand it. But you young society women drive yourselves as if you had to."

"What is a society woman?" I inquired. "I have never known what it means."

"You wouldn't," he said cheerfully. "All right. Let's see that pulse."

CHAPTER XXXI

I went out that same evening, against Maggie's protests; and of all the strange events of last summer, I think nothing was more eerie than the situation in which I found myself that night. I had waited until then, for I wanted to see one Samuel Dunne, plasterer, and it was likely that he worked through the day.

Why did I go? I hardly know. Certainly he had told all he knew at the trial. But I was grasping at straws just then; and I wondered, too, how he was getting along, this elderly man who had lost both wife and child, and had been crippled himself by Allen's car.

On that one point I was reassured at once. There was nothing impoverished about the apartment building when I found it, a plain old red brick house, past its grandeur and now made into flats. Nor was anything further from my preconception of Samuel Dunne than the rotund little man who, after some delay, answered the bell on the top floor. Answered it after an odd fashion too, for he did not throw open the door. He opened it a foot or so, squeezed through and closed it carefully behind him. I saw that he was very lame in one leg.

"I'm sorry," he said, blinking in the light. "We've started."

I had not the remotest idea what he meant.

"I don't want to disturb you, Mr. Dunne. Can I talk to you? Just a few minutes."

He could see me better then. He looked surprised, and he smiled a little.

"I'm sorry, miss," he said. "I thought you'd come for something else. If it's work you want done I can take your name and come to see you."

"I can talk here. It's not about work."

He looked embarrassed and rather puzzled.

"I'd be glad to talk to you," he said, "but you see we've started. They'll be needing me." He saw my face and smiled again. "It's a séance," he explained. "Just a small circle of friends. I have lost my wife and a daughter, and now and then I get messages. Nothing important, but it's a comfort."

I liked him, and clearly his messages, wherever they came from, had helped him. He looked quite cheerful, if a trifle abashed.

"Maybe you don't believe in such things," he said. "That's because you don't know. Most people don't know."

I made a quick decision.

"I might learn," I said. "Is your sitting private, or could I join it?"

He looked doubtful. Then he opened the door an inch or so, looked in, and closed it again.

"It would be all right, I guess. Nothing has really commenced." He hesitated. "It's customary to pay fifty cents," he said sheepishly. "One of our neighbors is the medium, and it gives her a little something."

I found a half dollar in my bag, and he pocketed it in businesslike fashion.

"Just go in quietly,' he told me. "There's a chair by the door. It's pretty dark."

It was dark. The only light was from a small red bulb in a corner, and I still have no idea who were in that room. There were, perhaps, a dozen people, sitting in silence, while in an armchair there seemed to be a woman, asleep and breathing stertorously. There was the odor of flowers in the air, and after some time I located them. They were on the floor in the center of the circle.

Mr. Dunne sat down beside me. The silence continued. Once a man sneezed, and there was a small stir of disapproval. Then Mr. Dunne spoke aloud, in a quiet voice.

"I'm afraid we've disturbed the vibrations," he said. "Let us sing."

He started a hymn, and the others joined in. It was a familiar one, and I found myself singing too. I had a quick thought of some of the people I knew, seeing me in that environment singing. Then the singing ceased and there was another silence. The woman in the chair was breathing normally now, and seemed to be sound asleep. Suddenly she stirred and sat up, I think with her eyes closed.

"Good evening, friends," she said, in a heavy semimasculine voice.

"Good evening, doctor," said the other shadowy figures; and Mr. Dunne leaned toward me.

"Her control," he whispered. "He was a doctor down near the Bowery in the old days."

"I am glad to see so many of you gathered here tonight," the voice went on. "I hope the conditions are good. There is a new presence. If she is in accord—"

This seemed to be a question, and Mr. Dunne nudged me.

"I am in accord," I said, as best I could.

"Then all is well," said the voice. "Sam, Verna is here. She says not to take that new contract. There is something wrong about it. You will lose money."

"Thank you, doctor," said Mr. Dunne. "I wasn't sure myself. Tell her I won't take it."

For a time Sam lost Verna. There were many other messages. A Martha was not to go south. A woman near me, who seemed to be holding a handkerchief to her eyes, was told that Jean was all right. "All right and very happy, mother." It seemed to me trivial and more than a little shocking; made out of neighborhood stuff which anyone could know. There was apparently an Emily whom nobody knew. Then suddenly I heard my name.

"Marcia," said the voice.

"I am here," I managed, out of my utter surprise. "Do you want me?"

"There is a message for you. The trouble is not over. Do you understand that? It is not over. There is more trouble coming."

I gasped. Mr. Dunne leaned over.

"Keep on talking," he said. "Keep the vibrations going. Say something."

"What sort of trouble?" I asked, my heart thumping. "We have had so much. Who is in danger?"

But there was no answer. The medium put her hand to her chest, gasped as though it hurt her, and then leaned back in her chair and began the heavy breathing again. The séance was over.

I got out before the lights were turned on. It was customary, Mr. Dunne said, to give her a few minutes' rest in the darkness first. He came with me into the hall, solicitous and anxious.

"I'm sorry about the trouble," he said. "From what she said, you've had some already."

"Yes," I replied. "How—how did she know my name, Mr. Dunne?"

He smiled at me cheerily.

"They know everything," he said. "Funny thing about that contract. But Verna knows. She's a better businessman than I am, even now. You said you wanted to talk to me, didn't you?"

But I was confused and uncomfortable.

"I've only recently heard of your accident," I said. "I really came to see if you are getting along all right."

"Fine," he said cheerfully. "Mr. Page took good care of that, and I've got a little business of my own. The leg's a nuisance, but you can get used to anything, you know."

He shook hands with me and went briskly back into the room. The lights were on by that time, and there was considerable talking and even some laughter. Apparently one man had put his foot through his straw hat! But I went quickly down the stairs and out into the street.

I had been gone almost a week from Sunset. When I got back, William met me at the train and said the house had been quiet and that everyone was well. I had a bath and breakfast, and then went out onto the upper porch, where I lay back in my steamer chair while Maggie tucked blankets around me. It was magnificently cool, and for a time I was content merely to lie there, looking out over the water.

It was Maggie who, looking down at the beach, said that one of the crows was dead.

"Looks like it broke its neck," she said. "I always did say they were bad luck."

"One of them has already had it, I should say," I observed idly.

It was comforting to be cool again, cool and clean, after the city. The sun shone on the bay, on the white sails of a yacht race beyond the islands, on motorboats and launches. There was no sign of Allen's cruiser, but the *Sea Witch* was in the harbor and I knew that Howard Brooks was still about.

I tried not to think; to rest and watch the gulls, and forget that world where men were driven mad by women and ran down other women and killed them. I wanted to forget the Langdon Page who had been engaged to somebody named Emily Forrester and had gone crazy over Juliette. I tried not to see that picture of him, looking straight into the camera, as he left for the penitentiary.

I could not have been very successful. When the sheriff came to see me that same afternoon, he eyed me closely, his head tilted to one side.

"Humph!" he said. "Looking sort of washed out, aren't you? Detective business sort of wearing on you, eh?"

"What do you mean by detective business?" I inquired unsuspectingly.

He sat down on the rail, which creaked under his weight.

"Listen, young lady," he said. "Too many things are happening around here for me to run any risks with you. I telephoned down to New York when I learned you'd gone, and I know pretty much what you did. All except the library stunt. That's got me puzzled. Looks as if you could get books enough around here without that."

He knew that I had not gone to the library for books, but he did not say so. He gave me one of his searching glances and smiled.

"Not ready to talk yet?" he said. "All right. D'you mind if I look over that room upstairs again?"

"Everybody's been over it, again and again. Besides, it's been cleaned."

He looked disappointed.

"Like mother, like child!" he said. "Why didn't you leave it alone? Way it probably looks now, might be any room anywhere. What's the sense of cleaning it anyhow. Nobody ever

271

sees it."

He went up, but he was there only a short time. When he came downstairs again he took a turn or two about the porch, his hands in his pockets, before he spoke at all.

"Trouble with a case like this," he said, "there are too many leads and too few clues—if I know a clue when I see it, which I begin to doubt. There's a reason for everything we've got. That's sure. And we've got plenty of motive. Too much motive. Far as I can make out, quite a few folks on this island wanted Juliette Ransom out of the way. Fred's not the only one. Take Lucy Hutchinson now. She's not sure yet that Bob didn't do it, although she's beginning to doubt it. As for the others, what about this Pell fellow, for instance? He gets hurt. He's carried to a hospital by somebody unknown, he gets well, and by the great horn spoon, he doesn't come back. He's got a five-thousand-dollar trailer here, and does he claim it? He does not."

He went on. There were no actual clues, no prints, latent or otherwise, no bullets, no weapons unless the golf club was one, and its handle had been wiped clean. The lock to the toolshed had been broken by somebody, but by the time they got it three or four people had handled it. Jordan had put in a local call the night she was killed, but it could not be traced. But there was one thing they'd all overlooked, and as he said, he always came right back to it.

"That's the hatchet you and Maggie found upstairs," he said. "Your brother didn't bring it; according to both you and that Maggie of yours, it was there before he came. It wasn't bought in town either. So we have one of two guesses: either Juliette and the Jordan woman brought it, or it was carried in through the window. My guess is that the women brought it, and if we knew why they did it we'd know a lot more about this case. We'd know still more if we knew why, having brought it, they didn't use it."

"They may not have had a chance," I told him. "Part of the time the rooms were locked and the key hidden in my room. Then when they did get in, they might not have had time. But there's another thing to think of," I added. "Whatever was there may have been gone."

272

He grinned, for the first time.

"Got the makings of a good policeman, haven't you?" he said. "Well, I'll agree that there was probably something there, and that somebody made a darned good try to get it. We don't know that he got it." He turned his blue eyes on me. "If he got it," he said, "who was it tore up those rooms of yours in New York?"

"Who told you about that?"

"You ought to know," he said, his eyes twinkling. "You ought to know a lot of things. Understand you've got spiritualist on me!"

I could only look at him, and he chuckled. Then he sobered again.

"Now see here, Marcia," he said, "we've got to have a showdown, sooner or later. What about this fellow Dunne? And why did you go to see him?" When I said nothing he made a gesture. "You can't play with a man's life," he said gravely. "Things look pretty bad for Fred Martin. Arthur's cleared, and there's nobody else. But Allen Pell leaves the hospital and disappears. Why? Is he afraid of somebody? Or what is he hiding? And why? Isn't it time you spoke up?"

But I could not answer him. All I could say was that I did not know, and a few minutes later I heard him slam out of the house and knew that he was both angry and suspicious.

CHAPTER XXXII

It was that night that Doctor Jamieson was killed.

I can write that now. Even a few weeks ago I could not.
Perhaps the most tragic thing about death is that one gets used
to it. The strangeness wears off; the empty place is gradually
filled. There is a new man in the village already. He drives the
doctor's car, and I suppose he knows more modern medicine
than Doctor Jamieson knew existed. He has installed a small
laboratory in the room where the old doctor used to keep his
fishing tackle and the rubber boots he wore for country cases;
and already the people on the island are accepting him; as if
there had been no murder, as if he had not stepped into a dead
man's shoes.

For it was murder. He was found by the side of the main
road, his car drawn up beside the wall of the Pendexter place,
as if he had stopped it there; and there was a bullet wound in
his heart. The gun had been fired at close range; but there was
no weapon in sight. He was slumped down in the seat, his body
slightly turned to the left, as though he had been talking to
someone. Indeed one arm hung down over the door, as if he
had put out a hand too late. Or even as though he had been
merely resting it, after his casual fashion, on the top of the
door.

He was discovered at half past eight. It was the night of the
masquerade ball at the club, given for the local charities, and
dozens of cars must have passed him on their way to this dinner
or that preceding it. As it turned out, it was Marjorie Pendexter
and Howard Brooks who finally discovered him.

Howard was driving, and the car was only ten yards beyond

their gate. Marjorie noticed it first. They had passed it by that time, but she tried to look back.

"Wasn't that the doctor's car?" she asked.

"Looked like it," said Howard. "We'd better stop. He may be having engine trouble."

They backed up and got out, two fantastic figures, Marjorie as the Queen of Sheba and Howard as a medieval knight in tin armor. Cars continued to pass them, but no one stopped. It was by the light of one of them that they saw he was in the driving seat.

"He's sick," said Marjorie. "Doctor! Doctor Jamieson!"

He did not move, and Howard searched for a match in those preposterous clothes of his and could not find one. He reached over and got some blood on his hand, and he stood quite still for a minute.

"See here," he said. "I think he's hurt somehow. You take the car and go on. Get the ambulance. I'll go back to the house and try to locate that doctor at the hotel."

But he did not go back to the house. He watched her drive off, her high jeweled headdress on the seat beside her. Then having saved her that initial shock, he hailed the next car. Unfortunately it was the Deans, also on their way to the dinner, and he knew that Agnes Dean had a bad heart. He stood, rather at a loss, while the car lights gleamed on his armor and he searched for a handkerchief to wipe his hand.

"Man here seems to be sick," he said. "If Mrs. Dean would drive on I'd be glad if you'd stand by. I'll have to telephone and I don't like to leave him."

They arranged it that way. Agnes Dean went on, under protest, and Mansfield got out. He was dressed as an ambassador of some sort, with a broad red ribbon across his shirt front, a row of decorations, and a wig. Also he had matches, and he lit one and looked inside the car.

"Good God, it's the doctor!" he said.

"Yes. I think he's been shot."

The match went out. Mansfield Dean stood still in the darkness, not moving, not speaking.

"If you'll stay here I'll go back to the house and telephone for the police," Howard said. And he added grimly: "It looks like another murder."

"You think he's dead?"

"I know he's dead," said Howard.

I had not gone to the ball. My visit to New York had left me in no mood for parties. But that was the story as it gradually reached the club that night. The ball went on. The band played, a few of the younger people danced; but there was no grand march that night, and certainly no gaiety. Out on the road a space had been roped off. Police kept the traffic moving, and once more state troopers and the local officers were gathered around a body. At half past nine the sheriff came, his siren going wildly. There were two deputies with him, and he was out of the car before it had come to a stop.

They stood back and let him through, for it was a county case again. He had his own flashlight, although the place was alive with them, and he stood for some time and gazed down at the dead man.

"The doc!" he said huskily. "Somebody's going to suffer for this if I have to send him to hell myself."

The place was swarming with men. The police photographer was taking photographs, his bulbs flickering. Detectives were examining the car, the road, the path. Others worked their way through the shrubbery searching for a weapon. And the doctor sat slumped in his seat, like a tired man taking a long rest.

They found no weapon. They found exactly nothing. The wound had been instantly fatal. The bullet had gone through the heart. But one or two things were developed, at that.

He had stopped the car himself. The brake was on. And he had suspected no danger. He had made no move to get out, or to defend himself. Someone had stopped him. He had turned the car to the side of the road, and been killed without a struggle.

"So there we were," the sheriff said later. "He knew who killed him, most likely; but he didn't expect it. He was going back to town after seeing Dorothy Martin. He hadn't even had his dinner."

No one had heard a shot, but who does hear a shot in these days of backfiring? He had not been robbed. His worn old wallet was in his pocket, the small black book in which he kept

277

a record of his calls. When a doctor finally arrived he fixed the hour of death as something after eight o'clock, but that was merely approximate.

"That was the situation we faced," said the sheriff. "Anybody could have done it. Only, who wanted to do it?"

Fortunately Doctor Jamieson was a widower. His only son was married and lived in Boston. But his elderly housekeeper, Mrs. Woods, was heartbroken.

"Who would want to do such a thing?" she asked, with bewildered tear-stained eyes. "He had no enemies. Everybody liked him."

She had some information. For a week or so the doctor had been worried. He had eaten very little, and long after she had gone to bed she would hear him moving about below, "as if he was walking the floor."

They went through his papers that night, sitting at that cluttered desk of his; an old roll-top with its upper ledge crowded with samples of all sorts, where he used to search for malted milk tablets for me when I was a child. There were a few letters from the son. "Dear Dad: I'm sorry about the delay in thanking you for the check. I've been out day and night hunting another job, but—"

They were all like that, and when I heard that, some time later, I remembered the years he had worked, his old mud-spattered car, and his neat clothes, never new. He had forty dollars on deposit when they found his bankbook. But they found nothing else. His professional cards and records, a few receipted bills, the usual blank prescription pad, but that was all.

Open on the desk was a medical magazine, with an article on the use of some new drug or other. He had marked a part of it with a blue pencil. And in the wastebasket, crumpled up and also written in pencil, was the beginning of a letter. Rather it looked like an attempt to draft a letter. It had no address, and it contained only seven words, with one incomplete.

"I find myself in an impossible pos—"

Either he had abandoned the idea then or sent off another letter. There was no doubt in anyone's mind that the word was to have been "position," and one of the detectives spoke up.

"If there'd been a gun," he said, "I'd say that was the beginning of a suicide note."

They even debated the idea, sitting around his office that night. He had been worried. He hadn't eaten. They had found an insurance policy, and he might have wanted it for his boy. Suppose the gun had been in the car and someone had picked it up? It was far-fetched, but possible.

They got Mrs. Woods again and asked her.

"What about a gun? Did he own one?"

"He had two, a rifle and a shotgun."

"A revolver? Or an automatic?"

"No, sir. He never owned any."

She went back. She was making coffee for them, cutting bread and butter, and crying as she did it.

"Well, that's that."

But the note puzzled them. For whom was it intended? What was the impossible position in which he had found himself? Had he known something so dangerous that he had been killed to suppress it? They went back over his books, but the names in them comprised nine-tenths of the neighborhood, including the summer colony.

When they went back to the dining room Mrs. Woods was there. She poured the coffee and they ate hungrily, as men must eat, even in the midst of death. She seemed distracted, however, and finally she made up her mind.

"I do know something," she said. "The doctor told me not to tell it, but now he's gone—"

They stared at her. The room was suddenly quiet.

"That's all right, Mrs. Woods," said the sheriff. "It can't hurt him now, you know."

She still hesitated.

"It's about a visitor he had one night a day or so ago. He was here a long time. I didn't let him in. The doctor did that. He drove him away when he left, too. But they were both sort of excited. I could hear them."

"Then you didn't see who it was?"

"Well, I did and I didn't. Not to be sure anyhow. But they passed the kitchen window on the way out to the garage at the back. That was about ten o'clock. I can't be sure, but I thought

279

it was the painter fellow; the one who disappeared."

They dissembled as well as they could, according to the sheriff later. It was a bombshell among them, but they kept on with their coffee and bread and butter. Only the sheriff spoke.

"I see," he said. "When did the doctor ask you not to say he had been here?"

"That was the next morning. I said: 'Wasn't that that painter last night? The one they've been looking for?' He was pretty much upset. He didn't say it was or it wasn't. He said: 'A doctor's house is like a priest's, Mrs. Woods. I don't want any talking about who sees me here.' Then he looked straight at me and said: 'There was nobody here last night, Mrs. Woods.' I said, 'Yes, sir,' and—well, that's all I know."

Nothing of this was brought out at the inquest, our third during the summer. The murder had taken place on Saturday night, and the inquest was held on Monday. It was strange to sit there for the third time, and not see Doctor Jamieson presiding behind the desk. Strange, too, to know that in a few days the room would be filled with children, back after the long holiday.

The authorities were not telling all they knew this time. The inquest actually brought out little beyond the fact and method of death. The unfinished note was not produced, nor was Mrs. Woods called. Marjorie and Howard testified, as did Mansfield Dean. The autopsy had shown nothing not known before. The dead man had been shot with a .32 automatic; the bullet had pierced the heart and lodged in the cushion more or less behind him and to the right. No weapon had been found.

The doctor had visited Dorothy Martin, still in bed and still nervously collapsed. He had left there at a quarter to eight, which would have brought his car to where it was found some ten minutes later. Before he saw Dorothy he had made a call in the interior of the island, at a farmhouse there, and had seemed silent but not depressed. Both places had offered him supper, but he had said he had an appointment and had to get home.

There was no record of any such appointment on his pad. His evening practice drifted in and out, usually without prearrangement. As a matter of fact, the waiting room had been filled while he still sat slumped in his car where he was discovered.

Howard Brooks told about finding the body, and Mansfield Dean of staying by it. The rest was purely routine. The usual verdict was brought in, People went home to lunch, and our new mystery was apparently no closer to solution than the others.

But there was another thing which the police had suppressed. On the car door at the right was a full set of fingerprints, and they were not the doctor's.

CHAPTER XXXIII

I cannot write much about that third funeral. The doctor's son had come, a thin harassed-looking man with a wife and two small children. I could not help feeling that, for all his grief, the insurance money would be a godsend. Practically all the island attended, and the grave was piled high with flowers. From where I stood in the churchyard I could see the other two graves, and fresh white chrysanthemums on Juliette's, that mysterious weekly tribute which still continued. Then it was over, and the crowd dispersed, leaving the doctor at last to an unbroken sleep.

Just as I find I cannot write about the doctor's funeral, so I cannot here set down my own state of mind at that time. And as if to add to the confusion and terror, the bells in the house started to ring again. The one from my room to Maggie's rang that same night. I had not touched it, and the first knowledge I had was the sound of a falling body in her room. She had forgotten that her foot was tied to her bed!

The bay was quiet during those days, for the end of the season was approaching. Mike now brought in early dahlias instead of roses from the garden. The nights were cold, with a hint of frost. The grass was turning brown, instead of the bright green of spring, and there was a touch of color already on some of the trees. Lying wretched and sick at heart in the late summer sunshine I could see now and then the sleek head of a seal and knew that they would soon be back, to lie out on familiar rocks, to bark and quarrel and play, through the long cold winter.

I did not think much during that brief interval. I did not dare to think. I knew now of that night in the doctor's office after his death, and Mrs. Woods's statement. And I knew something more. I knew that Allen Pell had been on the island the night of the murder.

One afternoon, a day or two after the funeral, Lucy Hutchinson came to see me again. She wandered in after her usual fashion, looking subdued but also relieved.

"It's a ghastly thing," she said. "But at last I've got that nonsense about Bob and Juliette out of my mind. When that happened Saturday night Bob was trying to look like a Roman emperor, and swearing all over the place."

She lit a cigarette and gave me a hard direct look.

"I suppose you've heard about the mysterious masked man at the ball?" she inquired.

"What do you mean? What mysterious man at the ball?"

"Not exactly at it. Lurking on the edges, I should say. You know how it is at a thing like that. Masks never fool any one. And we know everybody. He wasn't really in costume. He had a black domino and a hood. He stayed outside on the terrace. I thought he was looking for someone."

"He would have had to have a ticket, Lucy."

"Not if he came by water. Or over a fence."

"Are you trying to tell me that somebody crashed the party? I don't believe it."

"I am trying to tell you," she said quietly, "that Allen Pell was on this island that night." And she added, "You can ask Marjorie Pendexter about it. I saw her talking to him."

I was completely panicky when she went away. Little by little I saw the case against him building up, and was helpless. Then, with a suddenness which almost destroyed me, Arthur was once more involved in the mystery.

Mike was preparing for the winter. He does his gardener's housekeeping then, tidies up his mulch heap behind the garage, goes over his tools and cleans out the toolshed. That day he was getting ready to whitewash it. He moved out the lighter stuff, and then pulled out the heavy lawn roller.

I was in the grounds when I saw him come outside. He had something in his hand and was examining it. When he saw me he slipped it into his pocket; but I had a sudden feeling of apprehension. Mike was devoted to us, but he was integrity to the unpleasant point, and I did not like the look on his face.

I went toward him at once.

"What was that, Mike? What did you find?"

"It wasn't anything. How about that iris down by the pond, miss? It's not—"

"Mike! Let me see what you put in your pocket."

He took it out, unwillingly, but he would not let me touch it. It was Arthur's gold key ring, and I suddenly felt weak in the knees.

Mike looked me straight in the face.

"Reckon sheriff's got to see this, miss."

"Mike," I said desperately, "you can't do this to us. Not to Mr. Arthur, or to me. You know he didn't do any of these dreadful things."

He shook his head.

"I'm sorry, miss. I left that roller out the night somebody broke into the shed, and I put it back the next morning. This was under it just now, when I moved it."

There was nothing I could do. Mike simply put the ring back into his pocket, and went austerely and I thought unhappily back to work.

He took it to the police station that same evening. He had taken no one in the household into his confidence, but after his early supper I saw him dressed in his best clothes, starting for the town. He walked slowly, like a man going to an unpleasant duty, and there was something inexorable about him, like the majesty of the law.

There must be such a thing as the inertia of despair, for during the next day or two I was about as useless as a person in a cataleptic fit; that is, I was conscious of what was going on around me, but I was entirely unable to move. The police seemed to have made no further move about Arthur's key ring. The sheriff did not come in, and there was no word whatever from Allen.

Things went on much as before. Fred Martin was still protesting his innocence in the jail at Clinton, his hard muscles growing soft and his face pale and anxious. And Dorothy, up and around now, with Mrs. Curtis to help her, was clutching

285

her baby fiercely in her arms and looking out on an unfriendly world with wide tragic eyes. Then one day Mrs. Pendexter came to see me and roused me from my apathy.

She brought some hothouse grapes and the usual local gossip. Eliza Edwards claimed that Helen Jordan's room in her house was haunted. Agnes Dean had taken the shock of the doctor's death badly, and was in bed again. This family was going to Tuxedo and that one to Lenox.

Under it all she was not quite herself. She looked strained, like the rest of us; but she had aged that summer. There was no alacrity in her movements, although her tongue was as sharp as ever.

"Pack of fools, running away from trouble," she remarked. "Even that future son-in-law of mine. If you ask me, he knows more than he's letting on. He's deep, but I see through him. As to that girl of mine, what's she doing moping around? I've got more life in me today than she has, at whatever age she says she is."

She finished her tea and got up.

"You ask Howard Brooks what he doing sneaking a bundle out of my house the night the doctor was killed," she said. "Money or no money, I don't want any killers in the family. And tell Lizzie that tea was so feeble that it ought to have been kept in bed."

Before she left she told me that Marjorie and Howard Brooks were leaving soon, to join a house party at the races.

"Don't know what's happening to the young people today," she complained. "Can't seen to stay put for more than a minute. If you want to see Howard you'd better do it soon."

She climbed into her high car and drove away, a stiff, indomitable little figure in an outrageous hat; and left me to make what sense I could out of what she had told me.

As a result I tried to see Marjorie that same night. She was dining out, however, and the next morning I walked to the Pendexter place, going bareheaded and surprising her on the terrace. She had a book in her lap, but she was not reading. She was sitting listlessly in a long chair, and looking out to where the *Sea Witch*, magnificent in white paint and glittering brass, swung at its anchor.

I probably startled her, but she greeted me placidly enough.

"Hello, Marcia," she said. "Mind if I don't move? That's a good chair. Well, I suppose the season is over. I won't be sorry. It's been a hellish summer."

I nodded and took a cigarette from the box beside her.

"Your mother says you are leaving soon."

"Yes, thank God," she said fervently.

She looked at me.

"You look shot to pieces," she said with her customary candor. "Don't lose your looks, Marcia. That's about all we have," she added, smiling faintly. "Looks. That's why women like Juliette thrive. They take care of themselves. You and I—"

She shrugged and let it go at that.

But she had given me the opening I needed. I threw away my cigarette and confronted her squarely.

"That's what I came to talk about," I said. "Not about Juliette, but about what's happened since. You knew Allen Pell was Langdon Page. So did Howard. I want to know why he went to the charity ball the other night."

She tried to look surprised.

"Did he?"

"He did, and I think you know it."

She stirred uneasily.

"I wish you wouldn't imagine things," she said. "If he went it was probably to see you. He's in love with you. That's no news to you, of course."

"How do you know all that?" I inquired, rather grimly. "You do know he was there. And I don't think it was to see me. He could have done that at Sunset."

She moved restlessly in her chair.

"I wish you'd leave me alone," she said querulously. "Yes, I knew he was there; but that's all I do know. He and Howard were old friends. When Howard asked me for a domino and mask I found them for him. That's all."

That was probably Mrs. Pendexter's bundle, although it was not much help just then.

"But why go to the ball all alone?" I persisted. "It sounds ridiculous. He was hiding from the police, or so he told me.

287

Then he goes, badly disguised, to a thing like that! Didn't Howard explain?"

"Howard doesn't do much explaining," she said, not looking at me.

"Well, I think he has some to do. He knew Langdon Page. He knew he was here on the island. When I tried to find out who Pell was Howard took the yacht out the next morning for a cruise! And I've wondered since about a lot of things, Marjorie. Who around here but you two knew that Langdon Page had a prison record? That his prints were on file?"

She sat bolt upright and stared at me.

"You're not trying to connect Howard with these murders?" she demanded.

"I haven't said that. But whoever attacked Langdon Page and then took him to a hospital knew his prints were on record. He went back to that trailer and wiped it clean."

She lay back in her chair. The color had faded out of her face, and she seemed on the verge of collapse.

"Not Howard," she said. "O my God, not Howard."

That was all there was to that interview. She was plainly beyond more questioning. I tried, but she only shook her head. In the end I called the butler and got her some brandy, but as I left I could feel her eyes, enormous in her pale face, following me like those of a scared child.

I came back home, to this porch, to the monotony of high tide and low tide, dawn and sunset. It seemed as though the world had suddenly stood still; that everything had stopped and only my mind went on, feverishly active.

Nevertheless, there was tragedy in the making during that interval. No more murder, thank heaven, but real trouble; the sheriff with Arthur's key ring locked in his office safe, and those letters of his about a dog going their slow way to the dead letter office and back to Mamie, in his office. And even before that one of the minor miracles of modern criminology: those photographs of the fingerprints from the doctor's car on their way to Washington. A machine started, a slow quiet movement, inevitable as fate itself, and then a card dropping.

A thousand miles away at the doctor's funeral a reverent voice intoning: *"I am the resurrection and the life, saith the Lord;*

he that believeth in me, though he were dead, yet shall he live."
And in Washington, in his shirt sleeves—for the day was hot—
a small man with spectacles picking up that card, examining it
and carrying it away.

"Here it is," he said.

There was no excitement. The card might send a man to his
death, but there it was merely routine. Less than an hour later,
from another room in the building, a longish telegram went to
Russell Shand, and Shand took it to the District Attorney.

Bullard read the message and looked up, angrily flushed.

"What does that prove?" he said. "That this Page—or
Pell—killed some people with his car! Any drunken fool does
that. We know he saw the doctor and rode in that car of his.
Why wouldn't his prints be on it? We'll get him, but then
what? If we keep on we'll have half the people of this county in
jail."

"Who put them there?" said the sheriff belligerently.
"You've been playing to the newspapers ever since this thing
broke, Bullard. Now, by the great horn spoon, suppose you let
somebody else have a chance?"

He went to New York a day or two later. This time the police
there were playing ball, as he put it. He did not have to go to the
library, as I had. They had the files and the records of the trial.
They gave him a small room somewhere, and when he finally
emerged, hot and dirty, he hauled a small newspaper clipping
from his pocket and showed it to them.

"Got any idea where that would come from?" he said.

They had none. They examined it curiously.

"What about it?" they said. "His marriage was off. That
wouldn't be news. He'd gone up for eight years."

"I was thinking," said the sheriff, "about that ad on the
other side. I've got a hunch that when I find who was selling
those pups, I'll have got somewhere in this case."

They laughed. They had been polite that day, but he was still
a country sheriff to them, "stepping high over plowed
ground," as he said.

He did not come back at once. He went over Juliette's
apartment again, and one day the harassed young man let him
into our house, in response to a wire from me. He spent some

time in the basement, which because of its barred windows had not been wired, and I believe he came up smiling. And he saw Samuel Dunne in the red brick house and even sat in at one of the meetings.

"Darndest thing I ever saw," he told me later. "If everybody didn't have an Aunt Mary I'd think I heard from the old lady. Least it sounded like her. She told me to go back home and mind my own business!"

The evening before he left he went to see Arthur at his apartment. Arthur and Mary Lou were dressing for dinner on some hotel roof to escape the heat, and Mary Lou absolutely refused to leave the two men together. "What concerns Arthur concerns me," she said. "Only I wish you'd let him alone. Fred Martin did those murders, and you know it."

There was no use in temporizing. Russell Shand got out that key ring and put it on a table.

"Thought you'd like this back Arthur," he said.

Mary Lou was fixing her hair at a mirror, but she saw Arthur's face and turned. She looked from one man to the other, and it was she who broke the silence.

"Where did you find it?"

"Mike found it in the toolshed." He looked at Arthur, and then unexpectedly he put out his hand.

"Kind of awkward, losing a bunch of keys," he said quietly. "I lost mine once, and I went around like a hen with her head off until I found them."

He went away at once, leaving Arthur staring after him. A wise and kindly man, our sheriff. "I sort of thought I'd better leave," he told me afterwards. "Looked like Mary Lou was getting fixed to kiss me, and I'd kept the record clean up to then."

CHAPTER XXXIV

He came back the next day. Not alone. He had two New York detectives with him. They took a drawing room and sat up half the night, discussing the case. The alarm for Allen—he was still Allen to me—was out in earnest now. Once again radio and teletype were busy. There was an intensive search going on, this time with a grim determination and a dogged persistence that were new.

Only Russell Shand kept his head.

"Sure I want to find him," he told Bullard. "I haven't said yet I want to see him convicted; that's all. And I'd hold onto Martin. A day or two more won't hurt him."

For as the facts became known, as such facts do become known, there was a rising demand that Fred Martin be released. The Clinton Paper had an editorial on the subject.

"We have the anomalous situation of one man being held for a murder, while an intensive search goes on for another individual suspected of the same crime; a man, moreover, who already has a conviction for manslaughter to his credit. Granting that Fred Martin had a possible motive, his past record is clean. He married a second time under a misapprehension, but there is nothing essentially criminal in such an act. On the other hand, the man Page—or Pell, as he called himself—was not only in the vicinity during all three murders. He had known Juliette Ransom well. He undoubtedly knew Helen Jordan, the second victim, and was afraid of what she might tell, and his fingerprints have been found on the murder car owned by Doctor Jamieson.

"Compared with all this, the case against Fred Martin becomes negligible."

It was on the second day after his return that the sheriff brought one of the detectives to the house. Probably Bullard had been riding him hard, for he was grim and unsmiling.

"Sorry, Marcia," he said. "This is Mr. Warren. He's working with us. He wants to ask you some questions."

I was trembling, but at least I kept my voice steady. There was a fire in the library, for the weather had turned cold, and the sheriff stood in front of it, not talking but watching me.

"Just tell him everything, Marcia," he said. "We know most of it anyhow."

I could not do that, but I went as far as I could.

I told of my first meeting with Allen, and of going to the trailer for tea; but when I explained the reason for going back to the camp the next night, the detective stopped me.

"What do you think he meant, that he would let no innocent man go to the chair?"

"I thought he knew something he had not told me."

He looked significantly at the sheriff; but he was gazing serenely out a window.

"I see. And did he say why he wanted an alibi for your brother?"

"He didn't think he was guilty."

"Still, wasn't that rather unusual? Unless he actually knew your brother was innocent?"

"How could he know that? He didn't even know Arthur."

"He might know who *was* guilty, Miss Lloyd."

There was more, of course. Some of it I have forgotten. At last he came directly to the point.

"You don't know where he is now? Pell, I mean."

"No."

"Just how often have you seen him?"

"I don't know exactly. Five or six times."

"When did you see him last?"

I did not mention the cruiser. I could not.

"I was giving a dinner. I went out onto the porch and he was there. I had only a minute to talk to him. People were arriving."

"And the date?"

I gave it to him and he wrote it down. Then he leaned forward.

"What was that talk about, Miss Lloyd? Please be accurate. You may have to repeat this under oath."

He looked surprised when I told him.

"He wanted you to leave the island? Did he say why?"

"He seemed to think I wasn't safe here."

Warren sat still, drumming with his fingers on the arm of his chair. The sheriff smiled for the first time.

"I told you, Warren," he said. "Too many things don't jibe. Why did he want Marcia to leave the island? So he wouldn't kill her? Who put that hatchet I told you about in the room upstairs? Who in hades knocked Pell out and then carted him off to a hospital? And why didn't he kill the doctor when he made that call on him, if he was going to kill him at all? They were out together in that same car."

Warren was silent.

"What's more," the sheriff went on, "a man can kill people with his car and not be a killer. Look at that key ring! If the gardener here had found it a month or so ago it would have caused Arthur Lloyd a lot of trouble. But Arthur Lloyd was no killer. We've had one attack and one murder since, with a clear alibi for him in both cases. As it is—"

"What about the key ring?" I gasped.

The sheriff looked at me and smiled.

"It's like this, Marcia. I expect it was Arthur who found that body up the creek. Just happened on it, most likely. Well, what would he be likely to do? He knew there was a good circumstantial case against him. What's more, he was a lawyer and he knew that without a body there was no murder, in the eyes of the law. No corpus delicti."

"You mean that he buried her?" I asked weakly.

"That's about it. Mike had the keys to the toolshed that night, so he broke in and got a spade. It stood out like a sore thumb all along that whoever buried her did it decently. She wasn't just tossed in and covered up. It was a fool thing to do, probably, but after all she'd been his wife. Then after he did it he found he'd lost his keys! Must have been a pretty tough situation for him, when you think about it."

I could imagine that now. Poor Arthur! I found my lips trembling. The detective looked almost shocked.

"Took a good-sized chance, sheriff, didn't you?" he said. "If

293

you knew all that—"

The sheriff smiled.

"I know these people," he said. "You don't."

The detective got up. It was apparent that he disapproved of all this. These were not the hard-boiled methods of a big city. All this nonsense about knowing people! Who knew anybody else when it came to murder?

He cleared his throat.

"We might look at those rooms, sheriff," he said. "You've got that hatchet on your brain!"

I went up with them. It was a bright cold day, with the sun pouring in; and nothing could have been more normal than the hospital suite appeared, now set in order again. The wallpaper was as fresh as the day it had been put on, twenty-odd years ago. In the nurse's room the cot was neatly made up, and the trunks and boxes were closed and in their places. The broken china had been removed, but the toys remained, and on top of a wardrobe Arthur's old cage still stood, mute reminder of the white mice he had kept, and which had filled in his convalescence from everything, from whooping cough to mumps.

I stood there looking at it. It reminded me of something, but I could not think what it was. Mother had loathed the creatures, but I had liked them. It had been one of my virtues in Arthur's eyes. Then what—

The men examined the other room carefully. I could hear them raising the window, and even turning back the rug. When they reappeared it was the sheriff who spoke.

"That night Maggie was hurt up here, Marcia," he said. "She ever remember any more about it?"

"She thinks she was walking in her sleep. She has an idea she was in that room when she was struck."

"What part of the room?"

"In the corner by the bed there."

I went to the doorway and showed him, and he went back again and rapped on the wall. It was solid, and he looked baffled.

"What was she doing there?" he asked. "Or does she remember?"

"She thinks she was on her knees, as though she was looking

for something. But she doesn't know what it was."

They went away soon after that, Mr. Warren looking faintly amused and mildly superior.

"There's your hatchet!" he said, as they got into the sheriff's car. "A sleepwalker! You'll probably find that she carried it up there herself."

"Might be," said the sheriff. "Only trouble with that, she's a peace-loving woman, and it's kind of hard to think of her carrying it about here with her. Then, too, where did she get it? They don't stock that kind in town."

I was left, still trying to remember about Arthur's mouse cage. That afternoon something happened which drove all thought of it out of my head. William, bringing me my tea in the morning room at five o'clock, told me about it. He put down the tray, lifted and replaced the sliced lemon, coughed apologetically, and said:

"I understand they have found the man they were looking for, miss."

"What man?" I said, my heart sinking.

"The painter. Mr. Pell."

I still do not know how he learned it. I never have known how our secrets, such as they are, are always known by our servants before we learn them. But I do know that I dropped the empty tea cup and broke it to pieces.

"Where did they find him?"

"Well, they didn't exactly find him, miss." He had stooped and was picking bits of china from the floor. "That's one of the old Dresden cups. Your mother thought a lot of those cups," he said, with reproach in his voice.

"What do you mean?" I said frantically. "Get up, William, and look at me. What is this story you are trying to tell me?"

He looked hurt.

"He wasn't exactly found," he repeated, straightening stiffly. "I understand he walked into the courthouse at Clinton and gave himself up, miss."

I sat there, staring at him. I believe he brought a brush and pan and gathered up the scattered pieces of the cup. I think he spoke to me, and I answered. But I remember nothing until Maggie found me with my tea untouched and my face gray, and with William's help got me upstairs and into my room. There she put me to bed, an electric pad at my feet—"They're like ice, miss"—and brought me some whisky in a glass.

She asked no questions. She merely mothered me. When I was breathing better she stood over the bed and put a hand on my forehead, as she had done so often when I was a child.

"I expect he's all right," she said, in her expressionless voice. "That Russell Shand is no fool. They'd have arrested Arthur if it hadn't been for him. There's a lot of stuff nobody knows yet. When that comes out—"

"Oh, Maggie!" I said, and cried as I had not cried for years, with my head on her stiffly starched breast.

The details came in slowly. On that afternoon, at two o'clock, a man walked into the courthouse. The place was strange to him, and he asked for the sheriff's office. The sheriff was out, and after some hesitation he inquired for Bullard. He was neat enough, but he looked tired and dusty; and the secretary in the District Attorney's outer office looked at him askance.

"He's busy," she said. "He's in conference."

Allen smiled, as if something amused him.

"You might take in my name anyhow—or a stick of dynamite!" he said. "You'll find the effect will be about the same."

It was. Bullard was inside with a half dozen men: two deputy sheriffs, a reporter or two, a county detective, and one of the men from New York. The desk was littered, and in the resulting rush for the door papers were scattered all over the floor. The two deputies got out first and caught Allen by the arms. He stood perfectly still, and they looked a little foolish.

"I understand you are looking for me," he said. "The name is Page. Langdon Page."

"You dirty so-and-so!" said the New York man furiously. "What's the idea anyhow? If you think you're going to softsoap yourself out of this mess—"

"There's a young lady in the room," said Allen, grinning at him. "You might remember that. I suppose there is some place else to go?"

"And how!" said the New York detective derisively.

CHAPTER XXXV

I did not know all this at the time. Bad as things were, I did not believe for a moment that they could hold him for the murders. He had broken his parole, and now he had surrendered. He would be taken back; years would pass, and he might still be there in prison, locked up away from the open he had loved so much. Any dreams I might have had had died hard that night.

To make matters worse, the house was strange again. After a series of bright days a fog had come in, crawling along the surface of the water and gradually blotting out the islands. As always it brought in a raw dampness, and in spite of the electric heating pad I shivered in my bed.

I did not sleep much, but I dozed at intervals, rousing with the jerk which means tense nerves. It was only eleven o'clock when I heard Chu-Chu growling, and sat up in bed. The house was very still, the servants sleeping. As I sat up I realized that the bells were ringing again.

I still have no explanation. It was not late. Perhaps Samuel Dunne and that eerie circle of his was sitting that night, hearing from Verna, or Emily or Jean. Perhaps they even liberated some force which reached the house. Whatever that explanation may be I only know that, lying wide awake after the bells had stopped and the house was quiet once more, I remembered what I had forgotten about the mouse cage; and so took the first step toward solving our mystery.

It came to me suddenly, as a forgotten word will spring into the mind. I was a child again, lying in bed in the quarantine room. There was scarlet fever about, and I had a sore throat. As a result I had been banished upstairs, dragging my feet and carrying a doll.

"How long is it to be this time, mother?"

"Not long, if you're a good girl."

Even now the injustice of that rankles; as if being a good girl had anything to do with it! Mother had a sheet wrung out of carbolic solution hung over the doorway at the top of the stairs, and Arthur was severely banished. It turned out, however, to be merely a cold, and in due time I was restored to the family again. But in the interval something had occurred.

Arthur brought me his mice to amuse me. He crawled up the drain pipe one night, holding a string in his teeth. Once inside he carefully hauled up something I could not see, and at last it emerged triumphantly. It was the mouse cage.

"Thought you'd like to watch them," he said, with feigned indifference. "They smell a bit, but they're lively."

It was a princely gesture from a big brother to a small sister. For hours that night I watched them. Then I decided to open the door and let them out. That was fatal. I got all back but one, and when Maggie came in the next morning she was furious. I could still see her on the floor, looking under the beds for the wandering one, and threatening to tell Mother.

It was late in the morning when I heard a faint scuffling, and saw the mouse appear from a large hole in the corner of the wall, above the old baseboard. Maggie caught it, and she never did tell Mother.

I knew now. That corner was where Maggie had knelt the night she was attacked. She may even in her sleep have gone back to that incident. But what I was remembering was not that. The hole was gone, the wall intact! I had not thought of it for years.

At daylight I put on a dressing gown and went upstairs again. The fog had come in in earnest, and the gray-white light was poor. I was nervous when I turned on the lights, but no bell rang, and everything was quiet. I stood staring at the corner, unable to believe my eyes. There was no hole. No mouse could have hidden behind the baseboard, and the wall was neatly papered with the old familiar wallpaper, which had been there for more than twenty years.

It seemed incredible. I had not imagined that incident. I could still see Maggie, with the little creature by the tail and her whole soul revolting.

"You're a bad girl, Marcia. Just for this I'll drown the creature. Dirty nuisances they are, anyhow."

She had not drowned it, of course.

I went back to bed, but not to sleep; and it was then that I remembered Mrs. Curtis. At half past seven I called her up, and she seemed mildly surprised.

"Listen," I said. "When was it that Mr. Curtis found a leak in the roof over the hospital suite?"

"Three years ago. It was in the spring. That whole corner by one of the beds was soaked."

"What did you do about it?"

"Why, I told you at the time, Miss Marcia," she said reproachfully. "You paid the bill. We had to have the plaster fixed. And I found a roll of the old wallpaper and had it put on."

"Did they rip off the baseboard?"

"Rip off what?"

When she understood she was vague. She didn't know. She thought the baseboard had been left as it was. Only the plaster was damaged. I hung up, and sat thinking. Three years ago someone had broken into the house through a cellar window. Mrs. Curtis had discovered it and sent for her husband, and in going over the house they had found the leak and later on the plaster had been repaired.

Where did that take me? Who had entered the house that spring? Had come in a car, broken through the cellar window, and yet taken nothing away?

Had it been Juliette? She knew the house. She knew the hospital suite. She had been ill there at one time, years ago. She might even then have known of that hole behind the baseboard and used it for her own purposes. I had seen her once coming down the stairs, stepping cautiously so no one would hear her.

"Juliette! What on earth were you doing up there?"

She had looked uneasy.

"I was looking for something," she said querulously. "Good

299

gracious, Marcia, do I have to report everything I do?"

It was suddenly clear to me. Juliette, remembering that old hiding hole of hers and coming back, three years ago. Almost certainly Jordan with her, perhaps stopping in the village to buy provisions, where Eliza Edwards had seen her. The house cold and damp, the two women shivering, but at last something found, or something hidden. Hidden, of course, or why had she come back this summer?

How long had they stayed during that earlier visit? Not long, I thought. Perhaps only the night, with a breakfast of sorts; some coffee bought when Eliza saw Jordan, some bread and butter. Juliette's car could not be concealed for any length of time. So far possibly the rain had favored them, but the estates all about were probably being put in order, with gardeners at work. They had got away, as secretly as they had come.

I could see more, too. I could see that return of Juliette's this year, and the discovery that the wall had been repaired. It must have been a shock. They had brought a hatchet to pry out the baseboard and secure whatever was there. But they had to face a disturbing fact: that whatever was there might already have been found. Perhaps they asked some judicious questions. Indeed later I found they had done so. The result must have been comforting. If anything had been discovered the household knew nothing about it.

But they were not certain. The workmen might have found it and Mrs. Curtis have put it, with the other odds and ends, in the next room. She might have thought it unimportant; something left over from our childhood, like the mouse cage. What was it? Arthur had said that Juliette had owned a tin box and kept it locked. Perhaps—just perhaps—that was it.

Box or not, some things were easy to explain. Jordan had made a preliminary survey the day they came, finding the key where I had left it. I had seen her move the curtain. Then she had carried down the bad news to Juliette, lying waiting in her bed.

"There's no hole there, Julia. They've plastered it up."

"Good God! Do you suppose they found it?"

And Jordan looking at her with shrewd appraising eyes.

300

"You'd have heard about it if they had. You can bet on that."

They must have watched and waited afterwards, waiting for a chance to get back. When it came they were ready. They hadn't much time. They tore the place to pieces, one of them probably working, the other on guard. They found nothing, and in the end that search was their undoing. After it the room was padlocked, and they could not get in again.

I was in a fever of impatience that morning. My first impulse was to call Mike with a pickax and have him tear the wall open at once. Sober second thought made me change that. Whatever was there, it might be a part of the mystery. It might even explain our crimes. In the end I decided to get the sheriff and tell him what I knew.

I did not get him. Not for hours. He had gone home to get some sleep after that all day and night session and the telephone receiver had been left off the hook.

I know something now of that session. The other men coming and going, but Allen still in that chair, and Bullard shouting at him.

"She saw you on that path and recognized you. You had broken your parole, and she could send you back to the pen. Maybe you hated her anyhow. So you killed her."

"I did not kill her. I never killed any of those people."

"She told the Jordan woman about you, and the Jordan woman went to the police for protection. She was scared too. She carried away the letter that referred to you. Why did she do that, unless she was afraid of you?"

"Why should she be afraid of me? I never even saw her."

"I'm doing the questioning, not you, Page. And don't lie. We've got you, and you know it. You killed her and took that launch you'd rented and towed her out to sea."

"How do you know she was murdered. She might have fallen on the rocks."

"And then put a rope around her neck and towed herself! Why did you shoot Doctor Jamieson?"

"I didn't shoot him. I've never had a gun since I came to the island."

301

"What did he know, that he had to be put out of the way? What happened, the night you saw him, to make you decide to kill him?"

"We had a talk. I'm not going to discuss it. It was entirely friendly. He got out of his car and drove me to where I'd left my boat. He watched me while I rowed out to the cruiser. That's the last I saw of him."

"So he knew you were on a boat! He could turn you in whenever he wanted, so that ended him."

Now and then the sheriff put in a question. Compared with Bullard's fighting face, his was quiet.

"Tell me something, Page," he said. "What brought you here, anyhow, in that trailer thing of yours? This was the last place you'd naturally come, isn't it? You'd be likely to see someone you knew at any time?"

"That was the chance I—" He checked himself. "I had certain reasons. I don't like to hold out on you, sheriff. You've been damned decent to me. Let's say it was a personal matter."

"Better tell us, son."

He shook his head.

"Sorry, " he said laconically.

He was frank enough about some things, his release from prison and his desire to escape publicity. "I needed time to readjust," he said. He explained also the stay in Boston and the purchase of the trailer there; and he even smiled faintly about his pictures.

"I'd always liked to dabble with paint," he said, and let it go at that. Those were the lighter moments. They hammered at him, their faces grim and sweating. The New York men protested when at eight o'clock in the evening the sheriff sent out for food for him, and a package of cigarettes. At midnight Bullard retreated, exhausted, and the other men took over. But Russell Shand remained, watchful and alert.

"Why did you advise Marcia Lloyd to leave the island, Page?" he asked.

"It was no place for a woman, alone in that big house. I understood someone had broken into it."

"That's all?"

"That's all."

302

"Who took you to the hospital, and left you there?"

He hesitated at that, looked undecided.

"I don't know," he said. "I must have fallen and been knocked out. As for who picked me up—" He shrugged. "How could I know? I was unconscious. I don't remember anything for the next few days."

"Part of that's true, son; and part of it is a pretty poor lie. It was broad daylight, and you hit the back of your head. You know who did it. What was it? A fight?"

There was no answer to that. Shand went on:

"I'll grant that somebody picked you up. Even that's queer, though. There was a hospital right there in town, but what did he do? He took you a hundred miles, left you and then ran away? Think it over, Page. We don't like to convict innocent men in this state."

And then for a minute Page broke.

"Good God," he said. "Don't you suppose that I have thought it over?"

It went on and on. Asked why he had hidden since his recovery he was stubbornly silent. The same thing was true about breaking his parole. The room was bright with light and thick with smoke. He grew dizzy. Once or twice he dozed in his hard chair and they shook him awake. The New York men would have gone further, but Russell Shand was still there, and it was his case. If Shand waived extradition, they could take him back to the penitentiary, but that was probably all they could do. They sat or stood around, disapproval on their faces; and at four that morning he was put in a cell and they went back to their hotel to sleep.

"They'd have had him confessing everything from mayhem to arson if they'd had their way," the sheriff said later. "We were just a lot of softhearted hicks who'd never heard of a rubber hose!"

He was still asleep that day when at last I reached the sheriff by telephone and asked him to come over. He was still asleep when I told the sheriff that story, and when Mike put his garden pick through the wall. And he was still asleep when, after five minutes or so of noise and plaster dust, Russell Shand put his hand down inside the baseboard and withdrew a

303

locked tin box. He stood with it in his hands, lightly blowing the dirt from it.

"Smart girl, Marcia," he said, and grinned at me.

He did not open it there. To my wild disappointment he carried it away with him.

"Want the fingerprints, if any," he explained, "and a good locksmith to open it. You'll hear as soon as I can get here, after that. It's property, I suppose."

He warned us all to secrecy before he departed. Then I was left to face the endless day. The town was in a turmoil over Allen's surrender. People came and went. There was, it was said, a move to quash the indictment against Fred Martin at once, and Dorothy was out on the porch of her cottage, holding her baby and starry-eyed with relief.

It was no surprise when Mrs. Pendexter came in again that afternoon, her old eyes snapping.

"I had to get out of my house," she said. "Give me some tea, Marcia. Howard Brooks is having a fit, and Marjorie is locked in her room and won't speak to anybody. Didn't even know they knew the fellow. What did the idiot mean by giving himself up?"

"I don't know," I said drearily. "I suppose he knew they'd find him eventually."

She gave me a long hard look.

"See here," she said. "Ever think of Tony Rutherford in this case? He was wild about Juliette. I don't suppose that hurts you now, but he was straight off his head at one time."

I leaned back and laughed hysterically.

"Tony and Bob and Howard," I said. "Not to mention Arthur and Fred! Maybe they all got together and formed a syndicate to get rid of her. Maybe—"

"Stop it," she said sharply. "This is no time to get hysterical, Marcia. You've done pretty well so far, for a girl your age. I suppose Howard Brooks was crazy about her too, eh? Well, that doesn't surprise me any. He's a fool about a lot of things. But according to him this Page is innocent. He'd sooner believe I did it! I'm not so sure he doesn't at that. Knew I detested her."

She was less indignant after she had had her tea. She told

304

William his hair needed redyeing, which sent him out in misery, and talked to give me time to control myself. Agnes Dean was worse. She had a couple of nurses, and the doctor from Clinton was spending most of his time there. "And a nice bill that will be!" People were leaving as fast as they could get ready, Conrad and all the shops in town were losing money because of the season, shortened by the murders. And she herself would like to buy Page's trailer and start off in it.

"I'm getting on," she said, "and I've had a taste of excitement this summer. It's going to be hard to settle down."

It was just before she left that she came to what I think was the real object of her call. She jabbed furiously with one of her hatpins at the creation on top of her head.

"I remember that Page case," she said. "Papers were full of it. Seems to me I heard he was engaged to somebody at the time. Who was it?"

"I think her name was Emily Forrester."

"Never heard of her," she said, with a final jab. "But if I were you I'd have it looked into. Whoever she is, she wouldn't be too fond of Juliette, I imagine."

The remainder of the afternoon I sat under the sun umbrella in the garden. The fog had lifted, and save for the overflow from the pond and the rustle of fallen leaves, it was very quiet. The fish in the pool came up hopefully when they saw me, and then seeing my empty hands went about their own affairs.

I could not read, I could not even think. From where I sat I could see Pine Hill, already touched with yellow and red, and the Dean house above the road, almost hidden in its trees, where Agnes Dean was fighting for a life which meant little or nothing to her. Above, along the creek valley was the empty grave where my poor Arthur had buried the woman who had been his wife, and covered her face with leaves; and farther up in the hills was Loon Lake, where she had drifted, undiscovered, until the flood waters had carried her on.

None of our murders, not even that of Doctor Jamieson, had come so close as that one. She had been one of us. It was from that room upstairs, with the rose sheets on the bed and all her extravagant possessions about her, that she had gone out to her death. And somehow I felt guilty.

305

She had been in fear of her life. I knew that now. All that feverish talk with Arthur, her demand for a lump sum of money so that she could leave the country, had had terror behind it. If we could have done what she wanted we might have saved her, and perhaps the others. Should we have done it? We might have. The Deans might have bought the house. They had liked it. And Mother's pearls was still valuable, even in these days of cultured ones. If she had only been frank! But she never had been frank.

CHAPTER XXXVI

I was still thinking about her when Russell Shand came back that day. He came straight to me in the garden, looking sober, and pulled a paper out of his pocket. Before he opened it however he sat down and regarded me gravely.

"Just how fond of this Page are you, Marcia?" he said. "I've got an idea you've kind of fallen for him. That so?"

"I like him very much. I—I'm fond of him," I said.

I probably colored, for he glanced away. He filled his pipe before he spoke again.

"There was a string of pearls in that box," he said unexpectedly. "Among other things. I've had the jeweler in town look at them. He says they're worth a lot of money. Did she have anything of that sort?"

I was surprised. Whatever I had expected, it was not the anticlimax of hidden jewels.

"I don't know. I don't think so. Not if they are really good."

He considered that, eyeing his pipe.

"Well, let that rest," he said. "I don't know that they're important, except that she didn't seem the sort to hide anything like that away. Not if they belonged to her. See here, Marcia, there's a letter in that box that doesn't look so good for Page. It looks as though Mrs. Ransom was threatening to write to his girl and break off his engagement."

"How do you know that?"

"Letters. His letters to her, her letters to him."

I stared at him.

"Her letters to him! How did she get them?"

"Well," he said, not unreasonably, "he might have sent

307

them back. But one or two were pretty recent. To the time he was hurt in that accident, I mean. And there were some others—not from her and not important—that had only come in the day before the trouble, Saturday, and it was Sunday when it all happened."

"She had other letters of his?" I said, bewildered.

"She had."

He smoked for a minute or two in silence.

"I've been figuring that out ever since we opened the box," he said. "Looks to me that the minute she heard he was in trouble, she hotfooted it to his place, wherever he lived, and made a clean sweep. Maybe she hadn't much time. As I told you, there's stuff there of his that hadn't anything to do with her. But she was sure raising the devil with him. He'd gone off his head about her. When that was over he wrote and told her so; but she wasn't letting go. Not when he had the money he had. It's all there," he added. "Question is, would he hate her enough to wait three years and then kill her. There's hardly any feeling on earth that lasts that long, unless—"

He changed the subject abruptly. Among other things he had found her decree of divorce from Fred Martin, obtained in Florida.

"Dorothy's all right," he said. "So is the youngster. That's something anyhow. But the rest doesn't look so good for Page, Marcia. We might as well face it."

There were some bits of cheer, he went on. There were what he called pretty hot love letters from several men, and I gathered that some of them belonged to the summer colony on the island. "They must have been pretty darned uneasy," he commented. He did not name them. He sat for some time contemplating the fish in the pool. Then he went back to the pearls. They puzzled him evidently. The local man thought they might be worth anywhere from thirty to fifty thousand dollars. Of course, they might have brought her back. She wanted money to get out of the country, and there they were, tucked away in a tin box behind a wall.

"What gets me," he said, "is why she wanted to get out of the country. Who was she afraid of? Page? A man doesn't kill a woman because he got drunk and into trouble. As to these local fellows, she may have been trying to get money out of them; their letters for cash, if you get the idea. She may even have told somebody where they were. That would be Arthur's man on the roof, and maybe whoever hit Maggie. But I've looked over the field, and if there's a killer among them I ought to be selling neckties over at Milt Anderson's haberdashery. What about that necklace, Marcia? Would she steal a thing like that?"

I hesitated.

"I don't really know," I said. "I don't think so. And after all, pearls have identity. A jeweler who has matched a really good string would always know it."

He put down his pipe and looked at me.

"Now that's interesting," he said slowly. "Fellow would know them, would he?"

"I think so. Yes."

He rose heavily. He moved like a tired man that day, as indeed he was. He picked up his hat and, still holding it, stood looking over the low hedge to the bay.

"It would be interesting to know," he said, "if that necklace was in Page's desk or around his place when she rifled it. A present maybe for this girl he was going to marry. If that's what Mrs. Ransom went to get—But it doesn't sound right to me, somehow. She didn't go there for that. But what she did go for—" He drew a long breath. "She didn't lose any time over getting there," he added. "If she wasn't after the necklace, what was it? There's a lot in that box she wouldn't want the police or anybody else to see. But I've got an idea either she didn't find what she wanted, or she got it and destroyed it."

He left soon after that, going back to Clinton. For reasons of his own he did not mention the box to Bullard or the detectives. Instead he took it to Langdon Page that night in his cell, and saw him go pale when he showed him the pearls.

"Belong to you?" the sheriff asked.

"No. What would I be doing with things like that?"

"Ever see them before?"

"I'll not answer that, sheriff, if you don't mind."

Nevertheless, he looked shaken. He did not touch them. He did not apparently want to look at them. The only trace of interest he showed was when the sheriff said they could be traced. But it was when the sheriff handed him the clipping he had found under Helen Jordan's bed that Page showed the first real signs of anger. He got up and crumpled the thing in his hand, his face livid.

"I wish you would stop this damned snooping," he said, savagely. "I'm here. You've got me. What more do you want? What does it matter that my engagement was broken? I was in jail. I was going up for eight years. What has that got to do with this?"

"Men have killed women for things like that," Russell Shand said gravely.

"So I killed Juliette Ransom because of a broken engagement three years ago! Emily had never heard of her then. There was no marriage because there couldn't be a marriage. Get that through your thick head and leave it alone."

"You hadn't bought the necklace for Miss Forrester?"

"No. Definitely no."

The sheriff had to let it go at that. With the letters it was different. Allen—he was still Allen to me—glanced through them, at first hastily, then more carefully. If he was looking for something he did not find it. He put them down on the bed beside him—the cell had only one chair, and the sheriff was in it—and laughed contemptuously.

"What a fool a man can be!" he said. "I suppose she went after them as soon as—as soon as the papers had the story. She seems to have beaten the police, at that. They'd have taken those pearls and put them into safekeeping somewhere."

And that, the sheriff said later on, was where he got his first real light on the case.

He took away from that meeting what he called two hunches. One that Allen had hoped to find something among those papers which was not there; the other that he knew more about the pearls than he had admitted. But the sheriff had read that trial in New York from start to finish, and one thing had stuck out like a sore thumb. The one man on the island who had been a part of the party at the club on Long Island was Howard Brooks, and the next morning he got a boat and rowed himself out to the *Sea Witch*. The owner's flag was up, so he knew

310

Howard was there; and after some parley they let him aboard.

He found Howard on the deck, sipping moodily at a whisky and soda, and he looked uneasy when he saw the sheriff.

"Morning sheriff," he said. "Anything I can do for you? Drink?"

"I'll smoke instead," said the sheriff. "I suppose you know what I'm after."

"No idea," said Howard shortly. "Except that you fellows over at Clinton are crazy."

It was not a promising beginning. But the sheriff was not daunted. He sat there on the deck, with its chintz-covered chairs and its shining paintwork, and deliberately put all his cards on the table.

"That's the story, Brooks," he said when he had finished. "Bullard and these other fellows think Page is as guilty as hell. Maybe he is. I'm not so sure, myself. That's all."

Howard took another sip of his drink.

"I don't get you," he said. "What is it you want me to do?"

"Who's in Page's apartment in New York?"

"I haven't an idea. It was given up, and his stuff put into storage."

"Who did that?"

"I did," said Howard, not too graciously. "I saw him in the hospital, before the trial. He asked me to do it."

His suspicion of the sheriff gradually relaxed. He knew nothing of any pearls. He saw no letters from Juliette Ransom when he looked over the place. Of course the police had been there before him. He had bundled all the papers he found in a box and sent them with the furniture to the warehouse. There was nothing important among them.

"That depends on what may be important," said the sheriff. "I suppose I could get into that place?"

"I could. I rented it. Why?"

"Because I'd like to have a look at it. You were in a hurry. There might be something more. It's only a chance, but Godamighty, Brooks, if this fellow won't save himself somebody's got to do it for him."

As a result they went to New York on the train that night. The sheriff took the pearls along, although he said nothing to

311

Howard about it. In fact, they said little of anything. Howard evidently considered the whole proceeding useless, and was inclined to be annoyed. They ate dinner together almost in silence and separated at once, Howard to his drawing room, the sheriff to smoke his pipe on the observation platform and stare at the flying landscape without seeing it.

There was some delay in the morning. The keys were at Howard's office, and he had to wait until his staff arrived at nine o'clock. There was still further delay at the warehouse. The room was packed to the ceiling with furniture, trunks and boxes, and only coercion and bribery finally enabled them to have some of the stuff moved outside. Howard was still glum and non-co-operative; but he handed over the keys, and as the search continued he began to show interest.

The box of papers was the first. The sheriff examined it, sitting flat on the cement floor of the hall outside and going through everything scrupulously. There was a bundle of letters from "Emily," written in a rather unformed hand. He did not read them, but after glancing at one he stopped and wrote something in his notebook. The bills, paid and unpaid, he passed over quickly. There was no record of any necklace, but there was one for a pair of diamond earrings. They had cost twenty-five hundred dollars.

"I suppose Mrs. Ransom got them?" he observed, and Howard nodded.

Still nothing turned up. The desk was empty. So were the drawers of chests and other furniture. Howard began to look at his watch, and at last went away.

"If you're going through the trunks," he said, "I'll be at the office. He had a Jap who looked after him. He packed them. You won't be likely to find anything."

But the sheriff did find something that morning, sitting waist-high, as he put it, in a welter of masculine clothing, ties, riding boots, and undergarments. He found it in the pocket of a dressing gown, and as he sat there it was like seeing a great white light.

"I knew a lot from that minute," was his comment to me later. "Trouble was, it didn't help Page any. If I'd guessed right, things looked worse for him than ever. That is, he had a

312

real motive then for getting rid of her. Or for hating her, which might be the same thing."

He was hot on the scent by that time.

He did not go to Howard's office that afternoon. After some trouble he located the police officer who had seen the accident which killed Verna Dunne and her daughter, and the ambulance which had picked Page up out of the street. What he learned satisfied him, though.

"You're sure of that?" he asked the hospital intern.

"Sure. That's where I found him. He hadn't been moved."

"Didn't seem queer to you?"

"Well, I didn't think of it at the time. It looks funny, doesn't it? Still, with a jolt like that—"

"No jolt in the world would send him where he was, unless the car had turned over."

"Well, it hadn't done that. What's it all about anyhow? I suppose you mean he wasn't driving the car himself?"

"That's the idea."

"What happened to the other fellow?"

"That's what I'd like to know," said the sheriff grimly, and went about his business.

He spent the rest of the afternoon visiting the jewelers in town. It was a long tedious performance, but at last he got results.

"I'm not sure, but I think—Let me call somebody, will you?"

The sheriff waited. He looked about him. "Never knew there were that many diamonds in the world," he said, telling me about it after the case broke. At last somebody came. The pearls were identified, checked in a book, and the sheriff wrote a name in his notebook and met Howard at the train that night with an impassive face.

He said nothing of his afternoon activities. He gave him back his keys, and once more they ate together, in comparative silence. But the sheriff was profoundly anxious. So far as he could tell, he had only built up the case against Allen Langdon Page.

He was trusting nobody by that time. He slept with his wallet and notebook under his pillow in the train that night, and the

313

next morning he sealed the little book in an envelope and locked it away in his safe, along with the necklace and the tin box. Then, with the doors closed, he got on the long-distance wire.

It is part of the irony of such matters that while he was on the telephone Mamie found at last what he called the dog letter in the mail. "Dear Sir: In response to your inquiry—"

For he already knew, by that time.

Bullard came in to see him that morning. They had not broken Allen, and he was in a vile temper. He insisted on going over the case again, over everything from the fingerprints on the doctor's car to his ability to run a motorboat. The sheriff listened imperturbably.

"You've tried to block me in this case, Shand," said Bullard belligerently. "I've watched you all the way through. Things have come to a pretty pass when the sheriff of this county refuses to uphold the law. Some of these days—"

"Some of these days I wish you'd park your fat fanny outside this office," said the sheriff rudely. "I've got work to do."

Bullard was still spluttering when the telephone rang. It was long distance.

"All right," the sheriff said. "This is Shand. Get off the wire, Mamie. This is private."

He was not smiling while he listened.

"I see," he said. "When was that?"

He listened again, making a note on a pad before him. Then Bullard, idly watching and ready to renew the attack, saw his face change.

"Say that again," he said slowly.

When he hung up the receiver he had forgotten that Bullard was there. He picked up his hat and shot out of the office, and a moment later his old car was rattling down the street.

CHAPTER XXXVII

I knew nothing of all this at the time of course. The races were on, but the *Sea Witch* was still in the harbor. There was a rumor that Howard Brooks had been sent for, and had gone to Clinton in a towering rage. And Bob and Lucy were still next door, although they had been packed to go for a week.

The story of the tin box had got about. Also, rapidly as the summer colony was diminishing, at least a dozen people came in at odd intervals, and I had all I could do to parry their polite curiosity. Yes, there had been a box, but there were only some letters in it. Letters? What did I mean? Family letters? And how had I found it?"

I did my best. I told them what they already knew, that the hospital room had been broken into, and that I had remembered that the plaster had been repaired on the wall, and thought I would investigate. No, I had not seen the letters. The police had the box.

They had heard about the pearls too, and that was harder to evade.

"I don't know who starts these ridiculous stories," I said. "What pearls? I certainly haven't seen any."

They would go away at last, leaving me exhausted and short-tempered. It was hard to get rid of them. They were kind. They had been Mother's friends, or were my own. But into their comfortable and monotonous lives had come another mystery; not horrible this time. Nothing they had to refuse to face; but definitely exciting.

They drove away in their big and little cars, somewhat let down by my prosaic answers. I could almost hear what

315

they said.

"What do you think? If the police have those letters—"

"My dear, Marcia wasn't telling all she knew. Do you suppose that Arthur—?"

For there was still that story of Arthur's in their minds; Arthur slipping back to see Juliette; Arthur sleeping in the quarantine room, Arthur chasing an unknown man about the place in the middle of the night. And there was still an old distrust of him, never quite dead. He had married a cheap woman, and they had had to accept her.

Even before the sheriff had got to New York the story had reached the papers. It was entitled "Mysterious Tin Box" in the only one I ever saw. It was rather devastating. Whoever had talked, there was a full and inaccurate description of the bells ringing in the house, and more than an intimation that some ghostly visitant had led me to the wall.

It was on the evening of the day when Russell Shand got that mysterious long-distance call of his that I had a visit from Tony. He was as debonair as ever, even to the flower in his lapel; but under it I felt that he was anxious. He showed strain.

He had come to say good-bye, he told me. He was leaving the next day.

"Unless I'm arrested!" he added lightly.

"Arrested? Why?"

He shrugged his shoulders.

"Why not?" he said. "There were some letters of mine in that box."

He had lost his nonchalance by that time. He looked haggard, if that word could ever be applied to him. He stood in front of me, eyeing me with a new seriousness.

"I've been all sorts of a fool, Marcia," he said. "Probably the worst thing I ever did for myself was to let you go. I know you won't want to talk about it, but I've got to. I've not only let you down. I damn near cost Arthur his life. Only I'll say this: I'd never have let him go to trial."

I felt very strange. Not Tony! Not gay irresponsible Tony, with the flower in his lapel and his carefully tied black tie! My lips felt stiff.

"Are you trying to say—"

"I'm trying to say I knew Arthur didn't kill Juliette Ransom. I saw him get into that car when he left the island. I even got the number of the car. You see, I didn't know it was Arthur. To me it was just somebody who'd dropped on me out of a window, and damn' near got me at that."

It had been Tony on the roof!

He sat down then, and told me the story. It went back to that last night of Juliette's life, when I had left them together and gone outside. Juliette had not lost a minute. She had hidden a box in the attic, she told him, and now she couldn't get at it. The wall had been plastered.

"She had told me where it was, and asked me to get it; and like a fool I said I'd try. You see"—he looked at me unhappily—"I'd written her some letters years ago, and she'd kept them. She offered to give them back if I got the box, and I—well, I fell for it."

Apparently he had refused at first. He knew the old route by the trellis and up to the window, but he was no housebreaker. He didn't like the idea. But she was desperate, he said. She began to implore him. She was frightened about something. Her idea was to get the box, which had something in it she wanted, and then to get out of the country. And while he did not trust her, he saw she was in deadly earnest.

When he went out to call me that night he took a turn toward the garden first and looked up. He could still get up there, he saw; and the rest seemed easy. How could he know that Arthur was coming back that night? Was probably even then somewhere about the place? He went home and changed his clothes. Then he got a tire tool from his car and came back. Juliette had said she'd left a hatchet in the room. But he had an alarm. There was a light in the quarantine room, and he was uncertain what to do.

He wandered about for an hour or two. Then, maybe at three o'clock and feeling like all kinds of a lunatic, he climbed the trellis. The next minute somebody looked out and then began to get out of the window overhead.

"I was scared," he said. "Scared out of my wits. I ran and dodged, but the fellow kept after me. I was all in when he

317

lost me."

He had hidden in the shrubbery at the foot of the Dean place, he said. He heard Arthur still moving around, he did not know who he was. It seems to have occurred to Tony then that the whole situation was on the off side, as he put it; that whoever it was had had no more business in the house than he had. So far as he knew, the only man in the house was old William, and William could never have run like that.

In the end, as it turned out, he had reversed the previous state of affairs.

"He'd been after me," he said. "Then when he gave up I followed him along the road. I had worn tennis sneakers, so he never heard me. Anyhow he never looked back. When that car came along and he hailed it I thought maybe the driver was an accomplice. So I took his number. I still have it."

I sat very still. How simple it sounded! All that long agony, and Tony with the flower in his lapel as he told me; leaving the island the next day, going back to his work and his clubs, his dinners and dances, the whole frivolous structure of his life.

"You have nearly ruined us, Tony," I said.

"I'd never have let Arthur be convicted."

"You have already let him suffer intolerably. Why didn't you speak up at the time? That's what I can't forgive."

He looked uncomfortable.

"See here, Marcia," he said. "It wasn't a question only of myself. If I had testified I would have had to mention that infernal box of hers. And she told me there were other letters in it. Some from married men up here, that she meant to collect on. It's been straight hell, Marcia."

"Yes. It has been straight hell for everybody," I agreed. "And it's still straight hell for some of us."

He came over to where I sat, and stood looking down at me.

"I suppose it's no use, Marcia? It's all over, isn't it? Between you and me?"

"Yes," I said steadily. "I'm sorry, Tony. It's all over."

It was more nearly over than I knew.

The storm came that night: one of those autumnal disturbances which drive in from the open sea, bringing a heavy surf on the outer rocks and a swell in the bay which broke on our beach in miniature rollers. I remember that it washed in an empty gasoline drum, which at high tide beat against the wall until Mike in rubber boots waded out and salvaged it.

Another of the crows was dead on the porch the next morning. It may have struck one of the windows. Maggie said bad cess to it, but I felt rather grieved. It had had a sort of cocky impudence to it which had amused me, if anything could have amused me that summer.

But there had been a real tragedy also that night before, and one which left me chocked and grieved.

Agnes Dean had died. The night nurse had gone down for her late supper, and when she came back Agnes was dead. She had died alone, her face turned toward the photograph of her daughter, which always sat on the table beside her bed. Her thin tired face looked quite peaceful.

The nurse was young and excitable. She ran downstairs, finding Mansfield Dean in the library. It was late, but he had not gone to bed. He was sitting in front of a fire, his head bent, all his vitality drained out of him. At first she thought he was asleep. She went over and put a hand on his arm.

"I'm sorry, Mr. Dean. I—"

She began to cry, and he looked up at her.

"My wife?" he said thickly.

"Yes. Just now. Very quietly."

She was shaking, and he got up and put a big arm around her to steady her.

"It's all right, my dear," he said. "She would have wanted it like that."

He told her to stay downstairs for a while, and went up himself. She heard him close the door into Agnes's room, and then a silence. She began to grow frightened. It was uncanny, that silence; no servants called, no sending for a doctor, none of the usual quiet movement of a house after a death. She went up again and opened the door.

Mansfield Dean was on his knees beside the bed, and he held a revolver in his hand.

Her courage came back at once. She spoke sharply.

"Don't do that, Mr. Dean. That's cowardly."

He looked at her strangely. Then he got up, moving slowly and with a quiet deliberation.

"Yes," he said. "Don't worry, my dear. I'll not add to your troubles."

He went out then, still carrying the gun. But before he left he broke it and emptied it, as if to reassure her.

I did not know this then. All I knew was that Agnes Dean was dead. It was not unexpected, but the Deans had been a part of us, for a time at least. His big booming voice and his hearty hospitality had been a cheerful addition to the summer crowd. I had seen him on the golf links, playing execrable golf, but always pleasant, even humorous.

"How's that, Miss Lloyd? A little more twist to it and it would have gone back to the clubhouse!"

I had not known Agnes as well. She was much older than I, of course; and there were times when she stayed quietly at home and let him go out alone.

"My wife's not well," he would explain, looking worried. "I thought she'd better rest."

He had been gregarious. He had liked people. And now he was alone, with the aloneness of a man in trouble. He had plenty of friends but no intimates. With a woman I would have gone up to the house at once. A man was different.

The news came as usual with my breakfast tray, and I felt oppressed and sad. I had had a devastating night, what with Tony's story and the one thought that never left me: of Allen in that cell at Clinton. Once, too, I thought one of the bells rang, just before midnight. Although the day started badly, it was to be a red-letter one on my calendar, and will be one for the rest of my life.

For it was that day that the sheriff solved our murders.

He had known the answer since the long-distance call when he put Mamie off the telephone. "Get off the wire, Mamie. This is private," he had said; and listened gravely. But he had really known the answer before that; when he had made that last trip to New York with Howard Brooks.

He had stayed late at the courthouse the night before. Mamie was gone, the building empty. A cleaning woman came with her pail, and he sent her away. "The place is all right," he said. "If you have to earn your money go and clean up the office of our distinguished Districk Attorney. It needs it!"

On the desk in front of him was a rough transcription of the long-distance call, the statement of a New York jeweler, the medical magazine taken from Doctor Jamieson's office, and a map of the island. The map had four crosses on it; one for each of the murders, and one for the place where Allen had been attacked at the top of the path up Stony Creek. There was one thing more, and the sheriff concentrated on that. It was the note from the doctor's wastebasket: "I find myself in an impossible pos—"

He sat for a long time with that in his hand.

He had a few questions written down in front of him, and some of them he checked off. He knew the answers. Even before Mamie got the letter about the Pekingese pup he had known where the clipping came from. He had learned that in New York, at the storage warehouse. But he still had one or two.

Who had taken Jordan's body out to sea?

Why had Lucy met Juliette the morning she was killed?

Who had attacked Maggie?

Who had ransacked Juliette's apartment, and our New York house?

He sat over these for some time. Then—about midnight—he jammed on his hat and went to the jail. When he left he had the answers to two of them.

It was a wild night. He got five or six hours' sleep. Then early the next morning he put on his oilskins and a pair of rubber boots, and drove to the island again.

His case was ready.

At ten o'clock of that day he was waiting in his office, that sheet of paper in front of him, and Mamie keeping off the drifters who otherwise would have wandered in. He was still there when three men came into the room. They came sheepishly, Tony Rutherford, Howard Brooks and Bob Hutchinson. They had not come together, and they eyed each other with suspicion. The sheriff, however, was calm.

"Sit down, gentlemen," he said. "We'll make this as painless as possible. I may say that in that safe over there I

321

have some letters that will interest all of you, but nobody knows the combination but myself."

He smiled at their unhappy faces.

"Live and let live," he said. "I'm not saying some of you haven't run pretty close to the edge of the law. I know it, but Bullard doesn't. So let's get this over and done with. Now, Mr. Brooks—"

CHAPTER XXXVIII

I was at home that morning. The wind was driving the rain horizontally against the house, and I stood at a window, feeling that my life was as dreary and as hopeless as the weather outside. I was no child. Even if Allen cared for me there were probably years of imprisonment ahead of him; if indeed he escaped something worse.

At eleven o'clock Lucy Hutchinson came plodding once more through the rain. Her nonchalance was gone. She looked tired and almost dowdy.

"I had to come," she said. "I couldn't stay by myself any longer. They've sent for Bob, Marcia."

"Who?"

"The police. The sheriff."

I was stunned, but I tried to be helpful.

"That doesn't necessarily mean anything," I told her.

She did not relax.

"This damned rain!" she said. "Marcia, I knew Juliette had some letters from Bob. I met her that day to try to get them from her. If that comes out—"

I was nervous, and I turned on her rather sharply.

"Are you saying that you killed her?" I asked.

She stared at me.

"Good God, no," she said.

It was a bad morning. Lucy stayed, smoking incessantly. The surf continued to break against the wall, coming in thunderously, so that the house itself seemed to shake. Cars came and went along the Dean driveway on the hill, and at noon Mary Lou called up from New York. She seemed badly frightened,

323

and said that Arthur had had a telegram and had taken the late train the night before for Clinton.

"It's too silly," she said, with her voice quavering. "They've got the man who did it, haven't they? And Arthur's busy, Marcia. He's got a lot of business just now. If it's about that idiotic box you found—"

I kept my temper, although I was alarmed.

"They may want a statement about something from him," I told her.

She would not ring off. A statement about what? And what about the box anyhow? The papers were full of it. Was it really true, or just a newspaper story? How on earth did I know it was there? Had I seen what was in it? And what about the pearls? Were they there or not, and if so could I keep them? Why not? They were found in my house.

I hung up, feeling slightly stunned. Things must be happening in the courthouse at Clinton. Confidant as I was that the sheriff believed Allen innocent, I knew nothing of what had happened since he found the box. Nor were matters improved when Marjorie Pendexter telephoned.

"Marcia," she said excitedly. "Why on earth have they called Howard to Clinton? On a day like this?

"I didn't know they had."

"He went off early this morning, Marcia; you don't think he's mixed up in anything, do you?"

"I don't see how he could be."

"Let me know if you hear anything, will you?"

I promised I would; but I was badly shaken when, shortly before lunch, I heard the sheriff's voice on the wire.

"I don't like to ask you on a day like this, Marcia," he said. "But if you'll come over this afternoon I think we can clear this thing up."

"Clear it up! Then who—who's guilty?"

I could hear him chuckle over the telephone.

"Way my office looks now you'd think it was a corporation," he said. "How about three o'clock? If I'm not there just wait for me."

I drove over. Shall I ever forget it! The storm was worse, if possible. Near the bridge a tree had been blown down, and I had

324

to turn back and make a long detour. Even at that I was early. I sat for an hour in that cluttered office of his, with the safe locked and Mamie typing in the outer room, before he came in; and when he did there was no buoyancy in his step. He walked like a tired man. He nodded at me, took off his hat, sat down and lit his old pipe before he spoke at all.

"Well, Marcia," he said at last, "I guess we've finally got to the bottom of it."

I could only look at him.

"Maybe we'd better get at it from the start," he said, turning his swivel chair and looking out the window. "It's not a pretty story, but maybe it's understandable. A woman like Juliette Ransom can pretty well play hell with people's lives. There were some queer things too; like Arthur finding and burying the body. And we had a coincidence or two that balled things up for a while; Fred Martin being on the island, for instance. That fooled me at first, but—" he smiled for the first time—"it fooled Bullard too."

Then he began the story.

"I suppose I never did believe Arthur did it. Not after the first few days. You get to know a man after thirty-odd years, and he wasn't the type. Then I had to think. If he hadn't, who else around here would want to get rid of her? Plenty didn't like her, but that's different. Then, too, you've got to remember how she was killed. Nobody lay in wait for her with a gun. If Lucy Hutchinson hadn't left that golf club up there on the path maybe she wouldn't have been killed at all. In other words, it wasn't premeditated murder. Somebody just hit her!

"But they meant to kill her. Don't forget that."

He turned his office chair and looked at me.

"Well, there she was. She was dead. Maybe whoever did it was sorry, but it was too late. It was daylight, and she had to be got rid of. That fooled me for a long time. I've only just got it straight. She was no lightweight; and it took a pretty strong man to get her on that horse and get her down to the lake. If there had been a good prize fighter on the island I'd have arrested him as like as not, for that thing alone.

"Anyhow, there she was, and sometime during the search Arthur, who knew the lake and the creek, found her and buried her. That fooled me too, for a while. You see, I knew he was a lawyer, and that he'd know that if there was no body it would be pretty difficult to prove a murder.

"The Jordan matter didn't help any either. She was scared. She'd come to me and said she wanted to get out of your house. That sounded like Arthur too. I'd found the hat, you remember, and it didn't look too good. But the night Helen Jordan went to Eliza Edward's she left after her supper, locked her room, and telephoned somebody.

"I went over every pay call made in the town that night, but I couldn't find it. Here she was, a stranger in town. Outside of the hairdresser she hadn't spoken to a soul. Then who was it she had called?

"It stumped me. She went out and she didn't come back. It was clear as water that she'd arranged to meet somebody on the bay path somewhere, but who was it? It was almost certainly a man. I couldn't see a woman killing her and then putting that rope around her neck and dragging her out to sea at night, or any other time. But here again was somebody not ready for a murder, and not used to it either. He didn't even know enough to put a weight on her body!

"Well, you know about that. Her bag was found, and later she was. The one thing I couldn't see was why she had carried off that Jennifer letter. It was back in her room, locked in her suitcase, and her room was locked too. The letter wasn't important, but the postscript bothered me. 'Have just heard about L—. Do please be careful, Julie. You know what I mean.'

"Who was this L—, and why was Mrs. Ransom to be careful? What did this Jennifer woman know? Well, you know about that too. We found her finally, but she wasn't talking. She'll talk now," he added grimly. "If she doesn't I'll lock her up."

He filled his pipe again and lit it.

"All right," he said. "There we were. We had two women dead. One of them was a stranger here, the other hadn't been around for years. I didn't see the answer on the island, or anywhere near by. So you and I went to Juliette's apartment in New York.

"We didn't find much, except a clue to who this Jennifer

326

was. But I did have that old newspaper clipping. Somebody's marriage had been indefinitely postponed.

"Maybe that doesn't sound like much, but there might be a lot of heartbreak in it. The fellow's name began with 'L' too, Langdon Page. And don't forget I knew Juliette. I'd seen her around for six or seven summers. I'd seen that apartment of hers too. She was a troublemaker, all right, and here was trouble.

"I wasn't sure of anything, of course. It mightn't mean a thing. But as I've said I was drowning, and a leaf looked like a lifeboat to me. So I kind of kept after it now and then. I carried that clipping around, and every day or so I'd look at it.

"Then maybe the most curious thing of all happened. Somebody had hated Juliette and got rid of her. Helen Jordan had known too much—she was in the other woman's confidence—so that she had to be put away too. But by the great horn spoon, what was the idea of knocking out a fellow who called himself Allen Pell, parking him somewhere until night, wiping his fingerprints off that trailer of his, and then carting him a hundred miles to a hospital?

"That spoiled the picture. It just didn't fit anywhere. Why wipe those fingerprints off? Who did it? It wasn't Pell himself. I had an idea maybe Pell was dead. Then we got the word that he'd been taken to a hospital, and that didn't fit either. I couldn't see Pell, either as the killer or anything else.

"What it looked like was that somebody had hurt the fellow, and then had been damned sorry, if you know what I mean.

"Well, that didn't look like our killer. It looked at that time as though we had two different bits of trouble on our hands; Pell's injury and the murders. Three, if you count what had been going on at your house: the hatchet up there in the old attic, the way those rooms had been gone through, and Maggie getting hit on the head and knocked out. And by the way, I may as well tell you that it was Fred Martin who hit Maggie and knocked her out."

"Fred?" I said, astounded. "But why? He didn't even know her!"

"Well, Fred's sorry enough." The sheriff smiled again. "He thought she was a ghost! He'd heard those stories about your

327

house, and when she stood up in her nightgown he pretty nearly fainted. Then I guess he just lashed out at her."

Fred, he said, had been about the house for several nights, before Juliette was murdered, trying to see her. He meant to choke the truth out of her, according to his own statement. He was certain she had got a divorce somehow. She was marrying money when she married Arthur, and she wouldn't take a chance on losing it.

"Maybe he'd have killed her, if he got a chance; he's only human. However, somebody else did it for him, so that was that.

"However that may be, he knew she had some things hidden. She as much as told him so; and after the excitement of her death began to die down, he went to New York. His mother was sick. That's correct. But while he was there he got into her apartment, posing as a reporter and paying some bribery. There was nothing there, so he got the idea she had it with her. She'd made some crack about having letters that would blow the island wide open, and he thought maybe she had the record of her divorce among them.

"Anyhow he wanted to get to her room. He got into the house by that window, and— Well, that's what happened to Maggie. He was scared. He thought maybe he'd killed her. He carried her down and laid her in the hall, and then he beat it."

He got up and stood for a minute, looking out at the rain. When he turned he eyed me gravely.

"Then you came into it," he said. "All at once you shoot down to New York. It's hot. You look as washed out as though you'd been hung on a clothesline. But you go to New York anyhow. Jake Halliday, one of my deputies, sees you at the station here and tells me. So I call up the police there and have a man see what you're after. I felt pretty foolish when I heard you'd spent some of your time there at the public library!

"But you did something else, Marcia. You went to see a man named Samuel Dunne, and Halliday had no trouble about him. He and the neighbors were holding séances to get in touch with his wife and daughter, who had both been killed by a hit-and-run driver.

"I still couldn't see it, when Halliday called me up; but I sent

328

him back to the library, and he got the files you'd had. There was Dunne's story and all the rest of it. What's more, this Jennifer Dennison was mixed up with it, and so were Howard Brooks and Marjorie Pendexter. And here's something else. This Langdon Page had got out on parole early in June of this year, and then disappeared. He hadn't reported since.

"It began to look as though he was our man. Halliday had got the story from the papers. Page had been crazy about Juliette, and had been drinking heavily as a result. Well, a fellow who's been two or three years in the pen has time to get over a lot of things; especially love for a woman. But we had to remember this. She'd wrecked him. His engagement was broken. Maybe his business was gone. I didn't know about that.

"Maybe he'd brooded over this thing, his broken engagement and so on, until he wasn't normal. Still and all, it takes a good bit of brooding to make a man kill a woman for a reason like that, and after three years. It didn't quite jell, as my wife says.

"Anyhow we didn't have Pell, or Page, or whatever you want to call him. Halliday got a photograph of him, and the folks at the tourist camp identified him all right. He could have known Juliette was here. We found an item to that effect in one of the society columns. Maybe these fellows in the pen read the society column. They do some queer things. But we didn't have him and we couldn't find him. All we knew was that he'd been on the island.

"Bullard had Fred Martin by that time, and was off hell-bent for election! I kept telling him there were too many odds and ends left over, but you know him. He had Martin and he wasn't letting go. Then the doctor got killed, and there was that fingerprint on the side of the car. There was no use arguing that the print was on the right-hand door and the doctor had been shot from the left. We got the print identified, and it was Page's, alias Allen Pell!

"Well, you know that part of it. He'd disappeared and we couldn't locate him. Then one day he walked in and gave himself up, and I'd like to have seen Bullard's face! Page denied the crimes, but Bullard wouldn't even listen. He was all set to go again!

"But I wasn't satisfied. Page wasn't telling all he knew. That stuck out like a peg leg, and I got an idea he was protecting somebody. But who? He didn't know anybody much on the island except you—so far as I knew. He had known Marjorie Pendexter and the Brooks fellow, and he might have seen Fred Martin and Dorothy in Florida. He had a place there. But who else?

"Then that tin box turned up. I learned a lot from it. Not the letters from men. Mrs. Ransom had been doing some polite blackmailing, I was sure of that; but I couldn't see any of the men concerned killing her. But I did get some things that looked phony to me. The necklace was only one of them.

"What, for instance, had sent Juliette around to Page's apartment as soon as she could get there after that accident of his in New York? He'd run through a traffic light and killed two women and hurt a man. He was picked up unconscious and taken to a hospital; and it wasn't very long before the police went through his wallet and found out who he was. But she'd been there already! There was a letter or two in that box that he had received only the day before.

"Now that was a queer thing. She must have hotfooted it there pretty quick. The police were there three hours later, and they found his stuff scattered all over the place. His Jap slept out. There was nobody in the apartment. But less than three hours after he'd killed those people she was there! He was unconscious in a hospital, nobody knew anything about it. But apparently she did.

"You see what I mean. Not only was there something in his apartment she had to have. She knew about what had happened several hours before the morning papers had it.

"I didn't know then what she was after, but I was sure of one thing. She'd been in that car with him that night; and I wasn't so darned sure she hadn't been driving it. In that case—"

He stopped and drew on his pipe.

"In that case it was pretty bad news," he said slowly. "Suppose she was driving that car? Suppose, being a man, he took the rap for her? He may have hoped she'd come out and confess. When she didn't, what could he do? Accuse her? He had no proof, and I'd say he wasn't the man to hide behind any woman's petticoats. He might have been drunk, and she took the wheel. In that case he'd reason the punishment was up to him.

"But you can see where that left me. That gave him a motive for killing her; not premeditated murder, but rage and resentment. That was the kind of murder it had been! Not only that either. There was another reason for his wanting to kill her. I'll get to that later."

CHAPTER XXXIX

I sat still. My hands and feet were like ice, and it seemed to me that for hours I had been there, listening to the rain against the window, to the tap-tap of the typewriter outside, and to that inexorable voice, going on and on.

The sheriff looked at me sharply.

"Wait a minute," he said. "Don't jump at things, Marcia, I haven't said he was guilty. I've only said it looked like it."

I breathed again, and he got a piece of note paper out of his wallet and laid it out on the desk.

"Well," he said, "to make a long story short, I went down to New York again. I saw the police who'd found him after the car struck the pole, and I found the intern who'd picked him up out of the street. All I have to say is that if he was driving the car that night he took a flying leap from under the wheel, over the other seat and the door, and out on his head. It should have killed him, but it didn't. So what?"

I did not reply, and he sat looking at the paper before him.

"I didn't believe it," he said slowly. "I had the picture pretty well before I went down this last time. I knew she'd been at his apartment that night after the thing happened. My idea was that he had been hurt, but she wasn't. She got out of that car and ran, and nobody ever saw her. But when she reached home she started thinking. There was something in his place she had to get; and get it before the police arrived there.

"Did she get it, or not? It seemed to me part of the case turned on that. And if she did, where was it? If it was a letter she might have burned it. Chances were if she found it she did. But maybe she didn't. She was scared, and she kept on being

333

scared. She fired her maid and sent out to her old home for the Jordan woman. Remember what Helen Jordan wrote? 'She has something on her mind. She acts scared, and you know that isn't like her.'

"Well, later on she was more scared than ever. You can figure it like this. Page had gone up for eight years. Even with time off she had five years or more. But he's paroled, and all at once she wants to leave the country. Why? Was she afraid of him? He'd kept quiet through the trial. He knew she did it, but he'd kept quiet. What had happened in that interval to scare her?

"So far as I could make out, maybe two people knew she'd been in that car. One was Page. The other looked like the Dennison woman, from that letter of hers. But she wasn't afraid of the Dennison woman. Then who was she afraid of? Was it Page? Or was it somebody else? And here were Tony Rutherford and Bob Hutchinson and Howard Brooks all cluttering things up; not to mention Fred Martin and Arthur, and even you yourself!

"Well, there I was. I took a look at that house of yours on Park Avenue, and it wasn't hard to find out how it had been entered. Some bars had been sawed out of a basement window, and it looked like a professional job to me.

"Ever try to saw an iron bar? Well, it's not easy. They'd been sawed out and then set back into place with gum of some sort. Just to look at them, you'd never know they'd been touched.

"Now that was queer too, Marcia. There was quite a lot of stuff around, pictures and Oriental rugs and so on. But this fellow isn't interested. He goes up to what's got to be the room Juliette used to occupy there. A blind man would know it was hers, and it's there he looks things over!

"Well, we haven't many professional burglars on the island. But we did have one fellow who'd been in the pen. That was Page; and I reckon when we get all the pieces together we'll find Page sent somebody into that house of yours, to look for something. But don't hold it against him. Likely he had his reasons.

"Anyhow, the upshot was that I wasn't sure that Juliette

hadn't got what she went after that night after she'd killed those people. It wasn't in the box. That's sure. So I had a talk with the Brooks fellow, and he let me look over Page's things in the warehouse. At first it seemed like I'd gone up a blind alley. Then I found this, in the pocket of a dressing gown. She'd missed it, after all! If that's what she went to his apartment for, she completely forgot, in her panic, that if he had saved it at all it would have to be in his bag in the car."

He picked up the paper in front of him and gave it to me. My hands shook as I tried to hold it. It was in the square bold writing which had been familiar to me for so many years. "Dearest: If you'll leave the club at nine I'll meet you at the gate. Jennifer is sending me in her car. You can drive me back to town, and we can talk things over. Ever yours, Juliette."

I sat staring at it.

"She did it, then?" I said dully.

"She did it, and the Dennison woman knew about it," he agreed. "I've got the story from him. She claimed he'd been drinking and she took the wheel. She wanted him to break his engagement to this Emily Forrester—you might keep that name in mind—and he refused. Guess he'd seen through her by that time! Anyhow she was furious. Maybe she'd been drinking too, I don't know. But she stepped on the gas and went through the traffic light like a bat out of hell. When she knew what she had done she tried to turn a corner and hit a post. He went out, but she was behind the wheel and wasn't hurt. At least he thinks not. Nobody saw her. The street was dark, and she just slipped away."

He took a long breath and got his cold pipe going again.

"Well, that's it," he said. "Or it's part of it. I told you it's not a pretty story, and it isn't. All told, it took six lives before it was finished: those two women who were killed by the car, three here, and one more. Can you guess who it was?"

I shook my head. I felt sick and dizzy.

"Then I'll tell you," he said. "You saw that clipping, and I've mentioned the Forrester girl. How do you think she felt about this? Pretty hard on her, wasn't it? Here she was, all ready to marry Page; the trousseau bought, the invitations ready to go out. Then he gets eight years in the pen. That was a lifetime to her; and while I gather Page wasn't in love with her—he's a gentleman. He doesn't say so, but I get it—she *was* in love with him.

"Anyhow, she stood it for a good while. Then I don't know what happened. Maybe she learned about Juliette. Maybe she learned that he wasn't guilty, and had taken the rap for another woman. I wouldn't put it past Juliette to tell her herself! But she couldn't stand it. She—"

"You mean that Emily Forrester killed Juliette!" I gasped.

"I mean," he said, "that Emily Forrester killed herself."

I do not recall all that followed. Sitting there with my mind racing I was only aware that the case against Allen was building up, slowly and inexorably. The sheriff went on. The clipping had interested him from the start. He had sent out what he called the dog letters, in the hope of locating the Forrester girl.

"I had the whole United States to go over," he explained. "But if I could find who advertised those pups I'd find the girl. But when I did find out I knew who she was already. Got it out of some letters in the warehouse."

He got busy on the long-distance telephone when he came back, and it was then that he learned about that suicide of hers.

"Kind of knocked me out for a minute," he said. "There was the motive for Page, right enough; and I began to wonder if Bullard wasn't right, after all. But there was something else in that telephone call. I had to begin my thinking all over again. So—"

He did not go on. I heard footsteps in the hall outside, and Allen came in, a deputy sheriff beside him. My heart almost broke when I saw him, he was so changed, so gaunt and thin. He had been shaved and someone had brought him fresh linen, but his eyes looked sunken in his head.

The sheriff got up.

"Sit down, Page," he said. "I want you to tell Marcia here what you told me. Go easy with it. She's had a pretty bad time herself."

It was all incredible; the sheriff going out and taking the deputy with him, Mamie typing in the next room, the rain still washing down the windows, and Allen making no move toward me. Looking strained and awkward, and unsmiling as though

336

we were strangers; as though—

"I didn't want to do this, Marcia," he said. "It's the sheriff's idea. I—how much do you know?"

"Only that you never murdered anybody," I said, as steadily as I could.

He nodded, but still he did not come near me. Instead he went to the window and stood there, with his back to me. Then he apparently came to a decision, for he turned again.

"This is with gloves off," he said. "The truth, the whole truth and nothing but the truth, at last, my darling."

"Nothing will change me, Allen."

And at that use of his old name he gave me a faint twisted smile.

"I suppose a man's sins live after him," he said. "And it is the innocent who suffer. He told you about Emily?"

"Yes. I—I'm sorry."

"I killed her," he said. "I killed her, as surely as if I had fired that bullet myself. But that is my only murder, Marcia. I want you to know that."

He told me about her then, speaking in a sort of drab monotone as if he was afraid to let any emotion come to the surface. He had been engaged to her. The thing had drifted along. Perhaps he was never in love with her, but he was fond of her. He had meant to carry on.

Then he met Juliette, a few months before the wedding. Emily was a quiet girl, rather shy; and there was Juliette, his own age or older, reckless and fascinating.

"I'm not excusing myself," he said. "I went crazy about her."

But it did not last. He began to see her, I gathered, as the cheap woman Mary Lou had called her. She was not in love with him, but he could give her ease and security, and she wanted both. When he told her he was through she was like a madwoman. She wouldn't let him go, and toward the end she threatened to send his letters to Emily.

"I got tight that day," he said. "I didn't know what to do. And I guess you know what happened. She drove the car, and she killed Mrs. Dunne and her daughter."

When he came to he was in the hospital. He had been

337

identified, and Howard Brooks was sitting by the bed. He told Howard the facts, but later on thinking it over he decided to take the responsibility himself.

"I'd been drinking," he said. "It was my fault she had had to drive that night. I wasn't hiding behind her."

Howard had thought he was a fool, but was sworn to secrecy.

He stood trial and went to the penitentiary. He didn't care what happened to him by that time. The pen was not too bad. He worked in the library and tried painting in his leisure. After a time he got a few lessons. But life was over. He painted to keep sane. That was all.

Then after almost two years Emily shot herself. He had never dreamed of such a thing. It almost killed him. I gathered indeed that he almost killed himself. Not that he loved her. For the sheer tragedy of it. She had left a letter for her family, but none for him.

When his parole came it meant nothing to him.

"I had three deaths on my soul by that time," he said, still in that flat monotonous voice. "I didn't want to see anybody I knew. I wanted to lose myself, my name, my identity, everything. And I didn't want to stay in any one place. I'd been shut away for a long time. I wanted the sky and— Well, you understand, don't you?"

That was why he changed his name. His first name had been Allen anyhow, although it was never used; and he took Pell out of the telephone book. And that, too, was why he bought the trailer. At first he felt rather absurd. Later on he liked it. He was free. He would even sleep beside it on the ground, for the sheer relief of waking and seeing the stars overhead.

Then one day soon after he got it he saw a New York newspaper, and read that Juliette had come to the island.

He had not seen her since his release, but he gathered that his freedom had come as a shock to her.

"For more than one reason," he said. "She'd gone to my apartment that night after the accident and had taken her letters to me. But she had taken something else, Marcia. Emily's father was giving her some pearls as a wedding gift and had had the jeweler deliver them to me. She took them too."

The other reason, he said, was that she was afraid of him.

She had thought she had anywhere from five to eight years of security, but here he was, free again.

"She had a twisted sort of mind," he said. "I'd gone to the pen instead of her, she had stolen Emily's pearls, and now Emily was dead. She knew how she would feel under those circumstances, so she thought I would also. God knows all I wanted was never to see her again, but—"

She seems to have been genuinely alarmed. She had gone to Howard Brooks and told him she meant to leave the country, getting a lump sum from Arthur and also collecting on some love letters, Howard's among others. I have always been sure, too, that she meant to recover and sell the pearls.

But there she was, on the island, and Allen followed her there.

"Why?" I asked, puzzled. "I don't understand."

"I was afraid she would be killed. I told her that," he said, and went on.

He had met her on the bridle path one morning. He had tried to see her before, but he had failed. Maybe I remembered one night when I had looked out, and he was on the beach below. But this day they met face to face, and she looked ready to faint. She had even tried to ride past him, but he caught the bridle of her horse and stopped her.

"Don't be foolish," he told her. "I've got to talk to you. I'm not going to hurt you."

She was quieter after that. She said all she asked was to be allowed to leave America and live abroad. And she mentioned the pearls, as a sort of bribe! She would return the pearls to him; she would do anything, if he would only let her alone.

"The pearls!" he told her roughly. "They are not mine. Return them where they belong."

She gave him an amused half-smile. She was herself again by that time.

"I'll have to get them first," she told him. "Marcia Lloyd has them now, but she doesn't know it!"

He let her go then, but before she left he gave her a warning; and this time she seemed impressed.

"I'm telling you," he said contemptuously as he released the bridle. "You don't have to leave America on my account; but you'd better leave it in your own."

That was the last time he ever spoke to her. On the night before her death she had taken my car and driven up to the camp, perhaps to tell him that she was trying to get the pearls. He was not there. And when he saw her again she was lying dead on the bridle path, with Lucy's golf club beside her, and her hat and gloves not far away, on the ground.

He glanced at me and then looked away again. His hands were clenching the arms of his chair.

"What was I to do?" he said. "There she was and nobody could bring her back to life. I wasn't afraid for myself, but I knew what would happen if she was found there. So I—"

"You put her into the lake?" I said, horrified.

"I put her into the lake," he said gravely.

I felt frozen. I must have made some movement, for he reached over and caught my hands.

"My poor darling," he said. "I know how it sounds, but I didn't kill her. You must believe that."

He went on after that break. He had carried Lucy's club up onto a hillside later on and buried it. The rains must have uncovered it. And he had had to tell Howard Brooks the story. Howard had been the first to see the danger.

"You damned fool!" he said bitterly. "If the story ever gets out, who will believe you didn't murder her? I'm not so sure myself!"

But Howard had stood by. They belonged to the same yacht club; Allen had a boat of his own somewhere. Both Howard and Marjorie had known he was on the island, although Marjorie had complicated matters later. She had been both jealous and suspicious. She knew Howard had once been interested in Juliette, and they had not dared to tell her the whole story, for obvious reasons.

"The whole story!" I asked desperately. "But what is it, Allen? Why don't you tell me? What *is* the story?"

He looked at me, his face stern and yet sad.

"I thought you knew," he said simply. "Mansfield Dean was Emily's stepfather."

I can still remember the shock of that minute. Not Mansfield Dean! Not that big booming kindly man, whose dead wife still lay in his house. I must have gone very pale. I know I got up, for the next minute Allen's arms were around me.

"My poor girl," he said. "I thought you knew. I thought the sheriff had told you. And it's all over now, darling. Try to remember that. It's all over."

I was crying unrestrainedly by that time. He still held me, but he seemed to be trying to explain something to me; that I must remember that Juliette's death had been on impulse, and that Jordan might have fallen or been pushed onto the rocks. But I really understood very little until he came to Doctor Jamieson's murder.

That, he said, had been cold and premeditated; and his voice hardened.

"I tried to warn him," he said. "I told him; but he thought he could take care of himself."

I looked at him in complete confusion.

"Told him what?" I asked.

"The truth," he said grimly. "What he had guessed already. That Agnes Dean had been emotionally unbalanced since Emily's death. And was dangerous."

CHAPTER XL

So Agnes Dean was our killer. As I write this I am still filled with horror. I can see her in her black dress, with all the panoply of wealth about her, looking at me with tragic eyes.

"I think life ended for me then," she had said.

But not only her life, and Emily's. She had killed Juliette on that bridle path, picking up Lucy's club and swinging it with the strength of a madwoman. Then quite calmly she had gone away, and Allen had found the body.

Whether she meant to murder that day nobody knows. She was unarmed. Of course she had known of Juliette's part in the tragedy of Emily's suicide. The whole pitiful story was in her daughter's farewell note. Now, the sight of Juliette sitting on that log had driven her over the edge. There was Lucy's golf club. So she used it.

She apparently felt no remorse whatever.

"She killed Emily," she said, "and I killed her. An eye for an eye, Mansfield."

And after the first shock he had taken her into his arms and promised to protect her.

During that interval Allen had found the body, and he knew at once what had happened. He and Mansfield Dean were friendly, and Mansfield had been afraid of what might happen ever since Agnes had learned Juliette was on the island. Together they had tried to keep a watch on her. But that day she had slipped away early in the morning. She had seen Juliette going out in her riding clothes, and had taken the short cut up the creek.

The two men were frantic with anxiety. She could not live

343

long, and they wanted to save her the disgrace of discovery. Then, too, she seemed more normal after that. They thought it was over.

They retained their affectionate relations. Together they joined that ghastly search for Juliette's body, and when at last it was discovered, buried, they could not understand it. Because Mansfield Dean was a sentimental man, deeply stricken, he had ordered those anonymous flowers for the cemetery. That was one of the things the sheriff had learned in New York. He had been more successful than I had.

"Confidential order, sir," said a clerk. "Sorry."

"You'll be sorrier if you don't tell me, son," said the sheriff, and flashed his badge.

Then Jordan's death came, like lightning out of a clear sky. Agnes had apparently not known the woman. But both her husband and Allen believed now that Jordan had telephoned her the night she left Eliza Edwards's. Whether she accused Agnes of Juliette's murder and attempted blackmail, I do not know. It seems more likely that she accused Allen, and Agnes knew he was not guilty.

"Helen Jordan knew the whole story," he said. "Not only that Juliette had driven the car that night; but about Emily, and the Deans. I had warned Juliette about Mrs. Dean, but she said she wasn't afraid. She could manage any woman! I suppose Jordan believed I *had* killed Juliette. Anyhow the inquest was to be the next day, and she probably threatened to tell what she knew. That was the end, for her."

It was possible, though, he added, that Jordan's death was not premeditated. She might have slipped or been pushed off the path onto the rocks below. All he knew was that Agnes Dean drove her car back to the house that night and walked calmly into the library there.

"I've killed the Jordan woman," she said.

Mansfield had not believed her. There were intervals when she imagined things, and he had never heard of Helen Jordan.

"The Jordan woman? Who is she?" he asked.

"Juliette Ransom's maid," she said, and went on upstairs to her room.

He followed her. She was in bed by that time, with that

344

photograph of Emily beside her, and he began to be uneasy.

"See here," he said. "Is this true? Or did you imagine it?"

"Go and look on the rocks along the bay path," she told him, and picked up a book.

No one will ever know what the next few hours cost him. He found Jordan where Agnes had said, and he drove wildly up to the camp to find Allen. He was hardly rational himself by that time.

"She's killed another woman," he said. "What in God's name am I to do?"

Allen was stunned. His first thought was to make certain Jordan was dead and then leave her where she was. But Mansfield would not agree to it. He had been devoted to his wife, and he knew, too, that she had not long to live. He would confess himself, before he would let her suffer. In the meantime, he wanted to get rid of the body.

Allen wanted to tow it out to sea in his boat. He was accustomed to the water. Dean was stubborn about this.

"It's my job," he said. "Show me how to start the engine. That's all I want. I'll do the rest."

In the end it was arranged that way, Allen staying at the Dean house to watch Agnes, now in a state where she might wander out at any time; and Mansfield Dean to that ghastly task he had set himself.

It must have been a hideous experience. He knew nothing of death and less of the ocean, and noise of the engine in the quiet probably rolled like thunder in his ears. I had heard it myself that night, as it left the foot of Cooper's Lane.

But he did what he had set out to do. He found the body, but he could not beach the boat. He waded ashore and carried her out. She was dead and there was blood on her, and so he took the painter, knotted it around her neck and headed for the open sea, towing the body behind him. The whole experience was sickening, and there was one period of undiluted torture. That was after he had cut her loose, and the engine stopped.

He could not start it again. He worked over it, sweating profusely. And then something floated beside him, and he thought it was the body. He nearly went mad; and the thing stayed there, bobbing about within a few feet of him. When at last the engine started he was completely collapsed. He saw then that it had been a floating log, but he headed the boat toward shore and lay down in the bottom of it. He could not get his breath for a long time.

When he finally reached home Agnes was quietly sleeping in her bed.

He was never quite the same after that. All his effort was directed toward saving Agnes from herself. On the surface he had not changed. He carried on, but that vast vitality of his began to fail him. The day I met him on the Stony Creek path I had seen the change in him.

And then came another complication. Allen had fallen in love with me, and Arthur was in danger of being tried for murder. He did not know what to do. He left me at the path and turned to see Mansfield Dean, coming along in his car. Mansfield got out, and the two men walked together a few feet down the path. Allen had his hands in his pockets, and his head down.

"See here, Mr. Dean," he said. "I'm going to be honest with you. I've just seen Marcia Lloyd, and I can't let her brother go to trial."

"What do you mean by that?" Mansfield Dean said thickly. "By God, Page, if you let me down now—"

"I'll not let an innocent man go to the chair," said Allen.

Then Dean hit him! He still had his hands in his pockets, and he hadn't a chance. His head struck a stone, and he was out like a light.

Dean himself was horrified. He was fond of Allen, and although it was broad daylight, he could not leave him there. He might not be found for hours, if then.

"He did what he could," Allen said. "Put yourself in his place! He hadn't even meant to hit me. But now he had me on his hands, and he had to get rid of me somehow."

He did pretty well, all things considered. He got Allen into the back of the car and started with him to the local hospital. But he was thinking, and part way there he turned back. If Allen died, he wanted none of the local police about, to hear any final statement. And he did not want him identified if he lived.

346

"I was a pretty logical suspect for Juliette's murder, if the story came out. And Dean is a fair man. He didn't know what to do. I suppose he did the best he could. He hid his car—and me—on a wood road somewhere in the hills; and he took the key of the trailer out of my pocket and went back there that night. He cleaned it for fingerprints, locked it and went back to the car. It must have been a pretty wild night for him."

Allen was still unconscious when Dean reached the hospital, a hundred miles or so away; and as he said, I knew the rest of the story. He put some money into Allen's pocket, rang the night bell, and drove away as soon as the porter had gone for help.

"So there I was," he said. "I couldn't come back. How did I know he'd cleaned my prints off the trailer? All I knew was that the police were after me, probably for two murders. And I had to play against time. If Mrs. Dean died I could tell the truth. If not—"

He let that go. He had done the best thing he could think of, and sent a vagrant from the hospital with the note to me. But there was something else to be done. He had met me. He didn't want to serve the rest of his term for manslaughter, and there was something that would help to clear that up: Juliette's note to him that she would drive back to town with him from Long Island. She was dead now, and it could not hurt her.

"I suppose that's what she went to get, the night I was hurt," he said. "Even I had forgotten all this time that it couldn't have been there. I had an idea it was hidden with the pearls—unless she had destroyed it—and she said you had them and didn't know it."

He had got in touch with a burglar he had known in the pen, and had him go over the house, especially Juliette's former rooms. But there was nothing there; no letters, no pearls, and by that time there was a nation-wide search for him, and he expected to be picked up at any time.

It was then that he took to the sea again. He located the former captain of his yacht, told him as much as he dared, and through him bought a small secondhand cruiser. Howard Brooks had financed the deal. Allen was out of money, and did not dare to draw any. And he came back to the island.

347

"Partly to see you, my dear," he said, "and partly to see how things were going."

They were going badly. Dean had missed his revolver and was afraid Agnes meant to kill herself. He himself was worried about me, and about the doctor.

"She knew I liked you. She probably suspected I was in love with you, and she resented that. She thought it was disloyal to Emily. She may have thought I had told you too much. I was anxious about the doctor too. She had told Dean that the doctor was giving her medicine to make her talk. Whether it was true or not, if she thought it—"

However that might be, he had gone to the doctor and warned him. He had not told him all the story; merely that she was emotional and unbalanced, and possibly dangerous. But he thought the doctor knew a lot, and had guessed the rest. He had listened and nodded.

"I can take care of myself," he had said sturdily. "I've had to do it for a good many years."

A night or two later she had shot him.

She was dressed for a dinner party when she did it, and for the ball to follow. Not in costume, but wearing all her pearls, and a beautiful small tiara. Then she had sent her maid away and gone outside for air. Nobody saw her going down to the road in that black dress of hers, with a black wrap over it. When Dean came down she was back in the hall, inspecting herself in a mirror and entirely calm.

"How do I look?" she asked.

"You're always lovely to me, Agnes."

And that was all.

She had known the doctor would be coming back from Dorothy's and had gauged her time well. She had stopped his car in the road and shot him. It was probable, Allen thought, that she never spoke to him at all; and the first real knowledge Dean had of her guilt was the night she died. He found the gun under her mattress then, and the nurse had discovered him with it in his hand.

He had meant to kill himself, but the nurse had stopped him. The next morning in the rain he had gone up Stony Creek and buried it. He took the police there later on.

It was the doctor's murder that had decided Allen. Up to that time he had hoped that her heart would give out before she could do any more damage. Now he told Dean he was going to surrender himself. Dean had taken it hard.

"Give her a little time," he said. "For God's sake, Lang! She's dying! She can't do anything more. Let her go in peace."

And that he had done, sitting still under their questioning there in Bullard's office, feeling faint and exhausted, but still holding out. Then she died, that night in her sleep. Died just in time to escape Russell Shand, in dripping oilskins, confronting Mansfield Dean the next morning in his library. He had come back from burying the revolver, and one look at the sheriff's face was enough. He knew that the long struggle was over.

"Sorry to trouble you at such a time, Mr. Dean," Shand said quietly. "I guess you know why I'm here."

Mansfield Dean looked at him, his face gray but his head erect on his tired body.

"God works after his own fashion," he said strangely. "At least he has saved her this."

It was after he got that story that the sheriff went back to the courthouse. Though it was still early, Bullard was already behind his desk, looking busy and important, with a group of men around him.

"Just dropped in," said the sheriff, "to say it's all over. You can let Page go, and Martin too."

"You're crazy," said Bullard reddening.

"Well, you're a fool," said the sheriff cheerfully. "If the public knew about both of us we'd soon be out of office. As a matter of fact," he added, "our killer escaped last night. I got there this morning, but I was too late. She was gone."

"*She* was gone! What the devil do you mean?"

"She was dead," said the sheriff soberly.

He told them then, and they crowded around him—all but Bullard—and shook him by the hand. The New York men even asked him if he didn't want a job with them; but he refused with a grin.

"I'm only a country policeman," he said. "What would I do in the big town?"

He had his conference that morning: Bob, Tony, Howard,

and eventually Arthur. The tin box was on the table, and they were an anxious lot. At last he gave them back their letters, and then got up.

"I suppose it's no use reading a lecture to you fellows," he said. "Looks to me as though one woman had played you all for suckers. The good Lord makes a woman like that now and then. But you've done your best to clutter up this case. So if you don't mind getting the hell out of here, I'll get back to my real business."

They went out, grinning and sheepish; but Arthur stayed and the sheriff opened the tin box again.

"Something you and the Martins will be glad to have," he said. "She was divorced from Fred all right. She was your legal wife. But as one married man to another, I wouldn't tell Mary Lou there was ever a question of it."

And it speaks well, I think, for the Lloyd blood that Arthur managed to smile.

I am still here. Since I commenced this story the fall has come in earnest. The days are bright and even warm, but the nights are cold. At bedtime Maggie tucks me under an eiderdown, and puts a little blanket into Chu-Chu's bed. But the house is still and peaceful. No bells have rung since Agnes died. But I am not satisfied that they had any connection with our dreadful experiences, and I am sending for the electrician to come again tomorrow.

Except for a few die-hards, the summer people have gone. The house on the hill above Sunset is empty, but Mrs. Pendexter still drops in.

"I always did suspect that Dean woman," she says, with her usual shrewdness. "It had to be either her or her husband. The rest of us had wanted to kill Juliette for years, but hadn't done it. And I liked him."

I am much stronger. Soon the new doctor will let me go back to New York. He is very scientific. Every so often he jabs me and carries away some blood on a slide. He takes it back to the old doctor's house and into the laboratory. What does he see under the microscope? I wonder. The times when it chilled with horror or went sick with fright? I think not. He is a very material person.

As I finish this I can hear Mike in the garden, getting ready for the winter. He fills a wheelbarrow with leaves and dumps them on the mulch pile behind the toolshed, there to rot and grow rich in decay. And downstairs William is putting away the silver. He is looking forward to the winter, and my wedding. Every now and then he appears with a suggestion.

"I was thinking, miss. About the reception. Perhaps we'd better—"

He is younger than he has been for many years. So is Lizzie. So is Maggie, planning my clothes for me and already seeing me in white satin, and a veil, coming down the aisle. Her child. Her little girl, now grown up and a bride. How little we know about them, those faithful people who serve us through a lifetime.

Yesterday I took the car out. I stopped at the cemetery, and looked at those three tragic graves: Juliette's, Helen Jordan's and the doctor's. There are fresh flowers on all of them every week, and I understand the order is to go on. I passed the golf course too, and saw Fred Martin there as usual, his old cap on his head and his hands in his pockets, giving a lesson.

"See what you did that time?" he was asking. "Wonder to me you didn't bang that ball over to my house and hit the baby!"

He is crazy about the baby.

Now and then the sheriff drops in to see how I am getting along. He came only a day or two ago.

"Kind of got the habit," he said. "Now I've got to find out who stole Mrs. Pendexter's cook's overshoes out of the station wagon while she was at the movies. Well, I suppose that's life."

Then he saw my manuscript and eyed it.

"If that's a letter to your young man," he observed, "it's sure a long one."

"It's my attempt to tell what happened here this summer," I told him. "After all, people ought to know. About Allen, and everything."

He looked alarmed at first. Then he grinned.

"Put Bullard in," he said. "He's out of office soon, and he's got no comeback. I wish you'd seen his face that morning when I walked in and told him to let both Page and Martin go. It looked like a poached egg."

I saw him out, and as he went he cocked an eye up at the old hospital suite.

"If you're writing that story," he said, "you'd better call it 'The Wall.' That's what it looked like I was up against for a while. And, by the great horn spoon, part of the case was lying behind one all the time."

The postman whistled as he left, and I waited for my daily letter. I carried it out to the porch and read it there, with the seals in the bay and the gulls patiently fishing at the edge of the low tide. The sun was out and the bay was calm and still. There was a boy on the shore, throwing pebbles into the water, and I remembered Juliette doing the same thing and watching the little waves it had caused. "Like life," she said. "The damned things go on and on."

But it wasn't true, I thought. They went so far and then stopped; and everything was quiet again.

Standing there, I opened and read my letter.

"My darling—" it began.